One More Sunday

One More SUNDAY

John D. MacDonald

Alfred A. Knopf
New York

To the memory

of quiet Sunday mornings

in South Congregational Church

on Genesee Street in Utica, New York,

with my

grandfather, Edward Odell Dann,

my great-aunt, Emily Grace Williams,

my mother, Margarite Dann MacDonald,

my father, Eugene Andrew MacDonald,

and my sister, Doris Jean MacDonald

—now all at rest in Plot 63,

Lot 814 and contiguous Lot 6325,

in Forest Hill Cemetery

in Utica.

I know that a community of God-seekers is a great shelter for man. But directly this grows into an institution it is apt to give ready access to the Devil by its back-door.

RABINDRANATH TAGORE,
Letters to a Friend

It is becoming more and more obvious that it is not starvation, not microbes, not cancer, but man himself who is mankind's greatest danger, because he has no adequate protection against psychic epidemics, infinitely more devastating in their effect than the greatest natural catastrophes.

CARL JUNG

I believe more and more that God must not be judged on this earth. It is one of his sketches that has turned out badly.

VINCENT VAN GOGH

One More Sunday

One

The Reverend Doctor John Tinker Meadows stood silent and motionless at the pulpit of the great Tabernacle of the Eternal Church of the Believer, staring at the stained-glass window at the far end of the building, listening to the murmur and rustle of the enormous congregation as the sounds slowly diminished.

Once again the vast space was filled for an early-morning service, even in the heat of the sun belt in August. The three broad aisles which sloped down toward the altar rail at a slight angle cut the congregation into four equal portions, fifteen worshippers wide, sixty rows deep. Another thousand were over in the University theater, watching him on the big screen in closed-circuit color, and he knew that up in the control booth to the left of the stained glass, high above the entrance doors, the production manager and the director were watching the monitor sets, cueing the camera stations. The sound was being mixed with due regard for whichever camera was being used.

He felt a trickle of sweat on his ribs, under the cassock and surplice, and reacted with familiar exasperation toward the so-called experts who had designed the subterranean air conditioning. It had proven ample for the giant space even in midsummer, but had a built-in low-frequency rumble which made it impossible to use at full throttle when taping. Finn Efflander had someone working on a filter that might keep the rumble off the recording. But even were it working properly, he knew that by the end of the sermon his clothing would be sodden. He perspired heavily whenever and wherever he preached. His face would be wet and shiny in the closeups, partially defeating the efforts of makeup to give him the look of a younger Charlton Heston.

He was aware of a slight change of the light off to his left and realized that someone in the control booth had pressed one of the buttons which controlled the movement of the huge translucent, fire-resistant draperies, to move one of them slightly to cut off an edge of morning sun, making the interior light whiter and more luminous.

He heard a smothered giggle forty feet behind him, and he could imagine the stare his sister would direct at the offender. The choir of fifty young women, the Meadows Angels, was a constant discipline problem. Had they been selected more for voice quality and less for beauty, he guessed the problem would be lessened. But the Reverend Mary Margaret Meadows exerted an iron control which kept disorder at a minimum.

John Tinker Meadows knew that many in the congregation were seeing the service in person for the first time, after years of faithful membership and television viewing. To them the thrill of being in the same space, breathing the same air, as the famous elderly Reverend Matthew Meadows and his two talented children was only slightly dimmed by their being such tiny figures, so far away. And as the service proceeded, they would begin to realize that it was a lot longer than the fifty-minute version edited for broadcast.

It was time. When a child coughed, the church was so silent the small sound could be heard by everyone. He looked then at the congregation, feeling the tension and the expectation. He was a tall slender man with gray-blonde hair worn long at the sides, brushed back.

"O MIGHTY GOD, WHY HAVE YOU TURNED YOUR BACK ON THIS GOOD EARTH AND ON YOUR PEOPLE?"

The rich and resonant voice inherited from the old man filled the Tabernacle with a ripe and startling sound, perfectly amplified.

"What do we see around us?

"We see a sickness, a cancer, a corruption on every side.

"Through the same wondrous technology which allows us to send this service up to the satellite and back to the cable stations and into your homes, filth is being broadcast across the land. Squalid garbage, rated with X's, showing exposed genitalia, scenes of rape and incest and torture. Any child who can reach the dials on the television set can be immersed in this soul-stunting dirt.

"And we see this same seeping corruption in the books on the shelves of our libraries, paid for with public monies, with the tax money they demand from you as your ticket of admission to this wonderful culture around us! Cynical men in universities, in national magazines and newspapers, and on talk shows, praise novels which contain scenes that would gag a hyena.

"Perhaps we should be grateful that our public education system has been so gutted by the bureaucrats and unions, national and local, that the teachers no longer have time to teach reading. They are too busy turning out reports no one ever needs or reads. They are so busy our children can graduate without ever being able to write a sentence in acceptable English, or being able to read anything more difficult than comic books. Rejoice that much of the filth in our libraries is well beyond their abilities to comprehend.

"Perhaps teachers are being paid not to teach in the same way farmers are paid not to farm, able-bodied men paid not to work and politicians paid to pass legislation favoring themselves and the special-interest groups which bribe them.

"Once upon a time our nation was great. Now we sag into despair. The climate changes, the acid rains fall, the great floods and droughts impoverish millions, taking the savings of those who thought they could be provident in these times. We see all our silent factories, all the stacks without smoke, like monuments to a civilization past. Selfish owners refused to spend for modernization. Selfish unions struck for the highest wages in the world.

"We see rapists and murderers and armed robbers turned loose after a short exposure to that prison environment which gratifies all their hungers and teaches them new criminal arts.

"We see an endless tide of blacks and Hispanics entering our green land illegally, taking the bread out of the mouths of those few of us still willing to do hard manual labor.

"We see the abortionists slaying the people of the future.

"We see what little remaining wealth we have, squandered by the huge costs of maintaining lazy and overfed armies in distant lands where they are hated by the populace, and squandered by the Pentagon thieves who waste four dollars out of every five appropriated.

"Our air, rivers, lakes, land, bays and oceans become ever more toxic as the wastes of a plastic culture are dumped into them without authorization or control.

"We are afraid to walk our own streets at night, knowing that our police officers do not dare leave their cars to patrol on foot the shadows where hide the hoodlums, muggers, whores, addicts, drug vendors and maniacs.

"Rich men get richer in businesses which produce nothing tangible or useful—only bits of paper. Documents. Bonds and warrants and options and money management accounts. Mergers and spinoffs and liquidations."

He stopped and let the silence grow. He leaned forward and clasped his hands around the front edge of the lectern on the pulpit. His hands and wrists were outsized, larger than one would expect on a man of such leanness. He glanced down at the script and saw the margin notation indicating an extreme closeup, meaning that at that moment one of the cameramen was slowly zooming in on him using the longest lens on the TK-47 RCA computerized color camera.

"Do you think this is all something new in the world?" John Tinker Meadows asked in a half-whisper that carried to the remote corners of the Tabernacle. "Do you really think we live in exceptional times?" The sarcasm was clear.

"In Habakkuk's vision, the oracle proclaimed, *Outrage and violence, this is all I see, all is contention and discord flourishes. And so the law loses its hold, and justice never shows itself. Yes, the wicked man gets the better of the upright, and so justice seems to be distorted.*

"And the oracle said, *Trouble is coming to the man who amasses goods that are not his and loads himself with pledges.* And the oracle said, *Trouble is coming to the man who grossly exploits others for the sake of his house, to fix his nest on high and so evade the hand of misfortune.*"

Beginning with the hoarse whisper, he had been slowly increasing the volume and resonance of his voice as he straightened, knowing the long lens was slowly slowly backing away from the extreme closeup.

"*Trouble is coming to the man who builds a town with blood and founds a city on crime.*"

He looked at them from on high, gazing from side to side at the thousands before him. In a striking change he switched to a conversational tone of voice. With a troubled look he said, "So what do we do, my friends? Here we are, decent God-fearing people in a culture, in a world, going right down the tube. Do we pray and hope to inherit the earth? Do we grab guns and head for the hills? Do we tell ourselves things have to get better?"

After a pause he shouted, "NONE OF THE ABOVE!" He saw some of them jump. You could tell if you had them by the way some of them jumped. This was one of the good Sundays. Sometimes it worked better than other times. He had never achieved the consistency of the old man, who always made it work.

"We do not really live out there amid all that garbage. We live in the great peaceful country of the spirit. We live in the love of God and His only begotten son, and we live in the confidence that beyond that transition we call death there is eternal life for us who BELIEVE!

"You can turn your backs on the feckless, stinking, stubborn garbage of the world, its crimes and passions, its stench of victims and predators. I am not saying you cannot be touched in physical ways. You can. And those dear to you can be victims. I am telling you that you cannot ever be touched in that place where life means the most. This brute world can never touch your spirit, your soul. It can never defeat those who love God. You are weighed down by the burden of fear and apprehension as this physical world goes downhill in a hand basket. You can shrug off that hideous burden. You can live in a state of joy. Come down to the rail. You there, way in the back, you start it. Get up and walk down here. My father and my sister and I will receive you here, into the arms of Jesus Christ. And evil will never touch you. Never!"

He stared back and saw a few beginning to get up, to edge their way out of the long pews.

"That's right! Come down now! Acknowledge your God. Give Him a chance to heal you. To be saved means to be safe. When a drowning man is saved, he is brought to the shore, safe from the wild waters. Don't hang back. Don't tell yourself you'll think about it, and maybe try it next time. Will there be a next time? Will you have another chance? This is your chance. Now! Come on along. Move down the aisles to me, to us."

The Meadows Angels had begun to hum a cappella a medley of old familiar hymns. On cue they increased the volume as he stepped around the pulpit and followed his father and his sister down the few broad stairs to the level of the rail. All three aisles were reasonably full now, and all the familiar expressions were there. On some the beatific smile, on others the sidelong look of self-consciousness. On some a protective smirk. Others were without any expression, as though walking in a dream.

To John Tinker's dismay and annoyance, the old man was not taking part. He stood on the second broad stair from the bottom, looking up at the big curtains of woven glass fiber on the side windows, his lips moving as, with his right hand, he scratched the side of his neck. Mary Margaret gave John Tinker a glance and shrug of exasperation. She tugged at her father's arm and he pulled away and went back up. John Tinker thought at first that he was going back to his high-backed ornate chair, but instead the old man opened the narrow door under the choir loft and left. As this was not the first time it had happened, Nurse Minter had been posted at the other end of the underground corridor that led from the Tabernacle under the Garden of Mercy to the basement of the Manse.

There were a couple of hundred saved. The staff would take care of getting the names and addresses and other identifying information to feed into the master data base. John Tinker and Mary Margaret worked their way back and forth along the inside of the rail. Mary Margaret, from the pulpit, thanked God for those saved with a prayer which John Tinker felt ran five minutes longer than required. The collection was taken, swiftly and deftly. John Tinker gave a short and appropriate Bible reading, and Mary Margaret gave the benediction. They then stood side by side, high above the congregation, out of the reach of those who might want to approach and chat, until the Tabernacle was almost empty.

Then they went back through the narrow door and down six steps to the concrete tunnel which led for one hundred and fifty yards back to the Manse. The Manse, behind the Tabernacle and the Garden of Mercy, was on the rise of a limestone knoll. The corridor was lighted by fluorescent tubing which, in its effort to simulate daylight, gave off an odd pink glow.

"We should beef up that choir volume after the benediction," John Tinker said. "That many people always make too much noise leaving. All that shuffling and yammering."

"They can do that in the booth, can't they?"

"Of course they can. Provided somebody tells them to."

"Look, please don't get nasty with me just because he got out of control."

"What was he trying to do?"

"How could I possibly know? I don't think we can keep including him much longer, John. Maybe we should call a halt right now."

"All the old-timers expect to see him. And you have to admit, he really does look good, Mag."

"The doctor said Thursday that right now he's in better physical condition—blood pressure and pulse and respiration—than he was before his mind started to go. He said that's a fairly common phenomenon."

He pushed the door open and they went into the basement of the Manse. Willa Minter was waiting for them over by the elevator. She was a small square person, and John Tinker thought that in her uniform she looked like some sort of historical marker or monument. She had round pink cheeks, hair of a chemical yellow, and when she was upset she wore a servile grin that looked like some variant of guilt.

"He's settled down now," she said quickly. "He's taking a bath."

"With his celluloid duck?" John Tinker asked.

"John, please!" Mary Margaret said.

"Minter, does he realize he behaved badly?"

"Yes, of course. He was very upset about it. You see, he had a tummy upset and cramps and he had to go so bad he was afraid it would happen right there. It happened right after we got off the elevator, and the poor darling cried like a child he was so ashamed."

"Well, you better get back to him before he drowns," Mary Margaret said.

"Oh, he's awfully good in the tub. He really is. He loves to be clean. Squeaky clean."

She hesitated, still grinning, and headed for the stairs.

Once they were in the elevator, Mary Margaret said, "I thought you were very good today, John. As good as I ever heard."

"I had the feeling it was going well. This time Fred Stubbs did the first draft and then Spencer McKay and I worked it over. We'll use the original long version in *PathWays*, I think."

"John, could you get off at the third floor with me? I have a problem."

"Can't I get out of these clothes first?"

"Just a minute or two, please."

They got off at three, Mary Margaret moving with her characteristic lightness, agility and grace. She was a big woman, six feet tall, and he knew she outweighed him. Her fatness was a ripe, billowy, almost intrusive presence. In cassock and surplice she was as imposing as an oversized statue in a public park. She wore her dark gold hair in a glossy braid, curved and pinned into a regal tiara. Even with her strong features and with no makeup at all, at thirty-eight she gave off a flavor of total femininity, both fragrant and lusty.

He leaned wearily against the wall beside the elevator door and said, "Okay. What now?"

"It's Joe Deets again. Or should I say the Reverend Joseph Deets? I know you won't fire him. I really don't know how he does it, he's such an ugly little man. But now he's nailed another one of my Angels. Doreen Purves. She's been with us six months. She just turned eighteen. She's from a farm family near Waycross."

"You've talked to her?"

"Of course I've talked to her!"

"Don't get edgy, Mag. How'd she react?"

"First denials, and then she got very sloppy. Tears and hysteria. She claims she's in love with him. If we send her home she'll kill herself. She knows that she and the Reverend Deets are committing a sin, but she says they can't help it."

"Background?"

"She quit high school and went to work in a McDonald's. She got mixed up with a motorcycle gang and got pregnant and miscarried at five months. Her mother brought her to me. They've been church members for twenty years. She miscarried after her boyfriend got killed sliding under a truck on his cycle. She was in deep depression when she got here. She's been coming out of it nicely. Pretty little thing. Lovely untrained voice. And now this."

John Tinker Meadows sighed. "I'll tell Joe to cool it, for whatever good that might do. I'll threaten him."

"Thanks. I guess it's too much to hope to ask him to stay away from her. Just please make sure he keeps it very, very quiet. And there are a couple of other things, as long as we're talking."

"Mag! Later. Okay? God is love."

"Bless His holy name," she said obediently, and he got back into the elevator and went up to his suite on the fourth floor. It was refuge, a place of blues and grays and clean surfaces. A place of silence. There was a study, but he seldom used it, preferring either his office over in the Administration Building or, less frequently, the old man's office, over beyond the conference room, which he could enter directly from the living room of his suite.

He went straight to the bathroom, peeling off the sweaty white surplice with the broad gold trim and the sky-blue cassock. He kicked the garments toward the hamper, and before he turned on the shower he lowered himself to the floor and did his twenty fast push-ups, a routine so deeply embedded he seldom gave it any conscious thought. He was breathing deeply as he stepped into the steaming needles, and as he lathered himself with the pine soap he thought ahead to the private Sunday conference with Finn Efflander, going over the items Finn would bring up.

After he had dressed in sandals, tan slacks and a white knit shirt, he went into the study and accessed his schedule for the week on his personal terminal. The most important item was the weekday breakfast with the Senators.

Though he knew that Finn was next door in the conference room, waiting for him, he went over and stood at the big windows for a little while, looking out at a slice of the Meadows Center. He could see, beyond an angle of the Tabernacle, a portion of the giant, landscaped parking lot, and beyond it the divided boulevard that led toward the Lakemore interchange five miles away on the north-south Interstate. On the far side of the highway he could see, in the distance, a segment of the Meadows Mall and the large parking areas. Directly ahead of him were several of the University buildings—Administration, the Library and the Student Center.

Remembering that someone had mentioned the possibility of adding a wing to Administration, he turned idly to look at the colorful rendering of the whole Meadows Center, done in pastels from an aerial photograph taken for a magazine article. He experienced a moment of disorientation when he saw the blank wall near the fireplace where it had hung. He remembered that several weeks ago he'd had it taken down and rehung over in the lounge in Administration.

Over the past two years he had disposed of so many decorations and memorabilia, the suite had begun to look almost completely impersonal, like a suite in an elegant residential hotel. He did not care to wonder why he was doing this. He suspected it might be a reaction against the old man's practice of clinging to every possible artifact of success, framing everything frameable, mounting the mountable. But he did not care to speculate about it at any length or with any intensity. It made him feel uneasy to do so. He told himself he merely did not like clutter.

Without warning a dream edged back into his memory, and he did not know if he had dreamed it only once, or many times. It was a brief dream wherein he was standing on some high place in the same position as the Christus overlooking Rio, arms outstretched. It was very cold, but it was necessary he keep on standing there, without movement. It was imperative. Snow was blowing and clinging to his clothing and hair and eyebrows. Suddenly he was back at a distance looking at the statue of himself, watching the snow and the wind turn it white as marble. As the wind grew stronger, the white figure began to topple. It toppled so very slowly he realized it had to be of an immense size. It fell over onto the left hand and arm. They shattered with the bright clean sound of crystal smashing, and big transparent disks and segments of the arm went bouncing and rolling over a stony slope down toward the sea.

His eyes stung, and a single tear rolled down his left cheek. It startled him. Everything, he thought, is getting to be too damned much. The old man is going so fast. Every week he is worse. The days are too short. Privacy is almost impossible. Mag is becoming ever more difficult and contentious. And now Molly has begun making the little boring demands. Too much, too much, too much.

Two

Roy Owen sat in a small downtown hotel room in a city sixty miles southeast of Lakemore and the Meadows Center. He was drinking coffee and trying to read the newspaper, and found himself reading the same paragraph over and over without comprehension. He was waiting for Hanrahan, the private investigator, to arrive, and the anticipated interview was so alien to the patterns of his life that he kept thinking of it as a kind of charade, a game he had agreed, too hastily, to play.

Roy Owen was a small, trim, quiet man, conservative in dress and manner, hesitant in speech. He was in charge of the investment programs of three large no-load mutual funds headquartered in Hartford, Connecticut, and marketed nationally by General Services, Inc., which was associated in some obscure corporate manner with a large cable television enterprise.

There were twelve mutual funds in the General Services family of funds, five fund managers, with telephone switches permitted and even encouraged. The managers were in competition with each other insofar as annual fund performance was concerned. But there was not, as one of his colleagues termed it, any chickenshittery about staff meetings, advisers, committees and reviews. Top management did not care if you used chicken bones, the *I Ching*, witchcraft or IBM to decide when and what to sell, and when and what to buy. All they wanted was to have one individual on whom they could pin blame for bad performance, or pin medals for success. You could write your own expenses, visit the corporations, devise your own guidelines. Just avoid any conflict of interest, or any use of insider information. They would let you have a bad year, if it came after a bunch of good ones.

He had worked for a time with a mutual fund outfit where everybody looked over everybody else's shoulder, and you could expect to be given more advice than you needed or could use. It had made him very nervous and had given him a small temporary ulcer. He was content with this outfit.

He had a good assistant, Dave Wager, now watching the store, supervising the daily computation of per-share value, keeping a close and wary eye on the holdings in the three funds, well aware of how much of an emergency would require his phoning Roy.

Roy Owen had few illusions about himself. He knew that he did a very good job with the funds. And he did that good job because he relished winning and hated losing. Each year his base salary was sweetened on the basis of a complicated formula wherein his growth and income records were compared with the records of the Dow, Value Line, Standard and Poor 500, the Wilshire 5000 and several public funds comparable in size with his. He knew he was the sort of person people had to meet a dozen times before they began to remember his name. He enjoyed playing games and he enjoyed winning at whatever he played, be it handball, tennis or backgammon. In victory he was gentle and humble and self-deprecatory, carefully concealing the rush of pleasure he felt.

He was a graduate of the Wharton School and the loving father of Janie, aged six. His only concession to a certain independence of thought was a drooping pistolero mustache, shades darker than his hair, glinting brown-red in direct sunlight.

The investigator phoned and came up from the lobby and knocked on the door. When Owen opened it the fellow said, unnecessarily, "J. B. Hanrahan, Mr. Owen." He extended a large soft white hand. He was tall, sallow and thin, with bad posture and a watermelon belly. His thin dark hair was worn long at the left side and combed back across his bare skull and glued in place. He smelled of cigar. He wore green polyester trousers and a ranch shirt in faded yellow, with pearl buttons. A scar ran from the center of his forehead down through the outer edge of his right eyebrow and ended near his ear. At first glance the man looked both flamboyant and silly. Then Owen realized that Hanrahan was a chameleon hiding in the flower patch. He fitted into the sun-belt scene, a sickly old boy retired from almost any kind of office or factory work. The correct message was in the eyes of J. B. Hanrahan. They were a clear, unblinking green, like the eyes of a predatory waterbird standing in the frog pond.

He carried a plastic briefcase of imitation lizard, and said that, yes, he would like a cup of coffee if there was enough in the pot. Owen said he had ordered up coffee for two.

They sat at the small table by the window. Hanrahan said, "Glad you could come down. This is better than trying to do it by phone or in writing. I did just as good as the police did. I got nothing too. My inclination is to drop it right now and recommend you do the same. But she's your wife. Is or was.

"And you've put out a lot of money on me and got nothing back except what I told you already. And the police there in Lakemore could have told you that much. What I'm saying, Mr. Owen, I've run out of places to turn. If I knew more about the woman, maybe I could make a better guess about what could have happened."

"What kind of thing would you want to know?"

"Pretty personal, if you don't mind. More personal than what you told me at first."

"Such as what?"

"You and she get along good?"

He shrugged, trying to find the right words. "I don't imagine there are very many perfect marriages."

"Planning on splitting up?"

"Oh no! Nothing like that. It's just that Lindy has a lot more than her share of energy. After Janie was born, she got into a lot of volunteer work in Hartford. Library drive, blood bank, hospital foundation. Over a year ago she said she was getting tired of playing games where nobody kept score. She said that money is the device people use to keep score. An old friend told her about a job opening up on that magazine in New York called *Out Front.* The idea is that it's about people who are out in front, in the public eye. It wasn't difficult to make arrangements about Janie. Lindy's mother lives in a town house not two blocks from our place."

"You objected?"

"Look, I didn't like it then, when it started, and I didn't get to like it any better. She was going to come back home every weekend, but they have been sending her on special assignments, like this one. When I met her she was a young reporter on the Philadelphia *Bulletin*. My work is very interesting—to me. When I try to explain it to anybody except another market analyst, people begin to yawn. We have been living the same life a couple might live who had a friendly separation. And I don't like that magazine. It seems to try to make things sound dirty, no matter how innocent they might be."

"So she came down to make the Reverend Doctor John Tinker Meadows seem dirty?"

"She said there was some smoke and she was looking for fire. I don't like talking about personal things. I'm sorry. I'm not very good at it. Lindy and I were once upon a time good friends very much in love. Okay, lately I'd thought we were turning into pretty good friends, but I was wrong. I know I still love her. And I know Janie needs her badly, so badly she can't even let it show how much."

"Do you still feel, like you told me in the beginning, that the Church might have had something to do with her disappearance?"

"I don't know. That's what I wanted you to find out."

"The Meadows family has regular contacts with the press. This whole setup has become very important over the years. Why do you think she came down here and used a cover name?"

"I have no idea. She didn't say. Maybe she thought the name of the magazine would dry up any official or unofficial source. And if they found out she was using a false name, they could have assumed she was . . . more of a threat than she actually was. Big money is clout, Mr. Hanrahan. From what I've been able to read about this Eternal Church of the Believer, they seem to take in a lot of money."

Hanrahan smiled. The smile spread his pouched cheeks. It was a humorless smile, the grin of the basking shark. "Indeed they do. Yessiree bob, indeed they do. I better tell you a little more about those people."

He took a map from his dispatch case, moved the cups aside and spread it out on the table. Roy Owen hitched his chair closer to Hanrahan.

"Now this isn't to scale. It's just to give you the feel of the place. The Interstate is way over here to the west, and the city limits of Lakemore start two miles west of that. All of this, this whole shebang here, is the Meadows Center, located just about six miles east of the Interstate. I could have researched just how many hundreds or thousands of acres they've got, if there was any point to it.

"You can divide the whole thing into four parts. Right here is the

Eternal Church of the Believer, the Tabernacle, the Manse and these buildings here, Administration, Security Office, Communications and so on. That's the primary security area. You just don't get in there at all, and the fence line with the sensors and guard system, it butts up to the back side of the Tabernacle, so the public can get in the church, but the clergy and so on, they go out the back and they are in a secure area. They got a generator system in there, and their own water and sewage setup. In this here Communications Building they've got a couple of big mainframe computers in the basement, dug out of the limestone rock, that handle all the Church records and the University records and I suppose the records from the commercial area."

" 'Commercial area'?"

"I'll get to that in a minute. Now over here is the University complex. There are only about six hundred students and maybe fifty faculty, and anywhere else it would be called a college. It's still in the process of construction. Just about everything around there is being built up and added on to. And here to the north of the University grounds you've got the Meadows Settlements. Like a small city of retirement homes and homes where the employees live. That's all the secondary security area. Guards and gates to go through and so on, but not as tight as where the Manse and Communications are.

"You asked about the commercial area. This is it, all along the divided boulevard here for about three miles. This divided part of it is called Henrietta Boulevard after old Matthew Meadows' mother. It changes to two-lane when it gets to about two miles from the interchange, and changes back to State Road 433.

"This controlled commercial development is owned and managed by ECB Enterprises. ECB for Eternal Church and so on. What you have is the big Meadows Mall here, biggest mall in that end of the state. Along here are the big motels where the tourists and the pilgrims stay. And fast-food places, all leased from ECB. Lakemore Construction is the building arm of ECB. It builds commercial to the tenant's wishes, and it builds all the little houses in the Meadows Settlements according to several standard floor plans. Then there is Meadows Development, Inc. I'm not exactly sure what it does. Planning, maybe. The executive offices for the commercial side are on the second floor in the Mall. The Mall is the third grade of security area, just enough guards and patrols to keep order there and around the motel parking lots at night and so on.

"ECB Enterprises seems to own the Central Citizens Bank of Lakemore. Anyway, they bought a controlling interest back from the bank holding company that picked it up years ago, and they have a majority on the board of directors.

"What have I left out? Oh, maybe the most important part. In Communications they've got professional television and radio broadcast facilities, with first-class people. The early church service they had there this morning gets cut to fifty minutes and goes up to the transponders they've got on a couple of satellites, sent up there through the big GTE narrow-beam dishes on the roof of Communications, over at the end away from the heliport. It's a full hour when they get through with it, with five minutes of solicitations in front and in back of the service. From the satellite, either Tex-Tel or Westar, it goes to the cable and to the television stations that use it direct, so you might have a couple hundred stations putting that morning service on the air right now.

"They try to stay on twenty-four hours a day, seven days a week, television, radio, Bible lessons, talk shows, repeats, pageants, God only knows what. They have a lot of local talk shows scattered around, and for that they draw on their affiliated churches, about eighty of them. What happens, they get people to tithe, to send in ten percent of their income and sometimes even twenty and thirty percent.

"The money rolls in and the visitors roll in. Magazine and newspaper people, politicians, IRS, investigators from state and national committees, people writing books and lots and lots of hustlers. The big shots come in by private airplane and land on the strip back here beyond the hill where the Manse is. Some of them even get to stay in the Manse, which I understand is considered to be one of the finest small hotels in the world. At least it is staffed by people who used to work in fine hotels. ECB Enterprises has a couple of Gulfstream jets, a couple of small Beechcraft and a chopper—along with a little tower and a staff of ten to fly and maintain them."

"What do you mean about hustlers?"

"Big money attracts all kinds. Healers keep coming around to hitch a ride on the big bandwagon, but the Meadows family doesn't seem to want to get mixed up with any charismatics. They stay on the fundamentalist side of almost everything. And, of course, a lot of people come around who want to be licensed to sell souvenirs and trinkets. Those are handled by some kind of corporate subsidiary. Photographs, paintings, lapel pins, brooches, bumper stickers and insignia of their Society of Merit."

"Insignia?"

"There's lots of levels and degrees. Like if you give a hundred thousand dollars to the Church, you become a Founder of the Society of Merit, and you get a gold pin with diamonds, and you get to be flown in and stay at the Manse. The Manse looks a hundred years old, but it's only six. The people who want to sell stuff, they screen them very carefully. Just like they screen the people who apply for space in the Mall. I kept my eyes and my ears open, Mr. Owen, and the mail has to be trucked out there every single working day. Lots of bags of mail. There is a big mail room in Communications. Deposits go to the bank in an armored car. I can't make a guess because I don't have the figures on how many people contribute and tithe and so on. But from what they spend and how they live, they've got to be taking in more than two million a week. Maybe an awful lot more. And the Church is tax-exempt. It got the exemption back in 1946 when old Matthew broke away from the Baptists and started his own church. He had sixty parishioners to start with, and one old lady died and left everything to him. He used the money to go on radio."

"I've been watching the broadcasts. I see Matthew Meadows once in a while," Roy Owen said.

"Those are old repeats. He's got Alzheimer's disease. That's what they call senility these days. If they let him loose he wanders away and gets lost. What do you think of the television church services?"

"They seem very . . . well organized. Very attractive young people in the choir."

"The Angels. Some are students at Meadows University, and some of them work in the area, and some of them are kids in trouble that their folks bring and leave here. A lot of them live in a dormitory inside the primary security area beyond the Garden of Mercy. The ones who aren't in school and don't have regular jobs have to do odd jobs around the area to pay for their keep."

"You certainly learned a lot about it."

Hanrahan slowly folded the map and handed it to Roy Owen. "You can have it. It wasn't hard finding out how they are organized up there and what goes on. It isn't any kind of illegal setup. I kept asking how I could get a security guard job and if it was hard work once I got it. Security guards talk because it is very dull standing around."

"Why all the security? Why so much?"

"I wondered too, at first. But pretty soon I realized why it has to be.

John Tinker Meadows and his old man and his sister, they rope in their supporters by playing on their fears and on their hatreds and their loneliness. When you play that game with a big net, you are going to scoop up some people here and there who are pretty well unwrapped. Like they say, their elevators don't go to their top floors. There are metal detectors set into the frames of those big Tabernacle doors, and the guards are very good at quietly intercepting people going in. Six or eight times a year some loony tries to take a gun into church. Maybe God told them to blow John Tinker away, or take a shot at that big Sister Mary Margaret. Maybe in some sermon or other John Tinker told any Church member married to a sinner to pack up and get out. So the sinner brings a gun to get even. Or some nutcake decides he's so steeped in sin that the only way he can acknowledge it is blow his brains out during the service. By now do you know what I've been trying to tell you?"

"I . . . I guess I do, Mr. Hanrahan. It's a great big powerful organization and they are geared to repel boarders of any kind. With that sort of money coming in, they could make themselves immune to almost any kind of nuisance approach. My wife was just one person in a big crowd of . . . hustlers."

"And her chance of worming her way inside was zero, or the next thing to it. If they have to hire somebody to run the two-ton dishwashing machine in the Manse, they background them as carefully as the FBI and the CIA. Everybody working inside the primary security area has been cleared back to the cradle, and even so there is a lot of quiet surveillance going on."

Roy Owen took a card out of his wallet and slid it across to Hanrahan, saying, "Did I get it right when you phoned me?"

He pushed the card back. "Exactly right. Lenore Olan instead of Linda Owen. Amateurs tend to stick with the same initials. Room sixteen at the County Line Motel, which is way on the other side of Lakemore. That's where she stayed. And that's where whatever happened began, or began and ended."

Roy Owen was silent, remembering how Lindy had sounded when she'd phoned him on May sixth, that last Friday night he had heard her voice. Despondent was too strong a word. Listless and tired. "It isn't like I thought it would be," she had said. "There's a lot of stories here, but nothing *Out Front* would want to use. And maybe there's a nice juicy *Out Front* story behind the scenes, but I don't think I'm going to get it. If one lead works, I might stay a couple of days, maybe not. I don't know. Maybe I'll give up this line of work. Makes me feel just a little bit tacky. Now don't tell me how happy that makes you, or I just might not quit." He remembered hearing the soft husky sound of her yawning just before she said good night, told him she loved him and hung up.

"As I said in the written report, she phoned you on Friday night, Mr. Owen, and then she left the motel before dawn sometime during Saturday night. The motel owner didn't pay any attention particularly, because she was paid through Sunday. The room was empty and she and her rental car were gone. It was a cold trail by the time the police came into the picture. After you talked to her editor and said you couldn't reach her, they tried and then reported that she was a missing person."

"The report wasn't very clear about the car."

"Nothing is clear about the car. It was a Budget Ford on a corporate credit card. The license number was on the motel registration. When they traced it through Budget, they found out it had been brought here, to the airport lot. The keys and the rental agreement were in the glove compartment. The charge went through. By the time they found the car, it had been rented several times and it was down in Tampa. Car rental offices at airports have problems with people who cut it too close making their flight. They found the car in the airport lot on Monday, according to the charge they made on it, but nobody knows when it entered the lot. Apparently there was no parking ticket issued, or it was lost."

"So if something happened to her in Lakemore, somebody else drove the car down to this city, Mr. Hanrahan. And if she was the one who drove it down here, then something happened to her at this airport or at La Guardia, or in the city before she got to her apartment. Which was it?"

"She was Eastern Airlines coach, round trip, and her name did not show up on any of the manifests of any of the flights Saturday, Sunday or Monday, the seventh, eighth or ninth. The trail was ten days cold when the police got on it. And right now it's three months cold."

"I know. I realize that. But it is hell not to know. You keep thinking about it and wondering."

Hanrahan shrugged. "We've got fifty thousand kids disappearing every year and every year they come up with maybe two thousand unidentified bodies of kids. That means there are lots of people doing a lot of wondering. A lot of pain. I'm not trying to make yours sound like less. . . ."

"I realize that. I've got a month, a little less, of vacation. I'm in touch with my assistant. The market doesn't seem to be doing anything interesting. I don't want to be a damned fool, but I keep thinking that if I could find somebody she got friendly with the time she was here . . . and if that person might have noticed anything . . . I don't know why, but I keep thinking of going to that motel and staying in that same room."

"I can tell you it's not much of a place." He stood up. "There's nothing more I can do. I don't know what happened, if anything, and I don't know how to find out. I don't think that hanging around that area is going to do you any good. On the other hand it isn't going to do you any harm. And it will keep you from wondering if you could maybe have done something."

"I appreciate all your time and trouble, Mr. Hanrahan. What do I owe you?"

"Let's say you paid me up to date. This little conference was on the house."

Hanrahan shut the door quietly behind him, leaving a faint stale smell of cigar in the hotel room. Roy Owen looked at the crude map Hanrahan had given him. Manse. Mall. Tabernacle. Careful printing.

He folded the map and took his round-trip air ticket out of the zipper pocket in his carry-on case. The return reservation was open. He found the airline number in the yellow pages. The recorded message told him to please stay on the line, one of the agents would be with him shortly. They played zither music to him, a Hungarian tempo vaguely familiar. He thought about Lindy again and the soft sound she had made when she yawned into the phone in her motel room in Lakemore.

And he thought about Janie, about how strange she had been lately. The place to be was with the child. But what do you tell the child? Daddy couldn't find out anything about Mommy. Nobody knows anything about Mommy. Nobody knows where she is. Hell of a thing to try to explain to a child harboring some kind of fright, tucked far away inside her.

The zither music stopped and a voice said, "This is Caroline. May I help you?"

"Would that you could," he said.

"I beg your pardon?"

"I'm sorry. I guess I've changed my plans," he said, and put the phone back on the cradle.

Three

Finn Efflander sat alone in one of the leather chairs at the side of the long executive conference table. He had kicked a moccasin off and had one heel braced on the seat of his chair, his long fingers laced around his ankle, knee sharply bent. Idly and patiently he watched the interconnecting door to John Tinker Meadows' suite and waited for the man to come out. Behind Efflander, the door to the old man's office was open wide. Efflander had learned through observation and experiment that John Tinker Meadows was slightly more tolerant and flexible in his judgments when he could see into his father's office.

Efflander believed it was a daddy hangup, some suppressed guilt over taking over the store. All those plaques and citations on the wall, and all those pictures of a younger and more vital Matthew Meadows standing with the past and present celebrities of the world, all smiling out at John Tinker. Dr. Meadows and Sadat. Dr. Meadows and Churchill, Gary Cooper, Pat O'Brien, Herbert Armstrong, Harry Emerson Fosdick, Paul Harvey, Walter Cronkite, Tammy Bakker, Howard Cosell.

Finn Efflander exhaled slowly and deeply, reaffirming his posture and expression and appearance of languid ease, of mild amusement, of sleepy self-contempt. He could maintain this outward image when his bowels were turned to slime by anxieties, when his ears rang with tension, his mouth was dry, his hands wet, his heart banging. The look of total ease was his working armor, his costume. Basically impatient, he had taught himself a patience so endless it flattened those who tried to bargain with him and outwait him. Even when all his nerves were pulled so tight they sang, he could yawn and drawl and shuck around all afternoon. He was a long-limbed man in his early forties with pallid skin pocked with old acne scars. His cobweb-fine brown hair was receding rapidly. His eyes were hooded, his smile habitual, and he could make a brand-new custom suit look, within hours, as if he had bought it for three dollars from the Salvation Army.

The door swung open and John Tinker came striding in. Finn lowered his cramped leg and smiled and said, "People say you done good this morning."

John Tinker sat in the armchair at the head of the table and said, "It seemed as if I was getting a good feedback. It ran a little short. I left out a section of it. Didn't mean to. Just one of those things. I just checked the phone banks across the way. All the operators are busy. That's about the best way to keep score."

"I've got a sort of agenda, here, John, but not in any special order of importance."

"You always say that."

"Just one of my nervous mannerisms. Nicpac is after a donation."

"Because they did so great last time? Ha! And this isn't even an election year. What do you think?"

"Down the road I can see little continuing areas of vulnerability. Tax quibbles. Direct satellite broadcasting regulations, new rules on cable access. What we all want, Nicpac keeps saying, is less government regulation. So, through Nicpac, we help support our friends in the government. They are going after funds from everybody. PTL, Moral Majority, 700 Club, Worldwide Church of God, Trinity, CBN. But they are all a little edgy about giving because of the People for the American Way campaign, which keeps saying that organizations qualifying for tax-deductible gifts cannot participate directly or indirectly in any political campaign. And Nicpac is a political entity."

"What are they asking for?"

"Quarter mil."

"But they'll take a hundred thousand?"

"Gladly. Happily."

"So work it out with Joe Deets. It should come out of the Henrietta Fund, I think. Then we won't have trouble with those American Way fellows."

Finn nodded. He scribbled a note to himself. "Okay. We're turned down again on accreditation."

"But I thought you'd worked out something."

"I thought I had too, but we can't fit into that Non-Traditional designation either. It's full of art schools, diploma mills and such. So I've been on the phone with eight college presidents who share our problem. Between us we've come up with a list of thirty-four unaccredited institutions, and we've tentatively agreed that a new accrediting body is needed. NAROCU. Nah-ROW-koo."

"Nah what?"

"National Association of Religiously Oriented Colleges and Universities. If the nine of us come up with thirty thousand each and we tap the others for whatever they can stand still for, we can set up a headquarters, hire a couple of retired academics with respectable degrees and establish an accrediting procedure. We'll have some fair standards, of course. It will take a few years to establish some real plausibility, but in time we should be able to get a handle on our fair share of federal funds, and the degrees we grant will be more meaningful. Okay to run with it?"

"Good work. Good creative thinking!"

"But I want to ease out of it as soon as it starts to lift off the ground. I have enough to look after. Anyway, here's where we stand as of the Friday close." He took the familiar summary printout from his dispatch case and put it in front of John Tinker Meadows.

The printout covered all of the Church accounts, all of its assets in all of its various pockets, along with the bank and security accounts of the ECB Foundation, the Eternal Trust and all the smaller investment accounts. It revealed the gain since the previous accounting, showing the amounts added by both donations and market value increases. The grand total was quite unreal. It used to give John Tinker a fluttering feeling just under the heart, making it difficult for him to take a deep breath. But instead of triumph he now saw merely numbers. Lots of them, adding up to meaningless totals.

The second sheet of the printout was an interim profit-and-loss statement which covered all of the commercial operations and commercial entities.

"All in good health?" he asked.

"All thriving," said Efflander. "Just one small problem. One of the flying squadrons of the IRS is making Rolf Wintergarten nervous."

"He's being well paid to stay nervous," John said. "What is it this time?"

"A sly little variation. Here's the reasoning. They pulled the last year's personal tax returns of all our executive and administrative personnel. As you well know, every one of them tithes. They took the returns of the nine highest-paid people in the commercial end—construction, leasing, housing and so on—and the salaries came out close to one million total, so there is the question of the total tithe of a hundred thousand dollars."

"What question?"

"They say it can be called a kickback. We pay high salaries to reduce the profit on which we have to pay taxes, and then make those people kick back to the Church. They want to use that as a lever to pry open the whole contribution record, to make us prove to them that everybody tithes to the same extent—everybody who works for any direct or indirect entity of Meadows Center. In addition, they have the usual complaints about our overhead charges to the commercial entities. Share of the airstrip expenses, motor pool, overall maintenance, legal staff and so on."

"When are they going to give up?"

"They aren't being paid to give up."

"On all tax-paying portions of this complex, our books are clean and our practices are all within the law. As far as contributions to the Church are concerned, that is none of their business. Have you run this past the brothers Winchester?"

"Yes. Charley says that if we paid Wintergarten ten million a year and he tithed one million, we might be forced to discuss it with them on the basis we were translating potential profits into tax-free gifts. But there is no blatant example, and their reasoning, he says, is faulty. We can stonewall it all the way to the tax court, meanwhile being careful about any warrant to grab the books and records, so we can stonewall that too. But he says we just might mention it to the Senators this coming week."

"We'll arrange it so Charley can bring it up. I see you have brought your little tape player, and I assume it has something to do with what my sainted sister calls the Japanese nodules."

Finn smiled and pressed the play button, saying, "Now hear this."

John Tinker leaned back, eyes closed, making a fingertip tent as he composed himself to listen to this latest effort after so many failures. He heard the buzzing sound of a phone ringing somewhere, and then the heavy voice of a man saying, "Hello?" He sounded irritable and impatient.

"Is this Mr. Albert? Mr. Francis M. Albert?" a woman asked.

"Yes, yes. If you're selling, I'm not buying."

"Please hold the line. The Reverend Doctor Matthew Meadows would like to speak to you?"

"To me? What? What kind of a dumb joke are you . . ."

"Francis? This is your pastor speaking." John Tinker opened his eyes and leaned forward. It was the rich instrument of old—intimate, resonant, unmistakable.

"Reverend! It *is* you! I thought it was a joke that . . ."

"I called you, my son, because we here at the Church are worried about you. We haven't heard from you in ten months."

"Is it that long? Honest to God. I mean excuse me, I didn't mean to say that. Look, I didn't know it was so long."

"I have been worried about you, personally. I have been wondering if you might be in some kind of serious trouble, Francis. You and your wife have been members for six years. Is there trouble? Is there any way we can help you?"

"I don't know. I mean maybe. What happened, our daughter came down with some trouble of the spine. It's a long word and it means like it is disintegrating. And the treatments are killing us."

"Would that be Sharon or Karen?"

"Honest to God, you remember the names! Excuse me again. It's the little one. It's Sharon. She just turned eight. It's pitiful, she's being so brave about it. You wouldn't believe the expense."

"I can well imagine. And it would of course limit your tithe, Francis. But it should not eliminate it. You are not the sort of person looking for an excuse to stop supporting your Church. You and I have been together in the Church a long time, and we have both learned that no matter what you give, no matter how great your sacrifice, God will give you good fortune in far greater measure than your gift to Him."

"I know, I know. It's just that . . ."

"I would not want you to be opening up your life to greater misfortune by forsaking Him. Please let us know what we can do to help. We will be praying for little Sharon and for your whole family, Francis."

"I can't believe this has really happened! I never thought that a man as busy and important as you would have time for . . ."

"God is love."

"Uh . . . bless His holy name."

Finn turned the machine to rewind. John Tinker shook his head. He looked pale. "I never really thought that Japanese fellow could make it work."

"It's very eerie. This was a real conversation. Delinquents picked at random. Fifty calls. We counted only those where we could get through to the actual person. The calls were made over a three-day period. The resulting gifts averaged out two hundred and sixteen dollars per call. The lowest response was ten dollars, the highest fourteen hundred. Personal letters of thanks went out to each one, over your father's facsimile signature."

"I keep forgetting that technician's name."

"Mickey Oshiro. Here's a transcript of what you just heard. The portions that were canned have been highlighted in yellow. You can see that there are more of them than you would expect. Every voice pattern has been matched on a screen to the patterns lifted from your father's recorded sermons and Bible classes. The operator fills in the personal remarks on a phonetic keyboard and then at the right moment pushes *T* for transmit. She has to have a good memory for all the canned phrases. We put them on the key pad in a two-number code. And there is another code to imitate the way the voice drops at the end of a sentence, or goes up when a question is asked. It is all a product of voice synthesis, John. And very, very difficult for the operator. On lots of these calls she got rattled at the unexpected and had to break the connection and call back."

"You have just one operator?"

"Yes. Glinda Lopez. The other two I tried couldn't handle it. Glinda can just barely handle it. Understand, she is using a machine to talk in someone else's voice, without being detected or sounding false. The sweat runs right off her face. On the early ones she had the worst time. She bit her lip once and bled. But she's quick and smart and getting better with each call. She can't do an eight-hour shift of that. Nobody could. It's too intense."

"Maybe you could motivate her by giving her a percentage of what she brings in."

"That wouldn't work with her. She's not that sort of a person. She believes what she is saying. What Matthew Meadows is saying through her, through the machine. If I push her too hard she'll burn out, and then she might get cynical about jacking money out of people who can't afford to give it."

As he saw the change in John Tinker's expression, he knew at once that he had gone too far. The minister of God leaned toward him and said gently, "Perhaps you do not believe in the efficacy of prayer, old friend."

"I only meant . . ."

"An offering is a prayer to the Lord. You are sick at heart and you give up a piece of your life to be made whole again. Money is the way we measure the effort in our lives. The work we do is transmuted into gold, and in our gratitude we tithe the Church. We tithe God. We pray in gold. If you do not understand that at this late date, Finn . . ."

"Just clumsy wording. I'm sorry. I've burned out some of my people in the past. Their motivations change. They get cynical. I think it probably happens in every endeavor, John. It's part of the process of living and working. And believing."

"And you *do* believe?"

"Of course."

John Tinker Meadows looked directly into his eyes and Finn Efflander managed to endure that penetrating directness without looking away. And once again he wondered if John Tinker Meadows might be going mad. He seemed to be slowly, day by day, increasing the distance between himself and the people who ran his organization, the people he had to trust. At times like this, when John Tinker began talking about the necessity for faith, Finn felt alarm, as though he were alone in a room with an animal that had no idea of what its next move might be, and cared nothing about the consequences. He thought that it was time to talk to Mary Margaret again, to compare notes. There might come a day when this bleakness, this look of fury and outrage held in precarious control, might show itself from the pulpit.

It irritated Finn that this preacher his own age was able to cow him, to alarm him. In a highly successful business career he had dealt on even terms with men of far more power than John Tinker Meadows could wield. It was the suggestion of a destructive madness that made him so quick to try to mend any rift, he had decided. It was as though this whole Meadows empire which he had so carefully rebuilt out of the chaos was a castle of playing cards on a living-room rug, and John Tinker was a two-year-old playing in the same room, willful, destructive and unpredictable.

John Tinker sighed and relaxed and said, as though nothing at all had happened, "Something has come up. I don't think it's of any particular importance. Yesterday afternoon I had a long talk on the phone with Jeremy Rosen."

"The name seems to ring a bell."

"It should. He's a good friend of the Church. He's an Associate in the Society of Merit. And he's the chief executive officer of Burlington Communications, headquartered in New York. Last year when they picked up Farber Publishing, the magazine called *Out Front* was part of the package. Does that ring any bells?"

"Something about the police. Right! One of their people came down to write something about us and disappeared. Nothing to do with us, though it's a good guess she was going to write something unpleasant.

We gave our full cooperation. Sheriff Dockerty was very apologetic about the whole thing. What's up?"

"Jeremy has been reviewing the acquisitions. *Out Front* is beginning to make money sooner than anybody thought it would. He called in the managing editor to discuss budget and upcoming features. The editors are sending another investigative reporter down to try to open it all up again and see if there was any connection between the Church and her disappearance."

"But there wasn't!"

"You know that. I know that. But vicious gossip and hints of scandal sell magazines. And we are especially vulnerable. Those who have never found God, or who have turned their backs on Him, would like to destroy His true Church. Jeremy said that he could put a stop to it, but he would rather not because he was afraid that it would look as if we had brought pressure to bear on him. And he said there is a good relationship there between the editors and the reporters, and he feels that if he starts censoring their projects, the best ones might leave. I told him I understood his reluctance and I appreciated his warning us in advance. They're sending a woman again, sending her down sometime this week." He tugged his wallet out of his hip pocket and removed a scrap of paper that had been in with the currency.

"Her name is Carolyn Pennymark. Jeremy thinks she's about thirty years old. She was with the Washington *Post* before she went with *Out Front* about two years ago."

"If she checks into one of our motels, or makes a reservation, I'll be informed right away. Then what?"

"How would you suggest we handle it?"

With only momentary hesitation, Finn Efflander said, "I'll sic Jenny Albritton on her. Instant photo and thumbprint for her gold ID badge. Total charm. All the literature. Everything open to her except the mail room, the money room and the computer room. Access to you, too, of course. And maybe a little chopper ride around the reservation?"

"Good thinking. And by the way, Finn, are you reasonably sure that person, that Mrs. Owen who disappeared, had no kind of meaningful contact with any of our people?"

"She got into Administration and saw the Reverend Walter Macy for about three minutes. She had made an appointment to talk to him about a gift of property to the Church. One of our best security people, Eliot Erskine—he used to be on the Atlanta police force—thought she acted strange in some way, so he followed her into Walter's office after she had been in there not more than two minutes. She was rambling on and on to Walter about some icons her grandfather had brought from Russia before the Revolution, and when it became evident to Erskine that she was lying or confused, Walter told her to bring them in and they would have them appraised by professionals and she would be given the appraisal report so she could write them off as a gift. He thanked her for her generosity, and Erskine led her back out to where a terribly battered old pickup truck with a bearded driver was waiting for her. She told Erskine her car was being fixed."

"What day was that?"

"A Friday. She was on the gate report as a Miss Olan. Friday morning. May sixth. We've got no other record of her seeing anyone. And we would have if she had."

"I guess I have no reason to feel uneasy about this, but I do."

"I'll take care of things. Not to worry."

"You're invaluable to me, Finn. I don't know how I could manage without you at my side. Give the very highest priority to this voice synthesis, please. As soon as you think she is able, have this Lopez woman start training one or two more."

"Will do."

"God is love," John Tinker said, rising to his feet.

"Bless His holy name," murmured Finn.

Four

Joe Deets looked forward to Sunday afternoons. He spent them in his windowless office on the second floor of the Communications Building. A long desk had been built against one wall. He sat in a secretarial chair of pale oak and fake leather, with fat rubber tires. With one practiced shove of a foot, he could scoot along the desk from the terminals to the printers, and over to his own personal computer with its modems, two printers and eight-inch Winchester disks.

Sunday afternoons were fun time, investment time, the day for juggling money. There were eleven tax-exempt trust funds, all discretionary. They were divided among the trust departments of four New York City banks, three banks with three apiece, and one with two. A fifth bank served as a temporary receptacle, a way station between the Central Citizens Bank in Lakemore and the eleven trust funds.

It was his policy, proven by results, to keep all the funds invested at all times, moving from stocks to bonds to money market funds and back, long and short, depending on his sense of the marketplace. The securities analysis program on the big mainframe computer downstairs was wonderfully complex. It was tied into a market updating service so that after any business day he could print out each fund, showing current values and the percentage of change from the previous printout, the history of that particular investment and its rating in comparison to the performance of all other holdings in that fund and in all the funds under his control. Each week, after the infusion of new money, he apportioned it among the funds and set up the buy and sell orders. By tapping a very few keys on one of his terminals, he could print out the month-to-month history of each fund back to the day five years before when he had written the lengthy and intricate program that controlled the input and output and continual updating of these funds and all their transactions.

After proper safeguards had been built into the bank computer system for interbank transfers, he had been given a private access code which enabled him to make the transfers, and which also provided for a printout of his activities, if any, at the end of each working day for each bank involved.

Whenever he sent buy or sell instructions on any one of the eleven accounts, he sent simultaneous advice to the discount brokerage house which, by agreement with the banks, handled all ECB orders.

Through his personal computer, without the knowledge of anyone else in the world, he leased space in a mainframe computer in Virginia, space which he accessed with a variable code he knew was almost impossible to break. On each Sunday afternoon, after he had decided on his buys and sells for the following Monday morning, he put those recommendations into his privately leased space. Then he arranged for the ECB mainframe to access that same space with a simpler code, one which would not permit changes to be made in the stored information. It was printed out and always contained the ending phrase "Courtesy of Conover Resources" and the date.

Once all the transactions had been completed, Joe Deets would compute the total dollar volume of all buy and sell orders and transfer a tiny percentage of that total as an advisory fee to the bank account in Philadelphia of Conover Resources. That fee was moved in and out of the Conover account very quickly, ending up in a blind trust in a branch of the Bank of Nova Scotia in Freeport in the Bahamas. There, under the careful husbandry of Number 712-311, it had grown from the four hundred and fifty-one thousand dollars he had pilfered to over seven hundred and sixty-five thousand in the three and a half years since he had set it up.

There were times when he wished he had named the advisory company with a little less bravado. His mother's maiden name had been Clara Conover. And the dear old thing would have considered it a mortal sin to steal from any church, regardless of its beliefs.

Not really stealing, he thought. It's a computer game. When an auditor had become very curious, Deets had pointed out to the fellow that he had personally negotiated a fee with the discount broker which more than compensated for the tiny bite Conover took in return for its splendid advice. And Deets could point with a justified pride to the growth of the funds. As another way of sidetracking suspicion, he was always careful to have Conover make a couple of recommendations which he did not follow.

Also, of course, he was able to state, quite correctly, that he gave no orders for any portfolio changes without approval from his investment committee, composed of Efflander, Wintergarten and Charley Winchester.

Not theft at all, he thought. Just a bit of spice to keep the job from becoming too dull. Nick them for a tiny drop of blood every time the big beast walks by. A little adventure to keep the glands working. And if ever they did decide to get rid of him, by that time there should be so much money squirreled away, a man could live in one of the world's better places, with all the food, shelter, whiskey, music and women anyone could ever want. In the interim, a fellow could do quite well right here, bless you, Doreen darlin'. They would be more hesitant to get rid of him now that he was the Reverend Joseph Deets. It amused him every time he remembered the way it had been done. "Read these two books cover to cover, Mr. Deets. Write three thirty-minute sermons,

Mr. Deets. One on Peter and John before the Sanhedrin, one on the Seventy-fourth Psalm and one on Deuteronomy, Chapter 14, Verses 22 to 29. Write a five-minute prayer relating to each sermon, Mr. Deets. Memorize your sermons and your prayers. Practice the delivery. Tell us when you are ready and we will listen to you, the three of us, the Meadows family."

And so he had been ordained. They had declared him a minister of the Eternal Church of the Believer, and he had driven a hundred miles to a small church and there delivered his best sermon and best prayer. It had been duly noted in the next issue of *PathWays*. They had thought to bind a very valuable employee more closely to the Church, and perhaps to keep him on a shorter rein. They could not know it, but if they made any kind of successful attempt at keeping him out of mischief, he would end up slamming his head and fists against the walls, and hollering in tongues. Certain needs in certain people are beyond logical restraint. He knew that if he changed faiths and worked his way up to the huge red hat of a Cardinal, the hinges of his knees would still go weak at the sight of the gentle bobbling and swaying of the sweet parts of the young girls. Here he was in his forty-second year, and when he had been but thirty he had believed that in another dozen years the great surges and clenchings and breathlessness of need would diminish, slacken off to something manageable. But it had never left him and now he doubted it ever would. There was a beast in a cage in the back of his mind, in the shadows, pacing tirelessly to and fro, showing only the glint of a savage eyeball, the shine of a predator's fang. Yet a beast capable of the ultimate gentleness and patience with such as Doreen. Old cat and sweet mouse.

After he was certain of his selection, eleven buy orders, ten sell orders, he ran it through the Virginia computer service, retrieving it with the mainframe down below, and then printed it five times on the 200-cps impact printer on that coarse yellow paper which seemed to give the committee members more confidence than when he used the daisy-wheel Diablo and heavy bond to make it look as if a secretary had typed it on a Selectric.

He put the reports in blue Accopress binders and, at ten to five, he went outside and got on his bike and pedalled out through the gate and on down Henrietta Boulevard to the Meadows Mall, pumping at a leisurely pace, squinting into the light of the sun high in the west. It reflected off the distant metallic scurrying of cars and trucks on the elevated Interstate. He shoved his bike into a stanchion and chain-locked it in place, pushed a Mall door open and walked fifty yards through the air conditioning down the broad corridor toward the office area. He remembered the big fuss about being open on Sunday. The old man had said never. The tenants created more and more pressure. Once John Tinker had taken over, he had ordered the complex open from noon to eight in the evening, with later hours for the four cinema theaters, which could be separated from the rest of the Mall by big accordion gates.

He walked slowly and cheerfully, a gnarled, bowlegged man with the swaying walk of a farmer or a sailor. He had swarthy skin, deeply scored with weather wrinkles and smile wrinkles. He had big white teeth, which looked false, but were his own, and lusterless black hair cut short, which looked like a hairpiece, but was his own. He was tufted with coarse curly black hair down to his finger knuckles. He had a mild scratchy countryman's voice, and small bright pale gray eyes. He had a look of chronic contentment and amusement. He knew he was very good at what he did, but he felt that it was a special ability much like being a born linguist.

He could move from one computer language to another with total recall and no hesitation—from Fortran to Pascal to COBOL to Basic to Ada, but his preference was APL, the sophisticated language he had learned in the beginning, in 1974. He was able to see the shape of a whole program in his mind in any language, and could thus devise uniquely simple shortcuts. He had a knack for locating and eliminating the bugs in any program.

He knew he was lucky to be living during this brief period when these skills were rare and very marketable. Voice synthesis and computer-generated computer programs were going to render him, he believed, as obsolete as a hand-cranked adding machine.

But here and now, they had to keep him around and treat him nicely. He had young programmers working for him, constantly improving and expanding the usefulness of the huge data base of everyone who had ever evidenced any interest in the Church, constantly devising new indexes and cross-references so that printouts based on almost any aspect could be ordered.

He knew the younger men who worked for him were good, but not good enough to ever come upon the secret program he had embedded well inside the main data-base program. It operated in real time, and would never begin to take effect unless he failed to access it with a sixteen-digit variable code on the first day of each month at noon. If he ever left under his own power with kindly feelings toward all, he could erase that secret program in minutes. If he was forced out, the program would begin to take effect the next time he missed typing in the code.

It was, he knew, a simple and a deadly way to destroy all the information in a data base. It was founded on random transitions. Once the destruct program began to take effect, it would look at first like some sort of simple microchip failure, but by the time they realized there was no way to backtrack to the original data, all the storage would have turned to garbage. All the names of all the faithful would print out in Lower Slobovian, and all the files and records of the Eternal Church would be meaningless.

Lately, however, he had begun to wonder if it wasn't a poor way to repay the kindnesses of the Church by making his destruct signal so automatic. It wasn't really fair. Suppose one fine day he was run down by a madman in a pickup truck, or died of a sudden heart attack. The data base, product of his own skills and energies, the single essential factor in the Church's financial health, would self-destruct. As he smiled benignly at the Sunday shoppers, he suddenly realized how he could send his destruct signal from afar. Some of his best programming ideas came to him with a stunning abruptness. He could invent an unusual name and address. He could bury that imaginary person so deeply in the data-base program that it could hide there as a dreadful and elegant little trigger mechanism. It would come to life only when one of Jenny MacBeth's girls typed the new donor on the terminal screen and sent it through for filing in the main data base. The more he thought about it, the better he liked it. Then if they ever threw him out, he need only mail in a donation in that trigger name.

It needed very little refinement, he thought. And it would be a pleasant irony to use Clara Conover as the trigger name, giving her two strange middle initials to obviate the chance of any random duplication. Clara X. Y. Conover of 123 State Street, Middlebury, VT, with the proper ZIP. And the great computer, with its insectile sense of precision, would suicide the program only when that precise name and precise address were fed into its memory. Poor thing, that she had not lived long enough to see her adored son become a man of the cloth. He decided to set it up this coming week, and dismantle the one that needed once-a-month attention to keep it from activating.

He took the slow escalator up to the main mezzanine and walked down to the locked featureless door at the far end of the wide corridor. He pressed the bell button four times in rapid succession, the door buzzed at him and he pushed it open. He went through the secretarial office with its four work stations and four ubiquitous terminals and printers, hooded and silent. He went on through the open doorway in Rolf Wintergarten's office, smiling and saying, "Guys, your guru has arrived."

Charley Winchester, the head of the ECB legal team, sat in one of the leather armchairs, his heels propped on the coffee table. He was a fat white jowly man with horn-rimmed glasses so thick his eyes looked huge. He exuded a comfortable flavor of amiability. He had an interest in his fellow man that was so genuine everyone responded to it. Charley made everybody feel important.

Rolf Wintergarten was fifty, trying with some success to look thirty-eight. He was slim and trim, with good shoulders, a careful tan, soft contacts, designer clothing and blow-dried hair with a picturesque lock falling across his forehead. He worked with weights and ran two miles every day at first light. As was the case with the other top administrative personnel, Wintergarten had been ordained in the same manner as had Joe Deets. It gave them access to an especially generous set of health and retirement benefits, the same benefits that had made it relatively easy to induce the pastors of the affiliated churches to join with ECB.

Charley Winchester and his brother Clyde were the only two in the inner circle who had declined, politely, the opportunity to be ordained in the Church. Charley had pointed out, quite correctly, that under the right circumstances it could diminish the effectiveness of the brothers in a court of law. It was rumored that Charley had tried to make a joke of it, thus infuriating the old man.

He had said, "Being an officer of the court might be in direct conflict with being an officer of the Church, the way things are going lately." Levity in such matters was unthinkable.

"I think it's my turn," Wintergarten said. "Isn't it my turn?"

"Aren't we waiting for Finn?" Deets asked.

"Sent word he might be able to make it, but he'll be late, and so go ahead," Charley said.

Rolf bowed his head and Charley took his feet off the coffee table and sat up. Deets bowed his head. In a voice too loud and too oratorical for the circumstances, Rolf Wintergarten said, "Dear Lord, we beseech Thee to grant us wisdom in the administration of our appointed tasks, to give us the courage to make the hard decisions, to help us nurture the funds entrusted to the Eternal Church of the Believer by those who have come to Christ, to use it in ways which will enhance Thy kingdom and further the cause of Christianity. Amen."

"Hey, that's nice!" Charley said. "That's real nice!"

Wintergarten flushed and looked pleased. "It was longer, but Molly helped me cut it down. It's written out, so we can use it again sometime. Well, shall we get started? Joe?"

Joe Deets passed out two of the blue cardboard binders he had brought in his bicycle basket and opened a third one to follow along in case there were any questions. There seldom were. They were in the usual format. Weekly receipts from all sources. Operating expenses broken down into simplified categories. Grants-in-aid and charitable contributions paid out of current receipts. Lists of holdings in the trust accounts and in the money market funds. Cash in bank accounts. Each figure was preceded by the figure from the previous week, the week before that, and the same week for the prior year. The final sheet showed the recommended investment changes.

"Little mite heavy on cash?" Charley asked.

"John Tinker's orders. He wants to be able to use cash to make the best deal possible on the twenty-two hundred acres beyond the Settlements. But the cash is making money while it's waiting."

"I don't understand why he *wants* that much more land," Rolf said in a plaintive tone.

"Add two and two, and keep your ears open," Charley said. "This is my guess, and even though I don't think I'm far off, I don't want it repeated. Hell, I don't even have to say that to you two, do I? I base my guess on things he's had me checking out the last few months. I think what he has in mind for that area is one great big son of a bitch of a medical complex specializing in the degenerative diseases. Hospital, medical school, nursing school, research programs. The medical school and the nursing school will fit in with the University. It makes the Settlements a more attractive retirement area for Church members. Right now what have we got? A direct payroll of four hundred and something, not counting the University. Another two or three hundred there. Six hundred students. Then there's the indirect payroll. Your people, Rolf, and Lakemore Construction and Meadows Development. It's a class act. He gets a good medical insurance program out of it and a new way to tap the funds we can't touch, funds out there available for

support for medical facilities. It will enhance the standing and the reputation of the whole Meadows Center, provided he can attract top people
to staff the hospital and the medical school."

"Aha," Deets said. "Mystery solved. I wondered why we were cutting
so far back on the things the old man has always supported. Like Right
to Life and the Missions and World Hunger. Right now we could come
up with—need I say it?—a very substantial sum. But how is the old man
going to react to all this medical stuff? He's always told the flock to stay
away from doctors, except for bleeding wounds and broken bones."

Charley Winchester shook his head sadly. "The odds are against his
ever even knowing about it, Joe. He's deteriorating fast and the medical
center is a long-term project. Also, it's my guess there are a lot of people
who might have joined the Church if it hadn't been for that hangup the
old man has or had about medicine. Go down his road and you'd never
find out you were dying of diabetes."

Wintergarten, frowning, closed his folder, laid it down, and tapped it
lightly with his fingertips. "In management I've dealt with some large
figures. But these are a little too big for my comprehension."

"If he wants his medical complex, he'll get it," Charley said. "And
then maybe they can make you two reverends into honorary surgeons."

Joe Deets was visibly amused, but Rolf said, "I don't find that particularly funny, Winchester."

"Why don't you learn to laugh at yourself, Rolf?" Charley said. "It's
good for the digestion and the complexion."

"If a man doesn't take himself seriously, nobody else will."

Charley shook his head sadly. "Good grief, man. If I started taking
myself and my profession seriously, my brother Clyde would go into
hysterics. We're just plain old country lawyers, and we make a little deal
here, a little deal there, and keep everybody happy. Life's too short you
should get pissed off at a harmless remark."

"And I don't care for that kind of language in my office!"

Charley sighed and looked sadly at Deets. He shook his head and
turned to the approval sheet in the folder and scrawled his name.

Rolf Wintergarten said, "Don't you at least have an obligation to look
at the changes he wants to make?"

Charley shrugged. "Joe does a good job for us and I don't understand
most of this crap anyway."

"If you don't understand it, shouldn't you get off the committee?"

Charley stared at him. "Good God, man, you're even worse than your usual self. What's chewing on you anyway? Finn will go over it before he signs it, and he knows more about it than either of us. You think Joe is stealing?"

Rolf ignored him, opened the folder and looked at the list of changes. "You're putting almost a half million dollars into this United Industrial. I never heard of it. What do they do?"

"They made eleven percent on two hundred and fifty million in sales last year. There's over three million shares outstanding, so it isn't thin. They're into electronic defense equipment, coal stokers, surgical gloves and hospital supplies. Well managed, with a B-double-plus rating."

"So what is this Hillenbrand Industries? What's so good about that?"

Joe beamed at him. "This is your kind of thing, Rolf, because we all know how you like brand names. This mother owns the Batesville Casket Company, the largest manufacturer of burial caskets in the country. They own a company that makes electric hospital beds and electronic bedside cabinets. And they own American Tourister luggage. Sales of four hundred and twenty mil last year with profits of a little more than sixteen percent."

As Rolf took out his pen to sign the approval sheet, Charley stood up and said, "I guess I'll take my dirty mouth out of these sanctified environs, guys. Someday, Reverend Wintergarten, I want you to tell me where you get your shirts stuffed. See you, Joseph."

As soon as the door closed behind him, Wintergarten jumped up and said, "Why do they keep that man on? He's disgusting!"

"You know the answer as well as I do."

"What answer? He's coarse and irreverent."

"All his life Charley has had the knack of making friends, good friends. He has good friends in county government, in the city council, in the state legislature, in both houses of Congress and in a lot of the executive branches. And regardless of what you think of him, Rolf, he is one of the most likable men I've ever known."

"Not to me."

"Let me give you some advice. Charley and Clyde have been with the old man for over twenty years. Whatever it is between you two, it's chemical. Too bad. You're both good men. If push comes to shove, you are the one they'll have to dump."

Rolf stared at him. "You're serious?"

"Absolutely. So try to like him."

"I can't."

"Lately you're not acting like yourself."

"What is that supposed to mean?"

"It's an observation, pure and simple. You seem irritable and edgy. If there's something you want to tell anybody about—here I am, a certified man of the cloth."

"There's nothing especially wrong, Joe. I keep getting involved in a lot of small idiotic problems. I could shed a lot of them if I could find an assistant good enough to take some of the load. Leases to renegotiate, key people off sick, and this damned weather, hot as furnaces, going on forever, it seems."

"Summer can't go on forever. Nothing goes on forever. And if you stay patient, problems tend to go away in time."

He saw a sudden wetness of tears in Wintergarten's eyes before the man turned away and walked across the office. "You're probably right," he said.

"Don't try to force things. Just ride with the tide."

"Thanks, Joe. Thanks for the advice. I'll . . . try to make myself unwind, let down a little."

Joe watched him. Wintergarten was moving slowly, shoulders slumped. Forgotten for the time being was his recent practice of moving quickly. Quick turns of the head. Macho swing of the shoulders. Rapid gestures. It was a contrived body language designed to match the blow-dried hair, the magic drugstore tint. Fifty years old and into the second year of marriage to a twenty-six-year-old woman. Joe guessed that he had become suspicious of her. With cause. But too frightened of losing her to risk the sly investigations which would prove him cuckold.

Joe Deets had predicted the problem halfway through the party given by the Meadows family in the main lounge of the Manse a week after Rolf Wintergarten had brought his bride into the community, some three years after his childless wife, Angela, had died of electrocution when a sudden southern thunderstorm had draped live wires across her Mustang. Joe had liked Angela. She had been a narrow-faced, narrow-bodied woman with a wry perspective on the world, and a knack of making her somber husband seem almost lighthearted. Molly was quite different. Round face, big round breasts worn high, fatty little mouth, Boston accent and a direct and challenging look.

Halfway through the party Joe Deets had found himself alone with her, over by the slate fireplace. They looked at each other and they carried on one of those prefabricated conversations. I think you will like it here . . . I certainly hope I will, everybody seems so nice . . . We do get a lot of hot weather . . . I don't mind it hot; I hate snow and ice . . . I think you'll like the people here . . . They have been wonderful to me; I can see why Rolf enjoys it so much . . .

They made their mouths move, saying inanities, while they looked out of their caves, appraising each other, speculating—two beasts on either slope of a deep ravine, lifting their muzzles to snuff all aromas, no matter how faint.

Yes, he had decided at the time. I could manage it. We could manage it. With care and guile. Not now, but within a couple of months. But not worth it. Too much risk for too little reward. The eyes had looked up and out at him from under the black curl of the thick bangs, and the tiny pink tongue tip had moistened a corner of the small mouth. Someday, maybe. Depending.

Now, well over a year later, Deets had been hearing rumors. Nothing really specific. Sly wink. "Rolf's got maybe a little more than he can handle there."

As he walked back through the Mall, toward the exit where he had left his bicycle, he came face to face with a dark-haired young woman as she came hurrying out of a discount shoe store, carrying purse and shopping bag. She had an outsized mass of dark hair curled into small tight ringlets. She wore the white blouse, dark skirt and sensible shoes required of all female staff during duty hours at Administration, Communications and the University.

As she gasped and jumped back in surprise, he cried, "Patsy! How great to see you! You're looking fantastic!"

"Sure, Joe. Sure. I'm really, really great," she replied, sour and accusatory.

"But I mean it!" he said, striving for conviction and almost but not quite succeeding. Patsy Knox had dark circles under her eyes and there were new lines bracketing her red mouth. "How are you doing, Patsy?"

"How do you think I'm doing, you son of a bitch!"

"Hey!"

"Hey what? You got me moved over to that rotten Student Affairs Office. You got me moved off the kind of work I really like. You wouldn't return a phone call or answer a letter or anything. You *humiliated* me, you rotten little bastard!"

"Keep it down! Look, let's have a doughnut and coffee."

"I've got to get back. We're working on the files."

"What's ten minutes more? It's Sunday."

She thought, shrugged, said, "Why not?"

Where two corridors intersected there were small Formica tables behind a Chinese-red railing, and a self-service counter. It was like a small outdoor café indoors. He brought their tray back to the table where she waited.

As soon as he was seated she said, "I only said yes to this because it gives me a chance to tell you how bad you hurt me."

At least she was keeping her voice down. For that he was grateful. He shook his head sadly. "Patsy, Patsy, what kind of an attitude is that?"

"What kind do you expect? At first I was so damn dumb I thought you were really too busy all of a sudden to have any time for me. Joe, you came after me and you seduced me, and when there wasn't any more novelty to it, you dropped me like a hot rock. I learned a lot from you, pal."

The doughnut had given her a powdered-sugar mustache. He took her wrist and she yanked it away and said, "And then I heard about Doreen. Look, I was a little young for you. But *that* kid, my God, Joseph."

He grabbed her wrist again and held tight as she tried to pull away. "Listen to me. What we had together was very beautiful, Patsy. It was beautiful and it was important to me. You came along at just the right time in my life. We were very special, so special that we burned it all out too quickly. When things are over, people sense that they are over. You knew it and I knew it. And I won't let you spoil it for us at this late date, cheapen it, turn it into something it wasn't."

"My God, you're really good, aren't you?"

"My memories of you are precious. I wish you wouldn't try to spoil all that for both of us. I hate what you are doing to yourself."

"And I hate you!"

"Hate is corrosive. It destroys. You can't carry that much hate around inside you, Patsy, without harming yourself. And you are such a wonderful person, I just don't want to see you like this . . ."

"What you are is a lying sneak."

"I did not have you transferred. When it happened I suddenly realized it would be the best solution for both of us, so we wouldn't keep running into each other a dozen times a day. You have to believe me, Patsy darling. I know I hurt you, but it was done out of kindness, to keep from hurting you over a much longer period. I did love you, you know. Don't ever forget that."

She looked back into his eyes and he saw the fat tears form and spill. He felt the tension go out of the muscles in her forearm and wrist. He slid his hand down to enfold her hand. She took a deep shuddering breath. "Joe, where did we go wrong?"

"The flaw is in me, not in you. A failure of constancy, I guess. I can't seem to ever give myself completely to anyone. I tried with you. I really did."

"I almost believe you, Joseph," she said.

"Please try."

She put her Styrofoam cup down on the tray and stared at him and then, to his astonishment, gave him a wide strange grin, a savage grimace behind the tears.

She stood up and said, "No matter what, remember that I would never have done it if you hadn't cut me off so completely."

"Done what?"

"What I knew I had to do."

And she fled, almost running, leaving him sitting alone, filled with alarm. He watched her, and even as he was telling himself there was nothing she could do to damage him in any way, another part of his mind was taking a cool measurement of her, comparing her to all the memories of the others, realizing that even though he now retained the most specific and detailed memories of her every contour, every elegance, every blemish, in time these uniquenesses would blend into the general memory of all the others, would be submerged into acres of breasts, fields of buttocks, thickets of lips, forests of hair, and the huge, mournful, chanting choir of all their random sounds of love.

He dumped her half doughnut and the rest of the disposables into the hinged slot in the big orange bin. He felt suddenly weary, almost to the point of depression, and found himself half hoping that Doreen would not find it possible to sneak out this evening for their customary Sunday assignation. She was, as Patsy had pointed out, very, very young. She was so young she made him feel a foreigner in a strange country, having so little of the language that all he could talk about with her was the weather.

Five

The old man was in the worn tapestried wing chair by the windows when the Reverend Sister Mary Margaret Meadows came to see him after lunch. He was facing away from the big television set. The sound was off. On the screen motorcycles leaped silently from sandy knolls and churned through dark puddles, spraying sheets of water into the air.

He was a part of her life, an important and ineradicable piece of a lifelong past, now somehow washed ashore here on another planet—a less happy place. Seeing him dozing she could imagine that he would awaken, look quickly at her, spring out of the chair and be Poppa again as in the olden days, vibrant and laughing and strong. Those had been the days of gold, luminous in memory. Just the three kids, John the eldest, Paul the youngest and she the beloved daughter in the middle.

They always sat with Momma in the far right of the first pew on the right as you faced the pulpit. That was where he wanted them to be. They were, he always said, a part of his strength, almost the most important part.

There had been that strange certainty about it all, the total belief that everything would work out the way they wanted it. Poppa would be the pastor of the church that never stopped growing, and people would come long distances to hear the thunder and the sweetness of his voice. John Tinker and Paul would be his captains, the men at his right hand. Poor Paul. Poor Paul. She was to have become a missionary, famous for her strength and skill and faith, married to a man as strong as Poppa, bearing his children in primitive places of the world. But they were going to be healthy and strong. Then when Poppa and Momma were old, she would come back with her family and by then Paul and John Tinker would have families, and they would all be close together, and all take care of old Matthew and his wife.

The world did not seem to break apart with any huge dramatic flash and bang. It was odd, she thought, the way it just seemed to wear down, or wear out, or grind slowly to a duller and more halting pace. And the things that went wrong went too far wrong for fixing.

She moved quietly to a hassock and sat where she could look at his sleeping face. All the old strength was still there, in the bold bone structure, the heavy brow, the line of the jaw. But the face was like a castle where once a king had lived, a castle proud and impregnable. But the king had left, the pennons were rags, the gates open, moat dry, and an old wind sighed through the empty corridors.

She saw movement out of the corner of her eye, and turned as Nurse Willa Minter appeared in the doorway to the bedroom corridor, eyebrows raised in question, nervous grin coming and going. Would that the damned woman could stop the smirky look. But she was a jewel, of course, an irreplaceable jewel, regardless of what John Tinker thought of her.

Mary Margaret held a finger to her lips and Minter hesitated and then went away.

In childhood it had seemed to Mary Margaret that Matthew Meadows' rise to ever greater importance had taken a long, long time. Looking back now, she knew the time span had been surprisingly short. He had been a country preacher, packing his small church, resisting affiliation with any other sect, preaching his particular fundamentalist faith, going back to those minor prophets seldom included in the standard editions of the Old Testament, those clumsy and mysterious names—Habakkuk and Zephaniah—Malachi and Nahum—Obadiah and Amos. Then he was on the radio and the children in school began to treat Mary Margaret and her brothers with a new sharp focus of curiosity, mingled with a vague awe. Bigger churches, more staff, more money, more broadcasts, and at last this purchase of land at the end of nowhere, a huge parcel which even at the low cost per acre meant a great debt to pay off. Everybody thought Matthew Meadows had too big a dream. But the people listened on radio and on television and in big amphitheaters in great cities. The people listened and joined and tithed, and the dream came true sooner than anyone could have guessed. All Momma ever got to see was the skeletal framework of the Tabernacle and the architect's renderings of the four towers against the blue southern sky. And before she died there was a rumor that the Interstate might come by quite close to the Meadows Center, and it was rumored that Matthew had some good friends and disciples in high places who were going to make certain it would come close, so the pilgrims from afar could more readily come and see the wonders.

The very best times, she thought, were when she was young and she could look up at him preaching, and she could feel his voice and his presence and his gestures and his piercing eyes lifting the congregation, bringing them together up out of the pain and despair of their humdrum lives into the wonders of the spirit, the majesty of the soul, the promise of life everlasting. That feeling of being a part of something great and wonderful had always made her heart flutter and her breathing fast and shallow. She loved him. She loved his hands and his strength. She wanted him to be proud of her.

And then at the peak of his strength and power and influence, it all began to go bad for him. He and John Tinker and the Winchester brothers had flown out to Los Angeles in one of the Gulfstreams, and somehow he had become separated from the others in the terminal. He became quite lost. He could not remember the name of the hotel where they were staying, or even what city he was in. The airport police took him to an office and checked his identification, phoned the Center, using his telephone credit card, and learned the name of the hotel. John Tinker Meadows and the Winchester brothers were in the big suite, and very worried and upset. Charley Winchester came out to the airport in a cab and took him back to the hotel. When Matthew Meadows started to tell all of them what happened, he tried to make a joke of it, and then began sobbing.

But by then, of course, the family that was going to last practically forever was down to but the three of them. Paul had died far away and alone in a strange place. The people there should have told us in time for us to get to him before he died. We thought it was best for him to be there, in that place. I was never ashamed of him, even after what he did to himself. I never could really find out if Poppa was ashamed of Paul. I know John Tinker was. I hope Poppa wasn't ashamed of him, because if he was, Paul knew it. Even when he was at his worst, far away from everything and everybody, he was still aware of things like that.

We're just, none of us, at all like what we thought we would be, back there when the days were golden and long. The worst, I guess, was when Poppa began to fade on us. One moment his memory and his perception of time and place would be flawless, yet minutes later he would be totally confused about where he was, what day and year it was and who he was talking to.

They had to use guile and misdirection to keep him from contacting any of the pilgrims who came to visit the Tabernacle. He tried to run things as he always had, but he gave contradictory orders and orders that often made no sense, referring to problems solved and decisions made long ago. John Tinker took over, carefully and quietly so as not to make the old man angry. The old man wanted to preach and they had him do some sermons on tape in the studio. They were disasters. His voice was beginning to go. He forgot his train of thought and could not find his place in his notes. But he was so important to the national congregation, the Church administration was afraid that if his condition became known they would lose membership. He had become a symbol of the Church. There were over fifteen hundred splendid hours of Matthew Meadows on tape. John Tinker and Mary Margaret sat in on long and exhausting editing sessions. The final selections, over seven hundred hours, were adjusted for color, and then dupes were made on archival-quality tape and stored in the air-conditioned vaults. The old radio tapes were far more numerous, and almost as useful.

And so he was still there, smiling out at his congregation from their living-room television sets, hearty and inspiring, giving his Bible lessons, reading from the Gospel, bringing new converts to the Eternal Church of the Believer. Whenever Mary Margaret saw one of the old broadcasts, it twisted her heart.

They had taken him to three medical centers where diseases of aging were being studied. They said he had had some small strokes, and there was some minor damage from that. But the significant problem was detectable by brain scan, that pattern and configuration which indicated Alzheimer's disease, the most disabling form of senility, progressive and irreversible. Only a minor percentage of persons in their late sixties became senile, perhaps six to eight percent. And even in the nineties the percentage remained relatively small, peaking at perhaps twenty percent of those at very advanced age. Matthew Meadows, they said, was otherwise in remarkable physical condition for a man of sixty-nine. They could expect an increasing problem of communication, irrational behavior, confusion, more memory loss and, finally, a total impairment of memory and all mental processes, at which time it might be wise to institutionalize him.

After they had accepted the diagnosis, she and John Tinker had agreed that he could be cared for indefinitely at the Manse, in his own suite, surrounded by the great complex he had created. There was money enough. Equipment could be purchased and nurses employed who would keep his condition a secret known only to the family and their closest associates.

Now it seemed they might have to stop including him as a silent member of the trio at the altar. There was no problem about editing out any visible aberration from the tape while organizing it for broadcast, but it would be visible to the thousands at the Tabernacle and in the University auditorium, and they would speak about it in hushed tones to other thousands.

Watching his empty, sleeping face she thought about this new program John Tinker had devised, with the help of the Japanese computer specialist, Oshiro. They would rebuild the famous resonant voice of Matthew Meadows so that it could talk on the telephone to individual Church members. She had tried to talk John Tinker out of it. He said the apparent presence of the old man was essential to the health of the Church. She said it was an abomination, akin to having him stuffed and rigged with wires like a large puppet so that he could preach as well as speak. John Tinker had laughed at her.

Her father stirred and opened his eyes and looked without comprehension at the television screen. The Sunday-afternoon motorcycles were gone, replaced by a shapely young woman who stood poised against a pale sky, at the edge of a high platform. She jumped and, in slow motion, made an incredible series of spins and twists before she sliced neatly into the blue pool water.

He looked at her, and she saw the puzzled look in his eyes, and knew he was searching memory for her name.

"Ernie?" he said in his thin, uncertain voice.

The doctors had told them to be patient with him. Lately he had begun to think she was Ernestine, his elder sister, who had died of pneumonia several years before Mary Margaret had been born. She was surprised at how angry it made her to have him call her that. Ernestine was a few pictures in an old album, a fat young woman who frowned at the camera and who wore odd hats.

"It's Mary Margaret, Poppa."

"Of course. Mag. I'm sorry. Wasn't Ernie here yesterday? I remember she was telling me something about how a mouse got into Momma's sewing basket."

"Ernie hasn't been here in a long time."

"I messed my pants this morning," he said, making his voice small, looking down at the floor.

"I know."

"Willa told you! I told her not to tell."

"She had to tell us, Poppa. We had to ask her why you left the service the way you did."

"I left the service? Before it was over? Oh . . . I guess I did, because I had to go something terrible, Ernie."

"Mag."

"I'm sorry. I keep calling you Ernie. And . . . I guess she's dead. She's been dead a long, long time."

"Yes."

"They told me she went right to heaven to wait for the rest of us. I tried to imagine what it was like, where people could wait. Momma said it was probably like a big golden bus station with gold benches and a door where people come through into heaven. I used to wonder if there would be so many waiting she wouldn't see us when we came through the gate. Ernie would never wear her glasses. She said that being fat was enough. I didn't eat any lunch today. Willa ordered up milk toast but it was too mushy. I couldn't eat it. It made me feel sick to look at it even. I had a milk shake."

"Was it good, dear?"

"It was very good. They have very good milk shakes here. You like milk shakes. What you should do is move in here."

She sighed as she realized how many times they had gone through this same conversation. If she said she already lived there, he would become more confused and then he would become angry and frightened.

"I think that's a good idea, Poppa. Maybe I will move in here, if they have those good milk shakes."

"That would be nice, Ernie. Then I could see you oftener. Days go by when I don't see you at all, or see anybody except Willa."

"Well, until I can make arrangements to move in, I'll try to come and visit you oftener."

"Maybe I could come and see you. No, that isn't such a good idea. I'm safer in here. They can't get in here, but they keep trying."

"Who's trying to get in here, Poppa?"

"You know. I told you about them. The Antichrist. I don't want to talk about it. I told you that, too. How are the others?"

"The other who?"

"The other members of our family, Mag! What did you think I meant? Where's Paul? And where's your mother?"

"Paul is away. At school."

"He doesn't ever write me."

"He was never much for letter writing."

"I guess you're right."

She was afraid he was going to ask about her mother again, and there was no good way to handle it. She knew that if she lied, she merely added to his confusion. And the last time, when she had told him she was dead and how she died and how long she had been dead, he was overwhelmed by great waves of grief and loss, and he remembered how her dear face and body had dwindled to gray-yellow skin stretched over bone, how the radiology treatments had taken away her hair, her teeth, and any remaining will to live.

Poppa had always been opposed to doctors and hospitals, unable even to discuss them in any reasonable way. He said always that regular habits, a simple diet, a happy spirit and regular prayers to the Lord God would keep the body in fine fettle. Perhaps that would have worked with Momma too, but she could not cling to her happy spirit after Paul mutilated himself. It was as if all the family's luck and some of their shared love had rushed out with the blood from the severed arteries and veins. When he was put away, Momma mourned her last-born as if he had died, which in one sense he had. They had all planned to be so proud of him.

And it did not take long before she began to be tired, to lose weight, to lose the flesh tones of health. By the time Poppa relented and agreed to let her see the doctors, the things growing inside her had eaten away too much of her and she could not be saved, not by radiology, not by chemotherapy and not by earnest prayer.

But he did not ask about her mother, about Claire, his long-dead wife. He would probably ask about her the next time. She wondered how John Tinker handled it. They never visited him at the same time. It seemed to make him more confused to have them both there.

"Willa says there's going to be lamb stew for supper. That's really good news, Mag. I *love* lamb stew. With boiled onions in it. The real small kind. Are you going to come eat with us?"

"I wish I could. I'm sorry, Poppa. Not this evening, but soon. Okay?"

"That will be nice," he said. "And we won't have to talk about Claire at all, will we?"

It startled her. Sometimes he seemed to be aware of what had happened to him, and to remember all the past. She had spent the Sundays of her life listening to the sweet thunder of his voice. For most of her life he had known everything worth knowing.

She went to him, bent and kissed his lined forehead, patted his silk-clad shoulder. She glanced at the television screen. A man on a horse had a rope around the horns of an immature bull and he yanked it off its feet and ran to where it lay fallen.

"Don't you want the sound on?"

"No. They talk so fast I don't know what they're saying. I just like to watch them. I like to watch them do things."

She had to hurry to keep her date with John Tinker over in the projection room in Communications. He and Finn Efflander were there, waiting for her.

"Why am I in on this particular viewing, gentlemen?" she asked.

"We need another opinion on this one. We think he's a new tiger. And we need one to hold the show together," John Tinker said. "You do nicely, Mag. And I am getting a little bit better as time goes by. But Doctor Macy just does not have the spark, and neither do our visiting clergymen. We've got to try to fill the hole the old man left. We've got to get the people crying and carrying on."

"Who is this so-called tiger?"

"The Reverend Tom Daniel Birdy from down near Pensacola. Don't laugh at the name, sis. I sent a crew down there with the best portable equipment we could find."

Finn Efflander started the professional tape and stood by to adjust the volume before coming back and sitting on Mary Margaret's right. The picture was good. But the Reverend Birdy was picked up in the middle of a thoroughly pedestrian sermon. He read hesitantly from the Bible. He was a big brown rawboned man with coarse black hair, a broad face and features that made her wonder if there was some American Indian in his lineage.

"But he isn't at all . . ."

"Just sit quiet, Mag. Please. Trust us."

Within a few minutes Tom Daniel Birdy got down to the primary business at hand, the business of saving souls.

"I know what you've been doing in your dumb, sorry lives," he roared, glaring at his congregation. The sudden loudness made Mary Margaret jump.

"Ever' one of you. No exceptions. You and you way over there in the pink necktie. You've been having sick, rotten little thoughts." He was down from the pulpit, pacing back and forth behind the rail.

"Sick, dirty little pictures in your lonely mind. You're ashamed of yourself and you're so glad nobody can see into your head. How do you know nobody can? *God can!* You've got the anxieties, ever' one of you out there. Money worries eat on you. Job worries. Husband and wife worries. In every black heart there's a little voice asking questions. They gone catch me? They gone find out? Some of you are saddled with old folks, mean as snakes, and you are trying not to hate them because they're your folks, but you hate them anyway and you feel the guilts for hating your own kin. Some of you got kids worthless as crabgrass, prowling the streets, stealing and fighting and fornicatin' in parked cars with other kids worthless as they are. What's gone become of my kids? you ask. What's gone happen to my job? What's gone become of me anyways? I got more than I can carry. I'm all bent over double and stupid from the load of sweat and worry and hate and guilt and all the anxieties I got to carry around every living minute of every day, giving me the bad dreams and the bad sweats at night. The years are crowding on by and I'm running in place. Running my heart out and not gaining one simple inch. Is this all there is? Is this what it's all about?"

He stopped pacing and leaned back and smirked at them. It was a knowing and evil grin on his big rough dark face. A wheedling smirk. He lowered his voice to a husky, secretive rasp.

"And you been *doin'* things! You been grunting away at it in dark places, sweatin' and gaspin'. Pleasuring yourself, taking what isn't yours to take. Grabbing flesh and grabbing money while your soul leaks out of you like spit down a drain. In the back of your mind there is this oily slippery little thought that keeps saying to you, now maybe those preachers were right. Maybe there's a devil and a hell and eternal fire and all that. But nobody has ever proved it, have they? Nobody has ever come back to tell us all about the weird wild crazy sound of ten billion souls in an agony that never ends, all of them sizzling and screaming at once, screaming for all the rest of eternity, their throats wide open, the eyes starting out of their heads.

"I'M HERE TO TELL YOU ABOUT IT! BECAUSE I CAN HEAR THE SCREAMIN'!!"

He dropped his voice again. "Now how can it be possible that you black-hearted sinners—and you are ALL sinners just as I am, because the thought is the same as the deed—how can you shed all that daily anguish and pain and guilt and worry and fear, and sidestep that deep red pit of hell you've earned for yourself?"

He made use of silence. He shook his head slowly. "The answer is SO simple. The answer is SO easy. It's laid right out for you, right here in this Book. Want to know how it works? You have to walk all the way up here to me, carrying that big sick stinking load on your back. You got to come up here and give one big terrible heave of your shoulders and you turn that big load that's killing you . . . you turn that load over to the good Lord. *AND HE WILL TAKE IT ONTO HIS SHOULDERS.* He always has and He always will. You take all your burdens and you take your immortal soul and you put them right into His hands and you say, *LORD, I'VE HAD ENOUGH OF THIS! I PURE GIVE UP! I CAIN'T HANDLE IT NO MORE BY MYSELF! I'M YOURS FROM HERE ON IN AND FOR THE REST OF ETERNITY!*"

He smiled fondly at them all, and said in a soft voice, "Know what's going to happen? He's going to TAKE that load of fear and guilt and dirt and sickness off you. And all He is ever going to ask you in return is you got to live by HIS BOOK, by HIS RULES. The rules are easy. Any fool can follow the Ten Commandments if he puts his mind to it. His mind and his heart and his soul. BELIEVE every God-given word in this sacred Book. LIVE every day in His way, for His glory and for your own eternal joy in heaven. You will stand free, my friends. You will be born again, with no more guilt in you than a newborn child. You will be SAVED, and there isn't never going to be another thing that can happen to you on this side of the grave that can make you afraid, or unhappy, or guilty, or miserable, or sick at heart. *NOTHING!*

"I'm God's agent standing right here before you. He give me the right to tell you how to drop those burdens and help you drop them. So get yourself on up here, those of you new here today, those of you who got too scared and shy to try it last time you were here. TRY IT! IT WORKS! Those of you who've already been saved, you look around you now for the ones that want to come up and can't quite make up their mind, and you take them by the hand and bring them up to the Lord and you will be doubly blessed. Come on along! That's the way. That's it. One after the other. You been walking all your life, but you never took a walk that's going to mean so much, now and in the hereafter. Come scrub your soul. Scrub your life clean. Find the way life should be, and never has been for you. Gather in close, all of you. Bless you. Don't try to hold the tears back. They come natural, out of gratitude to the Lord. They're a true part of being reborn. Thank you, God. This is more souls than I had any right to expect. You've answered my prayers again. Now let's all bow our heads in a prayer of thanks for being able to heap all our burdens on the Lord God."

John Tinker stepped up and shut the tape off and turned to face her, arms folded. "Well?"

Mary Margaret realized she was sitting bolt upright on the edge of her chair, hands knotted in her lap, teeth biting into her underlip. She made herself relax and lean back. "Wow," she whispered.

"That was what I said too," John Tinker told her.

She frowned. "He's very crude but he's very, very strong. That's because he's absolutely sincere. He really knows that it's going to work. And he makes it work. Fantastic! I know that my faith is just as strong as his, but I can't project it like that. He's acting but at the same time he isn't. He's fabulous, Johnny."

"And who does he remind you of?"

"Of course! Poppa, when we were little. He wasn't as crude but he was just as strong. He could make them cry. He could make them flock up to be saved. He could make them believe. Where has this man been? Why haven't we heard of him before?"

Finn had the facts memorized, as usual. "He's forty-two, and within a month of John's age. He worked in a pulp mill in Florida. He was a brawler and a drunk. He was born again when he was twenty-two and he has never lost his faith. He says that he was converted by Matthew Meadows long ago. There's no good reason to doubt him. At twenty-two he was sentenced to ten years in Raiford State Prison for manslaughter committed before he was saved. Actually, he turned himself in. He did six of the ten years, came out on parole, worked for a few years and then began to preach. He worked out of a tent, moving along the Gulf Coast, saving souls. He arrived in the town where he now preaches about eight months ago. Their old preacher had died of a stroke. There was no strong affiliation. They call themselves the Central Church of the Living God. He isn't really interested in affiliating with us. He thinks he's doing just fine where he is. He seems to think we are too big and too rich and too important. The only reason he talked to us at all and let us tape is because your father was important in his life long ago."

"That's like Poppa too, John. Remember, all those people that were after him. But he wanted to be the head of his own church and build it himself."

"I remember, but I think we need this man," John Tinker said. "And we need him right now. Agreed?"

"Certainly!" she said.

"He'll be coming for a visit in a couple of weeks. We'll send a jet for him and put him up in the Manse, and let him sit in on services in the Tabernacle. I want everyone on staff to be very, very nice to him. If we can persuade him to join with us, we're going to have some kind of a ball team here."

"I hate it when you use sports talk," she said.

Finn Efflander excused himself and left.

John Tinker Meadows turned a chair around and sat astride it, his arms folded, resting on the top of the back, chin on his forearm, staring at her. "We don't have enough time for any kind of talk at all, sports talk or otherwise," he said.

"I know. I worry about you, Johnny."

"In what context, Mag?"

"When we do have a chance to talk, you get cross. Like now, you get that irritated look. Can't we talk like family anymore?"

"Maybe whenever we talk I can expect to be nagged."

"Isn't that what family members do to each other? Isn't it maybe what they are supposed to do?"

"Not exclusively."

"And if that is what you always expect from me, no wonder we never have any time to talk. If you expect to be nagged every time, I don't blame you for avoiding me."

"Okay, tell me why you worry about me."

"Your sermon today was very, very good. You seemed to pull everything together. You seemed to reach out to the people today, Johnny. You don't do that as often as you used to. You seem to be . . . spiritually distracted."

"I've got a great idea. Why don't you give all the sermons from now on, Mag?"

"Please. Please don't be ugly. I'm not your enemy. I want everything to be good for you. But you seem to be . . . going away from us lately, all of us. Like when you look out the back window of a car and there is somebody on the shoulder of the road, standing there, getting smaller and smaller and further away. You don't seem to have any fun anymore, any real joy or satisfaction. You don't realize how seldom you laugh."

"Maybe there's nothing funny going on lately."

"You push me away from you. You push away all the people who care the most for you. And there's another thing."

"I knew there would be. At least one. Or more."

"People are getting very wary of you. Nobody can guess how you are going to react to anything. I know you are really carrying the whole load of this place on your shoulders. We all know that. We all respect you for the job you're doing. Is there something wrong, something beyond all the weight of responsibility?"

"Maybe I'm just getting a little stale, Mag. Perhaps it has something to do with the old man. I don't know. Who is there to approve of the way I handle things? It made me feel good to please him, you know? Now he has no idea how well or badly I'm doing."

She looked down at her thumbnail, ugly, bitten down to the quick. Without looking up she said, "There's just the two of us, you know. I wonder about it a lot. What could have happened to us? Poppa wasn't demanding. He never leaned on us. You know that. Lately I've begun to realize that he was such a holy and dedicated man that he had absolute confidence in the three of us. He didn't really see us the way we are. Not ever." She looked up at him.

"And we weren't deserving? Is that what you're saying?"

"No, Johnny. I'm saying that the three of us, and maybe Momma too, we had to kind of . . . push ourselves upward to fill up the big image he had of us. To be better people than we ever were. And it was too much, maybe. It was too much for Paul, certainly. And maybe in ways we can't quite comprehend, it was too much for you and me too."

"And so you are saying that what is wrong with you and me, we have been role-playing to please Poppa, and now he's not there to be pleased anymore. What's there is a confused and troubled child. Mag, if we are not what we appear to be or what we think we are, what the hell are we? What are we supposed to do with our lives? Right now thousands and thousands of people depend on us for their faith and their happiness. Isn't that enough justification?"

"Have you thought about marriage?"

It startled him. "I thought this was supposed to be a serious and friendly conversation. What in the world are you talking about? That's a ridiculous idea. I was married once. Remember?"

"And Chris was an absolutely fabulous woman. How could anyone forget her? Everybody loved her. You are forty-two years old, Johnny, and Chris has been buried up there on the hillside next to our mother for nine years now. Nine years!"

He stared at her. "Got the bride picked out?"

"Tracy Bellwright."

He looked at her in total astonishment. "You are really something else! Who the hell is she? Have I heard that name?"

"She's the oldest Angel I have, and she's getting self-conscious about being twenty-eight among all those young kids. She's assistant to Dorothy Getts, the dean of women."

"Tall pretty blonde woman? Long hair?"

"She's more than pretty. I think she's beautiful. She's intelligent, Johnny, and she has a sweet disposition, a lovely voice, and she's a very healthy person. And she adores you."

"She should save her adoration for the Lord."

"You know what I mean. Don't put me off that way. There could be a lovely wedding in the Tabernacle. You two would be a wonderful-looking couple. We'd get fantastic coverage from the media. And I think the members of the Church would really like to have it happen."

"Mag, I do not really think I want to get married."

"It could keep you out of trouble."

"What is that supposed to mean?"

"Why do you have to ask? You know the kind of trouble I mean. I don't think you want to force me to describe it to you. The last time it happened it could have gotten out of hand and turned into really terrible trouble for you and the Church and all of us. You were lucky. We were all lucky. The Church was lucky. Sometimes, Johnny, people go looking for you and they can't find you anywhere. And I am reminded of what was going on two years ago. There's a rumor you're seeing a married woman. Can it be true? After the way you promised the last time, never again?"

"Are you losing your wits, Mag? Are you losing touch with reality?"

"Do you want to answer me, or do you want to sidestep the question? Are you messing around with someone?"

"No. I am not messing around with anyone."

"When you are tempted, Johnny, you are not exactly a pillar of strength. You've proved that more than once."

"And you manage to rekindle the memories once a month at least, don't you? Everybody else who knew anything about it has forgotten, all except Mary Margaret Meadows. Maybe it's the way you get your kicks, living in my past."

"I'm not going to let you make me angry, John Tinker. I think there are quite a few people who remember it. But that's beside the point. Lately you've been so irritable and restless and remote, and it makes me wonder how vulnerable you might be to some sort of trouble. Why don't you take a good look at Tracy Bellwright? She would make a really lovely bride, Johnny. She'd make you happy. And then there'd be somebody to really approve of the good things you do, to be proud of you for them, like that sermon this morning."

He stood up slowly and looked down at her and smiled. "Sis, how would you ever get to know anything about that kind of restlessness. Look at you! You've put all other kinds of temptation behind you with a knife and fork. Gluttony is one of the sins of the gratification of self. Until you can control your own hungers, sister, and your own insecurities, try to stay the hell out of my personal life. Okay?"

He strolled out of the small projection room, closing the door softly as he left. She sat quietly for a long time, and then remembered the trick she had learned in childhood. If you tried to catch the rolling tears with the tip of your tongue, they would stop.

He's going bad, she thought. Ever faster. Like something rotting away underneath the shiny outer skin. You'd have to cut into it to find the rot. For many now, he has become more and more a person playing a part. A person pretending to be the Reverend Doctor John Tinker Meadows. A polished performer with a saintly look who, on any Sunday, preaches to more people than ever listened to Jesus Christ in his whole lifetime. He wanted all this because it was Poppa's. He wanted it dreadfully. And each year that he took over more of it, he wanted it less. Now he has it all, and maybe he doesn't want it at all. So he's getting more reckless. What is the game with the loaded gun? Russian roulette. With Johnny it is woman roulette. The loaded situation, loaded with risk. Defying God and his own father. Maybe, in some warped way in his mind, they are one and the same. There are rumors. He knows I didn't make them up. And if they weren't true, he wouldn't have been so vile and nasty to me.

From memory she whispered aloud the second and third verses of the Thirty-sixth Psalm, the Jerusalem Bible translation used by all the faithful of the Eternal Church of the Believer.

"He sees himself with too flattering an eye to detect and detest his guilt; all he says tends to mischief and deceit, he has turned his back on wisdom."

So he's pretending to be something he isn't and so am I. Paul couldn't handle that kind of strain, and maybe he was the best of the three of us. I am handling it better than Johnny. Does that make me the worst of the three of us, or the strongest?

She got up and rewound the tape and settled back and watched the Reverend Tom Daniel Birdy again. And again he touched her heart.

Six

By nine-thirty on that Sunday evening, the Reverend Joseph Deets was reclining in familiar and delicious comfort in the small living room of his bachelor house in the Meadows Settlements at 11 Zedekiah Lane. The tract houses in that area of the Settlements were based upon the smallest and simplest floor plans, and were occupied for the most part by single people or childless couples who worked at the Center and rented rather than owned the small houses.

An old tape by the Modern Jazz Quartet was playing, and the intricate music was just within the range of audibility. All the draperies were closed. A floor lamp with a blue shade was the only light in the room, over by the couch. He was stretched out on his most expensive piece of furniture, a television chair with toggle controls which worked much like those on a hospital bed, raising and lowering the back and the knees to the most comfortable position. Within reach of his right hand was a small table with two glasses and a decent bottle of California Cabernet Sauvignon.

His old blue robe was open, and Doreen's head was tucked beneath the edge of his jaw, and her forearms were under his back, her fingers hooked back around the top of his shoulders. Her firm breasts were pressed flat against his wiry chest. She lay froglike, her body slack and deeply penetrated, utterly relaxed. Across her back and shoulders and rear was a featherweight mohair throw, shielding her from the faint chilly breath of the air-conditioning vent in the wall nearby.

He slid his two hands up under the throw, and with his workman clasp and closely trimmed fingernails, he traced slow patterns from the small of her back down around the solid gluteal cheeks and back up again, now and again detouring to trace the inner and outer lines of her velvet thighs, altering now and again the force of his touch, from a questing firmness to the lightest brushing stroke, but never changing the pattern or the rhythm. At last, as anticipated, she made a murky sound, almost a sound of complaint, and ground her head against his jaw, pulling at his shoulders with her hooked fingers. Her personal history, retrieved by him from the detailed data bank when he had first become curious about her, had not prepared him for her shyness, reluctance and fear. As he continued to caress her without haste, gently, he felt deep within her a tiny clenching, like the fist of a small sleepy child.

It had taken him a long, patient time to release her from the conditioning inflicted on her by her hearty motorcycle sweetheart, a fellow rough, selfish and hasty in his lovemaking. Now that she was over the effects of him, she was, Joe Deets thought, like a tidy little cauldron of some wonderfully fragrant sauce which sits there on the back of the stove with the blue flame turned very low under it, a few wisps of steam rising. At any time, day or night, one needed only to turn the blue flame up a half whisker and the cauldron would simmer, then bubble at the edges and soon lift into a rolling boil.

He smiled to himself, tilted her head up and found her lips, then began a more strategic stroking. She sighed, shifted, and then breathed more quickly and shallowly as her hips began small movements. He felt her approaching climax from a long way off, and he helped her over the edge and into it, relishing her soft mewing sounds.

Once again he had been able to wait her out, willing himself back from the very edge of his own release, so that when she was still, he remained within her just as he had been before, deep, hard as a hickory post, pulsing almost imperceptibly with each strong thud of his heart.

He felt the hot wax of her tears on the side of his throat.

"No need for crying, sweetness," he told her.

"I'd just plain kill myself if she sends me home."

"I told you how many times? She won't send you home."

"How can you be real sure, Joe? This is black, dirty, evil sin and she knows it and you know it. You are older, she said, than my own dad and that makes it worse even."

"In one sense it's sin, Doreen. Every night of my life I pray for forgiveness for what we're doing. I tell Him we're weak creatures and we just can't seem to help ourselves."

"That's what I told her. We're in love and we can't help it. She said you could help it if you wanted to. She said you've always been like this. She said you were always making it with young girls like me, and you don't really give a damn about me. All you care about, she said, is getting sex from young girls. And it is always the same for you."

"Not like this. Not really like this. Never before like this, believe me, love."

"She says it means your sin is worse than mine."

"It probably is."

"Because you're so old?"

With an inward wince he said, "That isn't what I meant. I'm a preacher, Doreen. That's what makes it worse. But sometimes providence moves in strange ways. I have enormous responsibilities to the Church. Crushing responsibilities. Until you came into my life I was sleeping badly, I had constant indigestion. Worry about my duties to the Church was slowly killing me. And if I can't carry on, there's nobody else who can do my work. It would be a terrible setback for the Church. Do you see what I'm driving at?"

"Maybe. I don't really know . . ."

"Doreen, darling, believe me, you came along at just the right time. You are important to the Church because with you I can relax. All my worries are eased. I sleep at night. I am using you, dear little heart, to keep myself sane and alive. I'm using you, for the good of the Church, and that is what is sinful."

She hugged him, clamping those strong farm-girl fingers into the flesh of his shoulders. "I love you, I love you, I love you so much, Joe!" she cried.

"I know," he said comfortably, and with great care he reached out to pour them some more red wine. The memory of Patsy Knox's fierce and angry eyes slid through his mind, leaving a residue, a taste of staleness. The tape had ended, leaving only the whispering hum of the air conditioning. A car moved slowly down the street, the glow of headlights appearing briefly against the draperies. When she rose up to drink her wine, her blonde hair lay in a tangle across her eyes. She peered through the hair at him, a small once-wary creature in a thicket, now conditioned to the ways of the captor.

He felt as if he were on the verge of some great new truth, but it turned to nothing when he tried to put it into words. Each one, in her own time, is the very best of them all, he thought. And that does not have much meaning. It will come to an end. There will be a final one—a last lady —and I will not know at the time that she is indeed the last one. This one could be the last one. A dear child. No regrets.

Roy Owen found the County Line Motel at noon on Monday, the eighth day of August. It was three miles west of the small city of Lakemore, and on the north side of the road. It was an old motel with no more than thirty rooms, a single-story structure in the shape of a U with the open end of the U facing the two-lane highway. It was a block building covered with pink stucco, and had a red tile roof. The pink was faded and cracked, and there were many broken tiles. There was a patch of brown grass on one part of the roof. Parking was inside the U, the cars facing the narrow roofed walkway which ran all the way around the interior of the U. There were two vans, a pickup and a step van parked in front of the units.

The office was oven hot. An overhead fan spun and buzzed at high speed. The woman was standing behind the high counter, weight on her forearms, dark hair hanging toward the magazine she was reading. When she heard the twang of the screen-door spring she straightened, tossing the sheaf of hair back, giving him a welcoming smile. She was a lean sun-browned woman with a hard shelf of brow, a crinkled and pleasantly simian smile, very dark eyes. Her shoulders gleamed with perspiration. He guessed she was about thirty.

"Can I help you?"

"Have you got a single room?"

She nodded and put the registration card and a ballpoint pen in front of him. "Twelve dollars plus tax. Just one night?"

"Is number sixteen vacant?"

She tilted her head and looked at him with a puzzled expression. "It's empty, yes. You can have it if you want it. The wall unit is working okay in that one, at least. The one in here rusted out a month ago and it's been an oven in here ever since. The postage stamps get all stuck together. The rooms are pretty much all alike. Why do you want that one?"

He couldn't think of any lie that made any sense at all. "There was a woman who stayed in that room three months ago."

"Oh boy, I thought I'd heard the last of *that*. After the police and that old boy with the scar, I thought that was the end. The mysterious Miss Olan. What good could it do you staying in that room anyway?"

He spread his hands in a hopeless shrug. "I don't have any idea at all. Maybe it's only because I know how she thinks, how she reacts to things. I've been married to her nine years this month, and I hired that investigator with the scar. I couldn't get down here sooner."

She turned his card around and looked at the name he had printed. "Of course. Owen. I remember now they said that was her real name. Mrs. Owen. It makes a person feel strange to have somebody come into your motel and use a false name. She was supposed to be some kind of a journalist or a writer."

"Supposed to be and she was. Trying to get some kind of new angle on the Meadows family for that magazine *Out Front.*"

"That's what I found out later."

"She was on assignment. It wasn't any kind of free-lance thing. She used to work for newspapers using her maiden name, Linda Rooney. Everybody called her Lindy."

She tossed her dark hair back, an impatient gesture, and she gave him a strange, flat, challenging look. "Okay, your wife is missing and that is too bad, but bad things can happen in this world to pretty little women who don't stay where they belong."

"You sound angry. Did you quarrel with her?"

"No. We don't have enough customers I can afford to quarrel with any of them, friend. I found out later she had lied about her name and I guess I do not appreciate people lying to me no matter what the reason. And maybe I've got some kind of old-timey feeling about a woman roaming around the countryside leaving her little kid at home."

He was puzzled. "She talked about Janie?"

"Not a word. She didn't act as if she had a kid or a husband. I saw in the paper about the little girl. Jeanie, is it?"

"Janie. She's six, staying with Lindy's mother."

"And so everybody thinks she's just fine. Having a ball. That arrangement is okay with you, Mr. Owen?"

He smiled and shook his head. "I get the feeling we're quarreling about something, but I don't know what."

She seemed to pull herself back from the edge of an inexplicable irritation with him. Her smile was wry. She combed her fingers back through her dark hair and said, "Don't mind me. It gets too hot in this office without the air conditioning. Look, your Lindy was certainly a cute little person. A petite blonde. I think I could get a lot of mileage out of being a little blonde person." She tilted her head, studied him. "I guess you two must have made a great-looking little couple."

"You keep talking about her in the past tense. Is that because you feel sure something happened to her?"

"Lots of women want to get away from their kids for good."

Before he had a chance to answer in anger, defending Lindy, the step van pulled up by the office door and a man in gray coveralls came in and put a key on the counter. "Peggy, that damn shower water doesn't hardly go down the drain at all. You have to stand in it up to your ankles. It's still running out in there."

"Thanks, Lew. I'll get Fred to check it out. Everything else okay?"

"Fine. See you next time around."

"Be looking for you."

As the man was climbing into his truck, she turned quickly to Roy, and said, "I don't know if anything happened to her. And I think it's a natural way for me to speak about her. She was here. Right. Just as Lew who just left was here. And when she was here she was a neat-looking little blonde person. Okay. I don't think you should read anything into the way I use the past tense or any other tense, okay?"

"Okay, sure. I'm sorry. I know why I'm jumpy. But I don't know why you are so damn cross. I never had to go looking for anybody before. The man I hired said it was a waste of time to come here. But . . . I guess I have to do everything I can. I don't know whether I should be with Janie up in Hartford. Maybe that would be best for her right now. But someday she's going to want to know that I did everything possible to find her mother. And I don't know why I have to keep justifying myself to you."

Her faint smile was bleak. "I'm not asking you to justify anything, Mr. Owen. If you decided to look for your wife, that's your business, isn't it."

His smile was rueful. "So I should be looking. You could say I'm entitled. But I don't know how. Did you have any particular impressions of her? Please, I need all the help I can get."

"She was a type we don't get here much."

"How so?"

"Well . . . two-hundred-dollar silk blouse. Italian shoes. Heavy gold chain. Expensive luggage. Which direction did you come in from? Did you come right down off the Interstate and over here through Lakemore?"

"I came up on the Interstate but I went the other way first, over through the Meadows Center, and then turned around and came back through the town, maybe ten miles from where I turned around."

"What you have to know, to see what I mean, is the history. When the Meadows Center was real small and little, before they began building the Tabernacle, the Interstate wasn't finished through here, and people came to the Center north or south on U.S. Route 21 and turned off onto the state road that runs right by here. So that made for a lot of business for us. The county and the city encouraged the Meadows Center people. We didn't realize they were going to turn into what is practically another city. Now all the pilgrims and tourists come down the Interstate and turn east and stay over there in the Meadows Center motels and eat over there and shop over there. This side of town is drying up and blowing away. You and your wife would be the kind of people who'd stay over there at the Center. That driver who just left his key, Lew, he stays here because he saves a few dollars and we keep it clean. Our customers used to be able to eat right across the road over there, but it's been boarded up so long now there's weeds up to your hip pockets. Some people say that bringing all that money and traffic to this area is a real good thing for everybody. I don't know. I really don't. The last two fairly nice restaurants in Lakemore folded last year. A lot of the stores went out of business. And we can't seem to get far enough ahead to replace this rotten broken air conditioner!"

"So your impression was that Lindy didn't belong here."

"I wasn't all that curious about her. She came and went at odd times in that rental car. When Dolly was sick—she works maid for us—I made up number sixteen a couple of times but your wife didn't leave anything around that gave me a clue. But I didn't feel like prying. Even if I had wondered about her, I couldn't open people's private stuff no matter what. I didn't give a damn what she did."

"Most people like Lindy. It just seems strange to me . . ."

"Don't let it worry you what I think or didn't think, okay? You want to ask me questions, I'll answer them as best I can."

"I really appreciate that. The man I hired to look into it, Mr. Hanrahan, in a written report he told me Lindy had been seen in an old red pickup truck with a driver who wore a big black beard. When I asked him about that on the phone he said it turned out to be somebody who gave her a ride for hire over to the Center when her rental car wouldn't start. He said it had no significance at all."

"I guess it didn't. I got her the ride, actually. He's not a dangerous person. People call him Moses. When you head toward town from here, the third place on your left is a yellow house with green trim. That's Mrs. Holroyd's place, and Moses lives out back of her barn in a yellow school bus he fixed up. Moses is very handy and he's strong as a bull. People who have odd jobs they need done, they get hold of Moses. He does a cash business. He's kind of buggy on religion. I mean he'll quote things to you from the Bible for almost no reason at all. But there's a lot of that going around lately. When a person wants to get hold of Moses, they phone Mrs. Holroyd and she goes out to the barn and tells him or leaves a message for him. The police, Sheriff Dockerty himself, he looked into it and, like I told him, it was because I got a ride for . . . your wife."

"Her car broke down?"

"On a Friday morning, the last Friday she was here. She came into the office very upset. She had an appointment to see somebody over at the Center. They were coming out from Lakemore to fix her car but it would take too long. Could she borrow one? I didn't have one to lend. Fred was out somewhere hunting down some kind of a valve for the plumbing. I asked her if maybe she shouldn't phone and change the appointment and she said it had been too hard getting the one she had. Then I remembered Moses and I told her if she didn't mind somebody pretty strange in a terrible old red pickup, maybe I could arrange something for her. She said she didn't mind at all, but please hurry. Moses was at Mrs. Holroyd's and he came by ten minutes later. I walked her out to the pickup and introduced them and she told him what she wanted. Drive her in, wait for her, bring her back. He nodded and away they went. I guess it was eleven o'clock by then. He dropped her off back here at two o'clock, a little bit after. She came into the office and I gave her the envelope the car repair people had left for her. She told me she had given Moses fifteen dollars and she was worried about whether it was enough. I told her it was enough. She seemed relaxed. She drove out soon after that and came back at about seven o'clock in the evening. She parked outside the door there and came in and asked me if there'd been any calls for her. When I said no, she seemed depressed. Right after that she made a long-distance call on her credit card."

"That was to me. Friday night. What did she do Saturday?"

She went out early Saturday morning and I don't remember seeing her again until I saw her drive in past the office alone at dusk Saturday night. On Sunday Dolly told me in midmorning that number sixteen was empty. The key was on the bureau. Her car and luggage were gone, and I didn't think anything of it. She'd paid through Sunday, and there wouldn't be any unpaid phone charges because you can't call long-distance from the rooms except through the switchboard and I place the call."

"Did she make many other long-distance calls?"

"All on a telephone credit card, to New York City. Maybe there were five or six while she was staying here."

"Did she make any on Saturday, her last day here?"

"Well, she tried. Several times, but I don't think she got through. I mean, the calls were so short I thought the other end was probably busy, or nobody home."

"Who did she have the appointment with?"

"Somebody in the Administration Building. Moses saw her go in there. That's all anybody seems to know. I don't think she would have told Moses. He isn't the sort of person you chat with, you know. I don't think he's retarded, but he isn't really . . . normal. Kids make fun of him. These days they seem to dump people out of asylums, right out on the street. A friend of mine was in New York last month and she told me about seeing lots of weird people wandering around the sidewalks, making gestures and talking to themselves. Do you want to pay by cash or credit card?"

"Visa?"

"Sure. Just let me know by noon tomorrow if you're going to stay longer. Here's the key, but if you want ice the machine is broken. If you come here to the office, I can let you have some from our refrigerator."

"I'm sorry if there was something I said that upset you."

"Believe me, please, nothing you said upset me."

"Then it was something between you and Lindy."

"Enjoy your stay," she said, and wheeled and went through the doorway into the living quarters beyond the office.

He parked in front of sixteen and carried his suitcase in. The room was stifling. He experimented with the air-conditioner controls until he found a reasonable compromise between noise and cooling. The room contained a chest of drawers, a small desk, a straight chair, an overstuffed wing chair, a double bed, two windows looking out on woodsy scrubland behind the motel. Sixteen was in the base of the U, one of the rooms furthest from the highway. His front window looked out at the grille of his rental car. There was a small closet alcove with hangers permanently affixed to the clothes bar, a small bath with tub and shower, scarred sink and toilet with a cracked lid, and two towels halfway between bath size and hand size. There was a grass rug in the room and bolted to the wall a framed lithograph of big-eyed Spanish-looking children.

He removed his shoes and stretched out on the bed, fingers laced behind his head. The room was beginning to cool off. The ceiling was made of twelve-inch squares of patterned white fiberboard. Above the foot of the bed was a curious yellow stain on the ceiling the shape of a dog's head, defacing three of the white squares.

She was here, he thought. Right here like this, looking up at the dog's head and wondering how it happened, just as I am wondering.

Once again he had the conviction Lindy was dead. It came at unexpected times, with no warning. As before, it made his eyes sting and his breath catch. He had tried to keep it from happening when he had gone over to Lindy's mother's place to tell Mrs. Rooney and his daughter about his plan to come down here and look around. But it had happened then and they had all clung to each other, weeping. He did not like to cry, or to even think of himself crying. He guessed that it was due to his always being smaller than his classmates. In the roughest games, they had never been able to make him cry.

The night before he had talked long-distance to Margaret Rooney after his interview with Hanrahan. She had sounded very depressed. He had talked to Janie. She said she had a new friend. Her name was Princess Jones and nobody could see her except Janie. She wore a little gold tiara with emeralds on it, lace dresses and shoes with high golden heels. She would introduce him to her when he came home, but he would have to promise to pretend he could see her.

So Lindy was dead and it was a hell of a waste. There was no one to blame for the delay in reporting it. Her editors had not become alarmed until he had phoned them about not hearing from her.

So he knew everything about her and at the same time very little about her. She was nearsighted and wore soft contacts. She'd had a full scholarship to Vassar and had graduated with honors. She was an only child. She slept in short flannel nightgowns summer and winter. She drank spritzers. Anything stronger made her ill. She made a point of doing things well, regardless of her own likes and dislikes. And so she cooked well and had kept the house clean and her daughter healthy and tidy. When she was a child a lawn chair had collapsed under her and pinched off almost half the little finger of her right hand. She carried that hand half curled into a fist. In her touch-typing she used the stub of that finger for the "p," the ";" and the "?". There was a typing callus on the end of that stunted finger. She wrote a sturdy and durable prose, and when moved could write in an effective and luminous style. She was afraid of air travel. She liked large thick white towels. She had a knack of sitting without random motions or nervous habits, and she had a direct, level, challenging stare many found disconcerting. She was shrewd with money, a canny bargainer. She played to win, and became cross when beaten at games. She was a skeptic, researching everything she heard that she did not believe. She became huge with Janie, reminding Roy of a penguin in the way she walked, leaning back to balance the load. She could thrive on six hours' sleep a night. She kept her weight right at or close to a hundred and five pounds.

He guessed he did not really know her because they had never solved their sexual puzzles. When there was a mutual satisfaction, it was more by accident than design. He had tried to talk about it to her but there was a primness in her that made her change the subject as soon as she could. He had always felt that in some deep and secret way she disapproved of him, of his maleness and his hungers. It was a wall between them which they managed to ignore most of the time. When he looked deeply into her eyes, before she looked away he would sometimes think he saw a stranger back in there, someone he did not know and would probably never meet.

He wondered if her repressed sexuality was the reason for her truly impressive energies. He had never seen her felled by exhaustion except after the long ordeal of birthing Janie. He felt certain those energies had not led her into someone else's bed. She would have thought it unpleasant, tacky and dishonest. Untidy at best.

"Lindy is dead!" It was an experiment, to say it aloud for the first time. Tears ran out of the corners of his eyes, blurring the dog-head image on the ceiling. He wondered if the tears were real and true, or if he was crying at the idea of himself losing her. He thumped the bed with his right fist, as hard as he could. He got up, wiped his eyes and slowed the air conditioning. The room was cool enough. The sky was a milky blue. The sun shadows out behind the motel had soft edges. He could see a plume of dust rising and decided there was a dirt road back there beyond the trees, paralleling the highway. He could see, beyond the trees and dust, part of the roof of a barn. The rest of the roof had blown off or fallen in.

He wondered at his own unfairness in feeling an annoyance, an anger at Lindy for subjecting him to these waves of sour realization. He was glad he no longer had to feel guilt about resenting her work because it had separated them. It had been only a partial separation. He could have kept on living with that arrangement indefinitely merely by not thinking about it too much or too often. By disappearing she had opened up areas in his head he did not care to deal with or think about. What will happen to me now? What will my life be like? What should I do with my life and my daughter's life? What is it going to be like, being a single parent? Can I give her enough security, enough sense of herself as a whole person? And the presence of this special problem, this special small person in the center of his life, made all his other questions seem trivial and self-consciously awkward. Have I been happy? Has this been a happy life? Have I ever felt a genuine joy? Moments of it, sure. New bike, new car, new bride. A very good guess on the direction a stock would take, and good timing in buying or selling, outguessing the market.

But, in truth, I was never a joyful person, and neither was Lindy. Maybe that was the trouble with us. Two earnest little people trying mechanically for wild delights. Janie has a capacity for joy. She can run and sing all day. I doubt Lindy ever did. I'll have to ask Mrs. Rooney what Lindy was like when she was little. Strange how Lindy never reminisces, and neither does Mrs. Rooney. Something wrong there. Something about Lindy's father. Something unpleasant that makes a wall across the past. I cannot let Janie lose that sense of joy, that ability to live without doubt or reservation.

The phone rang, startling him. It could only be Hanrahan. Nobody else knew he would be here in this particular room at the County Line Motel. He answered with a feeling of dread and hope.

"Hi," a woman said, her voice husky.

"Who is it?"

"Me. Up here at the office switchboard. Peggy Moon. After I got through crying I realized I owed you better than I gave you before. An explanation, at least."

"About Lindy?"

"Sort of. Yes and no. Mr. Owen, a person can have wounds that seem to be all healed and then that person finds out that they aren't, and it is sort of . . . discouraging. I mean, how long is it supposed to take to grow up?"

"I don't think I understand."

"Let me work my way up to it, okay."

"Want me to come up there?"

"Oh, God, no! I can talk over the phone about it, I think. In person, never."

"About 'it'?"

"My mother was a very pretty woman too. When I was about fifteen I began to wonder if she had been as pretty as I remembered, and so I got the old pictures out. She was really beautiful. So okay, why I was so shitty to you, Mr. Owen, your Janie got me to thinking about me when I was six. I guess they were trying to hide it from me or break it to me gently or something. First they said to me that my mom had gone away on a little trip. And then they said she was staying longer than she'd planned. But after school started the kids told me she was gone for good. She had been seeing a man. His name was Lester Moyers and he owned the Lakemore Lodge. He had been trying to sell it. She had been seeing him in the afternoon at one of the cottages at the Lodge. He was divorced. He sold the Lodge for cash money and they went away together. The big kids at school talked dirty about her. I tried to kill them all. I couldn't believe it. I couldn't believe she would ever go away and leave me, forever. She had held me and hugged me and rocked me and read me to sleep. Her hair always smelled so sweet. She called me Punkin. Oh, damn it, here I go again. Give me a minute."

"You don't have to tell me . . ."

"Shut up. I owe you. Okay. She never came back. She never wrote. Nobody that she knew ever saw her again. Not to this day, and that, my friend, was twenty-five years ago. So I know what Janie is going through. Little kids don't know from voluntary. Right? In my mind that Moyers man tied her hand and foot and drove her away in his red Studebaker, and he wouldn't let her get in touch with me and tell me how much she missed me, how much she loved me. I'm telling you all this for Janie's sake. Your wife should have stayed the hell home where she belonged. She just didn't realize how very precious she was to the kid. And to you. It meant more to her to be out in the world roaming around, feeling important. I grant you it is a different situation, but Janie is feeling just what I felt. A terrible kind of . . . desolation. Empty. Unloved. Sick at heart. It's worse than people dying, I think, because you don't know where they are at all in the world."

"I . . . I'm sorry. I didn't mean to . . . inflict anything on you."

"You didn't. Not really. It's been with me ever since I read about it in the paper and the police were here and your detective was here. It took the lid off. I thought the package was empty by now, but it wasn't. Don't be sorry. I was sorry I acted like I did and so I had to tell you. Like I said before, enjoy your stay."

On that same Monday morning Eliot Erskine lay prone near the crest of a ridge about eight miles southwest of the first exit south of the Lakemore exit on the north-south Interstate. He was in the heavy shade of a clump of longleaf pine. This time he had brought the spray and killed off the ants which had been stinging him from time to time on prior visits. From the ridge he could see the irregular blue patch of Burden Pond twelve hundred yards away, and beyond it on the far shore the dingy white of the old double-wide mobile home parked permanently among the big live oaks. The two vehicles were near it in the shade, a dark blue Ford van with heavily tinted windows and a yellow VW Rabbit convertible.

The spotting scope was positioned on its low tripod, and with the sixty-power lens, Erskine could see the vehicles and the trailer as though they were but sixty feet away. He was a stolid, persistent man, a professional who had become accustomed to the boredom of stakeouts. The idea was to make yourself as inconspicuous as possible and as comfortable as possible, and wait. His car was a half mile behind him, parked near a bridge. He had a sandwich wrapped in waxed paper and a thermos of cold Tab.

It had taken him several years to finally decide to leave the Atlanta force. He had been good out there on patrol. He knew it and they knew it. He had the citations to prove it, and the special letters in his file. But when you get to be a certain age and have a certain amount of rank and seniority, then they pull you in off the streets and put you in a room indoors all day, reading things and writing things that don't seem real, don't seem as if they have ever happened to anyone. He had never married. He had no small talk. He found it difficult to make friends. But he had reached the point where he realized they were going to keep him indoors in a room for fifteen more years and then retire him on a pension. He did not think he could stand that.

He began looking for work during his time off. Too many jobs seemed to involve walking around warehouses all night, turning a key in a time clock. Or standing in a shopping mall jewelry store all day. Or riding around a big campus in a gray patrol car. He decided there should be some good money involved. He had watched a lot of big money made in ways he did not entirely understand. It seemed to him that a good piece of money would make the retirement manageable. A man with a little money, a careful man, could travel and look at what the world was like lately. You didn't have to approve of it—just see what it was like.

Three years ago he was hired by the Security Section of the Meadows Center, hired by a stone-eyed man who had once been with the FBI, and approved for employment by a big lazy-looking man named Finn Efflander, provided his credentials checked out. The most difficult part of it was explaining to them why he had wanted to leave the Atlanta police. The stone-eyed man was named Rick Liddy. Two weeks after he went to work, Erskine went to Liddy with a handwritten list of the deficiencies in the security arrangements, and where they could be tightened up without any additional expenditure of money or any additions to the staff. Liddy took it without comment and a week later he made Erskine a supervisor charged with keeping things firm and tight, with the privilege of picking his own hours.

Erskine was a fair-skinned man with small pale eyes and a big chest, big thighs, pale freckled fists. He could have been thirty-five or fifty-five.

There was movement in the distance, and he turned quickly to look through the scope. The door had swung open and the woman had come out first, going down the two steps, laughing as she turned to look back up at the man. He brought them into sharper focus. She wore a little white tennis outfit, with red ruffles under the short skirt. Her companion put the padlock through the loop of the hasp, snapped it shut and tested it, then came down the two steps and took her in his arms. He turned her and pressed her back against the side of the mobile home, kissing her.

Erskine saw a scrub jay fly down to the dry mud edge of Burden Pond, look in every direction and then dip to drink. When he looked back at the couple, the kissing had stopped and she was opening the driver door of the yellow Rabbit.

It had taken him the first three weeks of February to track them to their hideaway. The hundred-and-eighty-acre piece had been willed to the Church by an old woman who had been born there in the farmhouse long gone. She had died at ninety-five, and the double-wide had belonged to her grandson. The big towers of Southway Power marched across the land, and the grandson had negotiated a drop line, transformer and take-off for the house trailer, in return for the easement. Erskine had followed one or the other of them, until finally he located the last gate. When they left one day, one at a time, he picked the padlock on the gate and drove in and down to the trailer, following the tracks, picked that padlock as well, and found the lovemaking spoor of the two of them, and the little electric heater still warm. That same day he located the spot on the ridge for the stakeout, reported his find and went back with the voice-actuated tape recorder and planted it under the floor near the wide bunk, and hid the mike in a dark, dusty corner.

They were frisky in March and April. And, thinking they were totally alone, sometimes on bright warm days they would come outside and make love on a blanket on the grass, or atop the old picnic table when the grass was wet. There was a lot of laughter on the tape, giggles and slaps. He took dozens of pictures of them on the blanket, using his Pentax with fast film, a sandbag to steady the twelve-hundred-millimeter lens. When he had a half dozen which showed both their faces in the same frame, along with some specifics of whatever they were doing at the time, he stopped bringing the camera, and stopped coming to the ridge when they were there. The bugs of summer kept them inside.

Today he was there because he had decided enough was enough. The man walked over to the Rabbit and bent to talk through the open window to the woman behind the wheel. Through the scope, from his posture, Erskine guessed they were quarreling again. The laughing times were over. They were well into the scuffling which, he thought, marked the beginning of the end.

The little yellow car drove away. Erskine made careful note of the precise time. The man stretched and yawned. The little Rabbit kicked up dust behind it as it scurried down the two miles of private road, occasionally lost from his view in the rolling country. It stopped out by the private gate and moved, stopped again, and then went on, turning left on State Road 454, heading toward the interchange and the Interstate north. The man walked down to the edge of the small lake. He picked up a stone and threw it out into the water. At last he drove away in the van, following the dirt road she had taken, the only road out of the property.

Erskine made note of the time, and then walked down the slope and around the pond. The double-wide was up on blocks. He wiggled under it, between two of the piles of blocks, and aimed his pocket flash at a battery-operated tape recorder perched atop a spare block. He backed the tape up a few revolutions, put it on playback, and the woman said, ". . . I know your problem, pal. I know it maybe better than you do. Let's go, huh?" Then there was the sound of footsteps and the slam of the door, the rattle of the hasp and lock. He rewound the tape and put the cassette in his shirt pocket. He wormed back out from under the trailer, taking the small recorder with him. He went inside and retrieved the microphone and short length of wire.

Before he left and relocked the door behind him, he stood and looked around the main room of the trailer. It had a sad and tawdry look about it, as do all rooms, somehow, of loveless love or sudden irritable murder, or child abuse, or solitary suicide. The cop life had taken him into too many rooms with this flavor.

As he walked back to pick up the scope and thermos and can of insect spray, he thought with satisfaction that it was very nice not to have had to go get court orders, and very nice not to have to triple-check every move you made so no little smartass lawyer with a mustache could make you look like a fool on the stand.

But he knew he was going to miss the pond, miss looking at the birds and the wind riffles and, on the calmest days, the reflections of the live oaks and the clouds. He wished he could own a piece of land exactly like that.

He clambered over the final fence and got into the fierce heat of his car. The wheel was almost too hot to touch. A bird came booming out of the brush just as he got up to speed, the bird moving too fast for identification. It hit the metal just above the middle of the windshield with a sickening thud, and when he looked back in the rearview mirror he saw the feathers filtering down like snow. It made him feel bad. It made him wish he had gotten to that point of intersection with the bird in flight a little earlier or a little later, not at that precise exact moment.

Victims, he thought, were birds and animals and people who arrived at the wrong place at the wrong time, usually in too big a hurry.

Seven

By eleven-thirty on Tuesday morning the guards had brought all the mail sacks into Receiving, and they had been opened and the contents dumped into the big bins on wheels, and the empty sacks had been put aside for pickup on Wednesday morning, when the next load of mail would come in.

Jenny MacBeth, the mail-room supervisor, prowled the big room, aware at all times of every phase of the processing, of every person under her control, their strengths and weaknesses. Jenny was a cushiony woman in her late thirties, with a narrow waist and an elaborate styling of her red-gold hair which made her small and delicate features look even smaller. She wore a pale blue pants suit and a blue-and-white scarf at her throat. By special permission from Finn Efflander she was wearing blue-and-white New Balance running shoes over thick white Orlon socks. She was very grateful to Finn because the concrete floor had begun to cause foot problems and had been spoiling what she had always considered to be her sunny disposition.

One of the girls working at First Sort was new, and so Jenny MacBeth watched her frequently and carefully. The task of the women at First Sort was to grasp batches of multi-shaped, multi-colored envelopes, adjust them address side up, whack the batch smartly against the table to align the edges and then run them through the slots where the spinning razor edges slashed them open.

The opened mail was then dropped into one of two outgoing boxes in front of each woman in First Sort, the box for envelopes that contained cash, check or money order, and the box for envelopes with no enclosure.

Mail with no enclosure went to Secondary Sort, where the letters were extracted, stapled to the envelopes and scanned. Those with a credit card name and number and an authorized donation were bucked over to the credit desk, where the receipt slips were made out, ready for mailing back to the donor. Mail containing no donation, only questions or comments, was sent to Outgoing Mail for analysis and, if considered necessary, response.

Incoming mail containing cash, checks or money orders was picked up from the boxes at First Sort by an Angel on quiet fiber-wheeled roller skates and taken to the cubicles where the terminal operators posted the donation to the proper account in the huge data bank. The couriers brought to the terminal operators the stapled mail and credit slips as well for posting. There were fifteen three-sided cubicles with computer terminals, and today there were fourteen operators. The couriers had to keep an eye on the backlog available to each operator and make certain there was no interruption due to lack of material to process.

The terminal operations were the heart of the input process. The first step was to type the donor name on the terminal. If the printed name began to flash on the phosphor screen, the operator knew it was a duplicated name and went then to the next key, the street address. As soon as that donor was identified, the short-form response appeared on the screen, sorted from the central data bank, and the operator would scroll down to the previous donation and add the new one, with date, amount and mode of payment.

If there was no flashing response and no further information, the operator knew it was a new donor. Basic information was added from the letter, and the packet was hand-stamped "NEW" so that after it had gone to Banking for the makeup of the deposit for the day, the letter would be sent to Outgoing Mail for a special letter of thanks with the facsimile signature of Matthew Meadows or John Tinker Meadows so well done it could not be told from an original signature.

After a time Jenny MacBeth realized the new girl at First Sort did not have to be watched. She gave the impression of moving without haste, which was a product of a deftness of hand and quickness of mind. Sometimes a woman at First Sort would make a very standard mistake. After whacking the aligned mail against the tabletop, she would insert the whacked side into the razor slot first, a move almost guaranteed to produce checks or cash or money orders mutilated by the spinning razors.

Over the whacking sounds of the stacks of mail and the muted chuckling sounds of the terminals, Jenny MacBeth controlled the room by snapping her exceptionally strong fingers. One pop indicated a terminal operator running short of work to process. Two pops meant outgoing boxes ready for unloading.

Whenever a woman had a problem, she raised her hand and Jenny was beside her in moments. A terminal operator raised her hand. Jenny leaned over her and looked at a screen loaded with garbage. The girl was one of the new operators.

"What did you run last, sweetie?" Jenny asked.

"A new donor, Miss MacBeth. And then it just . . ."

"But didn't we then keyboard Control and then F to put the new data in the bank? Or did we go hopping along to the next donor?"

"I'm sure I did like you said. Control and F."

"Clear your screen and do the new donor again, dear."

Jenny watched. It worked perfectly. She put a hand on the woman's shoulder, digging in with strong fingers. "Simple *estúpida*, lambie pie. We do not sit here dreaming of sweet kisses while our fingers go rattling all over the keyboard, do we? We sit here and we think of the work we are doing for the Eternal Church, don't we, cupcake?"

The woman winced as Jenny gave a final squeeze of emphasis and then moved around to where she could see the woman's face, to make sure there was a glint of tears in the young eyes.

"And what do we say now?" Jenny asked.

"I . . . I'm sorry, Miz MacBeth. I won't do it again."

"Of *course* you won't, sweetness. Now check to see if your new donor is safely nestled away in the data bank, and then go like mad because your incoming is loaded."

The Angel swooped by, taking a recorded batch of donations over to Banking, and Jenny made a mental note that the guard posted near Banking was keeping his eye on the swaying rump of the skater rather than on the money. As has been the practice at large busy racetracks for many years, the incoming cash was weighed rather than counted. One hundred in random one-dollar bills, weighed on a delicate and accurate scale, will weigh exactly the same as five hundred in fives or one thousand in tens, falling within a range on the scale which will deviate slightly depending on how much new or old money is involved, but will not show an incorrect figure. Add or take away one bill and the needle swings beyond the limits.

At the Banking table the money was weighed, banded, tabulated on deposit tape and made ready for armored pickup, along with the stacks of checks, money orders and the Visa and Mastercard slips.

She prowled the room, slanting her quick glances from side to side, pleased with the smoothness of the flow. All letters, after processing, went on through the double doors into Outgoing Mail, where there was not as much need for haste, where the more highly skilled word-processing operators selected the appropriate paragraphs from the sample letters and also extracted factual information from the letters and filed them in the data bank in the long-form file for each donor. A death, an illness, a promotion, a birth—all these went into the electronic memory on eight-inch Winchester disks which facilitated rapid retrieval, and held hundreds of millions of bytes of data. Joe Deets had been telling her that one day they would be switching over to bubble memory, whatever that was.

When Finn Efflander had been hired six years before he had insisted that a letter be sent out acknowledging every donation, and that the letters appear to be individually typed, and that the letters enhance the feeling of the members of the Church that they were a special and select group, spiritually superior to their unsaved neighbors, and meriting life everlasting beyond the grave. The material that went into *PathWays* was intended to reinforce this sense of unity within a national audience.

In the beginning they had thought Efflander's ideas too expensive and elaborate, but events had proved him right. Jenny MacBeth had believed in Efflander from the beginning, as had Matthew Meadows, knowing that close and intimate relationships with the flock made the Church strong. The radio Bible lessons, the complicated television schedules, the Bible Quiz Show, the guest sermons, the radio talk shows, the huge mailings of *PathWays*—all these in themselves were not enough. Through studies ordered by Efflander and carried out by Joe Deets, it had been proven that the direct mail and the phone contacts were the most cost-effective ways of increasing donations.

After the last woman at First Sort was finished, and after the last terminal operator had closed down her terminal and was free to go, and after the complete deposit was made up and double-checked and the totals in the various categories entered into the proper operating program in the mainframe computer, Jenny MacBeth, along with the armed guards, walked the bank bags out to Receiving and made certain the armored truck was on its way. She then walked back through her section, where the cleanup people were sweeping the bits of litter from the concrete floor, and on into Outgoing Mail, on into the brisk roar of over thirty Xerox Diablo 1640 Printers, all knocking out those treasured letters at forty characters per second.

She went through and up the wide stairs to Finn Efflander's office. It was twenty minutes before three. Finn's secretary smiled and motioned to her to go on in. Jenny rapped, went in and closed the door behind her. Finn nodded toward the chair beside his desk. He was on the phone, saying, ". . . Yes, I did talk to Reverend Joe, and he told me you could give me a demographic sort on the West Coast tithes, showing increases and decreases by age and family status. Listen, Henry. You work for Joe, not for me. So if you see problems and he didn't anticipate any problems, you should take it to him, okay?"

He hung up and reached out and she handed him the printout of the final total of donations by category. He studied it, lips pursed. "Not too bad, and not great."

"Economic conditions. Big campaigns by the competition."

He nodded and smiled. "All the usual excuses. I'm pleased with how well your section is operating, Jenny."

Her cheeks felt warm. "Thanks. I've got some good people right now. Not that they don't need watching." She started to get up and he waved her back into the chair.

"There might be some problems coming up, Jenny."

She was startled. "Such as?"

"Some problems of image, let's say. Some woman who came down to look for sin and sensation disappeared. Back in May. Now they are sending another woman down, supposedly a more experienced person. She works for the same magazine and our posture is complete cooperation."

"I heard about that first woman. Some people say she must have found out something. That's ridiculous. What is there to find out?"

"Maybe there is something you and I don't know about. Some little scam that somebody has figured out. Maybe some kind of sexual fun and games. But it would be melodramatic nonsense to suppose that the Eternal Church of the Believer is so weak and vulnerable we'd have to protect ourselves by having a magazine person killed."

"It's ridiculous, of course!"

"What do you think of our first assistant pastor, the Reverend Doctor Walter Macy?"

The abrupt change of subject confused her for a moment. When in doubt, she remembered, always repeat the question. "What do I think of him? I don't know. I haven't really thought about him. I don't really have any contact with him. Why do you ask?"

"Have you had any contact with Mrs. Macy?"

"I know her, of course. Alberta. She keeps trying to organize things. Tea parties for the hired help."

For a few moments he closed his eyes in thought, leaning back in his leather chair, fingers steepled. Then he looked at her, lips pursed, and finally said, "We've worked together for six years."

"I know. You gave me a real chance to show what I can do and I'm very grateful to you, Doctor Efflander."

"From now on, we better be Finn and Jenny to each other."

"I'd like that, sir. Just when we're alone, of course . . . Finn."

He nodded and said, "This is going to be a very personal conversation, Jenny."

"Does it have something to do with Reverend Macy and his wife?"

"Yes, it does. I'll work my way around to specifics. But first I want to know . . . how committed you are in every way to the doctrine of the Eternal Church of the Believer."

"Committed? I don't really know how to fit the way I feel to a word like that, Finn. If you work here you have to be a member. I tithe and I attend services and so on. I believe in the Church and in its teachings. I know you're not trying to trap me or anything. I guess I believe as much as the average member does. And I donate time to church work. But I guess I can't take much credit for that. It's sort of expected of me. Of everybody." She shrugged and smiled.

He returned her smile and said, "I believe in God, and in eternal life, and in Jesus Christ, my savior, but I do not necessarily believe that the Meadows family and this organization is the one and only way to salvation." He watched her reaction and said, "No, Jenny, you're right. This isn't any kind of a trick or a test. By telling you this, I would be endangering myself if I didn't feel that we can trust each other."

"Okay . . . Finn. I guess I think the way you do. I guess we've both known how the other person thinks, really. The thing I like the best about the whole setup is the job I've got. And the chance to work with you, because you let me have some authority and responsibility."

"As you know, Jenny, I was hired away from a position I thought very complex and demanding. I was assistant to the chief executive officer of a corporation with five plants, nine subsidiaries, ten product lines and eight operating unions. I was hired for half again what I was making and I am now working half again as hard as I was there. The demands of the job are what motivate me. I am a clown riding a seven-wheeled bicycle across a high wire to see if it can be done."

"But I . . ."

"Be patient with me, Jenny. I don't get much chance to talk with any kind of absolute frankness to anyone on the team—forgive the corny expression. I think we understand each other—to a certain extent. While at the same time respecting each other's privacy. Okay, so the Church keeps growing. In one sense increasing power means an increasing invulnerability to slings and arrows and so forth. But with increased power comes increased visibility. And the bigger a target is, the easier it is to hit it. With increased power and importance we have little people within the organization who want to expand their own importance by playing on the vulnerability of other people who also work here. I like to keep tabs on our areas of vulnerability. I have my own little network of people who tell me things. You are a valued member of that network, mostly because you never bother me with trivia. I know that when you tell me something, it is going to be useful. I was given a quote from Alberta Macy the other day. She said that when her husband becomes as important in the Church as he deserves, libertines like Joe Deets and John Tinker Meadows are going to be exposed and thrown out, and—understand I am using an exact quote—there'll be no room here for sexual deviates like Jenny MacBeth and Jenny Albritton."

The bright room seemed to darken for a moment, and Finn Efflander's head and face looked four or five times life size. His mouth was moving but she could not hear what he was saying. And then she could hear his words.

". . . are all right?"

"I'm all right. It's just such a foul, filthy thing for that woman to say about us. It made me feel faint. I'm okay now, Finn."

"And there is absolutely no truth to the accusation?"

"None. We share a house. You knew that. She's my best friend. I can't tell her about this. It would hurt her terribly."

"Let me explain something to you—a couple of things. First, it is my intention to protect my people from false accusations. That is one of the obligations of any kind of leadership. It would hurt my standing here and hurt me personally if I were to protect you and then find out later that Mrs. Macy could prove her statement. Wait a minute. Let me finish. My final observation is that you do your job well and your personal life is your own. I avoid making moral judgments on anyone for anything that doesn't affect their work."

She started to speak and he interrupted her. "Think it over for a little bit before you jump at it, Jenny."

She felt her face grow hot and she pretended to feel faint again and buried her face against her knees to hide the telltale blush. While she was hiding from him, her mind was racing. How could that damned woman have suspected? How could she prove anything?

"Consenting adults can pick any life style they choose," he said, "just so long as it is between the two of them."

"Can I explain something to you? Please? Will you try to understand?"

Smiling, he held up his hand, palm toward her. "I don't want to pry into your personal life."

Jenny MacBeth hesitated. He had interrupted her at exactly the wrong moment if he was seeking total disclosure. She realized the friendly little talk had been a form of manipulation. How could he foresee any chance of defending her? Whether he thought the accusation was true or false, it would make no difference. He would ridicule the accusation in any case.

She smiled disarmingly at him and said, "All I was going to say was that Jenny Albritton is the best friend I've ever had. I never had a woman as a close friend before. We live in our little house with absolutely no friction at all. If that's some form of deviation, then I plead guilty, Finn."

She sensed both relief and skepticism, and plunged ahead, now confident of her role. "I guess that you would have to know her history to know how insane that accusation is. She had a husband and a little boy who was retarded. Her husband worked for a newspaper. They were going to visit his sister one Sunday. The little boy was in a kiddy chair strapped to the front seat. A drunk hit them head on, killing her husband and son. All she got were sprains and bruises. They had just begun to get interested in the Eternal Church of the Believer. After that, she got more interested and it seemed to help her with her loss, so she came down here and got a job doing public relations, the same sort of work she had done before she was married.

"I was lonely too. I'd been engaged to a man who didn't want to get married until we had a certain amount in a joint savings account. After we got to that total, he drew it all out and packed and left town without a word. I'd told everybody we were going to be married. We'd set a date. We were living together. Everybody knew that. I couldn't face it. I tried to kill myself but they found me in time. An old man I had known for years made me go with him to his church when Matthew Meadows was the guest minister. And I went up to the rail, choking and sobbing, and was saved. I was born again. I needed it right then, at that time in my life. But now it is not as strong a need. I guess it's because I'm happy in my work and in having a good and loyal friend in Jenny Albritton. We became friendly and signed up for the house together. I'd been here over a year by then, nearer two. So neither of us had any social life. We told each other our life stories. We shop together, cook together, diet together, take a course in Spanish at the University together. We wash each other's hair, alter each other's clothes, and we buy presents for each other. So I guess it's easy to see how some strange little woman with a dirty little mind would get the wrong idea about us. If the right man should come along for either of us, it would change everything. We both know that and accept it."

She stopped, realizing that to go on too long would be a form of overkill. She shrugged and smiled and said, "Now you know my dreadful secret."

She realized he had tried to maneuver her, and it had come dangerously close to working. Efflander was an expert. And she knew that if he had tricked her into confession, their six-year relationship would suddenly have become a very different thing. He would pretend to understand, but in truth he would not. He would look at her in quite a different way. Maybe staying in the closet was a primitive reaction in San Francisco or Dallas, but it was certainly a necessity at Meadows Center.

"I understand," he said. "I quite understand." From his smile she could tell that his relief was total, and the skepticism she had seen before had vanished.

"I knew you would," she said. "That's why I thought I'd better explain how the way we live could give that woman the wrong impression."

"As I said before, Jenny, in a large organization growing ever larger, as this is, it is dangerous and unpleasant when ambitious people begin to set up little fiefdoms, little empires, and try to grab for more power. Walter Macy is a better operator than I realized. He's been playing up to the ministers of the affiliated churches. He's strengthened that organization. He audits their share of the tithes. He preaches in their churches. He pats them on the back. Matthew Meadows' sickness has left a power vacuum. Walter Macy is doing exactly the same sort of job on the affiliates that Matthew used to do. John Tinker hasn't been interested in filling it. Old Matthew buttered up the affiliated preachers. There's a resolution on the books that if and when a new pastor for the Meadows

Center Church is appointed, the appointment has to have the approval of a majority of the ministers of the affiliated churches. Also, like a footnote, any pastor of this Church can be deposed by a majority vote."

"But I don't know anything about . . ."

"I'm telling you things you don't know. Right? You are useful and valuable around here. I want you to understand where Walter and Alberta Macy are headed, how they are thinking. Whenever John Tinker gets in one of our jets and flies to Houston or Toronto, you can bet that Walter and Alberta are thinking that someday they will be the ones doing the flying, and staying in the presidential suites and ordering the very best wines. I am in their way. Joe Deets is in their way. John Tinker is in their way. They can cut me down to size by picking off my best people, like a sniper on a hill."

"And that's the way they wanted to get rid of me? To make a false accusation and have you fire me? That's scary. What if you believed that? And never asked me about it."

"Her remark about you was repeated to me by a person she feels she can trust implicitly. Either she was off guard when she said it or she said it to a person she knew would bring it to me. Or maybe she even asked that person to tell it to me. And it was reported to me as being a very positive statement."

"I'm glad it happened exactly this way, Finn. I'm so grateful to you for . . . confronting me with it."

"Confrontation is a management tool, Jenny. Direct contact can solve a lot of problems. I certainly wouldn't want to force you out of here, because you are one of the very few I can *really* depend on."

And that too, she thought, as she sat there smiling, is another management tool—developing loyalty through flattery and a hint of exclusivity. "I'll try to be worthy of your trust," she said.

He smiled. "We are in Rome and it is full of Romans. You may have noticed."

"I'm sorry I got angry," she said. "I suppose I'd better tell all this to Jenny."

"I expect you to."

"She's going to be really upset. We've made jokes about people wondering if we were more than good friends. But I really didn't think anybody actually thought so."

"Run along now. And don't worry about it. I'll do all the worrying. You just keep on doing your job and keeping your head down."

As she started toward the door he called her back and, grinning at her, said, "Have you figured out how to beat the system yet?"

"The system?"

"The incoming money, the deposits, the records. What else?"

"Mr. Efflander. Finn, I would never under any circumstances . . ."

"Stop kidding yourself, Jenny. And stop kidding me. Every intelligent person who works around a lot of raw cash tries to figure out ways to beat the system. What makes a good supervisor is an active imagination. You plan how to beat it, and plug that particular hole and try again. What's the best way to beat it right now?"

"I can't think of one. I've thought of about six since I took charge there, and I plugged up every hole. Right now I can't think of exactly how it could be done. But I'm beginning to get the ghost of an idea. It involves a conspiracy between my roller-skating Angel and one of the security guards."

"Keep thinking. It can be done. Count on it. Two of your people will get together and find a way."

She started to turn toward the door just as she realized that it would not be characteristic were she not to try to use this new relationship to her own advantage. She turned back toward him, biting her lip. "Finn, I do have one suggestion."

"Let's hear it."

"We do get little foul-ups from time to time because Mrs. Diskant, who is in charge of Outgoing Mail, is on exactly the same level of authority and responsibility as I am. I think she is a fine woman and she does a fine job. But if I were to be in charge of my own operation and of O.M. as well, the coordination would be better. And I would certainly not interfere in any way with how she handles that department. You could explain to her why this change of status was necessary and I'm sure she would understand."

"I will . . . give it serious consideration."

She beamed at him and said, "God is love."

Looking only mildly surprised, he said, "Bless His holy name."

Between five and nine-thirty on that Tuesday evening, Glinda Lopez had completed twenty-one more long-distance phone calls to Church members delinquent in their tithes. With the help of the keyboard, her good memory, the Japanese voice-synthesis modules and her quickness of wit and improvisation, she had spoken to them with the rich ripe personal tone and cadence and intimacy of the Reverend Doctor Matthew Meadows in his prime.

After he had turned off the special equipment, she and Mickey Oshiro had wandered out of Communications and over to sit in darkness on the raised circular edge of the Fountain of Memory in the Garden of Mercy. A faint blue light shone on the spray of water, reflecting on their faces. There was a tickle on the side of her throat and she whacked a mosquito, rolled it into a tiny moist ball between finger and thumb and dropped it into the fountain. The sweat of long nervous concentration had soaked through her blouse and dampened her sweater and the waistband of her skirt.

"Mick," she said in a dead voice, "I am really whipped. This makes me tireder than anything else ever did. I don't know if I can keep it up without getting ulcers or a heart attack or something. And he wants me to train somebody else. My God, how can I train somebody to do something I can just barely handle myself?"

"It'll get easier. Once you get used to controlling the phonemes for stress and inflection and pitch, it'll turn into fun."

"You keep saying that, pal. I don't think it is going to get any easier because somehow I really hate it."

"Come on, Glin. What's to hate?"

"He's a loony, that old man is. You know. You and Mr. Efflander had me over there in the Manse to meet him. Sometimes his voice would be okay, and then it would go all wavery and thin again. I remember, he was asking me if I was from the store. What store? Then I was supposed to be Chris."

"Chris? Chris who?" he asked.

"She was John Tinker's wife. She died years ago."

"I didn't know he'd ever been married."

"Oh sure. But it was a long time ago. She drowned. They were guests on a yacht in the Bahamas and it was at anchor. She got up in the night and fell overboard somehow and drowned. It was a very big news story at the time. I was in high school when it happened. Anyway, what I was trying to say is how I hate it that people really think I'm the old man. It makes me feel weird."

"How do you mean?"

"I am inside the old man's voice and I am driving it like a car with no brakes. I say things he never said and never will say."

"So it's an illusion, Glin. We both know it is. Efflander brought me here and he's paying me well to create and develop this illusion. To me it's just a technical problem. Match the old recordings of the voice. Match the speech curves. Devise a new keyboard language, with half-tone drops at the end of a sentence, half-tone raises at the end of a question. But I know why it bothers you. The person who operates the system has to have a lot of quick responses. And that means a lot of imagination. And what is getting in your way is all that imagination."

"It just feels wrong."

After thinking for a few moments he said, "How about this. They send out thousands and thousands of letters that look like originals, with a signature nobody can tell from real. Lots of people must think old Matthew actually signed their letter. Or John Tinker. I bet there are thousands of letters going out that John Tinker has never even read. So what's the difference?"

"Maybe no difference. Maybe all the difference in the world. Take that woman in Lubbock the other night. God! The one that told me her dead husband comes back almost every night and sits on the side of her bed and talks to her. So she asks, what about that? I can't answer. So I got confused and hit one of the responses I'd already used and so she asked if I was a recording. Somehow, Mick, you've got to give me more time to think. These people come up with weird things. I need to stall. Maybe . . . Hey, maybe a little bit of coughing?"

"Nice!" Mickey Oshiro said, after a few moments of thought. "Very nice. Some coughing and I can stretch it a little by having him apologize at the end."

"By then I can have my answer on the screen, ready to punch it through. Have we got room on the board?"

"Oceans of room. And I can add another circuit board if we have to."

"Then give me some more small talk, please. The way people talk to each other over the phone. Like 'That's very interesting' and 'I'm glad you brought that up' and something like 'Maybe you'd like to tell me a little more about what happened.' Just give me a new row on the bottom of the pad, all time killers. When the delay gets to be too long, I can hear them breathing and that gets me so upset I mess up what I'm trying to keyboard onto the screen."

"I can get that done by tomorrow afternoon."

"Good. But I want some time to practice with it."

A sudden flashlight beam dazzled them, making them squint and turn their eyes away from the light. A guard said, "Pardon me, Mrs. Lopez. You too, sir. I thought some of the kids had snuck in here from the school again somehow. It's like a game with them."

She said there was no harm done, and wasn't it a lovely night, and the guard agreed and walked away. She yawned and stood up and said, "Thanks for listening, Mick. I'm kind of unwinding, maybe down to the point where I can get some sleep. I wake up a lot lately."

As he stood up, she stretched and yawned again. She was a thin woman, almost scrawny, given to graceless poses, bad posture, nervous mannerisms—tugging at her hair, pinching her nose, pulling her ear-lobes, biting the edges of her fingernails.

They walked slowly to the pedestrian exit beside the main gate, where the guard said good night and let them out. For the first fifty feet beyond the gate, they were in the bright glare of the security floodlights, and as they neared the darkness she said, "Hey, don't walk me home or we could become an item."

"I beg your pardon?"

"An item. Didn't they used to say that in California? This place, honest to God, is the world's worst rumor factory. If people work together, talk together and then walk home together, they think something has to be going on."

"I see. And you wouldn't like that to happen?" He suddenly realized how that sounded and said, "I mean, you wouldn't like to have people talking like that."

"I really don't care. I was just making conversation, I guess. Anyway, they would probably decide it's not exactly earthshaking even if we were all buddy-buddy. The spic lady and the Jap genius. There's enough going on around here, we'd be one very small item. Page twenty-seven, half a column inch. Besides that, I think I can spend the rest of my life without becoming anybody's item."

They walked on. He coughed and said, "We haven't talked about anything personal. But I do know you are Mrs. Lopez."

"Would you like to know about Lopez? Okay. Lopez is six three and about as broad as that gate we went through back there. But I'm never going to see him again."

"I don't understand."

"Oh, I could go see him, but there's no point in it." She stopped in the darkness, the lights behind her. "Mick, you're absolutely right. We've never talked about anything but this crazy voice synthesis, not until tonight. Okay, it's a dull story. He was a very proud man. He didn't take anything from anybody. He worked in a foundry and got in a brawl. It wasn't his fault. A foreman worked him over with a piece of pipe while some other people held him. Then they left him on the floor until somebody finally realized something might be really wrong. It happened up in Rochester. Lots of brain damage. He's three years old for the rest of his life, and the company insurance takes care of the bills from the state institution. He doesn't know me and never will and so I will probably never see him again alive."

"I'm very, very sorry, Glinda."

"Don't be. I seldom ever think about him. Those guys killed him. It's that simple. And that might be one of the things that make this synthesis program so hard for me to do."

He stood, looking at her, the distant light aslant across his face, a square, broad-bodied man with a round cheerful face, and black bangs that came down almost to his eyebrows. "I think I see what you mean, what the connection is. Your husband can't talk anymore. Doctor Meadows can't talk anymore."

"Thanks for the psychiatric analysis, Oshiro."

"Look, I was only trying to . . ."

"I know. Hey, I'm sorry. I'm really, really pooped, and when I'm pooped I get cross. You are a nice guy for a computer specialist. I never knew any Japanese person before. I was kind of edgy around you at first, but then you turned out to be just like anybody else. Don't you have any personal problems? We can work on those too."

"No problems, Glin. Too busy for problems. I worked with the Votrax Type-'N-Talk and the Telesensory Prose 2000. I worked with Pisoni and Nusbaum at Indiana, then back out to Silicon Valley. Our little outfit is called MacroMix. There's just five of us. We all worked for bigger outfits. We thought we might get rich, but it isn't happening yet. We design. We don't manufacture. Consultant contracts like this keep us going. And keep us learning. I dream that I am running along a beach, running like hell to keep away from a huge wave curling over me. The running is the learning. What we all believe, the five of us, is that one day, probably with a thirty-two-bit microprocessor, there will be a super program which will be able to be programmed to keep improving itself. Meanwhile, run, run, run."

"You have to realize I haven't any idea what you're talking about, Mick."

"What brought you here?"

"Me? It was kind of the end of the world for me. I tried Lopez's priest. I converted when I married Lopez. The priest couldn't seem to get hold of how desperate I felt. I loved Lopez, and for God's sake they had him in diapers, saying 'Gooo.' How do you rebuild your life? Then one evening I had the television on, it was a cable broadcast, and the Reverend Doctor John Tinker Meadows was sitting behind a desk. They zoomed the camera until his whole face filled the screen, and he looked right at me! He looked right into my eyes and he said very gently, 'You are sick at heart, aren't you?' And I answered him! What kind of a nut talks to a television set? The tears busted right out of my eyes and ran down my face and I said, 'Yes, yes I am!' 'You are in despair,' he said. 'You don't know what to do with your life. Nobody cares how deep you are in black depression. I am holding my hand out to you. If you take it, I can help you climb out of the pit into the sunshine.' So . . . okay. I took his hand. I wrote for the literature. I joined the Church. I took Bible lessons. I tithed ten percent. But I began to begin to feel myself sort of slipping backward. It all seemed sort of secondhand. So I quit my job and came down here." She lowered her voice. "It isn't perfect. What is? I'm down here. The sun isn't exactly shining yet, but maybe it will. I can live with myself better than I could before. I pray a lot. I believe. I really believe that God is love, bless His holy name. He will watch over me. What do you believe, Oshiro?"

"I . . . I guess I believe in the miracle of silicon. For thousands of years we've been savages living in the darkness. Now there is a bright light beginning to shine across the world, and we are standing in it, blinking and scratching and looking around. I believe that through this new communication man is evolving into something different. Not better and not worse. Different. And I am proud to be one of the pioneers. Maybe my God is speaking to us through silicon."

"I like working with you, whatever."

"I'll be around a while longer. You are one smart lady and you make the work more fun. You pick up on things, and you make pretty good suggestions."

"The calls still tear me up too much. Like tonight that old boy in Memphis wondering if he could send in ten percent of his food stamps. Maybe . . . maybe I don't want to get used to it. Maybe I'm resisting that because I think I probably will. And then it will be a job and I can use half my mind to keep track of what I'm doing." She sighed. She put her hand on his shoulder. "Good night, Mickey. And thanks for listening."

They stood awkwardly for a moment, alone together in the darkness, immobilized perhaps by what she had said about their becoming an item, but wanting a way to say good night that involved touching, involved human contact. And on simultaneous impulse they thrust out their right hands, and shook hands, and both laughed aloud because they recognized the parody of it, and the friendship.

And then off they went, she to a small room with hot plate, a room in the wing of the dormitory the University did not yet need to occupy. It was an inexpensive arrangement and it hastened the day when she would have the lawyers paid off in full, the ones who had negotiated the lifelong institutional support for Lopez.

He went on his half-mile walk through the warm night down to the pleasant room they had provided for him in the Meadows Center Motor House. He stopped first in the dining room, and as he ate his light, late supper and read his book, his concentration was marred by the recurrent memory of the tension in her voice, the agitation arising from this strange assignment. He felt that she had been trapped and he wished he could find some path out of the trap for her. He felt that he understood her, and he tried not to feel pity for her, an emotion she did not need and would certainly resent. Perhaps his sense of identification was the product of the soft warm night, and of being alone. He told himself that in many ways she was a grotesque, all those nervous mannerisms, awkward postures. But her eyes were lovely, and lost.

Six heavy men in their sixties were led to a table near Oshiro's. After they were given menus they put them aside and five of them bowed their heads over their folded hands. The sixth one, sitting at the end of the table, stared at the ceiling and proclaimed in a loud honking voice, "O Lord, we have come all the way here from San Antone, Texas, to visit the home office of Your Church and Your Tabernacle, and we have come to ask Your blessings on all the ventures and enterprises that us six brethren here gathered together are involved in. We want You to know, as You probably already know, that we've been tithing off the gross, not off the net. Ever' tenth bar'l of oil and ever' tenth foot of gas and ever' tenth head of cattle has been turned into cash money and given to Your Church to help in its mission to save us God-fearing Christians from the dee-structive and traitorous acts and schemes of the socialists who have wormed their way into power in our nation's capital, and from their field agents who wander through the land demanding fool things and fool reports from honest and productive businessmen who want only to . . ."

But by that time the voice had faded because Oshiro had signed his tab, left his tip, picked up his book and walked out—past the others in the dining room who were staring at the honker, transfixed, some of them with fork poised halfway between meal and mouth.

When he was in his room, he turned on the bed lamp and then went over and stood at the window and looked out at the four big floodlighted spires of the Tabernacle. It could very well become too much for Glinda Lopez to handle—this electronic deception, talking in the voice of the old reverend, extracting money from the people. Along with cynicism would come a simple destruction of faith. And she could not continue to do anything she did not believe in. She was, quite simply, that kind of person—the best and most valuable kind.

And what *do* you believe in, Oshiro?

As I told her, I believe in hundreds of thousands of circuits in a chip smaller than my front tooth. I believe in the magic of bubble memory and in the upcoming greater magic of amino acids with memory-storage capacity. I believe in instant retrieval and in all the people of the world locked into a network that can provide every one of them with communication with every other one of them, as well as with all the knowledge man has thus far amassed. Maybe believing that it will all work is no greater or less than believing in a God who watches the plight of every sparrow—a God rumored to have a plan so comprehensive the reason for every sickening disaster will one day fall into place and be made clear to us. Every sickening disaster and every enormous triumph. In that sense, silicon is one of the faces of God, and so is atomic fusion. We worship at our own strange temples.

Eight

Annalee Purves had mail-ordered some bed sheets from Spiegel in Chicago, and so every now and then she would go to a front window of the farmhouse and look down the long dusty slope of the narrow driveway and see the red flag still up on the mailbox and wonder how late this Wednesday delivery would be.

She was waiting for the confirmation of her order. Maybe they had changed the route again.

Anvil thunderheads were building in the west, sun-white on the tops of them, ominous blue-black underneath. They cut off the late-afternoon sun. The air was close and still, and at times a gust of wind would turn the leaves over and spin up the dust.

The house seemed very empty lately. It helped to leave the television on, and hear people laughing and talking even if you were paying no attention to what they were doing. Both the men were working—her husband, Hub, down at the airfreight depot in Waycross, and son Dave hauling sand and gravel over near Bickley. Annalee had lost her job back in February when the BuyRite chain had closed its local outlet. But it hadn't worked out too badly. She'd put in a large kitchen garden in the spring, with Dave's help. Hub and Dave had replaced the broken wire fencing around the chicken yard and they had gone back to chickens, even though she really hated the stupid messy things, pecking the weakest to death every chance they got.

With Doreen gone, up at Meadows Center, out of trouble at last, it seemed to Annalee more like the early days of her marriage, back twenty years when she'd been eighteen. But back then she'd had to put up with Hub's mother. It was Hub's mother's house and the old lady wanted it kept just so. Everything had to shine at all times. Once upon a time it had been a real farm, seven people living on it and working it and living off it. But no longer. It was too small for the way you had to farm these days. Red Layberry down the road worked some of it on shares, and that brought in a little. Not much, but welcome. As Hub said, it made the difference between Christmas.

If Dave moved out—he was going with that pretty little DeAngelis girl—then no two ways about it, she would have to go back to work somewhere somehow. Maybe this time Hub would listen to reason and agree to sell the place. Then maybe they could find a little place in Waycross where the electric and taxes and oil bill didn't eat you up.

When next she looked out, the flag was down. As she started to walk down the long driveway she heard the first bump of thunder and a hard gust of wind rattled her jeans against her ankles. By the time she was halfway back with the mail, blue lightning lit up the world and the crash of thunder was almost simultaneous. She ran through the first fat drops that pocked the dust and tapped against her hair and shoulders. She trotted across the porch and into the house, gasping for breath. The hard rain had begun. She sat at the little table in the living room to look at the mail. When she tried to turn on the table lamp she realized the television had gone silent, the power off.

She moved her chair closer to the window. Three catalogues, a bank statement, a letter for Dave from California. Nothing from Spiegel. And finally a letter to Mr. and Mrs. Purves, RR 3 Box 88, Bickley, GA. No return address. The date stamp on the envelope indicated it was from Lakemore. So it had something to do with Doreen but it certainly wasn't Doreen's writing. This was block printing, very carefully done as if somebody had used a ruler to make the lines.

She opened it and found a large sheet of ruled yellow paper, torn so carelessly from a pad that one corner was missing. She read the printed message twice before she began to comprehend it:

A WIERD LITTLE REVEREND JOE DEETS
IS FUCKING DOREEN YOUR DAUGHTER
EVERY CHANCET HE GETS, WHICH IS LIKE
ALL THE TIME.

A FRIEND

PS HE IS OVER FORTY.

A dumb joke, she thought. A sick dumb joke. It just could not be true. Doreen was a Meadows Angel. Just a week ago Sunday they had a lovely picture of her, singing. Her face filled the whole screen and they kept the camera on her for maybe twenty seconds. She had seen the tear on Doreen's cheek. She had never seen her daughter look so beautiful, in living color.

The Reverend Matthew Meadows would never let anything like that go on at Meadows Center. And neither would John Tinker Meadows or the Reverend Sister Mary Margaret Meadows. But maybe they didn't even know about it. Doreen could be sly. When she was a tiny little girl she could look you right in the eye and shake her head and say, "I didn't do it. Davey did it." She could say it so innocent, even when you'd seen her do it, seen her break the dish.

Sly like me, Annalee thought. A punishment from God come back again on me for getting away with it before, so long ago that sometimes a whole month can go by without me thinking back to it, back to those days when I must have been crazy, doing everything he told me to do. Sometimes I wonder where he is, if he is still alive.

They'd had to sit there, she and Hub, and tell Mary Margaret Meadows every last bit about all Doreen's troubles. The pregnancy and the motorcycles and the pills and the pot, and getting jailed two hundred miles from home. Then the boy getting killed like that, and Doreen losing the baby.

It was the next day that she and Hub had been called in to talk to Mary Margaret and John Tinker Meadows, with Doreen waiting on a bench in the hall outside the conference room. John Tinker Meadows had said solemnly that they had decided, with some misgivings, to take her in. She would be in a protected environment where she would have every chance to develop into Christian maturity. She would be given work to do around the Administration and Communications buildings. She would live in a University dormitory, and she would have to take courses in Homemaking, the History of Christianity and Missionary Service. She would have Bible lessons and choir practice. She would have plain healthy food and compulsory exercise and she would be kept busy at all times.

They can't know about it, Annalee thought. Maybe it isn't even happening. Maybe some girl in the choir is jealous of her. Maybe it's from some boy she won't have anything to do with.

She was always sly. And guess who she gets that from. My God, how close I came to turning my whole life into nothing. If Hub hadn't come along just when he did, where would I be now? Probably dead. Dying in the midst of sin and burning in hell forever.

Whenever she was deeply troubled she went to the nearest mirror. The television came back on, advertising baby powder. It was her way of reaffirming some contact with reality, to look in the hall mirror. She saw herself, a faded woman with frightened eyes, straight pale hair, a small pouch under her chin, lips sucked flat.

"What are we going to do?" she whispered. The "we" was the woman in the mirror and the woman watching her. The "we" was certainly not Annalee and Hub. And even more definitely, not Annalee and her son. Dave had gone after the motorcycle people and had spent five days in the hospital and had come out with his face looking different. He was a different person when he came out. A little bit quieter, probably for the rest of his life.

Maybe this Deets person was assigned to supervise Doreen's spiritual welfare but lost his head over her. It wasn't beyond possibility. Doreen's looks are the best of mine and the best of Hub's family. And she has a beautiful little body. Men began watching her when she was twelve. Later on the phone rang all the time. She isn't a bad girl. She's just easily led. She's pretty and she's weak and she's very loving. It's a terrible combination.

She dropped to her knees in the hallway and said, "Dear God, please help me figure out what's best to do. This could ruin her life just as bad as that motorcycle boy. Maybe she's praying to you too, because this is a terrible sin. If it's true."

She heard Hub's pickup coming up the drive. She jumped to her feet and ran and got the letter and the envelope, folded them, and put them in the back of the shallow drawer in the small table by the window, under a box of writing paper she hardly ever used because it had so many bright flowers on it there wasn't room enough to write.

He came into the back hall, soaked and stomping, pulling his work shoes and work shirt off. When she went to him, he kissed her and said, "Do you know, it came down so damned hard about ten miles south I had to pull clean off the road and stop? It's drowning your garden out there, and it's drove the chickens inside. Anything new?"

"Nothing, as usual. How was your day, hon?"

"Light. Real light. It's so light lately it's making me nervous. Too many people standing around drinking coffee out of that machine. Somebody may come by from the home office and clear some of us out."

"If they do, it won't be you."

Dave came home an hour later, muddy and exhausted. She served them supper at the kitchen table, and as she did so she felt like one of those women in the afternoon soap operas, being bright and cheerful so as to hide a dreadful secret from the others. And it was sort of like the kind of secrets women had on television. Not on those approved programs they always listed in *PathWays*. Whenever she was watching one that wasn't on the list she felt guilty, especially since they had taken Doreen in. It was always best to follow the rules of the Church.

That's what was so confusing about this new problem. The members of the Eternal Church of the Believer were all part of a very special group inside society at large. The Church told you never to donate money or goods to local or national causes like the March of Dimes or Easter Seals or the Salvation Army. Things like that. When you tithed your ten percent the Church gave part of that to the causes the Church knew were worthy. And when there was some great new need, the Church would ask for a second tithe. Sometimes it was very hard to find the money, but it was the way you confirmed your membership in the special group, your brotherhood and sisterhood with Believers all over the country and all over the world. As a Church member you had to live up to certain codes of dress and behavior. You did not seek medical help because it was a proven fact that faith kept the members healthier than all those people who had not found the true religion. The Church did not want you to join clubs or let your children join clubs. The Church was the only club anyone ever needed. You could not curse or drink hard liquor or register to vote or run for public office. You prayed for fifteen minutes every morning and another fifteen either during the day or at night when you went to bed. Sometimes during all the years she and Hub had been members, it had been difficult to live up to the rules of the Church. Sometimes you could not understand why certain rules were imposed on you. But in the end you realized every rule was there for a good reason.

You were not supposed to socialize with non-members of the Church because they represented the evil and decay of the outside world, and all of them had opinions and ideas which could contaminate a member if he or she was exposed over a long period of time.

You could not question the rule of segregation because it came down from the old Reverend Matthews and his son and his daughter—the only true representatives of God on this earth. You gave everything you were asked to give. It was as easy as that. In return God gave back to you health, a certainty of faith, a sense of belonging and an everlasting place in heaven. There was no personal problem here on earth that could not be eased by giving of your substance to the Church. Giving was prayer, the most effective kind.

God knew the sacrifices involved. Her very own blood brother and his wife and their three children were outsiders. They jeered at the Eternal Church. And so they had to remain outside her life forever, just as if they had died. If they ever did see the light and join the Church, then she could open her arms and take them all back into her family. For years she had hoped they would change. She had kept up their subscription to *PathWays* and she sent them the special messages that came down from the Meadows Center from time to time. Sometimes in the middle of the night she would cry very quietly so as not to wake Hub. They never even remembered her birthday anymore.

Doreen was living proof that the rules of the Church were right. She had mingled with outsiders and had been corrupted by them. Annalee had knelt in the cold on the hard floor, night after night, hour after hour, praying for Doreen to be released from the evil influences and return home to her family and her Church. When the accidental death and the miscarriage had happened, Annalee had wondered if this could have been a violent answer to her prayers. In the Old Testament sinners were often dealt with most savagely.

The doctor who had treated Doreen had recommended that she be given psychiatric care—some professional counseling at the very least. But Annalee and Hub had explained to the doctor that the rules of their Church forbade that sort of treatment. When Doreen, still frozen into a strange silence, had been well enough to travel, they had driven her up to the Meadows Center in the pickup truck to keep the appointment they had made with Mary Margaret Meadows.

She had thought they were saving Doreen's life and that she had been made whole again. And now this.

That night, after Hub began the soft and rhythmic snoring so familiar to her over the years, she lay staring up into darkness, thinking about Doreen. Doreen had been so quick, so lively. She could catch Davey even though he had been a year older and he could not catch her. It used to make him so furious. Annalee could see her daughter come running across the side field, running and grinning, her skinny brown knees pumping high, running right to Annalee and thudding into her, laughing and hugging. She remembered how perfect a baby Doreen had been, that little body so wondrously textured and shaped, so smooth and so delicate. Davey had been a rough, red, squalling baby. In the baby eyes of Doreen, Annalee had thought she could see all the secrets of a woman grown, smiling out at her.

Suppose it was true, that dreadful word in that note on yellow paper? If it was true, then everything was turned upside down. If something like that could exist *within* the structure of the Church, then was there anything left in the world which could be trusted?

Maybe this Deets was Satan in another form, invading the holy Church, tempting the weak. Hub had just turned forty, and he was younger than this so-called Reverend Deets, younger than the man who was reported to be bedding his daughter.

She could not tell Hub. He would just go up there and kill the man, minister or no. She finally knew what she would have to do. It was a simple plan and that meant it had more chance of working. She would say that she had been talking to Doreen during the day when the two men were at work. Several times. Girl talk, she would say, with a reassuring but mysterious smile. And she would tell them that it would probably be best if she went up there and spent a day or two with her. They could certainly take care of the garden and feed the chickens. Hub could drive her into Waycross and leave her at the bus station.

The important thing was to find out if the note was a lie, and the best way to do that would be to hand it right to Mary Margaret Meadows and watch her face as she read it. It was an awful thing to do, to make that wonderful woman read that terrible word in front of somebody, even when she was only reading it to herself, not out loud. If it was not a lie, there would be time to try to think of what to do next, and wonder if there was anything at all anyone could do.

On Thursday morning, August eleventh, by quarter to eight the temperature was nearing ninety degrees. One of the large white ECB limousines was parked in the shade of the hangar, the motor running to keep the air conditioner going. When Charley Winchester spotted the Gulfstream coming in over the low hills, coming down from the north, he and John Tinker Meadows got out of the cool limousine and strolled over to where the plane would stop, in front of the hangar.

There were just four passengers being brought in this time, two United States Senators and their administrative assistants. Charley knew all four men and he had briefed John Tinker. The senior of the two Senators was Marshall Howlett, and his aide was Jim Ricardi, who had been a Washington journalist. Lewis Train was bringing Robby Nathan, who had taught government at Yale.

"They're all strong people," Charley had said. "So we walk light and easy."

"Who needs who most?" John had asked.

"That's always a good question, isn't it?"

The four men came down the unfolded steps, Train in the lead, a jowly man with a big torso, cropped dark hair, a low forehead, a thin black line of mustache. The engines sighed into silence as the tractor came out to hook on and tow the aircraft into the relative cool of the hangar. As they were unable to adjust their schedules to stay over, the two aides carried dispatch cases, and the Senators were empty-handed.

Marshall Howlett was a delicate, scrubbed, burnished little bit of a man who looked twice as big on the television screens. He wore a pale suit of western cut and elevator boots. There was a gold buckle on the snakeskin band around his snowy Stetson.

Charley greeted them warmly and made the introductions. They got into the cool air of the white limousine, Charley beside the driver, the Senators in the back on either side of John Tinker, and the aides on the jump seats.

As none of the four had ever been to the Meadows Center before, Charley had the driver go slowly and take a roundabout route so that John Tinker could point out the various places of interest. The driver took them out Henrietta Boulevard past the Mall and then came back to the primary security area, through the vehicle gate and directly to the Manse.

"I had no idea there was so *much* of it!" Robby Nathan said.

"And still growing," Charley said, smiling back at him.

The conference table in the old man's large office on the fourth floor of the Manse had been set up for breakfast for six. It was a familiar routine. All the pictures, plaques, testimonials—the artifacts of a long and busy public life—tended to make guests more aware of the Church as a continuing entity, given special attention in the past by public men more celebrated than they had yet become.

The linen was white, the coffee steaming, the biscuits hot, bacon crisp, orange juice icy, melons superb, eggs to order, waffles golden, and the service swift and inconspicuous.

Conversation was general during breakfast, with comment about the Gross National Product, the continuing trend of corporate mergers and takeovers, the Mexican debt problem, the pitching in the National League, highway and bridge repair, the flood tide of summer reruns.

John Tinker Meadows was at the head of the table, his back to the bright windows, and Charley was at the other end. The two Senators had been seated where they could look over at the giant desk of the founder of the Church, at his high-backed black leather swivel chair, and at the glass cases full of the souvenirs of all the years of the old man's confident assumption of power and influence.

"What's the latest report on your father?" the dapper little cowboy Senator asked.

"No improvement," John Tinker said, shaking his head. "We were hoping he could stop by here and say hello to old friends, but this isn't one of his good days. He tires easily and he gets confused."

"I met him years ago in El Paso," Senator Howlett said. "An absolutely fascinating man. There were a lot of us at a big party, milling around, and even though he didn't say a word at first, suddenly everybody knew he was in the room. You could feel his presence. Must make it pretty hard to fill that big leather chair over there behind the desk."

John Tinker smiled and shrugged. "I don't try to." He could sense their uneasiness. Most laymen meeting a particular man of God for the first time in a social context never know just how to react to him. "My father had that fabulous magnetism that was so necessary when he began to build the Eternal Church of the Believer. I suppose in one sense the Church is not fully mature yet, in that it hasn't reached the growth we all anticipate. We're at the point where we have to use enhancements of personal magnetism. As you gentlemen surely know, we're at the point where colorless men, with enough technical support, can be elected to high office. Hair stylists. Voice coaches. Good speech writers. Skilled cameramen and producers. And all the lessons in gestures, proper pauses, variations in tone and emphasis. My father never needed a single bit of that. Gentlemen, I need it *all!* And I use it all." He smiled at them. "Sometimes I wonder if I am deceiving the faithful. And then I use that same rationalization men running for office probably use: it's all for the good of the people."

It was a joke which had always worked before, and it worked now with these men. Also it cued Charley into his first specific approach.

"Speaking of running for office, Marsh," Charley said, "and you too, Lewis. I want you both to know that regardless of any differences we may have had in the past, or any we might have between now and when you run again, you will have our support—generous support, through legal PAC channels, of course."

"Delighted to hear that," Lewis Train said, "and I am sure Marsh is too. No strings, Charley? No strings at all?"

"Just the usual invisible strings. I think you know what I mean. You gentlemen share the same beliefs and hopes and dreams that we have here, and share the vision of the future of the country that we all want. We know from your records that you will always vote our way on the fundamentals, on basic decency, abortion, school prayer, the American home, crime control, drug control, streamlining the criminal justice system, administering the entitlements systems in a fair and equitable way to eliminate cheaters."

Charley had passed it back to John Tinker, who said, "We're particularly interested in the criminal justice system. At last count by a reliable source, there were four hundred and seventy-two thousand lawyers practicing in this country. Is that too many? Or just enough? How big is the population of Japan? Forty million, fifty million? I heard recently there are more lawyers in the city of Philadelphia than in all of Japan. Maybe that's why they can build good cars and stereo sets cheaper than we can. If we have just enough lawyers in this land, then won't the law schools make sure that in future years we have too many? Would you say, Senators, that a country with too many lawyers might have too much litigation?"

Howlett said, "I have to admit a little bit of prejudice, being one myself. And so is Senator Train here. And the great majority of the legislative bodies in this country are jam-packed with lawyers. I'll buy that concept, Reverend. When a decent man who has been wronged in some civil matter has to wait seven or eight years to be heard, something is wrong. When major corporations with a good cash flow go into voluntary bankruptcy to protect the shareholders' assets from thousands of claims of damage allegedly done to the plaintiffs in past years, we all know that something is dreadfully wrong."

Lewis Train said to the little cowboy, "Marsh, I do believe we're going to hear about some kind of legal harassment from the government."

"Which is why we're here?" Marsh asked.

"Not at all," John Tinker said quickly. "The Eternal Church of the Believer is being constantly examined by tax collectors with help from legal specialists on the government payroll. But it's nothing we can't continue to handle just as we have in the past. The Winchester brothers and their cadre of smart young lawyers have always taken good care of the Church and there's no reason to assume they won't be able to continue to do so in the future."

Charley sighed heavily. "Thanks for the vote of confidence, John. But sometimes it do get a tad wearisome. The Reagan election made the fundamentalist churches sound too important in secular affairs, and so the tax people started coming down on us like a load of bricks, calling us political action groups and trying to pry away our legitimate tax exemption. Then along comes the mid-term election and it proved we didn't have the clout people thought we had. But the machinery to cut us down to size is still in place, and functioning."

"In all honesty," John Tinker said, right on cue, "the lines are a little bit blurred. Suppose a country preacher, which is how my daddy started out, gets up in the pulpit and thunders that little kids should have the right to pray in school. And in his county there are two men running for office. Jones is for prayer in schools and Smith is against it. Is the preacher urging his flock to vote for Jones? And does not this whole controversy cut across a lot of social lines? Abortion, busing, welfare, protective tariffs. It is my feeling that if people look to this Church for guidance, then the Church must express its opinion on many secular matters."

Jim Ricardi, Marshall Howlett's aide said, "When Jesus drove the money-changers out of the temple, was that a religious act or a political act?"

"It was a social act," John Tinker said. "It was a religious leader acting for the social good, because Jesus knew that Christianity could never thrive in a corrupt society."

Robby Nathan, the other aide, a chubby balding young man with a very deep voice, said, "Let me, as the devil's advocate for a moment, speak of fairness. This came up in my classes at Yale. Suppose Mr. Jones, who advocates no-fault divorce, is up against Mr. Smith, who is agin it. The churches use their donated funds to fight no-fault divorce, calling it a social evil. Several other organizations, which have no tax exemption, fight for it and try to get Jones elected. The people who are fighting Jones get a portion of their war fund picked up by Uncle Sam, as a charitable deduction. The people who are trying to get Jones elected have to use money that is all their own, that in fact is what they have left after paying taxes, so for the man in a fifty percent bracket, it costs him fifty dollars to give twenty-five to the cause. Unfair?"

"Good question. It so happens we do have a political action arm. It is called the Henrietta Fund, after my paternal grandmother, and it is made perfectly clear to all that any donation to it is not tax-exempt in any way, shape or manner. Through that fund we try to get men elected who are friendly to the causes in which we believe. We campaign for specific legislation. It is a healthy and sizable fund. We have a specialist here who has done wonders with all the Church funds and investments."

Charley stepped in and said, "On our commercial operations, and you saw some of them as we drove here from the airport, we pay tax on the same basis as any other business. ECB Enterprises, Lakemore Construction, Meadows Development and a slew of smaller things all pay what's due and are all subject to periodic IRS audit. Our executives tithe to the Church. Ten percent. In auditing their returns, the IRS has made the arbitrary judgment that the tithes in total are a kickback to the Church which works to keep our business profits low and our business taxes low. They are trying to use that as a lever to open up our donation records from the entire membership. We have to fight that all the way down the line. We have a perfect right to retain our exemption on the Church, the assets of the Church and the University. And, of course, if any individual Church member is unable to prove to the IRS his total annual gift we are more than glad to provide him with documentation from our records."

Robby Nathan spoke again. "Would this Henrietta Fund be as big and strong as it is were it not for the weight and prestige of the Church?"

John Tinker's quick smile was charming. He spread his hands in a big shrug and said, "Probably not. But no tax-exempt money goes into it. And it is expended on social matters and political matters. Are we to be totally muzzled by our government? Power equals responsibility and responsibility implies taking those actions deemed responsible. It's another good question, Robby. It helps clarify this whole area for all of us at this table. The Church is against crime, poverty, random dumping of toxic wastes, communism, sloth, indifference, police states, murder and littering the highways. In my sermons I touch on a whole list of social evils, from obscenity to adultery. In so doing, I am a political activist— because politics is the art of devising ways for men to live together in peace and in relative comfort. And with, of course, minimal interference from the State in matters that are not the business of the State."

"And as a matter of fact," Charley Winchester said, "we have almost as many checks and balances and safeguards as you fellows up there in our nation's capital—and by the way, we no longer believe that D.C. means Deliberately Confusing. We have a powerful advisory board formed of all the pastors of our affiliated churches. Over eighty of them now. We have an in-house steering committee, and we have the guidance of the Founders of the Society of Merit. We are supposed to keep their identities secret. There can never be more than twenty living members at any one time. But I thought you'd find it interesting, so I brought along a list you can look at, but not keep."

After Lewis Train studied it, he said, "Every one from the Fortune Five Hundred?"

"All but four," Charley said. "We get invaluable advice from it. It was old Doctor Meadows' idea to start that group. Those men have a financial and a spiritual investment in the Eternal Church."

"Speaking of our eighty-eight affiliated churches," John Tinker said, "I want to make a point about the causes we endorse and some of the causes endorsed by other church groups. We did not establish a lot of those churches. We picked them off. Quite a few of them came from national church organizations affiliated with the National Council of Churches, which is a part of the World Council of Churches. They were weak churches, discontented with the national church bureaucracy, and ready to split."

"Why," Senator Howlett asked, "in this era which we could call a time of the resurgence of the Christian religion, have these churches become so weak?"

John Tinker Meadows shrugged. "A lot of the church organizations have internal dissension. In the South we have the PCUS, the Presbyterian Church in the U.S., with over eight hundred thousand members. In the North they have the UPCUSA, the United Presbyterian Church in the U.S.A., with two and a half million members. They've been split apart since the Civil War. Back in 1969 they began to try to get together again, but a lot of the conservative members of both branches didn't like the sound of it. And we have been picking off some of their churches ever since. They did merge in June. But while they were fussing at each other, the Southern Church lost over a hundred and thirty thousand members, and the Northern Church lost three quarters of a million. Their dissension was our opportunity."

"I thought they'd have more members than that," Jim Ricardi said, frowning.

"We tend to think too much about membership totals," John Tinker said. "Fourteen million Southern Baptists. Ten million United Methodists. Forty-one million Catholics. Five and a half million Baptists in the National Baptist Convention." He shrugged. "We're one of the little ones. Over half a million. But growing faster than most because we make a better effort. We keep in better touch. The affiliated churches that decided to come in with us were quite weak. Now they are strong, so strong that the National Council of Churches keeps pecking at us, trying to find some leverage to make us give them back. They won't go back, for the same reason that so many members of the National Council of Churches tried to resign from the World Council of Churches, but it was voted down. A piece of every dollar that goes into the collection plates goes to the World Council of Churches with their headquarters abroad, and that World Council sends seed money to every Marxist revolutionary group in Latin America and in Africa. The World Council defends it on the grounds that the money goes for food and medicines, to help the poor, as Jesus Christ ordered us as Christians to do. But a lot of people believe, and I am among them, that if you provide food and medicine, it leaves the revolutionaries with more money for arms and terror.

"I bring this up only because you gentlemen might hear some strange things about the Eternal Church of the Believer from that big building they call the God Box. It might come directly or indirectly, but when it does, consider the source. The only revolution we sponsor is the return to Jesus Christ. And in this country that is long overdue."

Conversation returned to aimless generalities until finally Charley said, glancing at his watch, "I happen to know that Doctor Meadows here has a morning meeting coming up, and what I would like to do is take you fellows on a little walking tour of the Tabernacle and the Garden of Mercy before we head back to the plane."

They shook hands around, all smiling, all showing teeth. They would take their little tour, and when they were walking in the Garden of Mercy, a very pretty woman with a camera would recognize one of the Senators and would take their picture in the Garden with the Tabernacle as the background. Charley would get them to the jet in time to put them back in Washington a little after eleven-fifteen as promised. The color picture and the negative would go into the vault, properly labeled.

And just how did it go this time? John Tinker wondered. Pretty well. A few moments of tension. Not any more than usual. To his dismay he had almost lost his train of thought a couple of times while speaking to them. The same lines had been said perhaps too many times. He remembered his father saying to him long ago, "So far only four Senators and ten Members of the House have seen fit to answer our invitation to come see us. But we'll keep on asking. We'll always make it nice. No pressure. They'll tell the others. You'll see."

And now the grand total of Senators was over sixty, and he could not remember how many from the House of Representatives, some out of curiosity, some out of suspicion, some out of awe and a certain spiritual hunger. And many, of course, who had the natural politician's instinct to move in close to any kind of visible power.

Charley had said these two were on "useful" committees. The ones who didn't bring along any staff were almost always easier to handle, and would usually accept a touch of Charley's Wild Turkey or Finlandia vodka. His lines were getting a little tired and more difficult to say. He decided to put Spencer McKay to work on the problem and see if he could freshen it up a little. It went well, of course, but he was getting weary of it. It was the same kind of listlessness which seemed to have settled over everything. The Senators would go back to Washington and, in time, at the right time, they would have something to say about certain practices of the IRS as regards religious institutions.

Employees of the Manse were cleaning up the breakfast debris. He took a final cup of coffee back into his suite. A few minutes later his private line rang just once. He glanced at his watch. When it rang again, just once, five minutes later, he knew who it was and what she expected. He was tempted to ignore it. Yet she had promised to use that particular code only in emergency situations.

The affair was beginning to make him irritable. It was sliding slowly downhill—a familiar feeling. It had been one of his more idiotic risks. And she had been a little too obvious from the very beginning. His taste ran more to the shy and quiet ones, game difficult to stalk, especially for a public person. Maybe he had gotten into it this time not only out of boredom, or the sexual challenge of it, but also because Rolf Wintergarten was so openly adoring of his new, second wife, and Rolf was such a hardworking stuffed shirt, it seemed more like a bad script than a genuine, heartfelt affair. In fact it was so much like a bad soap opera that it had never seemed quite real to him, even when Molly lay under him, pumping and huffing. It seemed like some strange rehearsal, in which everything they said had already been written down and studied, and the camera crew, director, executive producer, script girl and the sound and lighting technicians stood by in readiness for the clap boards and the real take that somehow never happened.

So, with a deep sigh, and a leaden resignation, he went down and took one of the blue Ford vans from the motor pool and drove down to the Mall. He parked around in back, near the Sears service garage, and walked to the bank of telephones just inside that entrance to the Mall. As he looked for a coin in his pockets, three middle-aged women stopped and stood staring at him, jaws sagging, eyes wide.

"It is! It is! I told you!" the heaviest one said.

"Oh, Doctor Meadows!" the thin one said. "We're all members of the Church from Dayton, Ohio, and we all love you so much. If we run to the bookstore and buy copies of one of your books, will you sign them for us? Please?"

He smiled and nodded, nodded and smiled, shook their hands, found the coin for the phone, and then leaned against the wall by the plastic telephone shells, wishing he could, by an effort of will, disappear forever from the face of the earth without a trace, without a memory, with no knowledge of ever having lived. And with no slightest memory of his face, voice or existence remaining in the conscious mind of anyone on the planet, and no reference to him in any file or book or photograph. Death before birth.

Nine

Mrs. Holroyd told Roy Owen that Moses was doing some culvert work for a farmer a couple of miles up north of Lakemore, but she could see no objection to his going back to the barn and waiting for Moses by the school bus where he lived.

The converted bus showed considerable ingenuity. Homemade steps led down from a door cut into the back of the bus to a screened platform with a canvas roof peaked like a Chinese hat. On the platform was a small noisy refrigerator, a deck chair, two large floor fans, a table with a table lamp. A water pipe led down from the Holroyd house, and there was a hand pump to pump the water up to a big drum on a sturdy platform fastened to the side of the barn, about ten feet above ground level. A pipe led from the bottom of the drum to a shower head above a concrete slab, with a turnoff just above the shower head. A second pipe led into the curtained interior of the bus. The uncurtained windows had been spray-painted white on the inside.

Mrs. Holroyd had told him that Moses was a gem. He did any and all heavy work she asked of him, free of charge. He was very quiet, kept himself clean, did not drink and had no visitors. His red truck was, of course, a disgrace, but he kept it around behind the barn out of sight of the house and the road. "People say he's real strange, you know, kind of a religious nut, and don't I worry about him living on the property with me, but I tell them I feel a lot safer with Moses nearby than I would if he picked up and left."

Roy found a two-foot section of log in the tall grass nearby and rolled it over to the barn, upended it, and sat in the shade and the light August breeze, leaning back against the weathered gray wood of the barn, flecked with bits of color from the coats of paint which had long since bleached away. He thought he would tell Lindy about this, realizing at once that she was gone and there was nobody left to whom he could tell this sort of thing. During the three months she had been gone, it had happened often. He would be planning how he would tell Lindy: "Guess who I saw yesterday." "I heard that Red and Ellie are getting a divorce." "Let me tell you how Moses fixed up that old school bus." But there was no one to tell the small things to. And maybe that was the very best definition of loneliness, that those bits of trivia worth recounting set up the resonances of lives shared over the years so that the two of you looked at the incident from the same angle of reference, with no explanations needed.

Something tugged at memory and he recalled a New England summer long ago when he had caught mononucleosis—the kissing disease —in May of his last year in high school. He had been in bed during the graduation ceremonies, and the doctor had advised him against taking the summer job he had lined up before becoming ill and against any kind of strenuous exercise. "Be a slob," the doctor said. "Work at it until you get it right."

That summer had seemed endless, but from the first day of college until now, he had never been without constant obligations, overlapping and interwoven like the leaves of an artichoke, so that, in time, the obligations became the identity, and the self was hidden down in there somewhere, unexamined. He remembered reading long ago that some wise man had said the life unexamined is the life unlived. But what if you did not want to examine yourself? There was a certain comfort in being wrapped so tightly in obligation you were busy every minute, spending your free time in trying to organize your day and evening so that you could finish everything you were supposed to do.

Back on the motel bed, contemplating the idea of a life without Lindy at the center of it, he had felt himself drifting away, with no identity left beyond the extensive analyses of stock and bond issues filed on disks, and some old photographs in Lindy's albums, and something of himself in the way Janie looked around the eyes.

A rabbit came by and stopped close to him, in the grass where he had found the section of tree trunk. The rabbit did not look well. The dun brown fur looked lifeless, and it appeared to move more slowly than a rabbit should. He tried to remember the last time he had seen an animal in the wild. A raccoon face at the kitchen window of the rented cabin the summer before Janie was born?

The rabbit hunched its back and chewed at the wet grass where the log had been. It straightened and lifted its chin high and scratched the side of its throat with a hind foot. In the stillness he could hear the busy scruffing noise of that scratching. It was somehow reassuring, a homely gesture. It seemed to him that a sick or rabid animal would not chew grass and scratch its neck.

He sat and watched it crop and munch. Suddenly it sat straight up, forelegs against its chest, and seemed to aim its big ears down the slope beyond the barn. A dog was barking in the distance. The rabbit had a new awareness of Roy. No matter which way it turned, one wet brown eye watched him. It looked annoyed. It turned and hopped away, long hops, changing the angle of flight slightly at the end of each hop, an evasive maneuver practiced in such a halfhearted way it seemed to indicate the rabbit had come to believe the maneuver ineffective. Life was a crock, the rabbit said. Find some decent grass and there is some ugly giant sitting there staring at you.

"Sorry," Roy said. "Sorry about the whole thing. Hope you feel better soon."

And why am I sitting here on a log talking to a goddamn listless rabbit? Because the rabbit is helpless in its own way, as Lindy was helpless in her way. I am not very well either, but if I want to prove I am not mortally ill, I have to learn how to scratch the side of my neck with my hind foot.

Twenty minutes later the red truck came rattling and groaning along the drive. One front fender was gone. It looked as if it had been rolled down a rocky slope. It stopped behind the barn and Moses appeared a moment later. Roy Owen, as he got to his feet, found himself unprepared for the sheer size of this fellow. He was tall and broad and when he stood still, looking at Roy Owen, he seemed as immobile as any tree. He had the most total beard Roy had ever seen. It grew so high on his cheeks that all you saw were the dark unwinking eyes behind delicate little gold-rimmed glasses, a blunt brown tip of a nose and red lips. His black hair grew down across his forehead and was gathered into a rubber-band ponytail in back. Hair and beard were a kinky luxurious gleaming black, flecked with bits of gray. He wore a sweaty white T-shirt, overalls and black rubber boots caked with pale yellow mud. No small wonder, he thought, that Peggy Moon had prepared Lindy in advance for this apparition.

"You want work done?" the talking tree asked. The voice came from deep in the big chest, and the lips barely moved.

"Peggy Moon told me where I could find you."

It took many questions and answers before he accepted Roy's word that he was not from the police, not selling anything, just seeking a chance to talk to one of the people who had been among the last to see his wife before she disappeared.

"Little woman with light hair," Moses said. "Months ago."

"I'm trying to find out what happened to her."

After a thoughtful pause, Moses stared beyond Roy and said in a deeper voice, "Who has ever climbed the sky and caught her to bring her down from the clouds? Who has ever crossed the ocean and found her to bring her back in exchange for the finest gold? No one knows the way to her. No one can discover the path she treads."

"What are you trying to tell me?" Roy demanded.

"But the One who knows all knows her, he has grasped her with his own intellect, he has set the earth firm forever and filled it with four-footed beasts, he sends the light—and it goes, he recalls it—and trembling it obeys; the stars shine joyfully at their set times: when he calls them they answer, 'Here we are'; they gladly shine for their creator."

"Is that from the Bible?"

"It's from the Book of Baruch, a deuterocanonical book. It should have always been included in the Old Testament."

"It doesn't sound biblical."

He stared at Roy with what could have been contempt had the beard not covered the face so totally. "No thees and thous? I use the Jerusalem Bible, friend, just as do the misguided ones in the Eternal Church of the Believer. But they do not understand it."

"Are you some kind of a minister?"

"I am a prophet!"

"Well, that's really nice to know, and as far as I can recall this is the first time I ever met a prophet."

"Come back in fifteen minutes, friend. I have to clean up."

Roy took a slow walk along the shoulder of the highway. Cars and small trucks slammed by at high speed, ripping the grasses with the wind of passage, whirling up dust, and laying a hydrocarbon stink across the evening air. He came upon a dry and flattened toad on the eroded asphalt of the shoulder, looking like a silhouette symbol designed for a flag of some savage tribe of prehistory. It wiggled a flattened toe at him and the tiny shocking motion made him feel dizzy. The paper-thin toad and the browsing rabbit seemed partners in some eerie celebration of death and dying. The black ant came out from under the toe of the toad, refocusing reality. Life after death is a credo in the universe of the ant.

An oncoming car slowed, and then turned onto the shoulder and came directly at him. At first he stood in disbelief and, as it kept coming, he jumped wildly toward the ditch, turned his ankle on a hidden rock and fell into the wiry grass. He got up slowly, furious, brushing small grass seeds off his clothing. A woman with white hair as precise as metal shavings ran her window down and said, "Where is this Meadows Center Tabernacle?"

"Were you trying to kill me?" Roy demanded

"I think it's got to be the other side of the Interstate, Helen," the man behind the wheel bellowed. Roy then noticed the hearing-aid button in the woman's ear.

"If I hadn't jumped you would have hit me!"

"We promised Dad we'd get him to the Tabernacle before he dies," the woman said loudly.

An old man wrapped up in a blanket rose up and peered out the rear window. The rest of the seat was full of suitcases. The old man looked like a skull wrapped in gray paper.

"Then you better hurry!" Roy yelled.

"It's got to be the other side of the Interstate," the driver yelled, and he swerved back onto the pavement. The woman, before she closed her window, shrieked at Roy. "You've got seeds in your mustache!"

A panel truck swerved wildly around the car, narrowly missing a pair of oncoming motorcycles. The tourist car turned around in a driveway a couple of hundred yards from Roy, and came roaring back on the other side of the highway. The woman leaned across the driver and beamed and waved, and he found himself waving back. The old man had sunk down out of sight. Maybe, he thought, they had just missed the deadline. Nebraska plates. A long motor trip into dying. He clawed the seeds out of his mustache, and as he walked, the pain in his ankle slowly subsided. When he reached the school bus he could walk without limping.

Moses wore a fresh white T-shirt and faded blue bib overalls. His hair and beard were damp and matted. The concrete slab under the shower head was wet. The sun was just disappearing and the mosquitoes were beginning to prowl. Moses held the screen door open for Roy Owen. A ratty old bucket seat from a car, now mounted on a wooden box, had been brought out onto the screened platform, and Moses waved him into it as though offering a throne. Roy accepted some hot tea. It was strong and served in a thick ceramic mug with a bas-relief of a Disney duck on the side of it. Moses had the one with the mouse.

"I've been remembering," Moses said. "Sometimes it is easier to remember than it is other times. She did not complain about the truck the way other people do. She gave me fifteen dollars for my trouble. She wanted me to name a price but if I had done so, it would have interfered with her freedom of choice. That is what is important. Freedom. If she gave me five or fifty, it would make no difference to me. Or she could have given me nothing. It was up to her to make a choice."

One floor fan was on, whirring and turning back and forth, aiming first at Moses and then at Roy, like a spectator at a match.

"Do you have any idea what happened to her?"

"A stubborn heart will come to a bad end at last, and whoever loves danger will perish in it. A stubborn heart is weighed down with troubles, the sinner heaps sin on sin. There is no cure for a proud man's malady, since an evil growth has taken root in him. The heart of a sensible man will reflect on parables. An attentive ear is the sage's dream."

"Are you telling me Lindy had a stubborn heart and loved danger? What am I supposed to be learning from all these quotations?"

"Do not meddle with matters that are beyond you; what you have been taught already exceeds the scope of the human mind. For many have been misled by their own presumption, and wrongheaded opinions have warped their ideas."

"I have been taught nothing so far."

"That quotation was from Ecclesiasticus. Not Ecclesiastes. It was never approved for the Jewish canon of scripture, even though it was originally written in Hebrew and then translated into Greek in 132 B.C. by the author's grandson. The name means The Church's Book."

Roy took a deep breath and let it out slowly. "Mr. Moses, if we met under other circumstances, I am sure I would find all this very, very interesting. You are a true scholar of the scriptures. But what I want to know is if you remember where you drove my wife."

"On our way back to the County Line Motel, I told her that an evil growth called pride had taken root inside John Tinker Meadows. In the Second Letter of John it is written, 'Watch yourselves, or all our work will be lost and not get the reward it deserves. If anybody does not keep within the teaching of Christ but goes beyond it, he cannot have God with him: only those who keep to what he taught can have the Father and the Son with them. If anyone comes to you bringing a different doctrine, you must not receive him in your house or even give him a greeting. To greet him would make you a partner in his wicked work.' "

"Why did you tell her that?"

"A name can be dishonored by he who bears it. She had gone to speak to John. She had gone to greet him, and I told her that it would make her a partner in his wicked work. But then she told me she did not see him. She said she had talked to someone else. I do not remember if she told me. I let her off at the gate. They did not want me to come even that far, or wait there for her. The guards came out and told me to move along. I told them I was waiting for the woman who had just entered their building. They insisted. And so I got out of the truck and confronted them and I spoke some verses in a loud voice. They were strong verses and the guards went away. They kept looking back at me, but they went away."

"You sound like an educated man."

"That was in another life. In this life everything I have comes from the Book." He took it from the small table and handed it over to Roy, holding it with care. It was a thick, ragged, dog-eared copy of the Jerusalem Bible, Reader's Edition, a paperback with a cover printed to look like fabric. "I spent seven years with this Book," he said. "I got up at first light to read it. I walked back and forth in the cell saying the words out loud. This is the third copy, and in another year this one will have to be replaced. Many parts are getting hard to read, but I can shut my eyes and see any page in this Book and read it from the picture I see in my head."

"That's fascinating. Did my wife spend very long in that building?"

"Not very long. Not as long as I expected. She told me she might be an hour, but it was much, much less than that."

"How did she seem on the way back to the motel?"

"She wanted to know why I was angry at John Tinker Meadows. That was after I quoted to her from the Book. I told her that all anger and all vengeance belong to the Lord. I told her that he was pretending to be a man of God. She said she would certainly like proof of that. I told her she had the proof. He had automobiles, airplanes, jewels, homes, fine clothes. I told her that he traveled all over the world living in fine hotels, drinking the rarest wines, eating the best food. Wasn't that proof enough? There was one holy man in that family. Just one."

"Matthew?"

He made a contemptuous snorting sound. "Only an actor, an entertainer, a salesman. The holy man was Paul, the third child, the second son. He tried to practice the true religion. He wandered through the countryside, preaching to anyone who would listen. He gave away all his goods and money. He stuck thorns through his flesh. He flogged himself with brambles. He trod barefoot on sharp stones. This was his land, all these fields and country roads. That's why I came here, to gain in wisdom just by being where he once was. I am his disciple and his prophet. They tried to treat him with strong medicines. They put him in a place where electricity was sent into his brain. But soon he was as holy as before. In some way—he never told me how—he had offended the Lord with his left hand. And so he cut it off. When his wound had healed, they put him in the same place where I was. A long, long way from here. They did not want him nearby. They did not want anyone bringing shame on their church by talking about crazy Paul. He preached to me. He gave me the first copy of this Book. He changed me from a madman, from a vicious person to a man of God. He fasted and became very thin. Then he had pneumonia. After he died I spent thirty-six hours on my knees, praying for myself. Not for him or for his soul. His soul was alive forever, nestled in the lap of eternity. I read the Book and I walk these roads and fields, and I think of Paul Meadows."

"And you told all of this to my wife?"

"No," he said, "and I have not told it to anyone else."

"Why me?"

"Because lately I have been wondering why I was sent here. It began to seem as if I would be wasting my life if I spent the rest of it living the way I live—working, reading, praying. It came to me that perhaps I was sent here to make their church remember Paul. There are some good people in that church, betrayed by their leaders. If I can make them remember what Paul stood for, they could be saved. I do not really know. I think I should try to preach about Paul or he will be forgotten. He told me if I ever came to this area I should not speak of him or try to talk to anyone in his family. He did not explain. I have begun to think that he was testing me, trying to find out if I am strong enough to disobey his orders."

"Why were you in there, in that place?"

"Because the court said I was legally insane at the time of the commission of the crime."

"What was the crime?"

"Paul asked me that too. I could not remember. I used to try to remember, but I gave up long ago."

"But now you are okay?"

"I was released. I wonder if that was part of the plan. I was on medication for years. Through Paul I found the strength to just pretend I was taking it. I would keep it in my cheek until they were gone. Then I began to be able to read the Book and remember the words. One day they let a lot of us go. They took us in a bus and let us out in front of a big building in Youngstown. We were supposed to go inside and they would find a place to live for all of us, and food stamps and maybe some work. There was talk that the asylum had run out of funds to care for us. The others went in and I walked down the street and around a corner. I felt that Paul was with me."

"What is your full name?"

"I don't know. I used to have it on a card but I lost it. Paul had started to call me Moses. I think because of my beard. When I first came here people came to see me and ask questions. But I did not know any of the answers and finally they stopped coming."

Roy Owen measured the distance to the screen door off to his left, and wondered how quickly he could get out through it, and if his ankle was well enough for a fast sprint to his car.

"I want to ask you something, Moses. You can't remember what kind of a crime you committed. My wife disappeared that same weekend. Do you think there is any chance that . . . well, you might have done the same sort of thing again. That you could have . . . hurt her?"

He was silent and thoughtful for so long that Roy slowly relaxed. "I don't think there is any chance of that, Mr. Owen. Mr. Dockerty—he's the sheriff in Lakemore—he's a very nice man. I think he knows who I am. He took my fingerprints after I first came here and I think they found out that way. I think he knows what I must have done a long time ago. Mr. Dockerty came to see me after that woman had disappeared and he had found out I had driven her from the motel to the Meadows Center and back. He wanted to know if I had noticed whether anybody seemed particularly interested in her, or asked about her, or followed us. I hadn't seen anything like that. I don't blame you for asking me what you did. But if I'd done a crime of that kind, I think they would have asked me different questions. And more of them."

"Moses, I want to thank you for your help."

Both men stood up, and as Roy backed out the door, Moses looked beyond him into the shadows of night and said, in a particularly loud voice, "I will punish the ministers, the royal princes and all those who dress themselves in foreign style. On that day I mean to punish all those who are near the throne, those who fill the palace of their lord with violence and deceit. On that day—it is the Lord who speaks—a shout shall be raised from the Fish Gate, from the new town, howls, from the hills a great uproar. Men of the Mortar, howl! For the whole brood of Canaan has been destroyed, the weighers of silver are all wiped out."

Moses went back and sat down and opened his Book, and Roy sensed the man was no longer aware of him. As he walked to his car Mrs. Holroyd came out into the night, holding her clenched hands to her chest.

"Mr. Owen? Good heavens, what *was* that?"

"Sort of like a prayer, I guess."

"He's been praying a lot louder lately. It makes me worry."

"I think he's okay. He's a little bit crazy, and maybe we all are. But I think he's harmless enough."

"I can't remember anybody else staying as long with him as you just did."

"I guess that about all I can say, Mrs. Holroyd, is that this has been one of those strange days. He seems to think everything is part of a plan, and today I was part of it too."

He drove over to the Meadows Center, bought the last *Wall Street Journal* from the stand in the lobby of the Motor House and ate a solitary dinner in a corner of the dining room. He found a couple of situations which troubled him—a steep decline in one issue on what seemed to be extraordinary volume, and an unfriendly takeover situation involving another issue in which they had a heavy investment.

He phoned his executive assistant at home and he said, "Not to worry, Roy. On EGK, they're going to come out with very bad earnings for the last quarter, down nearly fifty percent, and when I heard the first whisper, I moved our stop-loss order up a couple of notches and we were sold out of it at eleven yesterday morning. I'm letting it sit in Continental for a while, okay?"

"Very much okay. And what about that oil takeover?"

"It's moving up on the tender offer and I give it another two and a half or three points and I think that right there we could nail down the profit we've got in it in the options market. But it's your decision, of course."

"Let's stay a while and keep a close watch on it. Find out which way the wind is blowing on arbitrage, and I'll get back to you tomorrow."

"Early tomorrow, because if we're going to move, we better do it before the weekend, Roy. How . . . how are things going?"

"Today I had a conversation with a rabbit."

"With a what?"

"A bunny. You know. Hop, hop."

"I guess I'm not following you too well."

"Then I had a long talk with a prophet. A prophet like in the Bible. A man who knows what's going to happen next."

"I'd say let's hire him, but I don't know what you're talking about."

"That makes two of us."

"Roy, how is . . . the other thing going? Are you having any luck at all?"

"Not so far."

"How long will you stay down there?"

"I don't know yet. Good night, Dave."

Back at the County Line Motel, big moths were hurling themselves at the outside floods near the office. Roy Owen parked and walked on back to the office, just to tell Peggy Moon that he had seen Moses and talked to him, and to thank her for helping.

A cheerful, angular man, burned deep brown, was standing on a stepladder, hammering a board into the side of a wooden frame which contained a small shiny air-conditioning unit. An assortment of bugs were inside the office, circling the lights.

He turned and smiled down at Roy. "Help you, friend?"

"I'm in sixteen. My name is Owen. I just wanted to thank your wife for helping me locate Moses."

The man flailed at a beetle near his ear and said, "Damn things came in when there was a hole here after I took out the old busted one. This is smaller, but I hope it'll do the trick. Anyway, friend, I never have had one of those."

"One of those what?"

"Wives. Nearly had one once, but when it came right down to it she decided I was on the shiftless side. I'm Fred Moon. Peggy's my sister. Hold on a minute. I'm about to plug this in and then I'll call her in to help me enjoy it."

He finished the hammering, caulked the crack next to the side of the plastic housing of the air conditioner and then plugged the machine in. It made a chattering roar. He silenced the chattering by moving the vents until it stopped. But the roar didn't stop.

"Noisy little devil, but that's cold air it's putting out." He climbed down, folded the ladder and leaned it against the wall, went behind the counter and opened a door and yelled, "Peggy! Come see what we got!"

She came trotting in. She looked startled for a moment when she saw Roy, and when she nodded and spoke to him before she focused on the new piece of equipment, it looked to him as though there was a sudden blush under her dark tan.

"It's real loud," Fred said.

"I don't care if it sounds like a marching band. This office collects heat all day long. Wow! Feel that. What have we got left to pay on it, Freddy?"

"Got to reline the brakes on his old Pontiac."

She turned to Roy, and said proudly, "My brother is one of the best shade tree mechanics around. It's been the difference between saving this place and losing it."

"Surely is noisy, though," Fred said. He carried the ladder out into the night. Peggy came up with a spray can and slew most of the indoor bugs.

"Get on okay with Moses?" she asked.

"He kept quoting from that Bible of his, and I couldn't understand much of it. I thought he was trying to tell me something, but I couldn't figure out what. All he could tell me about Lindy was that she was inside the building at the Center a lot less time than she expected to be, and she didn't get to see John Tinker Meadows. I suspect that was who she wanted to talk to."

"I can't believe I'm really going to be comfortable in here the rest of the summer. Now if we can just get us a new ice machine. What happens in this climate, things rust out. They quit and you look on the inside and there's nothing holding them together but rust. You know, it would be crazy to think that Moses had anything to do with your wife disappearing. Somebody had to drive that car all the way to the city and find some way of getting back, without attracting attention. Moses just couldn't manage that, and he doesn't have any friends who'd help him out on anything like that. Wherever he goes, people remember him."

"Have you got a few minutes?"

"Of course. Look, about my phoning you . . ."

"I want to tell you I'm glad you did. I feel so helpless about Janie that I try to tell myself the problem will take care of itself. And I learned from you that it won't. I tend to get . . . emotionally lazy about responsibilities like that. But I wanted to ask you about something else. I know how much Lindy depended on research. You can bet that by the time she came down here she knew everything that had ever been published about the Meadows family and the Eternal Church. Moses told me that the family tried to hush up the trouble they had with the younger son, Paul. I just wondered if she could have been looking into that."

"We wouldn't know anything special, Fred and me. We never really got into that Eternal Church. We were interested in it, of course. I mean, if somebody had started a ten-million-dollar zoo in the county, everybody would have been interested. But practically anybody would know as much about Paul as we do. How much did you find out from Moses? I heard he was in the place where they sent Paul, up in Ohio, I think."

"I know he was the youngest son and I know he died of pneumonia after he fasted for a long time. They put him in there because he went crazy and cut off his left hand. And I know he was kind to Moses and had a lot of influence on him."

"Okay, I can fill in a little. Let me see. John Tinker must be forty-two by now, and Mary Margaret about thirty-eight, so if Paul had lived, he'd be thirty-five, thirty-six, around in there. I'm thirty-one right now. I'm trying to work out when it happened. When the Church came in and bought all that land out there around the Meadows Center, there were a couple of old houses on it, and the family moved into one, and the people that were closest to the family moved into the other. The first thing they did was put up one of those great big aluminum buildings that look like half of a long huge pipe. They put in big fans to keep the air moving through it from end to end, and they bought hundreds of folding chairs and an electric organ. Our parents took both of us there one Sunday because the young boy was going to preach. That was Paul, and I guess if I was seven or eight, he was about twelve years old. I never heard *anything* like it anywhere before or since. It made me all-over goose bumps, listening to him. And he made me cry and he made lots of people cry. They said he had the gift, and he got it from his father, old Matthew Meadows. Fred and I, we wanted to go back there, but our dad wouldn't let us. He said it wasn't any kind of religion he wanted any of his kin to have anything to do with. He said it was hysterics. He said it turned everybody into crazy people."

She turned and looked at Fred, who had just come in. "We're talking about Paul Meadows and how he preached that Sunday." She looked over her shoulder at Roy. "Fred might be able to remember things I've forgotten. If you want to hear them."

"Of course I do. I'm wondering if my wife found out anything about Paul that could . . . endanger her life."

Fred frowned and hopped up to sit on the counter, and said, "I wouldn't think so. It's been over and done with a long time ago, and that Meadows Church is too big to be hurt by any kind of gossip. That kid preached up a storm. We heard him once in person and then they had him on the radio and Peggy and I listened a couple of times when we weren't supposed to listen at all. But then they stopped using him. We heard he was sick."

"Don't you remember?" Peggy said. "We heard he got sort of strange and they couldn't let him preach because once he started they didn't have any way to stop him. He just wouldn't stop. Everybody could walk out of the church and he would keep right on, they said. Then he got a big kitchen cleaver and chopped his left hand right off at the wrist and nearly bled to death. So they had to send him up to an institution that specialized in whatever it was was wrong with him, and then after he was gone maybe four or five years, he died. If I had to guess, I'd say he was sent up there when he was eighteen."

"Closer to twenty," Fred said.

"Then that would make him twenty-four or -five when he died. And I can remember that they had that huge funeral service for him on the very day of my twenty-first birthday. So you're right, Fred. Closer to twenty."

"Was it pretty much common knowledge that they sent him to a mental institution?"

They looked at each other. Fred frowned and said, "There was always talk about Paul Meadows. His father ordained him when he was about thirteen, and people said that was a mistake. Sometimes when he preached he would stick needles through his arm to show the power of prayer and faith. But I never saw him do that. Old Matthew never seemed to notice how weird the kid was becoming."

"Did the family try to keep the whole thing quiet?"

"Maybe they tried," Fred said. "I guess they did. But it was a small town then and it's still a small town. We all heard he died of pneumonia and complications."

"Moses verified that when Roy talked to him," Peggy said.

"And Moses told me he's going to start preaching the Gospel according to Paul Meadows."

Fred shrugged. "He'll never get to do it in the Tabernacle, and I don't think any kind of street-corner preaching is going to bother John Tinker and Mary Margaret."

"It must have been a sensation around here when he chopped his hand off. Were there any rumors about why?"

Fred gave his sister a wink that screwed up half his face and said, "Take a walk, lady."

"Oh sure," she said. "The menfolk want to talk dirty."

"Maybe this is just barroom talk with everybody beered up, and maybe it isn't. But my old man, he used to say that it was a real good idea to keep your woman away from the traveling tent shows. He said it was common knowledge those hellfire preachers could get their glands all stirred up enough so they could be took off into the bushes all ready to sing Praise the Lord. The talk around this area was that there was some woman they had teaching Bible at the Meadows Center, before they'd started the college. She was about thirty-five then, a big hearty good-looking woman, and she got purely turned on by Paul and his preaching and his strange ways. So they say she got to him, and she got past all that sanctity but they didn't do any actual screwing. I guess that was to come later. But she got him to doing a few things to her and for her, and that's how come his left hand offended him and so he cut it the hell off."

"What was her name? What happened to her?"

"Hilda something. German name. I can't recall it. But she was gone like at first light the next day, so I guess Paul told his daddy why he did what he did. They say she went to California. I don't know for sure. Hell, that was long ago. She'd be coming up on sixty years old by now.

There'd be nothing there worth digging into for any magazine. Poor old Paul just couldn't handle the pleasures of the flesh. I think it's true because it *sounds* true. You know what I mean?"

"I know. Thanks. I appreciate it. Moses told me that a police officer named Dockerty had checked him out. I want to be very certain that there's no chance Moses could have . . . hurt Lindy. Do you think he'd talk to me?"

Peggy came back in saying, "It's too hot anywhere but here, men, so knock off the man talk. I heard what you asked, Roy. You better hurry, though. Wil Dockerty retires the end of this month." She went over and stood in front of the full blast of the noisy little air conditioner. "No, don't touch that thing! I want to turn blue. Did you two decide Paul's history has anything to do with your wife disappearing?"

"I would say absolutely nothing at all," Roy said. "I don't even know what I am supposed to be looking for. Strange things, I guess. Things that might hurt the Meadows family."

"The history of Paul Meadows is strange enough," Fred said, "but trying to hurt the Eternal Church with that old story would be like throwing puffed rice at an elephant. Or like me, Peggy, the time I tried to beat up that meathead you were married to for about twenty minutes. And ended up with a concussion."

"Oh shut up, Freddy," she said wearily.

"Well, I want to thank you for your help," Roy said. "I better be heading back to my room."

"I'll walk you over. Fred, no comment. Please."

The night seemed especially warm after the success of the little air conditioner. They walked across the coarse grass in the middle of the compound. Something went scuttling away, rattling the grass, making her jump. "One of those little black lizards that came in from Cuba," she said. "They've chased out the kind we used to have." A truck droned by. They stopped and looked at the sky, but there were only a few stars visible beyond the mist.

Lots of worlds, he thought. The rabbit and the Moons and I and the black Cuban lizard are in one world. That flat toad is in another. Moses is in still another, an older place somehow. Older, not newer. Lindy is in some kind of world. And up there are tons of junk between me and the stars, circling, circling, either beeping or dead, but junk regardless, like that golf ball on the moon.

"Talk to your kid today?"

"Yes. I made it person-to-person to make her feel important. And I must confess it saved me at least ten minutes of aimless chatter with her grandma."

"How did she sound?"

"I don't know. Draggy. Polite. A little listless. But she gave me a telephone kiss. A squeaky one, and when I told her I love her, she told me she loves me, a good sign, I guess. She seems to be choosing her words more carefully. And talking more slowly these days."

"I remember. You have to be careful. People can cast spells if you are not careful. So you walk and talk and sit and eat and get ready for bed very, very carefully. It keeps the bad out."

He put his hand on her shoulder. "You and Fred are good people."

"Glad we have you conned," she said, and laughed. It was a nervous sound. She popped a quick kiss on his cheek and said good night when she was thirty feet away, heading for the office.

An airplane droned by, so high the sound of it was entangled with the summer sound of the tree toads and insects. People going by up there at seven hundred and fifty feet per second. Encapsulated in their roaring lounge, taking some of them toward something important, and taking others away from something dear. He wanted to be up there drinking coffee and reading one of those glossy airplane magazines about Hindus, mockingbirds and the best restaurants in Dayton, Ohio. He wanted to be up there heading for a city he had never seen before.

Ten

The Reverend Doctor F. Walter Macy waited in his small office in the Administration Building for Mary Margaret Meadows to arrive. She had phoned saying she wanted to see him in his office, and that she would be along as soon as she could arrange it. She had not stated a time, and the phone call had come forty minutes before.

He was working on an old sermon which he had recently updated, shortened and had retyped. He was using colored pencils to indicate the particular emotions he wished to project. The underlining reminded him: red for anger, blue for grief, yellow for spiritual ecstasy, green for contempt. It had been typed using an IBM element called ORATOR, the largest typeface available in their offices. On Sunday morning he would deliver the sermon in the Affiliated Eternal Church of the Believer in Newmont, South Carolina. Finn Efflander had assigned him a Beech-craft and a pilot, pointing out that the landing strip at Newmont was not certified for jets. Leave at seven-thirty Sunday morning, back by at least one in the afternoon.

He had tried to work on the sermon the night before, Thursday night, at home, but Alberta had been in one of her moods, walking around and around him, whacking with her feather duster at things that did not need dusting, muttering and mumbling.

And so he had to stop and listen to it all again, about how here he was, the Reverend Doctor F. Walter Macy, the First Assistant Pastor of the Holy Tabernacle of the Eternal Church of the Believer, second only to John Tinker and Mary Margaret in the active religious hierarchy, and here they were, living in this dumb, dreary little house at 15 Malachi Road. So what if it is one of the big floor plans, it is still out here where the help live, and by all rights we should be living in the Manse. There's room there for us even now, and if they'd come to their senses and put that old coot away somewhere like they did the nutty son, there'd be more than enough.

As usual, the more she talked, the more she got into the spirit of it. She came around in front of him and stood over him, bending forward slightly from the waist, a plain-faced woman with lifeless gray hair and a face that became mottled when she was agitated.

"Oh, you're a bear for work, aren't you, Reverend Walter? The television talk show and the radio talk show, and all the Bible lessons on tape, and giving guest sermons at some God-forgotten place every other Sunday. All my life I've gotten second best and third best and fourth best. Stand back and let others go first. Now, by God, that you've earned a place at the top, we're still on the outside of everything. Over there in the Manse, I wouldn't even have to cook if I didn't feel like doing it, or make beds or clean! You keep telling me to be patient. Well, I just don't feel like being patient anymore! I've stood by you all these years working my fingers to the bone and you've been telling me we'd get to the top. This is the top, isn't it? And there's no payoff."

She bent over further, so close that he could feel the fine spray of spittle as Alberta yelled, eyes bulging, "You do anything those damn Meadowses tell you! It isn't patience, mister. It's plain spinelessness. You like being walked on. It's a sickness! What you are, Walter Macy, you are just plain weak!"

She began to cry out of anger, and whirled and went back through the house, hooing and hawing as she went, and he heard the slam of the bedroom door.

He reread the parts of the sermon he had worked on, sighed, put it aside and went on back to where she waited. He wrote the sermons and she wrote their domestic scripts, their scenes and torments. He had always known this. This script called for certain words and actions on his part.

He tapped on the door and said, softly, "Alberta? Bertie?"

"Go away!"

"I have to talk to you, dear. I have to explain. Please."

When there was no answer, he opened the bedroom door. She was on her bed, her back toward the door. He went and sat on the edge of the bed, behind her. He patted and stroked her shoulder, and in a mild and gentle voice he told her they had to move very, very slowly, that to assert his rights too soon might cause disaster. He told her that he had planned everything very carefully so there would be no chance of things going wrong for them. If it works out, he told her, or rather *when* it works out, he would be the head of the Church.

After a predictable period of stroking and murmuring, she gave a great sigh and turned her tear-streaked face toward him and said she was sorry she had been so cross. Up until a few years ago this sort of scene had been one of the preludes to their lovemaking. Never passionate, she had, however, taken some pleasure from the act, he believed. But a few years ago it had begun to give her so much discomfort she had told him they had better not do that anymore. His disappointment was not quite genuine, and more intended to flatter than to argue for resumption. In a short time his vague desire for her faded completely away, and there was no longer any need to try to elicit some response from her slack white flesh.

After they had kissed and they had each apologized for making the other one unhappy, she went into the bathroom and washed her face and combed her hair. She came out and sat beside him on the edge of the bed and patted his arm and said, "Have you talked to Mary Margaret about . . . you know what?"

"Alberta, dearest, I don't even know if that is the right thing to do at this juncture."

"You keep telling me she's on your side."

"This is a very delicate matter. One has to anticipate what her choices will be, and which ones she will elect to take."

"Whatever the hell that means. I don't have the advantages of education you've got."

"It means that he is her brother, her only living brother. She has no husband. She has no lover. Her father is alive but beyond her reach. Sometimes it is not wise to be the bearer of bad tidings. She is the nearest thing to female royalty we have, and they have been known to order the messenger strangled."

"She wouldn't dare try to get rid of you! The affiliated ministers wouldn't allow it! Besides, after nothing at all happened after you told that magazine woman . . ."

"Hold it!" he shouted, glaring at her.

"Well, please excuse me for living. You said you were . . ."

"I said I was going to try to get in touch with that woman, yes. I was planning to send her a message through somebody I trust that I wanted to talk to her. But on second thought, I decided that it was not a valid idea."

"Why not? Wouldn't she want to know John Tinker is an adulterer? A hypocrite."

"Those people are very skeptical. They would consider the source. So I was trying to think of the proper person to go to her and tell her what was going on when all of a sudden she apparently went back to New York. Now, of course, we know she disappeared."

She stared at him for a moment, eyes narrow and lips compressed. "I don't understand why you told me you were going to talk to that woman, and then told me you did."

"Dearest, I am guilty, I guess, of raising false hopes. I should have made it clear that it was what I intended to do. I wanted you to be happy and hopeful. So I raised false hopes. I'm sorry."

"Anyway, you promised me you would tell your precious Mary Margaret Meadows about it."

"What proof do I have, Bertie? The phone lines apparently got crossed somehow and I heard them making a date, and the way they talked, it was evident what they had in mind."

" 'Evident what they had in mind,' " she said in a prissy voice, mocking him. "Tell me exactly what she said."

"I told you before. Once was enough. I don't have to say it again."

"You better tell me Molly Wintergarten's exact words, Walter, or we are going to have a lot more trouble."

"It's a kind of sickness to want to hear that kind of talk."

"But you're sure it was her."

"Absolutely."

"So say it again, damn you!"

He sighed. "She said to him on the phone, 'Tink, I am going to fuck you blind today.'"

"You told me you were going to try to get proof."

"After mature consideration, I decided it wasn't such a great idea. I decided it was better to wait for them to get careless. People like that always do."

"And suppose they don't?"

"Alberta, dearest, I happen to know that another woman is being sent down from the same filthy magazine. And I am going to try to arrange for my trusted friend to make contact with her, making quite sure she will never know the information came from me."

"It's a disgusting situation. He is a disgusting man. Mr. Efflander and Charley Winchester and Mary Margaret have been protecting him for years. And so did the old man before his mind began to go." She bent closer to him, eyes narrow. "If only you had more gumption, if only you had spoken out a few years ago. The years are going by and we're stuck here in this—"

"Hey," he said softly, noticing the new mottling of her face, the red blotches appearing. "Hey, don't get all worked up again. Everything is going to work out just fine."

And she had quieted down at once, much to his relief. They then took an evening walk through the Settlements, making a point of speaking most pleasantly to everyone they met.

Now he had finished the work on the sermon. He knew it would go well. He was wondering what other chore he could begin, when Mary Margaret rapped twice and came in, smiling, and sat in the big chair across the desk from him. She was wearing another one of those cover-everything dresses she ordered from Honolulu, apparently by the dozen. Sometimes he found himself wondering what she looked like under all the fabric. Very moist and pink and rubbery, he suspected. Like a big baby fresh out of the bath.

For years they had been allies, she and Walter Macy and the old man against Finn and John Tinker and Joe Deets. They had tried to make allies of the Winchester brothers, but Charley was too clever to take sides in any factional split, and whatever Charley did, Clyde did. Walter Macy felt he had another ally in Walker McGaw, who produced and directed the talk shows, and who, with patient coaching, had managed to correct a lot of Walter Macy's mistakes. He had reduced the scope of the gestures, dropped the voice range, taught Walter how to speak to the lens as though speaking to a dear friend. And, of course, come right down to it, the affiliated ministers were on Walter's side. They thought they were on the side of Matthew Meadows, but they did not yet know that he was never going to be able to take the pulpit again.

"Walter, I hear you are off to South Carolina this Sunday."

"That's right."

"I know you plan pretty well in advance. Can you give me an idea of how far you're scheduled into the future?"

He found the folder in his drawer and took the top sheet out and handed it across to her. She studied it, biting her underlip. "Way into November. Okay, you keep those dates, but don't make any more past that point."

"Why not? What do you mean?"

"I've talked this over with John Tinker and Finn. We've decided that we want you to drop the Bible lessons and the radio talk show and the cable panel show. We'll fill in with other personnel."

"Does somebody think I'm getting too much exposure?"

She stared at him. "What an odd idea! Of course not! Everybody knows how hard you work, Walter dear, and why. This change of plans is contingent on our being able to convince a minister he should move here to headquarters and pick up a big share of the preaching load, especially in the Tabernacle."

"Who is he?"

"He's the Reverend Tom Daniel Birdy. He has a little church in a little town down near Pensacola. He's apparently self-ordained. He was born again before he was sent to prison and he spent a lot of years there and got out and started saving souls, in a little traveling tent show. He's really, really fabulous, Walter. You wouldn't have heard my father when he was young, as I did. But I know you heard Paul, those few years he preached. The Reverend Birdy is crude, but he's got it all. He's very dubious about joining in with us, but John says we really need him. And we thought the best thing to do would be to put him in your hands so you can groom him, knock off the rough edges. That is, if he comes with us."

"Why do we need him?" Walter asked in a harsh voice. "He sounds like some kind of a hooligan to me, a man with no religious background or education."

She looked at him, and in a fraction of a second she saw a depth of purpose and ambition she had never before recognized. She had thought of him as a pleasant, bumbling, hardworking man. He was a big man, imposing enough, with a mild psoriasis that kept his face and forehead red and slightly scaly. He wore glasses with big black frames. He had big curving white sideburns and a pulpit delivery that could rattle the windows. He could preach a good rousing sermon and bring a reasonable number flocking up to the rail to be saved. He was, of course, endlessly and unctuously political, as was his meechy little wife, Alberta, who looked as if she had selected every one of her three or four sedate outfits at a Salvation Army sale. Mary Margaret did not like Alberta, and she had tolerated Walter because she had good uses for him. She had huffed upon the flames of what she had thought was a minor streak of ambition, letting him know she was on his side, arranging special sermons in the Tabernacle for him so that he would believe she was furthering his ambition to one day run the Chruch.

She had felt she could safely do this because he was no real danger to John Tinker or anyone. There was something indefinably hollow about him. The ecclesiastical bombast of his sermons was too patterned, too mannered, his gestures too formal, and too practiced, his very tears too automatic. When the old man had been out of sorts, and when John Tinker was traveling, it was Walter who had shared the Tabernacle pulpit with her, and Walter who, in return for that great favor, had worked his head off on the scut work of the Church, making certain they stayed on the air and on cable twenty-four hours of every day in the week.

With this new awareness of what was behind the façade, Mary Margaret changed direction so rapidly she wondered if he could hear her wheels spinning. "Well yes, of course, he is a bit of a barbarian, Walter dear, but we decided that with you to teach him how to give a decent sermon, we would have a very useful stand-in."

" 'Stand-in?' " he said blankly.

"Someone to help us out! Someone to help you and me, so that John

Tinker will be free to attend some international meetings he has his heart set on. And in any case, if he proves to be impossible, you will just have to help us find someone else."

Though his eyes looked uneasy behind the thick lenses, she sensed she had relaxed him a little and lessened his alarm. She vowed she would be more careful with him in the future. She wondered if it was that desolate little Alberta pushing him from behind, keeping him dissatisfied with his lot. If they'd had any kids, all that ambition could've been focused on them instead of on Walter.

"It might be a good idea if John Tinker had a nice long rest," Walter said.

She frowned at him, thinking this an uncharacteristic boldness. "What would make you say that?"

"I would say, from observing him, that he no longer takes the great joy in his calling that he once did."

"There is a lot of responsibility involved in running a multimillion-dollar enterprise. My brother has a lot to think about."

"I'm sure he does. And I'm sure he wishes he could lead a more private life. They know his face in every city in the land. I get a little of that, of course. But not the way he does." He shrugged. "I look like too many other overweight middle-aged men."

"Walter, you are a very distinguished-looking man, and we are all proud of you and the job you're doing. And if Tom Birdy agrees to join us, we will count on you to take him under your wing. Okay?"

"Of course, Mary M. There's nothing you could ask me that I wouldn't try to do as well as I possibly can. When will I know?"

"I hope by the time you get back here Sunday. Get in touch with me." She turned in the doorway and looked back at him. "If you heard it, you know that John Tinker preached beautifully on Sunday."

"I heard it. It was very good. Very. It's too bad we don't often hear him do as well."

She looked at him for a long moment, wondering if he should be brought to task for a minor impertinence, and then decided against it. Walter had always slipped his little knife into Johnny whenever he had a chance. She shrugged, smiled, waved her small pink hand and left.

On that Friday he walked home with every intention of telling Alberta about this new development. But as he walked and thought, the closer he got to his house, the more unpleasant the idea became. She would take it the wrong way. And so he told her the morning had been uneventful.

It had been a mistake mentioning to her his intention to talk to the magazine woman, but at least he'd had those second thoughts about mentioning the tapes and photographs Erskine had gotten for him, documenting John Tinker's wickedness with Molly Wintergarten. He shivered as he thought of how many times he had come close to telling her about the materials and how he had planned to use them. He had even thought at times of showing her one or two of the most explicit photographs just to see her stunned by the shock of it. They had always been open with each other. When you were writing a sermon and you suddenly thought of some interesting departure, you could go back to the first part of it and take out what did not conform to the new idea. But life was written day by day and hour by hour, with no way to go back and change any part of it. The moving finger writes. He decided that it would be a tactical error to try to tell the new woman from that magazine about the diversions enjoyed by John Tinker Meadows. There are times when you want to leave the moving finger with nothing at all to write.

He looked across at his wife as she ate her lunch, reading from a book as she ate. He had never liked watching her chew. She moved her underjaw a little bit from side to side as well as up and down. A strand of mouse-gray hair hung down on her forehead. Without looking up from her book, she stuck her underlip out and blew the hair away. The sharp exhalation ejected a tiny green piece of chewed lettuce. He watched it throughout its arc and fall. It landed next to the salt, which she would use and he could not. He got up abruptly and told her he was going for a little walk around the area before heading for the office. She nodded absently and turned back to her book.

Two blocks from his house a pair of Angels passed him, arms locked, giggling. Blue skirts, white blouses, sensible shoes, bright hair bobbing at the napes of their necks. He lengthened his stride to keep them in view longer, to watch the flex of their smooth calves, the pretty swing of their young hips. He thought of Joe Deets with hatred and a despairing envy. The beast was always there, just below the surface. That lust in the heart, which Jimmy Carter had admitted. The mind made its foul and secret images, leafing through them at such bewildering speed, it was as though it would be unbearable to dwell upon such grotesque perversions too clearly or at too great length.

The mind could not be restrained from working its foul inventions involving a thousand mouths, a great wetness, the aching spasms. But in time, little by little, he could bring himself back from the edge of the pit. The Angels were out of sight, around a distant corner and beyond the tall hedge. The last of the fragrances of their bodies and hair had drifted away on the slow movement of the heated air, and he forced himself to think of gray stones, bones breaking, iron fists—of images as far from the soft warmth of young flesh as possible—reining himself in with a hard and steady pressure.

With familiar resignation he promised the Lord a full hour of prayer to pay for the few minutes of erotic admiration of the bodies of the young girls. It was always disciplined prayer, kneeling motionless on a hard surface, keeping the mind focused on the task at hand, that of not only asking forgiveness for weakness, but vowing next time to meet the sweet perfumed tauntings of the devil with greater strength. And at the end of the hour of prayer he would remember to thank the Lord for having given him this great weakness of the flesh so that he was better able to comprehend, with humility, the weaknesses of his parishioners who told him of acts so scruffy and so horrid it made him dizzy to listen to them.

As he walked slowly along he tried to compose the structure of the long prayer he would make in atonement for the sins of the mind. But he could not find a beginning, or think of a suitable biblical reference. Far back in his mind, like a worm living inside what had once been a healthy structure, he held the suspicion that there would be no prayer this time.

He walked into the small park at the far end of Zedekiah Lane and sat on a concrete-and-cypress bench in the shade, out of the glare of the early-afternoon sunlight. With the nail of the little finger of his left hand he carefully picked a loose scrap of skin from his forehead. He wondered if reflected sunshine would be good for his psoriasis. In a few minutes he counted his pulse. It was eighty-two. He wondered what his pressure might be.

He knew he was using the trivial concerns of the body to distract him from the mortal sickness of his soul. He thought of the casual sinning committed with apparent unconcern by John Tinker Meadows and Joseph Deets, and he tried to convince himself that their sins, because there was no repentance or atonement, were greater than his own. But he knew the argument was forlorn. He found himself wishing he had not destroyed the photographs and tapes of John Meadows and Mrs.

Wintergarten. He could no longer lock himself away and look at the pictures while listening to the tapes. It had been one way of diverting his attention from his own problem, that problem so great that he was afraid that if he ever thought it through, step by step, the pressure would blow his heart apart. He wondered idly if he might be able to buy—without risk of course—materials as stimulating as the ones he had destroyed, and he wondered if they would help blur the sharp agony of his spirit.

His father had died at fifty-three. Walter was now fifty-four. For many years he had thought that were he to suddenly begin to die, if that great crushing pain they spoke of began to squeeze his chest and cripple his left arm, he could not know whether he would go gratefully to Jesus, or whether his last thoughts might be instead of an intense regret that through all his life he had averted his eyes from the young bosoms and lips and behinds and prayed to God to help him resist temptation. In the act of dying he might try to tell himself that he had lived his life the way it was supposed to be lived, as a man of God. The proper way. The decent way. God's way.

For all the years of his life he had averted his eyes, used prayer to cleanse his mind. He had not rolled and snorted in strange beds as had so many others he could name. He had not defiled his own marriage. The devil had approached him in female form many times. He had coveted. That was a sin, of course. But he had resisted, and that was strength.

But now was it all to be wiped out because of one incident which happened more by accident than design? Was all the rest of his life to be discarded just because of that?

He realized he was arguing with the Lord, and he was being angry with the Lord. But it was no good, of course. It was far too late to try to set up scales and balances.

The sin he had committed gave him the terrible assurance that when this sun became a nova and the earth a cinder, F. Walter Macy would still be turning slowly, slowly on the iron spit, his indestructible flesh basted each moment in lava, his eyes bulging forever as he howled his torment and his remorse and his agony.

He could contemplate the inevitable punishment for the act, yet he could not let any slightest specific memory of that time enter his mind. If it did, he felt that he would scream and become mad.

It struck him as most odd that he could divert his attention from his secret pain by making such vivid pictures in his head of things he had never seen that he became aroused. He knew he could probably never pray again, not the way he used to. And with prayer denied him as diversion, he escaped into erotic fantasy. Jenny MacBeth and Jenny Albritton, rolling and stretching and stroking in their languid sensual ease. Joe Deets, bucking away at the sweet flesh of the blonde Angel, defiling her with his vileness.

He used to think that because he could so vividly imagine the doing of evil, he was thus stronger than other men in being able to resist performing it. He now knew that had been but vanity, and it had been his way of rationalizing a certain sickness in his mind. He wondered if it was that very sickness which had propelled him into the Church in an attempt to escape the consequences of the diseased imaginings. But now he knew that any sense of escape had been illusion. He had been entrapped. Everything was changed. There was nowhere to run. And if there was a refuge, he could never run fast enough. The patient and eternal fires of hell were awaiting Walter Macy.

Sheriff Wil Dockerty found Roy Owen waiting to see him when he came back from the Kiwanis meeting on Friday afternoon. He looked at the messages Myrna had left for him and then told her to send Mr. Owen in. Ever since he had found out the man was staying at the Moons' motel, he had been expecting Owen to come see him.

He was a little surprised at the size of him. These little bitty blonde women usually turned up married to big men. Dockerty had learned that you go slow and easy with small men. They are quick to take offense, easy to rile. But this one had a steady gaze. He looked calm and smart. The mustache was a statement, apparently.

"Like some coffee, Mr. Owen?"

When he said yes, the Sheriff shouted out to Myrna, and she came in moments later with two big white steaming mugs. "Drink myself too much of this stuff all my life," Dockerty said, pushing the sugar across the desk to where Roy Owen could reach it. It was a green metal desk in a small room with gray walls, a metal table piled high with file folders, a single window looking out onto a segment of parking lot and a long angular slice of one of Lakemore's downtown streets. Sheriff Dockerty was a big flabby old man with large white hands covered with brown spots, and a head totally bald, and equally spotted. His breathing was shallow and audible.

"Come down to find out if we know what we're doing down here, did you?"

"Not really."

"Satisfied with Hanrahan's report, were you? Don't look surprised. He's a pro. He checked in with me just as he's supposed to. And if he'd come up with anything he would have come back to us with it."

"Whose jurisdiction is it?"

"Mine, by default. The city limits go right to the county line over to the west, and the county line is about a hundred yards past the Moons' motel. But we work together on just about everything. Couple of years back the city council and the county commissioners got together and combined a lot of our functions, to save money. The city is kind of drying up lately, and the county has got a lot of structure out there at Meadows Center they don't get any ad valorem on."

"Do you think my wife is alive?"

"I'll put it this way. I do if you do."

"I don't," Owen said without hesitation. "I would say the only possibilities would be total amnesia, and that is a very rare thing, I understand, or somebody holding her as a captive. That doesn't make sense either. So I think she's dead. It's hard to get used to saying that word. I don't like the thought of never knowing what happened. What do you think happened to her?"

"From the pictures that were sent down, and from talking to Peggy Moon and her brother, she was a pretty little woman with blonde hair and a good figure. I keep wondering if she didn't have somebody with her when she left to drive on down to the airport, or if she picked up somebody along the way."

"I would rule that out, Sheriff. She wasn't a damn fool. She never picked up hitchhikers. If she picked anybody up, or took anybody along with her, it was somebody she knew. I keep thinking about one little thing that seems uncharacteristic. Lindy is . . . was a very tidy person. I mean she followed the rules. All the little rules. I am staying in that room. There is a sign on the inside of the door above the dead bolt that says 'Please Leave Key in the Office When You Check Out.' You can't miss it. She would have left the key in the office."

"I remember seeing the sign. How many people ignore it? In most motels you leave the key in the room."

"Lots of people ignore it, sure. Not Lindy. I think somebody checked her out. I think somebody put her and her luggage in that rental car and drove away. The maid found the key in the room and the luggage was gone. Lindy just wouldn't have done it that way."

"It's not a hell of a lot to go on."

"There never has been a hell of a lot to go on."

"Because it was a cold trail by the time we got the word on it."

"What about Moses?"

"He's not bothering anybody and he didn't bother her."

"He isn't exactly an ordinary person, Sheriff."

Sheriff Dockerty got up and went over to the metal table and fumbled through the file folders, dug one out from underneath a stack, slapped the dust from it and came back to his chair.

He opened it and recited, "Born July 20, 1943, William McVay Davisson, only child of James and Ethel Davisson."

"He said he committed a crime and he can't remember what it was."

"He was a brilliant and erratic kid. He was through high school when he was fourteen and they didn't let him go away to school because they thought he was too young. I don't think the parents were too stable either. The mother died after a minor operation. A blood clot in the lung. The father went into deep depression and shot himself in the head. There was a lot of money involved. This was not a likable kid. And very strange. So the aunt and uncle, the mother's relatives, got themselves appointed guardians and they had the kid committed to a private mental institution. After he found he couldn't get out, he went into a"—he checked the folder again and said the word carefully—"cat-a-ton-ic state and didn't come out of it until years later. Then he was violent and they kept him sedated. And finally he was well enough for release, three years ago. The money was gone. After he showed up here I was able to check back because he could remember the name of the place, and they had a fingerprint record. If there was any crime, it was something he imagined he did. He said he couldn't remember it, but I got the idea he thought he had killed his folks, and that's why he was put away. They said he'd been a good patient for a long time, quiet and cooperative. When the money stopped coming in, they let him go. They notified the relatives, and got no answer."

"You don't consider him at all dangerous?"

"They didn't, and they're experts. He keeps to himself and works hard. He does a cash business. He's in demand for all kinds of chores nobody else wants to do. And he helps Mrs. Holroyd. I've always felt that just because somebody looks and acts different than the rest of us, there's no need to hassle them."

"Thanks for telling me all this, Sheriff."

The Sheriff smiled. "If you'd come in here pounding on my desk and demanding action, I wouldn't have told you a thing. Look, I've given the disappearance of your missus a lot of thought and a lot of legwork. What it comes down to, there are a lot of pretty women between eighteen and thirty-five disappear in this country every month of the year. With too many of them it's a case of being stupid and going alone to a bar and having a couple of drinks and letting somebody drive them home. Only they don't make it home. They make it into a shallow grave thirty feet off the road, or they make it into the middle of a vacant lot. There's a lot of brush and woods and fields around here. There's drifters and there's some home-grown men capable of rape and murder. I don't want to upset you, Mr. Owen."

"Go right ahead, please."

"The thing about that kind of crime, it's usually sloppy. Even if the rape is intentional, often the murder isn't. Ditch the body and get the hell out. But somebody had to go to a lot of trouble to clean this up. She had to be checked out of the motel. They had to dispose of a body and two suitcases and a train case and a purse and a little typewriter. They had to put that rental car right where the rental people would find it and think their customer hadn't left enough time to stop at the rental desk. There's one thing I wanted to know about Linda Owen and didn't have any way to check it out. The magazine people couldn't answer my question, but you probably can. Was she a strong woman, physically? I mean in the sense she would put up a fight?"

"Oh yes. She was only five foot one and weighed a hundred and five pounds, but she was a diet and exercise nut. She jogged whenever she could, and she had a rowing machine she used to keep her waist slim and her stomach flat. And she was very quick, very coordinated. She was good at games."

The Sheriff leaned back, closed his eyes, placed his folded hands on his broad stomach.

"Sheriff?"

"Just give me a couple minutes here, Mr. Owen."

Roy Owen composed himself, wondering if Dockerty had some kind of sleep disorder.

The Sheriff straightened up, sighing heavily. "Now let's try this. This was a northern woman down here, blonde wavy hair, gold jewelry, makeup, fancy clothes and a rental car. She was a woman working for a magazine that prints a lot of sexy garbage. She was using a false name.

She was under cover, if that's the right word. Now we're all country down here, pretty much. You go show her to the average working man here in this county and tell him what she was doing for a living, and he'd figure her for a part-time hooker."

"Now just a . . ."

"Hold it! You know she wasn't. And from what you say, I know she wasn't. We've got enough tourists coming here these days, the lines get kind of blurred, and it wouldn't be as obvious as it used to be, but somebody could have made some kind of bad judgment about her and tried to follow it up, and used some muscle and all of a sudden found out he'd used more than he'd wanted to, and there he is with a dead woman on his hands. But I kind of think that whole idea would depend on his knowing why she was here and who she was working for. He would have had to think she was playing it cute."

"What if she did find out something that could hurt the Church?"

"Like what? There's a little diddling going on here and there like there is in any big organization you can name. As far as the money part is concerned, I was raised up with Charley and Clyde Winchester and those two are good old boys. They make sure everything runs fair and honest. Anyway, as near as I could find out, she didn't even get close to anybody who could tell her much of anything. That Friday Moses drove her to the Administration Building, she got in to see Walter Macy, he's the assistant pastor at the Tabernacle and he handles a lot of scut work. And she acted so kind of strange Eliot Erskine followed her on into Walter's office. She wasn't there more than three minutes. She said she had some kind of Russian religious items she wanted to donate to the Church, and Reverend Walter told her he'd see what he could do, and Erskine marched her right on back out, and she got in the old red pickup and that was that."

"Erskine?"

"Used to be a cop in Atlanta. Good man, they say. Second in command of security at the Meadows Center. Rick Liddy is in charge. He was with the FBI. They keep it pretty tight. They buy good equipment. On the other hand, we just don't know where she was all day Saturday. Peggy Moon says she saw Mrs. Owen drive in and back out a couple of times, but she didn't pay much attention. Weekends there is one hell of a lot of traffic in the area of the Meadows Center, guided tours and indoctrination, and movies about the Eternal Church and all that, to say nothing of the services and the panel shows and those little carnival things they put on for the kids. I couldn't find anybody who noticed her anywhere at all that Saturday."

"Thanks for giving me so much time."

The Sheriff smiled and yawned. "Come the end of this month, that's all I'm going to have. Time. And I can't hardly wait to stop doing any damn thing at all, except eat and sleep and walk my dogs and work on my 1938 Rolls-Royce. Any luck at all and I can get that sucker back on the road again."

They said goodbye and as Roy was leaving Dockerty called him back and said, "I could have given you the wrong impression about how I give Moses a lot of leeway. I want to be honest with you. If the people in charge of Meadows Center come to me, or to the fellow who takes my job next month, and says Moses is a thorn in their side, then we roust him out of the county and maybe out of the state. It is a practical world, Mr. Owen, and we have to do practical things."

"I understand. Thanks."

Eleven

The Reverend Joseph Deets had dressed very carefully for what might become a disastrous confrontation. After he had donned what he called his God Suit, backward collar and all, and examined his image in the mirror, he decided it might be better to wear a more casual outfit. He knew he would be more comfortable, and that might make the difference. Gray polyester slacks, white moccasins and a blue denim shirt with four pockets and short sleeves, worn outside the slacks. He was annoyed and amused to discover that every few minutes he would inadvertently take a very deep breath.

He bicycled over to Henrietta Boulevard and turned west, past the Meadows Mall, over to the first motel that had been built at the Center. Now it was the least expensive. It was a three-story rectangle without elevators, with the cheapest accommodations on the third floor, and in front, near the boulevard traffic. He stopped at the desk and learned that she was in 322.

While he climbed the stairs to the third floor he tried to plan some way of handling it. But he knew it could not be planned. He would have to adjust to her reaction to him, playing his tunes by ear.

The voice on the phone had sounded so frail, uncertain and so young that he had thought it might be one of Patsy Knox's friends playing a wicked trick on him.

"I'm Doreen's mother," she said. "I came on the bus. I've got to talk to you."

"Where are you now?"

"I'm at the EconoWay Motor House. I want to come to your office. I asked and they told me you have an office in the Communications Building, but they wouldn't let me come in without permission from you. The policeman said you could arrange it."

"You wait there, Mrs. Purves, and I'll take care of it."

And now, he thought, as he raised his hand to tap at her door, I must face some overweight, red-faced countrywoman with murder in her little gimlet eyes, and a small mustache on her upper lip.

He heard the rattle of the safety chain and then the door swung open and the woman looked at him expectantly. He suffered a moment or two of disorientation, as though some warp in time had sent him to Doreen's world twenty years in the future: her waist thickened, eyes faded, thighs and upper arms heavier, blonde hair going gray, a pouch under the chin, lines across the throat and forehead and around the mouth. A pretty woman with a faded look.

"You brought the paper so I can go see Reverend Deets?"

"I'm Joe Deets, Mrs. Purves."

Surprise immobilized her for a moment, and then she tried to slam the door on him, but it hit his shoe and bounded back, slipping away from her fingertips. As he moved into the room, she backed away, her eyes wide. He turned and closed the door behind him.

"I don't want to talk to you here!"

"I don't have a private office. People are in and out all the time. It wouldn't be a good place, really. You sounded as if it's important and private. So I decided to come over and see you. What do you want to talk to me about?"

She started to speak, then turned and hurried over to her purse, opened it, took out a sheet from a yellow legal pad, folded twice, and started to hand it to him, then seemed to try to throw it at him. It fell at his feet. She rubbed her hand on the thigh of her skirt as though something had come off on it from that piece of paper. She wore a beige skirt, nylons, brown sandals with high heels, a white blouse with long sleeves and ruffles at the throat and wrists. He could see the beige jacket to the suit hanging in the closet alcove, wrinkled across the rump from the bus ride. Her suitcase was on a luggage rack by the closet alcove. It was a small room with a single window, a single bed, two chairs, a desk, rosebud wallpaper, and a Panasonic portable television set chained to a massive steel ring screwed to the wall.

He opened the letter and read it, seeing out of the corner of his eye that she had turned away from him. In profile she had the same high round little rump and slightly swaybacked stance as her daughter.

"I know who wrote this, of course," he said.

"How would you know that?" she asked sharply.

"It's not difficult to figure out. She worked for me for a time. I'm the computer specialist here. She had such an obvious crush on me it became embarrassing and I had her transferred over to clerical work at the University. Her name is Patsy Knox. If you confront her, I'm sure she'll admit it. She's not a very good liar."

"Why would she do that?"

He shrugged. "Anger, jealousy, impulsiveness."

"Have you been doing . . . what that letter says?"

"Who else have you showed it to?"

"I thought I'd go right to Sister Mary Margaret, because she helped us get Doreen accepted here and she and Doctor John Tinker Meadows told us how Doreen would be treated here. But . . . I just couldn't give it to her and stand there and watch her read it. I couldn't."

"I know what you mean. How did Mr. Purves react?"

"Nobody has seen it except me and the person who wrote it. And you. Unless, of course, they showed it to somebody before they mailed it. I don't know what to do. I never come up against anything like this before. I mean we had that trouble with Doreen—"

"I know about that," he said. He moved over and sat in the chair near the window and waved her toward the bed. She moved back and sat on the edge of the bed, ankles together, knees clamped together, her clenched hands resting on her thighs. He noticed that her hands looked chapped, the knuckles swollen.

"Well, have you been doing . . . what it says?"

"Annalee, we're here to think about Doreen's welfare, isn't that right?"

"Of course, but . . ."

"What was she like when she was little?"

"What? Oh, she was a wonderful child. She was a wonderful baby. She smiled all the time. She hardly ever cried. And she was a wonderful loving child. She was a happy child. Dave, he's a year older, he was cranky. He nearly drove us crazy crying. Why should I be telling you what she was like?"

"So that together, between us, we can find some answers."

"To what? You're doing it to her or you're not."

"I know what she was like when you brought her here. Sullen, silent, depressed. She moved and looked like a person with some sort of terminal illness, like a cancer."

"We were both scared, Hub and me. Both of us were scared about that. The doctor who took care of her after she lost the baby, after her boyfriend was killed, said she ought to have professional help. He meant some kind of psychiatrist, I guess. But I told him that it was against our faith. When she just seemed to get worse, we decided to turn to the Church. We've been members a long, long time."

"I know. Sometimes I wonder if we shouldn't relax our standards a little bit when it comes to emergency situations. People who go into depression after a tragic accident should have some access to appropriate care. We may be changing that stance in the future. There are plans to build a big hospital and medical center here, with emphasis on geriatric care, and probably a medical school. Then perhaps the Church will be willing to accept the use of special medicines in the case of emotional shock and depression. Psychic energizers they are called. And then of course there are drugs such as Valium which, used in moderation, can take the sharp edge off grief and loss. Yes, I would predict that there is going to be some liberalization of the past rules. Soon, but not yet."

"Well . . . we thought she would do just fine here."

"And she has! Let me tell you about last Saturday. I go everywhere by bicycle. I came here on my bike. I don't own a car. If I have to have one, I guess I could get one from the car pool, but come to think of it, I guess my license has expired. Anyway, there is a road that starts up beyond the Settlements, a narrow, winding little asphalt road. I told Doreen about my early-morning rides and she begged to come with me, and so she borrowed a bike and she was there waiting for me at six-thirty at this end of the little road. We rode for about an hour and then we leaned the bikes against an old tree, and while I rested in the shade, she went walking ahead to see what was over the brow of the next little hill. She disappeared from view and suddenly there she was again, running downhill toward me, running like the wind. It startled me. I thought something horrible the other side of the hill had frightened her. But she was running and laughing all the way down the hill, and she collapsed breathless on the grass there in the shade, still laughing. I asked her what had struck her so funny and she had no answer to it. She said she had just felt like it, that's all. She wanted to run and she wanted to laugh because she felt like it."

In silence Annalee stared down at her hands. Then she looked over at him without raising her head. "That's what she used to do when she was little. Then when she got in with those bike people and started staying out all night, and coming home acting funny from the stuff she was using, it like to broke my heart right in two. She was like a different person, so quiet and sullen-like, and never smiling, and even using bad language on me and her daddy. I prayed to God night after night to get Doreen back to like she used to be before she got mixed up with that gang. What I was afraid of most, God would kill her on one of those machines going a hundred and ten miles an hour, squashed like a bug against a tree or a truck or a bridge. I prayed to him to give her a chance to repent before she died, so she wouldn't spend all eternity in hellfire. She'd lost her faith. And my own faith was beginning to feel a little bit shaky. I'm glad you told me about her running. That's the way she used to be." She stared beyond him, out the window, into space, her eyes narrowed. "I used to wonder if it was something passed down to her."

"From whom?"

She looked startled. "I didn't mean to say that."

"From you?"

Her voice trembled. "It is something I am never going to talk about to a living soul the rest of my life."

"But it was something a little bit like her running around with the motorcycle people?"

"Maybe. I don't know. Let me alone. Could be it was all Hub's fault, the trouble with Doreen."

"In what way?"

"I guess I don't want to talk about it."

"I thought we were here to work out what's best for Doreen."

She sighed and shrugged, spreading her hands in a gesture of helplessness. "It's probably nothing. When she was seven, eight, nine. Around that age, Hub used to tease her to come give him a movie kiss. And she'd hug him tight around the neck and kiss him on the mouth for a long, long time. It was innocent fun with Hub. It was a game they played. She was his daughter. But it worried me that she began to get big up here when she was so young. And she became a woman when she was a month past her twelfth birthday. I couldn't blame that on Hub because I was that way too. And that's part of the reason I got into . . . never mind."

She stopped talking and stared at him with an exasperated expression and a little snort of frustration. "I didn't come here to the Center to have you talk and talk and talk and not say nothing at all. You probably think I'm some kind of dumb farmer-woman. Maybe I am but I'm not that dumb. You're not going to talk me out of anything. Are you sleeping with my daughter or aren't you?"

He knew then that she was a more formidable opponent than he had anticipated. There was a good toughness there, a directness that was going to require every bit of persuasion he could muster. And he had the feeling that it was not going to work, that nothing he said to her was going to change anything.

"I'm waiting," she said.

"Annalee, I'm a foolish man and I'm a weak man. Please believe me when I say that I am going to give you all the answers, but I want you to let me go at it in my own way, because it may be the only way I will ever get you to understand."

"You will never make me understand a man like you sleeping with my daughter."

"Do you know what a hypothetical question is?"

"I don't think so."

"Lawyers ask hypothetical questions when they cross-examine somebody in court, some criminal. 'What if,' they say. 'What if the prosecution can prove you were at the scene of the crime that night?'"

"You want me to change my question so it's hyp . . . hyp . . ."

"Hypothetical. No. I want to change the question around and ask you what will happen if what's in that letter is true?"

"You will burn in hell forever!"

"Aside from that."

"Don't you care about that?"

"When I am finally judged, Annalee, I hope that I will be judged on the basis of my entire life experience."

"You are confusing me."

"If that letter is true, nobody here at Meadows Center knows about it. If that letter is true, and if it were made public, they would have to send Doreen home. And if that letter were true and they sent Doreen home, she would probably kill herself. She tells me that she would, and I don't think she's bluffing. First she would sink back into depression, and then she would kill herself."

She leaned toward him and she hit her thigh with her clenched fist, a thud of bone against muscle. "You *are* telling me it's true, aren't you? Damn you! Why? She's just a kid. She's so innocent. You're older than me. Older than Hub. You're not handsome and you're not tall. You're kind of an ugly wrinkly bowlegged man, like some kind of farmhand. Those little pale eyes and that scratchy voice. What in the name of Jesus Christ could a sweet pretty girl see in you? How in God's name did it ever happen the first time?"

"If it happened."

"Play your dumb game. It doesn't work anymore. Just tell me why it happened."

"This is not a game. Don't think of it as a game. This is the real world, and foolish acts in the real world can make horrid things happen. What will happen if you, out of anger and pain and righteousness, take your daughter Doreen home with you, after telling Mary Margaret why you are doing it? What will happen if you tell Hub and her brother what happened to her up here?"

She looked startled and awed. "It would really kill Hub. It really would. He would have to come up here and kill you. Like he tried to kill her boyfriend the week before he died, after he found out Doreen was pregnant."

"Can't you talk quietly to your husband? Can't you explain things to him?"

She thought for a moment. "I think we used to talk a lot, when we were going together and after we were married, before the kids came along. The way I remember it, we used to talk about . . . well, things that are important, like time and God and love. But I can't remember what either of us said. I just remember sitting in the hammock and talking. Now we don't talk like that. We haven't for a long time. I wouldn't know how to begin with him. And I don't think he wants to talk about anything anymore. He is on edge. There's too many men been fired where he works and still not enough work, and in the night he'll get up and walk around the house and sit in the dark. It's like he's getting ready for some kind of explosion. I don't know. I'm not explaining it right. All I know is that if I tried to tell him about Doreen, I would get it half said and he would be gone. He wouldn't hear another word and he wouldn't talk about it. He would just drive up here ninety miles an hour and do what he would think he had to do. Please tell me what happened. I can't understand how it could happen."

"We haven't looked at all the probable results yet, Annalee."

"I guess not, and they would throw you right out of the Church and I guess that's what's bothering you, isn't it? I don't know what you're trying to talk me into, but that's what's so important to you."

He hoped his laugh was convincing. At least it startled her. "Mrs. Purves, I am a computer expert. As such, I am very well paid. I am a programmer of the very first order. They don't want to lose me because I am as near to being essential as any person in Administration can get. They ordained me as a device to make me less likely to leave. It puts me under a very generous retirement and pension program. It adds to the plausibility of the Church, I guess, to have the top people called the Reverend this and the Reverend that. But if you blow this whole situation wide open, they will have to ask me to leave, regardless of how badly they need my services. In a certain sense, I will be sorry to leave. It's a pleasant environment, an interesting challenge. But the major problems are solved. It may very well be time for me to move along. I would say that, on the average, I get three good offers a year from industry. I would have no trouble. I would have some regrets. But I would be doing interesting and important work within a month."

She stared at him. "Don't you believe in the Church?"

"I believe in God. I believe in some of the doctrine of the Eternal Church of the Believer. I don't take the rest of it too seriously. The rules of the Church that are made by men and not by God can be imperfect, just as men must be imperfect."

"Don't you think that seducing my daughter is a vile and horrible sin that will send you to the lowest pits of hell?"

"I'm not convinced it will. But let's continue with the consequences, if you don't mind. We are constantly subject to close and careful inspection by the media. So many newspaper, television, radio and magazine people come here that news conferences by the Reverend Doctor John Tinker Meadows occur frequently. Did you know that?"

"I know that they all want to tear the Church down. They are the Antichrist. Socialist rabble. That's what Matthew Meadows always calls them."

"I do not really believe you can expose me and take your daughter away without the media people hearing about it."

"Why would they? Are you saying you'd tell them?"

"Of course not. You said you couldn't control your husband if you told him about this. Violence usually gets press attention. The Church is always vulnerable, you know. Coverage of this sort of thing could only hurt the Church. And as I've told you, if Doreen leaves here and goes back into depression, she could kill herself. You know how the Eternal Church feels about suicide. And that would hurt you and your husband and all the friends she's made here. It would hurt me too, desperately, but that is of no importance in your considerations. Even if it doesn't come out, if I am forced to resign, that too would hurt the Church. I say that without arrogance. I know what my contribution is."

She rocked slowly forward and back, eyes closed, arms folded across her middle. "You could be an agent of Satan," she said. She looked at him in that disconcertingly direct way. "Tell me how it began. That's what I can't understand at all."

"I knew her history, of course. It was all in the restricted section of the detailed data base. I'm in charge of that, so when I found that one of the Angels assigned to Communications seemed dreadfully depressed, I learned her name and took a look at the file on my terminal."

"Why would that be any of your business anyway?"

"It wasn't, I guess. I have a lot of curiosity about people. I really like people. When I was a kid, I thought I might become a psychologist or a psychiatrist. A year and a half ago we had one of the students at Meadows University kill herself. I always thought it could have been prevented if somebody had talked to her about her listlessness and depression."

"So this whole thing was just to cheer Doreen up? I mean that's really some kind of big sacrifice for you, Rev'ren'."

"There's really no need to be sarcastic. Whether you can believe it or not, we are both, you and I, troubled people who have Doreen's best interests at heart. After I read the file, then I began to understand why she was so down. Why her hair looked so lifeless and her skin was grainy, and why she moved in such a listless way. I found myself worrying about her. If there is one thing I do well, aside from my work in computers, it is getting people to talk. It took a long time with Doreen. I moved her to my own department, without permission, I might add. She was suspicious of me. She was suspicious of everybody. She mourned her lost child and her dead boyfriend, and she was lonely here. Finally the dam began to break. I did a lot of listening. It all came tumbling out. There is a strange thing about talking your troubles out. As you talk them out, just the act of thinking of the right words gives you a different slant on your misery. I am a good listener. I really listen. To be truthful, I had thought she would be a dreary young girl. Her troubles were actually trite. I did not expect any special kind of intelligence. But I found she is a bright child. I call her a child, but eighteen is hardly that anymore. She is a woman who has had some blows which could have proved mortal. She could have been on that cycle with her friend when it slid under the truck, you know. She told me how close she had been to being with him on that ride that night. She didn't go because she was sick to her stomach."

"She never told me that."

"I don't think she told anyone until she told me. And she told me she had decided there was no God. If there was, He would not let such terrible things happen. There is no God. Life is accidental. A God worth loving would not have killed Mike. Her loss of faith was tormenting her. I talked to her about God's plan being too complex for the mortal mind to comprehend. We talked often, and she seemed to become more willing to listen. She began to come out of depression. We took long walks in the early morning. It was a slow process. She began to depend upon me and she began to trust me."

"That was a mistake, wasn't it?"

"Annalee, you keep asking me how it all started, and I wonder if you really want to know, or if you want a chance to make snide remarks. If that's what you want, we can call it quits right now. Do whatever you please. Strike out at everybody." He stood up.

He had spoken harshly. All games have stakes, he thought. And you can bet a little here and a little there, and dribble away any capital you might have. Or you can pick a number and bet everything on it. And do a little praying.

He had almost reached the door when she said, "No. I'm sorry. I really think it was a terrible mistake she made, learning to trust you. I think you were after her from the very beginning. But please come back and sit down and tell me. Please."

He returned to the chair and smiled sadly and said, "None of this is easy for me either. Just bear in mind that I was *not* after your daughter from the very beginning. You have to realize that. And if you are expecting some kind of a peep show, Annalee, I am not going to oblige you."

"I don't know what you . . ."

"The details of this so-called seduction are personal and private. No one has the need or the right to know them."

"But *why* did it happen?" she pleaded. "*How* could she let you do it?"

"She was grateful to me for starting her back on the road to being alive once more. She respected me, I guess. I think that she wanted to find some way of showing her appreciation and her . . . affection. And, God help me, I gave her a way to show it."

"Where did it happen?"

"At my little house in the Settlements. Late at night."

"What was she doing in your house late at night."

"We had been having what I guess you would call theological arguments, about the existence of a deity, and life after death. She walked up after the evening meal, after dark. I had asked her to come there because I wanted to show her something I had purchased. I have an IBM Personal Computer at home. I had bought a program called 'The Word.' I paid about two hundred dollars for it. It came on seven five-inch disks which contain the entire King James version of the Bible. It is marketed by Bible Research Systems in Austin, Texas. There are four and a half million bytes of information in the Bible, so it lends itself to a useful program. The disks are double-sided, double-density. The information is very tightly compacted on the disks. Best of all it has a data base management system on one disk."

"I can't understand all that."

"Sorry. What it means is that you can order the program to search through the whole text, very rapidly. I had been playing with it the previous evening. There is an index of two hundred subjects. For example, I would ask it to search for every reference that had to do with 'Forgiveness' and print that out on the little Epson printer I use. It is very fast. I knew of her awareness of sin and her conviction that if there was a God, He would never forgive her. So I asked her to come up and she did, and I had the program search the Bible for references to 'Loss of Faith.' She was really fascinated. And the performance of the program was impressive. At about nine-thirty we had one of those violent June thunderstorms. As a precaution I turned the IBM off, and it was a good thing I did, because not five minutes later the electricity failed. I found the candles and lit them. She pored over the printout about 'Forgiveness.' I was sitting beside her. She was so lovely in candlelight I felt as if my heart turned over in my chest. I am a silly man and a weak man. It is despicable to take wicked advantage of a vulnerable young girl. I suspect I have more than my share of masculine urges, and that is one of the crosses I bear. God help me, I reached for her, put my arms around her. She was very startled. She resisted for a moment, looking into my eyes, and then she let out a long sigh and moved closer and I kissed her."

After a long silence she said, "All right. So it happened once. It started with a moment of weakness. I can understand that. And she's impressionable. But that's no reason for it to go on and on, is it? Did it have to keep on happening?"

"Mrs. Purves, Annalee, I just hope I can explain this to you."

"I hope you can too."

"I am not going to go into any intimate detail. That wouldn't be fair to you or to Doreen."

"Are you going to tell me she didn't want it to stop there?"

"Not at all. She didn't care one way or the other."

"You can't mean that! She had to care."

"I mean it. I was astonished in the light of her personal history to discover she was sexually very inhibited, very ignorant. There was absolutely no pleasure in it for her. She was like a mechanical doll, going through the motions she learned from that boyfriend, Mike. He was her only previous relationship. He was impatient and brutal and ignorant, and he had destroyed her chance to have any pleasure out of physical love. Do you understand that?"

"Yes," she said in a barely audible voice.

"And, my dear woman, you see before you a man who succumbed to the Pygmalion syndrome."

"What is that?"

"Did you see *My Fair Lady*?"

"Three times. It wasn't on the forbidden list."

"An older man can find himself under a terrible compulsion to teach a young girl important things. It is a kind of arrogance masking itself as generosity and kindliness. I happen to think that kind of physical pleasure is the closest thing to heaven we ever find on earth. And so I fought the terrible temptation to see if I could help her find that kind of pleasure. I fought it and I lost."

"You're rotten! You're really a rotten person."

"Guilty. Rotten, licentious, wicked. A libertine, seducer of ignorant young girls. Bound for hell in a basket. Anything you want to call me, I'm guilty."

"But don't you even—"

"Now let's look at the other side of this crazy coin, Annalee. It is a custom these days to talk of scenarios. What would the scenario have been had Patsy Knox never sent you that note? Doreen and I would have continued our relationship for a time. We would have continued to be very discreet. And then, little by little, I would have loosened any hold I might have over her. Right now she thinks she loves me more than life itself. But it isn't love, of course. It's a physical infatuation, the by-product of a healthy young body and a lot of care and gentleness and patience and understanding. She feels great guilt, because she has found her way back to the Eternal Church and she knows we are sinning. However, she knows she found forgiveness for the sins in her past, and I am certain she will find forgiveness for what is happening now. She is healthy and alive and her eyes sparkle. She has learned to enjoy physical love, and that will help her in the marriage she will make one day. I love to hear her laugh. I love the funny little jokes she makes up. She believes that we are both deep in a sin we cannot help and cannot stop committing, and that we will go on like this forever. Not so. On many bases we have far too little in common. In my own time, with utmost kindness, I am going to push her away. I will do it, I swear, in such a way it will become her idea. I cannot really believe I have harmed her in any way. Can you understand that?"

"I'm trying to."

"Does she know you're here?"

"Oh no! I didn't want to see her until after I found out for sure what's been going on."

"So the ball is in your court, as they say. You can destroy a lot of people, and probably lose your daughter *and* your husband, or you can have a nice visit with Doreen, and say nothing about our talk, and tell her you came up to see how she's getting along. Then you can go back home and pick up your life and you have my word this will end."

"When? How soon?"

"That will depend on how much she resists breaking off our friend-ship. Anyway, it shouldn't last past Christmas."

"Christmas!" she said, in agitation.

"But it's only four months off," he said.

"All right then, but there's something I have to know."

"I don't know what you mean. What sort of thing?"

"I was going to ask you if you have other women too. But I guess I don't want to know that."

"While the affair continues, Annalee, I am faithful to Doreen. I could profess my great and undying love, but that would be another lie. I have a lot of affection for her. She is a pleasant person and she is not intellectually demanding. After a full day of the kind of work I do, I find her sweet and restful."

"But if . . . if I just let it keep going on . . . then I am committing a sin too. Like being in a conspiracy. Like sitting out in the car when somebody is robbing a bank. Oh God. I don't know. I don't know what to do."

She put her hands to her face and began rocking from side to side, sobbing aloud.

He went quickly to the bed and sat beside her and took hold of her wrists, pulled her hands down from her face. She fought him for a few moments and then went slack, her face turned away, while she made snuffling, choking sounds.

"Annalee, please. I want to recite something to you, something I memorized when I was young and I've never forgotten it. It was written a very long time ago. This is it. *Such, be said, O King, seems to me the present life of man on earth in comparison with that time which is unknown to us, as when you are sitting at supper with your warriors and counselors in the season of winter, the hall being warmed by a fire blazing on the hearth in the center, the storms of the wintry rains or snows raging without; and then a sparrow entering the house should swiftly flit across the hall, entering at one door and quickly disappearing at the other. The time that it is within, it is safe from the wintry blast, but the narrow bounds of warmth and shelter are passed in a little moment and then the bird vanishes out of sight, returning again into the winter's night from which it has just emerged. So this life of man appears for a short interval; but of what went before or what is to follow, we are utterly ignorant.*"

She had controlled her sobs in order to listen, and before he had finished it she had turned to him, frowning, her face blotched, eyes still streaming her tears.

"B-but," she said, "that is all so . . . cold and empty. You think life is nothing more than that? It's so scary. How can you stand going on if you think that's what we are? Just kind of . . . nothing."

She had ceased any resistance. The back of her right hand rested in the palm of his left hand and, by accident, his thumb pressed against the pulse in her wrist. He felt the soft steady pump of her heart against the ball of his thumb.

From its hiding place in the thicket, the ancient one-eyed beast awakened and lifted its head slightly, testing the forest breeze for the familiar scents, listening for the crackle of a twig as the prey approached.

Oh no, he thought. You talk about wickedness and contemplate this act. And even as you contemplate it, you are telling yourself, in a kindly tone, like an uncle, that this would be an absolutely certain way of sealing her lips. She's been readied by all the talk, by all the churn of emotions, by her own fears and uncertainties. In a matter of minutes it could begin, and all her protestations would be listless, her voice small, her body slack with only token resistance.

He remembered when he was little his uncle had a brown Studebaker, and on the dashboard was affixed, by a suction cup, a red rubber head of the devil, bounding about on a spring. It was always facing forward, through the windshield, but it turned around easily and whenever he rode with his uncle at some point in the trip he would turn the devil head around. It bobbed on the spring, grinning its devil grin, jaws agape, revealing the red rubber tongue. The eyes were tiny glass marbles, milky white, with black spots for pupils. He remembered his uncle saying one day, "If you play with your dink, Joey, that there is the fellow who's going to come get you and take you away."

He felt new tension in her hands and wrists and he saw from her widened eyes and suddenly compressed lips that she had sensed what he was thinking about. Looking into her eyes, he knew that she knew that it could probably happen, right here, right now, on this narrow motel bed in the sacred ambience of the Meadows Center, close enough to the Tabernacle to hear the electronic chimes on the hour and half hour.

Her mouth made the shape of a soundless "no."

He released her and stood up and went to the window and looked out. "The point is our utter ignorance," he said.

"What?"

"The point of the quotation. We have no certain way of knowing."

"Faith makes you certain. Really certain. 'Never yield to evil, practice good and you will have an everlasting home, for Jehovah loves what is right and never deserts the devout.' "

He turned and smiled at her. "Nothing is easy, except to people who are too dumb to care. You and I care about many, many of the same things and have many values in common."

"And there's a lot we don't have in common."

"What are you going to do?"

"I don't know yet. I'm going to think about everything you said. I am going to pray for guidance. And then I'll decide."

"I hope you'll be merciful, Annalee."

"I hope so too, Joe Deets. But in the end I'll do what I have to do. I'll do what Jesus Christ tells me to do."

He had the bleak feeling that he had lost this game. He had been close to winning it, but there was a signal in the righteous little lift of her chin.

"Maybe you could pray with me?" he said gently, remembering the movie about the godfather and the offer that couldn't be refused.

"You're not fit to pray words over me," she said. "But if you want to kneel down, you can stay here while I pray."

She got down and knelt and turned so that her folded hands rested, childlike, on the side of the single bed. He knelt by the chair.

"Dear Lord, I have been a faithful member of Your flock for a long time, ever since I was forgiven and I was healed a long time ago. I have been leading a decent Christian life and following all Your laws all the time, in my home and my marriage. I prayed to You to save my daughter Doreen when she was wicked and had lost sight of You. I prayed to You to give her back to the Church and her loving family. Now I don't know what to do or which way to turn. The man kneeling here with me pretends to be a minister of Your Church, but he is not."

Her voice was small, frail, young, and somehow confident that it was being heard. The silence lasted so long he wondered if she was through. And then she began again.

"Maybe even Satan can do Your work sometimes, Lord. This man kneeling with me as if he is praying helped bring Doreen back to You. Now she feels a terrible guilt because this agent of Satan has taught her to enjoy the pleasures of the flesh with him. He is a wicked old man. He tells me that if I expose him, I will be destroying several lives, and solving nothing. He tells me that is more important than the sin I am committing of doing nothing to save her from the sins of the flesh. This agent of Satan is an empty man. There is no soul inside of him. There are only tricks and deceits. He does not believe in You or in hell or in salvation. He does not understand how precious are Your laws, and how joyful is the chance of eternal life. I feel sorry for him. For a little while, long ago,

I was as empty as he is, and as consumed by pleasure. But I found my way back to You. I think it is too late for him, but if it is in Your mercy I pray to You to open his eyes as You opened mine long ago. And I pray to You to give me a small share of Your wisdom so that I may be guided toward what I must do. And please keep me from hating him, even though I can hate what he is doing." There was a long silence. She seemed to him to be waiting for something to come to her. And then she said, "Amen," and got up slowly.

As he got up, he found that his eyes were stinging, and a single tear had spilled. He did not want her to notice that. He had the strange feeling that for a moment, through her trust and innocence, he had been privileged to look beyond a curtain that had been drawn across a secret window all of his life. It had parted, just for a moment, too quickly for him to see and comprehend what was behind it. He was conscious only of a visceral feeling of expectancy, a flicker of unearned joy.

"Thank you for letting me stay," he said.

"That's okay. If I can't make up my mind, I'll pray again, and keep praying until I know what to do."

"Thanks for praying for me."

"You're the worst kind of sinner, Joe Deets. You are the kind who think there is no such a thing as sin. You think that the only sin is getting caught."

As he walked slowly down the corridor toward the stairs, he heard her put the chain back on the door. Damned old fool, he thought. You should have peeled her out of those travel clothes when you sensed there might be the tiny little chance she wouldn't fight it off. You've studied women long enough to know when to move in. It would have been the best insurance you could buy. What's all this genteel reluctance, Joe boy? Face it. After years of trying, you have finally found your stopping place, finally found something so wonderfully rotten that even you wouldn't do it. Perhaps there is some hope for you after all.

He did not let himself think about his reaction to her prayer. It had no place in his life. Before he got on the bicycle, he put his hand in his left hip pocket and took out the note dear darling Patsy had sent the woman. He wondered if, by now, Annalee had discovered it was missing. Not having it at hand should decrease any desire to blow the whistle. He started to tear it up, hesitated, put it back in his pocket. He wanted to see Patsy Knox's face when he showed it to her. Then he would tear it up.

He went directly back to his office, put Annalee and Doreen out of his mind and began work on the report he was writing to John Tinker with a copy to Finn Efflander about the feasibility of decentralizing the membership records. For an initial cost of $13,500 for a Vanguard 8000, with printer and ten-megabyte hard disk, they could equip the fifty largest of the affiliated churches for a total outlay of $675,000. The bigger churches were getting restive about sending the entire collection away and getting half of it back. This way each church could record its own total contribution received in the pledge envelopes, and prepare the necessary receipt for the church member to prove his tax-free gift. The proper percentage could be sent along, and by setting up modem connections between the mainframe and the decentralized computers, they would have a close check on finances and they could also verify mainframe data base records against the regional records. He wanted to work up a sample program to demonstrate how it could be done. But as he worked on the program, setting it up in Pascal, he discovered several ways his ideas could be improved and expanded to take care of other problems of administration.

Fingernails walking lightly across the back of his neck startled him and he snapped his head around and looked up at the pretty smiling face of Doreen Purves.

"Hey, guess what!" she said.

He looked at his watch. It was twenty past nine, and he realized he was very hungry for the dinner he had missed. "I give up. What?"

"My mom is here! She took me to dinner at the motel across from where she's staying."

"Why did she come to see you?"

"I guess just to kind of check up on how I'm doing. Hey, how long have you been here? Did you eat or anything?"

"I guess I forgot about it."

"What are you doing there?"

"Just a program for the affiliated churches."

She moved around to face him, half sitting on the wide shelf that held the computer equipment. "Can you quit?"

"Let me see." He printed the long list, tore it off the printer, studied it and scowled at it. Lots of clumsy steps. But a reasonable stopping place. When he was done, the revision would make it efficient and elegant. He stored it and turned off the computer and the printer. "I'm through for now."

"Okay, whyn't you bike over and pick up some fried chicken and chocolate shakes. I'm starved again. We ate at six. I'll wait for you at your place."

Over the kitchen picnic, Doreen said, "You know, when I saw her coming toward me after practice, I was really, really scared. I thought: Oh my God, she knows about me and Joe. It would really kill her. You know that? She couldn't handle it. And there's no way I could make her see that you're the best thing ever happened in my life."

"But it was just a visit."

"I guess so. Well, hell, I was a basket case when they brought me up here. I wanted to be dead, and I would have killed myself if I'd had the energy. Why am I telling you all this? You know how I was, better than anybody. Anyway, she acted funny. She looked at me funny. There's something on her mind, but I know it isn't us. We had a wonderful visit, Joe. It looks like my brother will be marrying the DeAngelis girl. Barbara. She's very pretty and nice. But they don't want to risk trying to get their own place in times like these, so they want to move in with Mom and Daddy, which is fine with them. Even though Barbara works, it will still mean more help and more company for Mom. I hope Barbara helps with the chickens. Mom hates those chickens. She can't stand them. My dad is okay too. They fired three guys from where he works, but they kept him on."

"When is she going back?"

"Her bus leaves at three tomorrow and she'll be home by about eight o'clock. She's going to come to choir practice. I showed her my room. I thought she'd ask me why I didn't have a roommate like they told her I would have. I'd hate to have to tell her all the tricks I had to pull to get a room alone."

"There's some chocolate on your chin, love."

"Thanks," she said. "Sorry." She dabbed it away, frowned and said, "About three or four times I looked over at her and caught her looking at me funny, as if she was trying to figure something out. I don't know what. She asked me a lot of times if I was happy. I told her I was happier than I had ever been, and it just about killed me not being able to tell her why. When I said good night to her about fifteen minutes ago in front of her place, she took me by the wrist and held on so hard it hurt. And she said like, 'Remember, Doreen, all your father and I want for you is for you to be happy and lead a good Christian life.' I guess I'm leading a good Christian life with one little exception, huh?"

"Just one exception."

"Gee, I wish you could meet her, or at least get a look at her. She's a real pretty woman. She's worked hard all her life, but it doesn't show, you know what I mean?"

"I think so."

"You could look in on choir practice maybe. She's about my size but a little heavier here and there, and she's a blonde too but she's getting quite a lot of gray in with it. I told her she ought to use a rinse, and she said maybe she would. She says my old dog misses me something terrible. Old Brownie. He sleeps on my bed and looks out the window for me at school bus time. I wish I could have him here. The only person he ever bit was Mike, and Mike kicked him so hard he went howling down the road. And I hit Mike and Mike hit me, and I went home howling too. Some great scene, huh?"

He looked across the table at her and said in a low tone, "I have a different kind of scene in mind for you, young lady."

"You do, huh? Like for instance what?"

He didn't answer her. He just smiled into her eyes and watched the changes. He watched her mouth swell and soften, her head tilt of its own weight, her eyes grow heavy-lidded, her breathing deepen and slow.

"Like what?" she whispered.

"Come see," he said.

Twelve

On Monday, August fifteenth, a large tropical storm, big enough to fill most of the Gulf of Mexico, recovered from two days of indecision. The weather people had named it Harold. The velocity of the winds at the center increased almost to hurricane force, and the entire storm system abruptly headed north-northeast at increasing speed, making landfall along the entire north coast of the Gulf, from eastern Texas to Pensacola.

It carried an enormous amount of water, and by Tuesday afternoon heavy rains were falling on Lakemore and Meadows Center. The sky was so dark the Boulevard lights went on automatically. Dozens of counties in six states experienced severe flooding during a twelve-hour period with rains of anywhere from five to twelve inches.

The giant storm brought tornadoes, high winds, electrical storms which mangled trailer parks, sucked roofs off frame houses and barns, toppled power lines and blew recreational vehicles off the highways.

In midafternoon when the rain was as heavy as any he had ever heard, Roy Owen sat at the small desk in unit sixteen of the County Line Motel going over the eight pounds of computer printout and corporate financial statements Dave had sent down from Hartford by Federal Express. He had arranged for their computers to be programmed to give him the ratios he thought significant—the market volume in each issue expressed as a percentage of the shares available, and related to the daily increases or decreases in the daily quote. And he paid close attention to the internal ratios of the corporations whose stock they held in the three funds. Ratios of sales to gross to net and to debt structure. He was a specialist in the different ways bad news could be weasel-worded in the footnotes to the financial statements. And he depended a great deal on the Value Line rating system.

Peggy Moon knocked and he let her in. Her dark hair was curly damp. She had clean sheets over her arm, wrapped in plastic to keep the rain off. "I'm really sorry, Roy, but that dang Dolly didn't show up, and I'm running way late, and all I got time to do is change the sheets and pillowcases, okay? If it won't bother you."

"It won't bother me. Go ahead."

He sat back in the chair by the desk and glanced over at her as she stripped the bed. She moved in an overly energetic slapdash manner, whipping the used bedding off, yanking up the corners of the mattress to tuck the bottom sheet under.

She stopped suddenly and came over to the desk. "Hey, I don't remember that lamp."

"I got it at the Meadows Mall, at Sears. I'll leave it here when I go. I needed a better light on these papers."

"You don't really have to leave it. Say, why all those green stripes on those sheets?"

"Standard computer printout paper, Peggy. When you have to read a column all the way across, it makes it easier not to get mixed up."

"What is all that stuff?"

"Sort of an analysis of the securities we hold in three different mutual funds. I'm seeing if we should sell anything or buy anything."

"Looks like big figures."

"We're not really large compared to some of the funds. Right now the total of the three is close to four hundred million."

She cocked her head and said, "You decide what all that money should be invested in?"

"With a little help from my friends."

"I think I should have been calling you Mr. Owen instead of Roy."

"It's not my money, Peggy."

"But isn't it a terrible responsibility for you?"

"I'm used to it. I like it. Whether it's a bull market, a bear market or a flat market, you just have to work out your strategy and try to do a little better than the guys over at Fidelity, or Columbia or Vanguard. You have to use every kind of computer analysis you think is worth anything, and beyond that, you fly by the seat of your pants. Right now we're coming to the end of a long-term bull market. My gut feeling is to lock in all the gains on the volatile issues and . . ." He stopped as he realized from her expression she had but the faintest idea of what he was talking about. He shrugged. "It's a living."

She laughed and as she started to speak the electricity went off. The window air conditioner ground to a stop. The storm seemed twice as loud as before. He could feel the building shudder as hard rain was whipped against the rear windows. The dim gray storm light filled the room. She went over and opened the front draperies a few inches and peered out.

"Hey, it's turning into a lake out there." She came back to the bed and finished making it, giving it a final pat.

She said, "I saved you until last, thinking maybe you'd go out."

"In this?"

"Well, it's just in the last hour it's gotten this bad."

As she finished speaking there was a vivid blue-white flash of lightning, so close it made a cracking sound. The thunder followed immediately, a huge bang with any after-echoes lost in the roar of rain.

She sat on the edge of the big shabby wing chair and he could see in the gray light how wide her eyes were. "And you better not go out in this," he said.

"Thanks. That was *close!* I hope it wasn't the office."

She went over and peered out the window again. "Looks okay from what I can see. Oh, it hit that big live oak the other side of the highway. Come look!"

Intermittently, through the blowing curtains of rain, he could see big limbs canted down toward the ground, the white of shattered wood where they had been joined. One limb seemed to be across the far lane of the road.

She went over and sat again in the upholstered wing chair, and he turned the straight desk chair to face her. She flinched as more lightning struck, not as close as the previous discharge. "How long are you going to stay, Roy?"

"I don't really know. Are you going to need the room?"

"I didn't mean that. I was just asking."

"Okay, you were just asking. What I have, I guess, is a kind of dumb reluctance to go back North. When I go back up there, Lindy will be missing out of the life I had up there. I was never with her down here. But the longer I stay down here, the tougher it is on Janie. This is . . . there's a word for it . . . oh, a hiatus. I was thinking last night, maybe I could make some kind of long-term arrangement down here. Get a private phone line, and put in a personal computer and a modem and stay in touch with the markets. And maybe go get Janie and bring her down. I wouldn't be getting all the daily gossip and rumor, but maybe that's just as well. I've never needed a lot of people around."

"But you'll have to go back."

"Sooner or later. Sure. But I'm not going to force anything. I just have the feeling there is something I am going to find out about Lindy, by being here. And maybe Janie has to be told what really happened."

She had to speak up to be heard over a louder roar of the rain. "I wish I could get out of here."

"You don't like it here?"

She made an all-encompassing gesture. "This is all we got, Fred and me. We can scratch out a living, but I don't know for how long. Trying to sell it would be like giving it away. Look at all the spots on the arm of this chair. And the burn. It makes me feel helpless because it keeps on going downhill, with no money ever to catch up. I ought to have the guts to walk away from it. But Fred's the only family I've got left. He loves to putter. This old place will just keep on sliding downhill. All the action is the other side of the Interstate." She scowled. "Basically, I guess I just don't like this kind of work. And they say that when you don't like what you do, you get cranky and you get lines and you get older faster. I look at myself and I look a lot older than thirty-one."

"No boyfriends?"

"Don't patronize me, Roy. I married a real charmer. And it got annulled, for reasons I won't go into, except to say I wasn't the one at fault. Got the good old maiden name back. Who needs to be Peggy Endelbarger anyway? I met him over at the State University and got married and dropped out in the middle of my junior year."

"I wasn't patronizing you. I was trying to sound friendly."

She smiled. "So, okay. We're friends. Maybe all I'm trying to do is tell you that there doesn't seem to be any place anybody can go and find the best of all possible worlds. Okay?" She jumped up and went over to the window. "That office phone is probably ringing its fool head off. Fred won't hear it from the next room. He's getting a little bit deaf. It's letting up a little."

"Not noticeably."

"There's a roof most of the way, and I've got this plastic." After she had fashioned it into a cape, she looked solemnly at him and said, "Whatever you want, I hope it comes out okay for you."

"Thanks, Peggy."

He had wanted to say the same sort of thing to her, but before he could word it, she was out the door. The wind helped bang it shut. She trotted along, head lowered, clutching the cape, the used linens under her arm. She went out of sight off to his left and then reappeared heading out the left arm of the *U* toward the office. She ran well, he thought. Lithe and limber.

It happened to people, he thought. Like the little eddies you find in a trout stream, where some leaves get caught there and will go around and around and around until the next heavy rain breaks them free. People have such a reluctance to change their lives even when they know they should try. He could not imagine how great the misery must be for people to spend their entire working life doing something that bored them and irritated them. Maybe, he thought, that was in part the reason for the success of the Eternal Church of the Believer and all the other evangelical sects which had sprung up lately. It was a way out of a life of dreariness and despair. It made them part of some great shiny thing that overshadowed their workday, and gave them a source of both pride and a kind of humble arrogance. I am forever saved and you are forever damned. Hooray for me.

The Reverend Sister Mary Margaret Meadows sat in the living room of her suite on the third floor of the Manse, listening intently to the specialist on Alzheimer's disease who had flown over from London at her request, and with John Tinker's approval. They had sent one of the Gulfstreams to pick him up at Kennedy the night before, and had brought him back ahead of the storm front and domiciled him in the Manse. He was a tall plump man with a long bald narrow head, a tiny white goatee and glasses with yellow lenses. His name was Winton Narramore, and she had filed the name under the mnemonic clues Winton for Winston, Narramore for Narrow-more. He spoke in a rumbling monotone which made it difficult for her to concentrate.

The room was decorated in pink, white and maroon and the windows looked out toward the slope of the cemetery hill behind the Manse. She was wearing a long white dress patterned with pink, and she reclined on a chaise. He sat on a straight chair near the foot of the chaise.

"What we should do, I think," she said, "is I will tell you what I think you told me, and you can correct me."

"Of course."

"With various methods you can actually see the plaques and tangles of dead and dying nerves in the brain."

"Yes. In quite a few of the cases, more frequently in the more advanced ones."

"Only five percent of people over sixty-five in this country and England ever get senile dementia."

"Yes, but we have seen Alzheimer's in rare cases in the late thirties and early forties, and we have increasing evidence that there can be some genetic predisposition to the disease."

"Signals go along nerves by electrical means, but where two nerves meet, the signal is chemical. The transmitting nerve releases a package of . . . of . . ."

"A packet of neurotransmitters that bind it to the receptors on the nerve nearby. And the nerves specialize, apparently, with some able to dispatch and receive only specific neurotransmitters. One such chemical is acetylcholine."

"All right. I have that. Now then, you said a certain enzyme makes the neurotransmitter acetylcholine. And in autopsies on people like my father, you find the enzyme very, very reduced in the brain tissue."

"Yes."

"And the problem is with the transmitting nerves and not with the receptor nerves?"

"That is correct. Or at least up until now that is what we have come to believe."

"Then why can't you get that enzyme into his brain somehow?"

"Madam, it has been tried in England and in West Germany. The results have been almost imperceptible. Alzheimer's seems to be the result of the death of the cholinergic nerve cells deep in the brain below the cortex, way down in the medial septal nucleus, the diagonal band of Broca and particularly in the nucleus basalis of Meynert."

"I can't remember all that."

"There's no need for you to remember. What I am telling you is that we have taken the first few tiny steps toward what could be, someday, a solution—just as we use L-dopa to improve the production of the neurotransmitter dopamine in Parkinson's disease. It is not my wish to crush your hopes for your father, but I would say, after a brief examination, that he has deteriorated too much for any hope of improvement. The dead nerves will not regenerate. I would guess that fifteen or twenty years from now we might be able to give perceptible help to people in the first stages of Alzheimer's."

"What will happen to him?"

Narramore shrugged. "Any remaining motivation and drive will decline. There will be a severe blunting of affect, to the extent you may well see a shallow, fatuous euphoria. It is an atrophic process, and will end with a catatonic lack of response, incontinence and the need for constant nursing care."

"When?"

"From the history you have given me, I would suspect he also has some multi-infarct dementia which has hastened the decline. I would estimate eighteen months to two years before he reaches a total blunting, a vegetative state."

She closed her eyes tightly for a few moments, and then asked him, "Would a million dollars donated to your research efforts enable you to help Matthew Meadows in any way?"

"It's a great deal of money."

"The Gulfstream III which brought you down here from New York cost fourteen million dollars, Doctor."

"It would be very difficult for us to put an immediate one million dollars to effective use. We are way out at the far limits of a very esoteric area of research. We are dissecting brains which show a marked atrophy, with dilated ventricles and wide sulci. We use chemical analysis on the neurofibrillary tangles and the senile plaques, and also on those portions of the brain which seem to have remained in reasonable condition. At the same time we are following the progress of the disease in dozens of patients, administering tests, measuring behavior. We do not yet know the most basic fact, *why* brain cells are being lost. A million dollars would help, yes. It would be tucked away and the interest on it would enable us to train some young interns. But it would not give us any way to help your father. One hundred million dollars would not enable us to slow the destruction of the cells of his brain." He smiled in a sad way. "Your generosity makes it very tempting to lie to you."

"When he dies, Doctor, and when it can be made public what he died of, then I will see that you get a sizable grant for your work, provided you use his name in some way to identify it."

"That's very generous. I am grateful."

"I'm grateful to you for your straight talk, Doctor. I think we will be able to keep on taking care of him here."

"He will need nursing care twenty-four hours a day."

"That won't be a problem."

He hesitated. "I am probably stepping beyond the bounds of proper medical advice, but I can see how deeply this affects you." He tapped his temple with a forefinger. "The identity of a human being lies inside the skull. His personality, hopes, dreams, capacities for love and affection, everything that makes up the whole person. As the brain dies—as his is dying—the identity fades. He becomes someone else. When you are with him and try to think of him in the old terms, in the way he once was, you only punish yourself for no good reason, and you confuse that new limited being which has taken over his brain. The father you knew is dead."

"My father will live forever in heaven!" she said in the voice that could fill the Tabernacle.

He gave a little start of surprise and said, "Of course, of course." He stood up. "I would like to get back as soon as possible."

"Nothing is going to take off in this. Not until late tomorrow, I'd guess. But we'll do the best we can. Thank you again."

A moment after he left, the lights flickered and she knew that the power had failed and the Meadows Center generators had cut in almost instantaneously. She wept.

Rick Liddy sat behind his big walnut slate-top desk in his small concrete office on the ground floor of Communications and watched Eliot Erskine take off his transparent raincoat and shake the drops off it onto the gray carpet before hanging it up.

"Frog strangler out there," Liddy said. "Radio says nine inches in Lakemore since ten this morning. That comes to near two inches an hour."

During the three years Erskine had worked for Liddy, the two men had arrived at a moderately comfortable relationship. They were both loners, both dedicated to the law, both intent on keeping fit. They often worked out together at the University gym. They both liked neatness, liked the ends tied firm and tight. And they both sometimes wished they were back in actual law enforcement—even at lower pay and less comfortable living conditions. They trusted each other, as much as they were capable of trusting anyone.

Erskine had asked for the appointment with such formal ceremony that Liddy knew it was important. Before he sat down facing Liddy, Erskine put a canvas zipper bag on the desk with such care that Liddy knew it contained whatever the hell Erskine wanted to talk about.

Beyond Erskine, on the wall twelve feet away, was a large map of the Meadows Center areas, with all the security areas and stations marked in different color codes.

"This could take a little time," Erskine said.

"Who's going anywhere? I told the girl to hold the calls."

"In the last week in January, Rick, you put me on what I guess you could call part-time detached service to the Reverend F. Walter Macy. You told me you didn't know what it was about, but Macy wanted me to keep it to myself. Which I have. Until now. You told me that if what he wanted me to do interfered with my regular duties, I should come to you. I was able to handle it okay."

"Has Walter Macy released you to talk to me?"

"No, sir. It's just that I think I should."

Rick Liddy leaned back and frowned at Erskine. Liddy was a ruddy and muscular man with stone eyes and black hair parted precisely in the middle. Silence is at times a useful way of asking a question.

"I think I finished the job he asked me to do," Erskine said, "and I just don't see the point in keeping on with it. He's not going to get any more than he's got already."

"And you *do* know, Elly, that Macy is number one in line after the brother and sister. In one sense we're both working for him."

"Rick, I just don't know how to explain why I thought it was time to come to you unless I show you this stuff. There's another thing, too. Walter Macy ordered me not to keep any copies of anything. But when I realized what he wanted, I knew I had to save my own ass by saving at least some of it."

"Up until now, I've trusted your judgment," Liddy said.

"The way it all began, the way Walter told me it began, it seems that right after Christmas there was some kind of foul-up on the phone lines and he heard John Tinker Meadows making some kind of date with a woman, time and place unknown. He tried to find out about it on his own, but he was afraid John Tinker would discover that Walter was trying to tail him. So he got you to assign me, without telling you what he wanted me to do."

"So you tailed John Tinker Meadows. That's really beautiful."

Erskine unzipped the canvas case and took out a sheaf of color prints. He came around the desk saying, "I did the lab work myself, of course. Made extra prints of some of them, and turned the others and the negatives over to Doctor Macy. It took me three or four weeks to unravel it. It was kind of delicate work, because they hole up in a pretty remote spot. Here is a photograph of the old white double-wide trailer. The two cars are parked over there to the left of the picture beyond that stand of live oaks. Her yellow Rabbit convertible and the blue Ford van he draws out of the motor pool. That water in front is Burden Pond, and I took these from a little ridge up the hill from the pond, in the scrub-pine woods.

"Now here are a dozen I took with the twelve hundred lens when they'd come outdoors on nice winter days for what they call a little al fresco. I took maybe ten rolls of the outdoor fun and games but these show the faces best. It's like a sixty-power telescope."

"I know. Say! This here is Mrs. Wintergarten!"

"The very same."

"Oh Christ! Oh holy bleeding Christ!"

"They aren't in any special order."

Liddy went through them like a man playing a very slow game of solitaire. "Absolutely great ass on that woman," he murmured.

Erskine had gone back to his chair. He took out the little tape recorder and put a cassette on it. Before he pressed the key for playback, he said, "I wired the place and used a voice-actuated recorder. It didn't work real great. You miss the first word or half the first word every time it starts up again. I gave all the tapes to Doctor Macy, but before I did, I played them back and copied some parts of them on to this tape. I got about an hour here of this and that. I pulled the recorder and I haven't told Doctor Macy I'm quitting. This damned thing has turned into overkill. And it's boring, and, speaking as a police officer, he's got all he needs to make his case. The son of the founder is screwing an employee's wife."

"Where is this place?"

Erskine explained how to get there, and told him that it was land which had been donated to the Church.

"Let's hear what you've got."

Erskine turned it on. The fidelity was reasonably good. It was a rackety bed. In extremis, the woman liked to yell dirty words. Erskine had selected excerpts which confirmed identity through the specifics of their conversations.

"That's enough," Liddy said, and Erskine punched it off.

"What's happening is, it is winding down," Erskine said. "They used to do a lot of laughing and tell jokes and try a lot of different ways of doing it. I could tell about that from the way they would tell each other what to do next. But now they grouse and fight, and from the way they complain, the sex isn't as good as it was."

Liddy went back to one of the pictures and studied it. "That son of a gun is a lot better hung than I would have guessed. He's a real bull."

"When I first found out what was wanted of me, I didn't want to do it. I thought of coming right back to you."

"I would have told you to go right ahead."

"Why?"

"You never had to be political, Elly."

"Sometimes in Atlanta it seemed pretty political."

"Not like Uncle Sugar. The more you know about everybody around you, the longer you last. And the better you make out. Look at it the other way. You refuse to tail the big man, I back you up, then what happens when Walter Macy takes over?"

He picked up the Kodacolor prints and leafed through them again. "I heard rumors. But you know something? I thought he had more sense. My God, he's a national figure. He went after this like a schoolboy. Real dumb. If he wants some great ass on the side, the way to get it is line up somebody you can trust to go get it for you. And not here. In Vegas or L.A. or Houston. It's bush league to go sneaking off with the wife of one of your own people. It's dangerous. Worst of all, it's plain stupid."

"Agreed. Did I do right to stop at this point, Rick?"

"Without this here casework, no. With it, yes."

"What's his point, having me go on and on?"

Rick Liddy thought it over, rubbing his knuckles along the blue stubble on his jaw line. "Let's say he couldn't figure out what to do with it. If he wants to knock John Tinker out of there so he can move in, who does he take that crap to? Fat sister? She wouldn't forgive the messenger. He could take it right to John Tinker and tell him to move over, or else. Or else what? That's what John Tinker would ask him. Does he find some anonymous way to slip it to Rolf Wintergarten? So Rolf shoots his wife, and then John Tinker and then himself. And when all the laundry is hung out to dry, Walter Macy might find himself kicked out by Mary Margaret, who would be very likely to find out what he did and how he did it."

"This stuff is too raw for publication anywhere," Erskine said. "But maybe if some magazine had it locked in the vault, they could go ahead and do some action-proof articles on the Reverend Doctor John Tinker Meadows. Juicy ones."

"The sort of thing that Mrs. Owen from that *Out Front* magazine could have been looking for."

They were policemen and their minds worked in a police fashion, having been shaped and formed by early knowledge of the infinite capacity for evil and misadventure the human animal possesses. They sat silently, with Richard Liddy looking blindly at the security map that covered the blank wall, and Elly Erskine staring out at the curtain of rain beyond the windows and not seeing it.

Erskine spoke first. "I'd say she wasn't alone with him more than one and a half minutes before I went hurrying into his office. She didn't ring true. She set off all my bells."

"Ninety seconds isn't much time."

"Time enough to set something up."

After another long silence Erskine said, "And it could be why he can't let go, why he can't tell me to quit. He wants it to look to me and maybe to his wife as if he is still gathering information, and has never made any attempt to use it."

"Provided he let his wife know about it. What are we trying to do here?" Liddy asked irritably. "What have we got here anyway? Isn't this supposed to be some kind of church?"

"We're both members, Rick."

"We have to be. Sure. But aside from that, I would be anyway. It answers something for me. It fills up some kind of hole I used to have inside me. It means a lot to Martha and me. It means we'll never lose each other, no matter what. How about you?"

"I don't know. The time I feel the presence of God is when I take time off and walk across the countryside. The growing things and the birds and the small animals. It fits together into a plan that I don't think could ever have happened by accident. And I don't think I'm the end product of a series of accidents. The machinery is too complicated."

"Okay, so the Church is valuable and worth protecting and we are part of the machinery of protection, Elly. So where do we go from here?"

"I think I better tell Doctor Macy I have to beg off because you've given me some extra duty and I won't have enough time."

"And see how he acts?"

"If he gets really nasty mad, we've been thinking bad thoughts. If he just blusters around a little, or acts relieved, are you going to try to follow up on anything?"

"I don't know. I just don't know. I might go back through the records and see if I can find out where he was on the afternoon and night of the seventh of May."

"As employees and as members of the Church, Rick, isn't it our duty to eliminate him as a possible choice?"

"If we can. Yes. I guess so. He works hard. He puts in long hours. He does all those programs and he's forever going out of town as a guest preacher. I wish the old man was still functioning. He was fantastic. You came aboard in time to hear him, didn't you?"

"He was great. Let me put it this way: he was so great I don't want Walter Macy, like they say, wearing his moccasins."

"A strong church shouldn't depend on just one man."

They sat in silence, thinking of their shared dilemma.

Erskine got up. He told Rick to keep three or four of the photographs, just in case. Keep them in the vault. He said he'd bring Rick a dupe of the tape. He said he'd report on Doctor Macy's reaction. And, holding the canvas bag under his raincoat, he headed down the hall toward the torrent outside.

When the heavy rain began, Jenny Albritton had to suspend her guided tour of Meadows Center, cancel the helicopter flight and drive the female reporter from *Out Front* back to the Meadows Center Motor House. She parked and went in with her to make certain her deluxe reserved rooms on the second floor in the rear, overlooking the fields and farmlands, were now ready for occupancy.

As she had been taking the woman around, to the Tabernacle, the University grounds, the Settlements, the Mall, she had been trying to get some clues about her attitude toward the Eternal Church. Carolyn Pennymark was in her late twenties, Jenny guessed, with a mop of tangled chestnut-brown hair, a small delicate face with pointed nose and slightly receding chin, prominent upper teeth. She wore glasses with very large lavender lenses and thin silver frames. She was slender, except for a meatiness of hip and thigh, wore a wrinkled brown blouse, baggy khaki pants and running shoes. She carried a huge canvas shoulder bag, and when she asked questions of Jenny Albritton, she taped the question and the answer on a little mini-cassette Sony, and from time to time she took photographs, using a Leica so old that the white metal showed shiny where she held it and pressed the shutter and the film advance.

When Jenny had glanced sidelong at Carolyn Pennymark several times, she'd decided that the woman had the face of a surly fourteen-year-old boy, blank, skeptical, indifferent and clean of any suggestion of makeup. Jenny left her at a table in the motel coffee shop, saying she'd be back in a minute, and soon she returned from the desk carrying a large brown envelope. As she sat, she placed it in front of Miss Pennymark. "This is our press package, and I've added some other material that may help you understand us better. Now even though the Church organization had absolutely nothing to do with the . . . disappearance of your colleague, we want you to be our guest."

The Pennymark woman stared gloomily at her. "I don't like this shit, lady. I didn't come down on promo."

Jenny shrugged. "It's nothing I had anything to do with. Mr. Efflander talked yesterday to Mr. Jeremy Rosen."

"Who is Efflander and who is Rosen? Just for starters."

"Mr. Rosen runs the conglomerate that owns your magazine and he is a friend and supporter of the Eternal Church. Mr. Efflander is the chief administrative officer here. It's all been arranged. Look, I think I know how you feel. I've worked on newspapers."

"I bet you have."

"Are you trying to be rude, Miss Pennymark?"

"I'm not trying to be anything at all, pal. I don't have to be anything or do anything except look this freak farm over and write a story." The no-color eyes behind lavender lenses were unblinking.

"All right, so this is awkward for you."

"I didn't say that."

"I wouldn't have set it up this way."

"I don't care what you've set up. What I don't want is any more guided tour, okay? If you have one all set up, forget it. Guided tours have a funny smell. They steer you away from anything interesting."

Jenny Albritton looked down at her fists and took a deep breath. "What are you trying to be, for God's sake? Are you trying out for a part? You want to be Barbara Waawaa? Get off me a minute."

"I want us both to get everything clear."

"Hooray for clarity. You have a gold badge in there. Wear it in some kind of visible place on that ragbag blouse. You have the ID card with your picture. On the back of the card are the places you can't get into. The money room. The computer rooms. Upstairs in the Manse. Otherwise you can go clopping around in your army boots anywhere you please, and the hell with you!"

Pennymark smiled. "Hey, there's a living person inside there, huh? Thanks for all your help, Jenny baby. Anyway, don't sweat it. If anything gets published out of this, we can both be surprised."

"Mr. Efflander's arrangement with Mr. Rosen is that they will publish whatever you wish to write about the Meadows Center."

"How nice! I don't have any angle at all."

"Don't expect one from me."

"I wouldn't even ask. Lindy Rooney Owen is stale news. She has slipped off the end of page eighty-five. They teamed us three times, God only knows why. She never did hard news in her life. She was the kind that, on a paper, you would send her to cover the school board budget meeting. On *Out Front* they'd send her to find out why a star walked off a set and cost Warner's five mil, or if Rod Muscle in his new underwater special is futzing around with Marilyn Boobs who was all set to get married to Vinnie Invincible."

"So what are you doing on that magazine if you are such a red-hot investigative reporter, dearie?"

She smiled again. "God only knows. They must have bought me with all that money. Or maybe they wanted to look as if they had something to do with real news. Anyway, we've got no clue why Lindy Prettypants came down here. It was a self-assignment. And it probably had something to do with some kind of tea party or gala on the green. They told me at the office her husband is down here."

"I wouldn't know about that."

"Of course you wouldn't know about that because it doesn't have anything to do with PR. I know where he's staying."

"I'll tell you one thing that has to do with PR, Miss Pennymark. The Meadows family has always been totally cooperative with the media. There was no reason for her to use an assumed name and some kind of cover story down here."

"The reason would be what a pal of mine calls dramatic ignorance. That's what happens when people try to spice their lives with what they see on the tube. Cops try to act like Hill Street. PR ladies try to be Leslie Stahl. What's the generally accepted version around here of what happened to Lindy? That is, if you're not too pissed at me to tell me."

"I'll answer your questions because that's my job. I don't have to enjoy it. Nobody has any proof, of course, but the thing that seems most likely is that she left Saturday night or early Sunday morning to drive down to the city and catch her flight. Somebody got in the car with her somehow. Maybe she had car trouble. Maybe somebody forced her off the road. So they raped her and robbed her on some little lumber company road, buried her and her suitcases and stuff, then looked at the rental papers in the glove compartment and took the car down and left it in the airport parking lot and walked away."

Pennymark made a face, twisting her mouth. "Christ, what a dingy way for Miss Priss to die. Lindy was the kind of person, if there was a full-length mirror, she'd undress in the closet."

"Excuse me, dear, but you won't get much cooperation from the Church people here if you take the name of the Lord in vain, and if you use generally foul language."

Carolyn gave her a long expressionless stare, and then said, too sweetly, "Oh, do forgive me!"

"Of course." She looked at her watch. "And I've got miles to go before I sleep. I left you lots of background material. Just sign for anything you might want to eat or drink. I really think it would be very helpful to you to read the material, no matter what you think of the whole operation here. It will give you an . . . overview that will save you time."

" 'Overview.' I like that. That's real classy. I'll read it, just the way I've been reading everything I could get my hands on about all these electronic preachers ever since I found out I might be coming down here. My own overview. Of Falwell, Jim and Tammy Bakker, the Armstrongs, the Crystal Cathedral and all the rest of them."

"Maybe you should stay in this afternoon and this evening. The weather is looking terrible. I can pick you up for a helicopter ride tomorrow if you like."

"No like," Pennymark said. "I'll rip through this stuff and then maybe you can fix up a car for me to rent and a map of the area."

"Driving could get very difficult."

"Everything in this world can get very difficult sooner or later, love. Thanks for all the attention."

Carolyn Pennymark finished her coffee and went up and inspected her small suite. It looked out on heavy rain coming down, rain heavier than she had seen in a long time. She unpacked with the speed and efficiency of long practice, trying to remember the last time she'd had a suite all to herself. She stretched out on the bed nearest the window and called the office, asking the switchboard for Marty Gehman's extension.

"This is me, old buddy, down here in Bible country, with it all arranged for God to pick up the tab for everything. You wouldn't have been in on that, would you?"

"No way. It all went on at a level I will never attain, Carrie. So enjoy. It could never happen again."

"What I've got here is a darling little suite. Blue and gray and rugs you can lose your feet in, and big windows and a bathroom bigger than my place on Fifty-eighth. I was met by PR. Why do all the PR women look alike?"

"Like what?"

"You know. Every one I've practically ever met is blonde with long elegant legs, cornflower eyes, golden hair, big round boobs and a round little ass, both in constant bobbing motion. As many white teeth as a harpsichord. An infectious grin. And everything they say has an exclamation point after it."

"Baby, you sound like you were back to practicing your Joan Didion imitation."

"Okay, so I should save it for my book. Good thinking. Anyway, I had a note on my desk about where Lindy's husband is staying down here and I need it. It's the top sheet on the blue memo pad, okay?"

He came back on the line in a couple of minutes. "It is called the County Line Motel. And you got a pencil, I'll give you the number." After she had written it down, he said, "Otherwise, how are things?"

"I've got a lot of material here I am going to read. It is raining outside as hard as I ever saw. I keep hearing thunder bumping, and I can hear the chimes in their big Tabernacle through the sound of the rain. My early impression is that the money comes into this place like it was coming down a coal chute."

"You old enough to remember coal chutes?"

"Marty, I am old enough to read about everything. You know, it's kind of nice country around here. Rolling hills, meadows, orchards, reminds me of a part of France I was in once. It ought to be pretty when the sun comes out. If it ever does again."

"Carrie, you get any feeling of cover-up there?"

"They seem to be straining to prove there's nothing to hide. And all of us big-time magazine persons know that means one of two things. Either they have or they haven't."

"Shrewd, kid. Very shrewd."

She heard a cracking sound on the line and then a quick loud slam of thunder. "Hey, goodbye. Lightning too close!" She hung up. She had turned the bed light on. It was darker in the room.

She read all the literature. She had never had to take a speed-reading course. She came from a family of compulsive readers. If you didn't finish a book quickly enough, somebody took it when you weren't looking. The light kept flickering and the storm seemed anchored directly over the motel.

When the phone rang she answered it reluctantly and cautiously. "Miss Pennymark? Albritton here. I won't be able to provide a car, either rental or from our pool. I'm sorry."

"I'll give it a try."

"I thought you would," she said, and hung up.

There were four rental agencies. Delegates from the Congress of Christian Leadership, a thousand strong, were due to arrive late that afternoon, and the Hertz, Avis, Budget and Dollar agencies in Lakemore said they were completely out of cars of any kind.

She phoned the County Line Motel and a woman with a southern accent rang Roy Owen's room. When he answered, Carolyn said, "I don't want to stay on the phone too long because the lightning is scaring me witless. I never saw lightning like this anywhere. I'm a friend of Lindy's from the magazine down here to do a story on the investigation. I'm Carolyn Pennymark. I was going to get a car and come out there, but I can't rent one or borrow one. I'm at the Meadows Center Motor House, number two-four-two. If you're not too busy, and if you have a car, can you come in and talk?"

It was almost an hour before he arrived. She had finished the club sandwich and coffee she'd asked them to send up to the suite. She was brushing her hair when they rang up to tell her a Mr. Owen was there. She told them to send him up, and she unchained her door and left it ajar.

He was of the stature she expected, as Lindy had told her about Roy, but the mustache surprised her. Lindy hadn't mentioned that. But she should have expected it, she thought. It was a cliché among urban men, especially those in stocks and banking.

He apologized for taking so long, telling her of the floods in the road and going the long way around. He apologized for how his raincoat was dripping on her rug.

She gave him her warmest smile and said, "Lindy was very dear to me, Roy. I miss her terribly. We worked together many times and she was marvelous to work with. I know you've been staying here, trying to find out what happened. I wonder if you'd save me some precious time by telling me what you've done and what you think?"

It took him an hour. She had to ask very few questions. He had an orderly mind, and a better gift for description of people and their attitudes than she had expected from a stocks and bonds person. It did not bother him when she scribbled the occasional note.

"Would you have gone at it like she did?" he asked her.

"I suppose it would depend on what I was looking for."

"Scandal in high places. Sex, misuse of funds, whatever."

She shrugged. "I wouldn't lurk. Not my style. I go after people with questions. Hard questions. Lots of people. And pretty soon the answers don't fit as well as they did in the beginning. So I keep at them until somebody rats on the others."

"I wish she'd tried it your way, Miss Pennymark."

"You going to stop calling me Carrie, Roy?"

"Sorry. Maybe you could use your system to find out what happened to Lindy."

"When everybody says they don't know, my system doesn't work. I run out of questions too fast. You've been around here a while, Roy. I've read their handouts. I'm beginning to get some ideas about the whole operation, but I'd like to hear yours. I mean, is this whole Center a Good Thing, in caps?"

He frowned and got up and wandered over to look out at the rain, hands locked behind him. "Compared to what?"

"Now there's a direct answer if I ever heard one."

He turned, smiling. "I'm by nature a measurer. I measure things against things, ideas against ideas. When the weather changes and you can walk around out there with the pilgrims and go to services, you get the feeling you see a lot of very happy and relaxed faces. They smile at one another and nod and speak. They are emotional. They cry easily. They seem to be . . . opened up. There is kind of a temptation to be carried along with them into whatever it is that makes them feel so . . . so secure and so loved."

"Compared to what?"

He shrugged. "Compared to any city street, I guess. Or compared to the congregation in the Lutheran church my family attended when I was a boy. That seemed dim and remote and rigid compared to this."

"And there are religions where people whip each other and kill the infidels and so on. It can get pretty gummy, right?"

"I suppose."

"These national congregations are something brand-new under the sun, Roy. They have one hell of a lot of clout. I was listening to some of the sermons that get broadcast from satellites before I came down here. They are strong and they contain a lot of nonsense. Right to life. Abortion is murder. I got over any chance I ever had to fall for that syrup when I did a story on the way little kids have to be warehoused in the big cities. Unwanted and unloved. They're brought into the world and there are not enough people to hold them, walk them, talk to them, bounce them up and down. That's the way babies learn, you know. So what happens? Those kids don't learn to talk until they are between two and three. Most of them don't learn to walk before they are two because they get no training, no chance, no practice. They are warehoused in cribs where all the attendants can do is work from one end of the huge rooms to the other feeding and changing them and ignoring them. Know what I would like to do if I was queen of the world? I would take a couple of platoons of those big elegant steely-eyed broads who think babies are too dandy to be aborted, and make them work the warehouses for a year, telling them that their job would be to turn those infants into human beings, people who would not have stunted minds and stunted emotions, and who would not go out on the streets like animals to rob and kill the helpless."

She noticed the way he was staring at her. "Hey, I'm sorry. It made a big impression on me, and I keep on unloading every chance I get. Aside from that, the electronic preachers have a lot of other brands of shit. Amurrica for Amurricans. Everybody who really wants a job can find one. Let's drop the big one on the dirty red Commie menace. Keep that Jap junk off our highways. Help our poor hardworking millionaire farmers. Let's stop the press from destroying Amurrica by shaking the people's faith in their institutions. They don't miss a chance, Roy. They say the things they know will feed ignorance and hate and superstition because the listeners express their approval in money, and money buys more air time."

"Is all that in the handouts?" he asked.

"All carefully and delicately and persuasively said. But it's there if you look for it."

"People always find what they look for, Carrie."

"Excuse me all to hell, friend. Did I step on your toes?"

"No. Nothing like that. In my line of work you get suspicious of simplistic analyses. I get the impression they tell their congregations some good things too."

She slung her legs over the arm of the chair. "Okay, okay. I come from the grubby streets of the naked city. In my line of work you look for the worst and you find it all the time. So you get conditioned. They tell me I can go talk to anybody I want except old Matthew Meadows. Jenny

Whatever told me he's too far gone. So I can talk to John the Tinker, and fat sister and anybody else. But that won't have anything to do with Lindy, will it?"

"Nothing at all."

"Thanks a lot for your help, Roy."

"I remember Lindy mentioning you. You say you went on assignments with her?"

"That's right."

"I hate to say this. I was married to her and I never really felt as if I knew her. She was such a private person. And I was wondering how . . . I mean, if she was . . . well, when you were out of town with her if . . ."

"Why, practically every night Lindy and me, we'd go to a cocktail lounge or a disco and pick us up a couple of Travolta-type kids and bring them back to the room and purely bang them out of their little wits."

For a moment he looked startled, and then he laughed. "Okay. Okay. It isn't exactly what I was going to ask. I think I wanted to ask you if you ever got to know her. If you and she ever talked about me or being married, or if she was happy."

"Roy, believe me. I never got to know her. I thought she was just about the most repressed woman I ever came in contact with. She could rattle on for an hour about how Tuchman researched the fourteenth century, but if you told her she had pretty legs and a nice bod, she'd look at you as though you did something nasty on the rug. You know what? I couldn't believe she'd given birth to a kid because I could never quite imagine her screwing anybody. I think something messed her up when she was little."

"I've wondered about that."

She studied him, head tilted. "Makes for a pretty tough kind of marriage, huh?"

"We managed."

"Sure. Look, I think if I get somewhere among the holy, they can get me back here somehow. How about you drop me off at the Manse? Can you do that?"

"They won't let me drive through the gate. You'll get wet going from the gate to the entrance."

"Maybe there will be a Christian with an umbrella."

It was three-thirty when he dropped her off at the guard cubicle, and after she showed her credentials, a man took her inside and apparently phoned the Manse, because minutes later a man came trotting out of the Manse and opened an umbrella before coming to get Carolyn. When Roy saw that, he headed back toward the County Line Motel, hoping he could get through.

The Reverend Sister Mary Margaret Meadows had come down to the lounge and taken Carolyn Pennymark back up to her third-floor suite. As they talked generalities, Carolyn was trying to devise a way to describe this woman in this setting. A large woman. A very large woman. A very large pink woman with golden hair and a lovely smile and a contralto voice which could probably shatter beer mugs if she gave it a good try.

"Many many times," Mary Margaret said, "we get discouraged, but there would be no point at all in denying you people a chance to talk to us, would there?"

"Just what are 'you people'?"

"From the media, dear. We try our best to explain but then they go away and what they do . . . there's an expression you would know . . . oh yes, they take a cheap shot. That is to say, they take some very minor thing and make it sound as if we were rural barbarians down here. I think it is because of how quickly this all grew from practically nothing."

"May I take notes?"

"Of course, my dear. They don't ever stop to realize that maybe the Eternal Church of the Believer grew so fast from its small beginnings when my father was the only pastor because it said something to people they badly needed to hear. It gave them some simple rules which make life simpler in a terribly confusing era."

"And you agree with all those rules, Sister?"

"In essence, yes."

"In other words, you've sought no medical help for your father?"

Mary Margaret turned red with anger and visibly brought it under control. She smiled and said, "What was that phrase again? Cheap shot. You can take cheap shots and there is no way to stop you except by ordering you out, and I am not going to do that. I want to make you understand. Years and years ago Matthew Meadows had an older brother he worshipped. That brother went into the hospital with a fever. They said he would be out in a few days, but he died there, suddenly. A friend who stayed home with the same symptoms recovered quickly. I am not talking about logic now. Where the mind and the body are so inter-related, nobody really knows how much the mind has to do with curing the illnesses of the body. We do know, from independent surveys, that the Church membership is, on the whole, a healthier and longer-lived group than the public at large."

"There could be other variables."

"Of course. We know that. But we are slowly, slowly relaxing our stipulations about seeking medical help. It used to be you went to a doctor with an open wound or a broken bone. We are adding a little bit at a time. A sore that won't heal. A sudden weight loss. Great thirst combined with weariness. My father would never've let that happen but he . . . has not been in touch with these things lately."

"What about not voting, not belonging to clubs or political parties?"

"What about it? The world is very diverse. A willing and suggestible person can be talked into diffusing his energies in a dozen pointless directions. Most people would love a good reason to say no to solicita-tions, and we provide the reason. The Church is all the organization people really need, outside the home."

"This is a very elegant place to live."

"Is that a question? I would agree. Yes, it is. I find it quite pleasant. But not necessary to my spiritual health."

"How much money does the Church take in in a year?"

"I think that probably Mr. Efflander knows, and my brother, and Reverend Deets. But I pay very little attention to that. It's fair to tell you that if I did know, I wouldn't tell you."

"Why not?"

"I would tell you only if I could also tell you how much the Church spends each year in good works, and you would promise to publish both figures."

"Fair enough, I guess. Do you have any comment to make about the death of Linda Rooney Owen?"

Her eyes widened. "Did they find her body?"

"Not yet."

"Then legally it is a disappearance, isn't it?"

"Legally, yes."

"We live in strange times, Miss Pennymark. People find their lives so difficult, with so many demands for so few rewards, that they often just merely . . . walk away from their life and never return."

"Lindy was content with her life and her work. Would you have any idea why she came down here?"

"I must say I don't like people coming down here and pretending to be somebody they are not. It would indicate to me that they are after some kind of scandal that doesn't exist."

"Now just a minute, Sister. Are you trying to tell me that with that whole band of fifty golden Angels you keep on tap, young healthy and beautiful girls, and all the staff men around here and the students and visiting clergy and the guys from the stores and working in security, you never have any kind of trouble?"

"Of course there's problems from time to time. Human nature is a problem, Miss Pennymark, as you may have noticed in your travels. The more mature people are, the better they are able to manage their lives. But the problems of young people adjusting to life wasn't the reason Mrs. Owen came down here, was it?"

"I wouldn't think so. I don't know why she came."

"Are you happy in your work?"

"What? Well . . . sure."

"And you feel fulfilled by it?"

"Sister, I do what I do, and I do it better than most, and I take some satisfaction in that. I am like a very dependable dog. They throw a stick into a jungle and I can go in there and bring it back. Fulfilled has the sound of home and kiddies. The guys I work with, I can't see them in that context either."

"You like being your own person."

"Exactly."

"Is there room in your life for God?"

"Sister, I had eight little pins fastened together that dangled from here to here, celebrating perfect attendance at the Sunday School of the Salvation Baptist Church in Kingsport, Tennessee. I was the next to the youngest one of four girls, and we all wore all those pins, and they got married and I didn't. They go to church and I don't. And I go visit lots and lots of nephews and nieces and get along with them fine. I try to do unto others the way I always wish they would do unto me. All except the fawners and the fakers and the political animals. I show them no mercy. Do you believe?"

Mary Margaret looked startled. "What do you mean? Of course I believe!"

"Really, really, really? Way down in the bottom of your heart, you know the truth?"

Mary Margaret leaned toward her. "I believe in life everlasting, in God and Jesus Christ and the teachings in the Bible. I live according to what I believe in, and conduct myself accordingly. I have absolute confidence God is watching over me and that when I pray He is there to listen."

Carolyn looked down at her pad. There was nothing to take any notes about, not in that profession of faith. She had talked to very plausible scoundrels over the years, and to the most skilled and practiced liars. This giant woman had a total sincerity, an almost childish confidence in her faith and in an ultimate justice.

"Then I can ask you something that bothers me?"

"Of course."

"Lots of money comes in here from hundreds of thousands of donors. It comes pouring in. It's a flood. Okay. I don't think I'm being a cynic when I say that it's a good bet that little dribbles of it are being diverted into the wrong pockets. Not stealing, exactly. Bad judgment mostly. But it is happening. And according to what I read today, money is supposed to be a kind of prayer. Stealing a prayer would be the worst kind of sin, I guess. So here's the question. How do you keep on justifying your faith in the middle of a situation where there is so much money and so much power people are taking unfair advantage?"

Mary Margaret thought for a little while. "I had to cut that question into pieces. First of all, I don't have to go around justifying my faith. I have it. It has always been there. It is as real as my hands to me. Secondly, it would be presumptuous for me to judge anybody else. Judgment is the Lord's. And I am confident that when the time comes for each individual, he or she will be judged according to his or her life. It will be judged on balance. Our Church members are mostly wonderful people leading wonderful lives of service and joy. They will deserve heaven, just as I hope I will."

Carolyn Pennymark felt simultaneously moved and exasperated. She slapped her notebook shut and dropped the pencil into her oversized purse, and took out the Leica.

Mary Margaret flushed and said, "I take very bad pictures."

"I hope you won't mind if I try. I'll do my best to make it a good one."

"Do the people you work for expect this of you? And of me?"

"Yes, ma'am," she said, startling herself.

She moved in close as she had been taught and took three, with the light behind the woman on the third exposure, and the lens turned slightly out of focus. She thanked her. Mary Margaret phoned down to have a car brought around, and then she walked her down to the en-

trance. At the motel she tried to tip the driver but he refused it. She had
to run three steps through the roaring rain to get into shelter. When she
got up to the room she realized she was bone tired. She did not know
why she should be. Usually she had a great deal of energy, and it went
on and on for days without cease. Something about Mary Margaret had
tired her. It was almost as if she had worn herself out holding great doors
closed against some sort of invasion.

When she awoke it was past eleven and she was hungry. She hurried
down to the coffee shop. As she ate her waffle she looked at the three
middle-aged women at a nearby table. They sat in silence. Two of them
looked enough alike to be sisters. One of the sisters sat with tears slowly
leaking out of her eyes and rolling down her expressionless face. One
woman patted the weeper's hand from time to time, and the other one
reached and dabbed at the tears with a paper napkin.

They must come from all over, Carolyn thought. All over hell and
gone, bring their heartbreak right here to the Meadows family, knowing
that the pain will be helped. Confident it will be. And what a dreadful,
constant, nagging responsibility *that* has to be. Suffer the little people to
come unto Me. Maybe the weepers are the lucky ones. I can't even locate
the place where I hurt, or find out why. It only hurts when I don't laugh.

Thirteen

At four in the morning on Wed-
nesday, August seventeenth, the huge rains stopped so abruptly the
silence awakened many people at Meadows Center from sound sleep.

Glinda Lopez awoke from a dream about her husband, so vivid she
reached her arm out to touch him and rapped her fingers against the
dormitory wall close to her narrow bed. In the dream he had been trying
to tell her something. The words were at the back edge of her mind and
slipped away into darkness as she tried to recall them. Only the cadence
and timbre of his voice was left. There was a dampness on her pillow

and she knew she had been crying in her sleep, but she didn't know why, or for whom. She sat up and blew her nose. She could hear the subliminal thud of some college kid playing music at a forbidden time.

John Tinker Meadows had been wide awake when the rain stopped. He had been wondering whether he should go into the bathroom and get ten grains of Valium. He had slept heavily in the early part of the night and then awakened with the feeling that every nerve had been pulled to such a tightness it thrummed like silver wire. Was Tom Daniel Birdy trying to be cute, trying to improve the offer, or was he serious about going his own way? If he joined up, could he be eased into the number-two slot without upsetting Walter Macy? If Walter Macy got too upset, he would take it to the Council of the ministers of the affiliated churches. He had built up a power bloc which he could not use against any Meadows, but would certainly use against Birdy. And what good had it done to spend another fourteen thousand on the old man, bringing the famous British doctor over? Mary Margaret's idea. Just to tell them what they already knew.

Made for an interesting theological paradox. Where was the old man's soul these days? It certainly wasn't in his body. If it was, it had died. It was gone, thus disproving everything the old man had so earnestly believed. Maybe, if it had no self-awareness, the soul could still be there in his body. But if souls had no awareness of self whatsoever, what was the point in going to heaven? Where was the everlasting life? There had to be some kind of special limbo, jam-packed full of all the old people's souls. Their souls had fled, but their bodies were still tied to earth, just like all those people on machines all over the world in the hospitals, brain dead. Miracles of modern medicine. Maybe, he thought, that is exactly the kind of afterlife I want, one without any self-awareness at all. So where is my reward? And my punishment? What if all of it, every smidgin, is right here? Heaven and hell on earth. And, thinking of punishment, how much does Rolf know? Or suspect? Rolf's own damn fault for thinking he could marry all that rubbery vitality and keep it satisfied. Now we do it like enemies punishing each other. Take that! And that! So why not end it now? Tomorrow. She won't make a fuss. She's tired of it too. It shows. Whining when I can't wait long enough for her. Indifferent to my needs. Total self-absorption in the midst of passion, using me as she would use a vibrator for masturbation. Maybe the final sin is that of indifference. Subject for a sermon. Tell Spencer McKay to work it up.

He got up and took the Valium, and then went naked to the sliding doors and opened them and stepped from coolness out onto the shallow balcony. From that fourth-floor level he could see the perimeter lights, a dark silhouette outside a guard station, lifting the glow of a cigarette to his lips. The night air was warm and humid, and the bats were out, darting and dipping. He told himself it was time for a lasting vow of celibacy. Otherwise, the risks were too great and becoming greater. There was too much curiosity about him, too many people focusing on him in compulsive obsession. And in weary resignation he remembered he had vowed the same vow too many times before to have any belief he could keep it this time. Perhaps one of these days he would take a look at what's-her-name. Tracy something. What had Mag called her? The oldest Angel I've got. A Guardian Angel to keep me out of trouble. This last affair was not like the others. There wasn't any compelling desire to begin with. Went after Mrs. Wintergarten just to see if an affair this close to home could be managed. Found it could be. So? Tracy Bellwright! He could see the long blonde hair and the tall slender figure, but the face was blurred. Healthy and adoring. Extricate myself from this one and take a long rest and then see if I feel I can marry again. Mosquitoes began to whine around his ears, and he went back inside. As the Valium began to work, he yawned himself down into sleep.

The abrupt cessation of the heavy rain awoke Roy Owen. His sleep had been so profound he had no idea where he was. But soon in the faint seep of light around the drawn draperies he recognized the room, and remembered all of it, and realized that for the very first time he could recall, he could not find any plausible justification for his behavior. There was no good reason to stay on here. The rhythms of this life were so much less demanding he felt uneasy staying on. Things were gradually shifting out of focus up in Hartford. Too many changes in the portfolios where he had not followed the reasoning carefully, because he had not had the research materials at hand. An increasing chance of an ugly surprise. He had almost been caught in the Braniff thing, but his analysis of the cash flow indicated they couldn't make it, not for very much longer, not with that enormous expansion in a declining economic condition. So he had dumped it over three market days, taking a minor bruise, and had dictated the usual memo to himself indicating what his analysis had shown, and what his reasoning had been. They are always suspicious of a dump, suspecting insider information. A stupid rule, because it is a violation of the free market principle.

Time to head home. They'll never find Lindy. That's what the Sheriff was telling me.

When the end of the storm had awakened Peggy Moon she had discovered she was hungry. She put a robe on and went to the kitchen between the office and the owner's unit, and, squinting in the glare of fluorescence, she cut a wedge of sharp cheddar, poured herself a glass of skim milk and leaned back against the edge of the sink as she ate. As usual, she found herself thinking about Roy Owen, wondering about him. Such a nice quiet steady little guy. She couldn't imagine him being married to that burnished little woman, all glitter and polish and self-possession. Before the rain came, Roy had started taking long walks in the cool of the early morning, from first light until well past sunup. She wanted to walk with him, and wanted to ask him if she could. But she could not imagine why she was so reluctant. She could be back by check-out time. And there were never that many people to be checked out. And Fred would be up anyway to take care, if she wasn't back. Maybe he would be walking again this morning. She wondered what he thought about as he walked. The missing woman? Or maybe securities he wanted to buy and sell. Or maybe he thought about his little daughter, and the years of married life.

Down in Georgia, at the Purves farm, the rain had tapered off and stopped before midnight. Before they went to bed, Hub had put on his raincoat and boots and gone out with a flashlight to look at how high the water in the creek was getting. It had already covered half of her kitchen garden, and the three of them had picked everything pickable and ripe enough before the water reached it.

He came back in with his thinning hair soaked flat against his head and told them it was still coming up, but very slowly, and he didn't think it would do damage to anything else.

Before dawn the three of them were awakened by a thumping and grinding and breaking sound, and by the alarm of the chickens. When she went downstairs, after Hub and Dave had run out the back door, she found a couple of inches of dirty water covering the kitchen floor, and seeping into the living room, soaking and darkening the rug. She put on her rain cape and hood and went out into the yellow glare of the dooryard light, thinking that she would tell Hub and Dave to move the good furniture upstairs. There was a huge lake moving relentlessly across their property. It had knocked over the big hen house and rolled it over against the wire fence. She could see some drowned chickens wedged against the wire. More were roosting in the old peach trees. A sawhorse and a barn door from somewhere upstream came floating to jam against the wire, and as she watched, the back of her hand against her lips, the wire broke and the chicken house rolled through, smashing into the pump house and breaking it free of its foundation. She saw a chicken floating and it seemed to be moving, so she ran and grabbed it from a place where the water was up to her knees and she could feel the tug of it. The hen flopped loose in her hands, soaking wet, and something seemed to break inside Annalee. She screamed and, holding the chicken by the dead feet, she swung it against a fence post as hard as she could. Hub came running to her and she eluded him and kept yelling and slamming the chicken into wet feathered pulp, yelling, "I hate these goddamn chickens and this goddamn farm and every goddamn thing on it!"

Hub grabbed her and she dropped the chicken and turned into his arms, sobbing. "Honey," he said. "Honey, what's wrong with you! It's not that bad. We've had high water before. What's gone wrong?"

"Nothing. Everything. I don't know. I just don't know." She pushed herself away from him. "Come on. It's seeped up into the house. We got to take the television upstairs, and lots of other stuff. You and Dave take the big stuff and I'll gather up the little stuff."

"It won't come any higher."

"That's what you said last night. And look at how much damage we got! Just look at it!" And as she began to cry again, Hub led her, sloshing through high water, toward the back stoop, his arm around her waist.

When the silence awakened Jenny Albritton, and she realized the rain had finally stopped, she did not move for fear of awakening Jenny MacBeth. They were together like spoons, both on their left sides, and she was curled against Jenny MacBeth's back, her face near the nape of Jenny's neck, with Jenny's hair tickling her forehead. Jenny and Jenny, she thought, sometimes so entangled one forgot what belonged to who. And the name murmured with love could be hers or your own.

She thought about the quarrel. It had been the worst one they had ever had. It had come about because Jenny MacBeth had finally told her about the strange conversation with Efflander. She had been furious about not being told sooner. Jenny MacBeth said she didn't think it important enough. Jenny Albritton said that obviously Efflander knew of their relationship. Jenny MacBeth said that was a lot of nonsense, that nobody knew or needed to know. And Jenny Albritton said that was the trouble with their relationship, they had to keep it hidden from the world forever if they stayed here, and they should have the courage to quit their jobs and move to some place where they'd have more freedom. And Jenny MacBeth said she should make up her mind. She couldn't have it both ways. And they had good jobs and were well paid.

They had said ugly things to each other, things that brought tears, and then they had fallen into each other's arms, had slowly and tenderly undressed, and had made sweet, quiet, forgiving love for hours and hours.

Jenny MacBeth, who had begun this way of life long before she met Jenny Albritton, had told her that even though Jenny MacBeth, as the aggressor, would probably never change, she, Jenny Albritton, inasmuch as this was her first affair of this kind, could very probably, if she wished, resume her heterosexuality should she meet the right man. And it was this assurance by her older friend and lover that had made Jenny Albritton willing to continue the lesbian affair after the first seduction, with its accompanying remorse and guilt, and her aversion to the more intimate aspects of it, even though at times it made her feel as if her heart would leap out of her chest.

But now, with sweet Jenny MacBeth breathing deeply and steadily beside her, Jenny Albritton thought back to the events of the day, back to her irritation at that dreary little dirty-mouthed journalist who tried to look like some sort of urchin or combat veteran, and had acted as if Jenny Albritton was some sort of jolly cretin, amusing to a certain extent but definitely unimportant.

Such a ridiculous public image to create deliberately, she thought. Those little braless breasts waffling around under that ragamuffin blouse. Fatty hips and thighs in the brown army pants. That untended tangle of dark brown hair with that little-boy face looking out through those huge tinted glasses. A dreadful little person, she thought, needing some kind of discipline. She thought of the throat of Carolyn Pennymark, and she thought of those pale and puffy little lips, and quite unexpectedly she thought of what it would be like to kiss those insolent lips and rub the hidden nipples into erection, and she had such a sudden flash of what the love books call giddiness that it seemed to hollow her out with need and wanting.

Well now, she said to herself. Who would have thought it? Who would have guessed? So what would have happened to me if Jenny MacB. had told me after that first time that after a few months of it I would never be able to change back again? I would never have let it keep on, would I? No. Because, more idiot me, I wanted to hang on to all my hangups. She knew that. Smart old sly Jenny MacB. She's got me now, right where I want her. And this is how I am and how I will forever be and I can, thank God, stop being nervous about getting too old to have kids.

She smiled and kissed the nape of Jenny MacBeth's neck, too gently to awaken her.

The radio said on Thursday morning that the Central School was closed, as some of the rural roads were still under water, and two bridges had been closed for inspection by the state engineers. School had opened early, on the fifteenth, because of time lost in the spring during the teacher strike. Damage in the southwestern part of the state, two hundred miles from Lakemore, was so widespread and heavy the Governor along with the Governors of three other states had asked to have their states declared disaster areas. In the southwestern part of the state, thousands were homeless. Bruce Swain's mother brought her coffee over to the kitchen table and sat across from him as he picked listlessly at his eggs.

When she asked him what his plans were for the day, he looked at her in surprise and said, "Go hunt for Baron!"

"Honey, he's been gone now for ten days."

"This is eleven."

"Okay. Eleven days, and it strikes me that if he could have made it home, that storm would have driven him home. I was discussing that with your father last night."

"I heard you."

"Were you eavesdropping?"

"I was listening. What you said was a lot of crap."

"Brucie!"

"He's out there, Mom, and I'm going to keep on looking for him until I find him." He tried to stare her down, but his eyes filled. She got up and took her empty cup to the sink. She came back and bent and kissed the side of his forehead. "Okay. Keep looking, then, if that makes you feel better. Got to go to work, pal. Don't forget to lock up. And . . . good luck."

They had bought Baron for him for his third birthday, a small red hairy puppy that charged into his legs, knocked him down and licked his face. From small wriggling pup to big red setter—they had grown up together. His father said the house was no place for a dog. But Baron had always slept at the foot of Bruce's bed. Always. It was the established order of things. What if a nightmare woke you up and he wasn't there? And who was always waiting for the school bus, and knew exactly when it would arrive?

He dumped out what was left of the eggs and rinsed his plate off and put it in the dishwasher with his milk glass. He checked the doors to be sure they were locked and went into the carport. The front wheel of his bike looked mushy and he checked and found it was down to forty-five pounds. He pumped it back up to sixty-five. It was going to be one hot day. The sky was glassy gray without a distinct cloud, and the sun seemed to fill half of it. He had divided his known world into sectors, each big enough to take a full day to search.

Today he would cover one of the furthest-away areas, over the other side of Lakemore, out toward the county line, chain-locking the bike to trees when he went out across the fields, looking on every side, counting his steps, stopping and yelling, "BARR RUN, BARR RUN, BARR RUN," three times after each fifty steps, then listening to see if he heard an answering yelp. The dog could be caught up on something and wasting away, dying of thirst, broken leg, some terrible thing.

By noon according to his Hagar wristwatch, Bruce Swain was walking along a muddy dirt road that ran parallel to the state road. His bicycle was chained to a curve-warning sign not far beyond the County Line Motel. He thought he probably ought to go back home and make sandwiches, but it seemed like a very long way there and back again, maybe more than twelve miles in the heat. Anyway, he hadn't been very hungry lately. When you had turned ten you weren't like some little kid that starts whining when he doesn't eat on time.

He came to a place where a house had burned down a long time before. The stone foundation was falling into where the cellar had been, and there were trees growing in the cellar as big around as his leg. The old barn was still standing, most of it. Part of the roof had fallen in. First he searched the cellar area, calling the dog every few minutes. Then he thought he should try the barn, because a sick or injured dog might seek shelter in there. It was a shadowy place, a home for bats and rats and things that slithered and skittered. No luck. He went out behind the barn and in a few moments he became aware of a very faint but sickening smell.

He began moving this way and that, tracking it down. There was a fitful breeze. At times he could not smell it at all. But then it got stronger and stronger as it led him to a small open structure with a warped shingled roof. It seemed to have a floor too small for it, and then he realized that it was the old well for the farm, and somebody had put old boards across the low stone combing, and the storm had blown a couple of them off. There was room for a dog to fall in. He leaned over and snuffed the smell that came up from the black depth, and it drove him back with an almost physical impact. He coughed and gagged, and went away to sit on the trunk of a fallen tree, thirty feet upwind from the well. He knew it was the smell of something long dead. Eleven days was enough time. Baron had never roamed this far from home.

"It isn't Baron," he said aloud, and his voice sounded small and unsure in the silence of the dead farm. The dog could have chased something which darted into the well. A barn rat. The dog would fall to the bottom and die and the damn rat would run away, squealing its rat-laugh.

"Damn bastard rat," he said, feeling the tickle of a tear on his face, a shameful weakness.

He knew he was going to have to see down there. So, holding his breath, he took away one board at a time. But when he tried to see the bottom, there wasn't enough light. The well roof overhead kept it too shaded. He found a stone the size of a peach and tossed it in. As he listened for the sound, he forgot to keep breathing through his mouth. He breathed once through his nose and nearly threw up. The noise puzzled him. It wasn't the *ka-plunk* sound of falling into water, and it wasn't a stone-on-stone sound, and it wasn't a damp kind of thud. It was a metallic sound. In two parts. Bang-clatter.

So there had to be some way to get some light down there. He looked around, thought for a while and then went trotting through the heat, across the fields, to the motel.

A tall man was sitting on his heels in the shade of the roof over the motel walkway, using a small noisy compressor to operate a spray gun. He had newspapers spread out, and he was spraying some old wicker furniture a new bright brave blue. When he noticed Bruce he reached and turned off the compressor and smiled and said, "Rent you a nice room, buddy?"

"No, thanks. I'm Bruce Swain. We live over next to the Center. What I'm doing, I'm looking for Baron, my red setter. He's been gone eleven days."

The man stood up, wincing as he straightened his long legs. He shook hands and said, "I'm Fred Moon. Eleven days makes it pretty serious, huh? You walk here?"

"No. I got my bike chained down the road there."

"Your daddy wouldn't be Arden Swain, the optometrist?"

"That's my uncle. My dad works for the city. His name is Dale."

"Oh sure, I know him. I mean I know who he is, not like we're old pals or anything. If you're asking me if I saw any red setter eleven days ago, I don't think so."

"No. What I mean, I think I found him. I mean I'm kind of afraid I found him. Over there across that other road, way over."

"You *think* you found him? Let's go inside and get a cold one and talk this thing over, Bruce."

After he had taken his first long swallows of icy cola, Bruce explained about the terrible stink and not being able to see down in there. "First I got to see that it's him, and after that I'll talk to my dad about getting him up out of there and burying him back home where he belongs. Maybe it's a raccoon or a fox or a big rabbit or something like that."

"Now, a flashlight might not work, just aiming it straight down there," Mr. Moon said, "because in old wells what you get a lot of the time is a bunch of brush and vines growing out of the walls, out of the cracks between the old stones. Now, right here I've got this big old mother of a flashlight, and we can tie it on some long string, turn it on, and lower it down there. This lens part tips down a little, and the handle on top makes it perfect for the job."

"I can do it and bring the flashlight back, Mr. Moon."

"You're big enough to call me Fred like everybody else, Bruce. Now, the stink is real bad?"

"It's really terrible. I nearly threw up."

"Okay, we'll take a couple of Peggy's dish towels here, and this little bottle I'll fill with rubbing alcohol, and when we get to the well, we soak a little into the towel and tie it around our noses and mouths."

"You really don't have to come along."

Fred Moon stared at him, then finished his soft drink and put the bottle on the counter. He nodded at Bruce. "You're afraid it will be your dog, and then you'll do a lot of crying and carrying on and you don't want anybody watching you."

"I . . . I guess so."

"If you didn't cry and carry on, you wouldn't be normal, and besides, I won't watch. Let me go in the office and tell Peggy where we're going.

Then, if it is your dog, what we'll do, we'll put your bike in the pickup and take it on home. Will anybody be there?"

"No."

"So we'll leave off the bike and I'll drop you at City Hall. Now we've got everything organized. We forget anything?"

"I don't think so."

Fifteen minutes later they reached the well and got the towels in place. Fred Moon lifted the edge of his and leaned over the well and said, "Hoooeeee! That is one powerful smell." He tied the cord to the flashlight and turned it on and began to lower it slowly.

"Whatever's down there is going to look pretty sorry," he said.

"I know," the boy said. "It's okay."

There was a lot of brush growing out between the stones of the sides. The light twisted slowly around and back, lighting a small portion of the old stones. It went down so far Fred began to wonder if he should have brought more cord. Then it touched something and tilted. He raised it free and let it slowly turn, let it touch an aluminum train case, a rotting hand and wrist, and then the ghastly face upturned.

The cord slipped out of his slack hand, and the light fell and tipped on its side, still burning in a few inches of water. Fred Moon scrambled back and turned and tore the towel off and threw up. Moments later, he heard the boy throw up. He wiped his sour mouth with the towel and went to the boy and said, "I guess neither one of us is cut out for this line of work."

"At least it . . . wasn't Baron," the boy said. That face down there was imprinted on his brain so vividly he could still see it no matter where he looked. And he knew he would never forget it, no matter how long he might live.

Carolyn Pennymark was stretched out on her bed, head propped up, the phone wedged between shoulder and jaw. "Hey, Marty? Little Red Roving Hood here. The rain quit and I have been up and down and around, and if there is anything else here, nobody else is going to find it either, so I better come in."

"Is that so? Really scoured it, huh? What did you come up with?"

"Just dumb junk. A rumor one of the computer geniuses is making it with one of the choir Angels, but it turns out she's the age of consent, so that's nothing even if I chased it down. Also, the old man is deep into

Alzheimer's, too far gone to ever make another appearance anywhere. It seems that John Tinker Meadows has a little history of messing around, but it has been nicely covered up in the past. There's talk they may put up a big medical school and hospital and so on, but it wouldn't make very exciting copy."

"So you want to head for the barn?"

"That's about it. I'm getting tired of the chimes."

"You sure it's time to come back?"

"Marty, what's wrong with you? Don't you trust me to tell you when a story is dead?"

"Certainly, doll. You know it's over when it's over. You can figure out the best way back and get started whenever."

"Thanks."

"Oh, by the way. It just came in over the wire a couple of minutes ago, some kid found a female body maybe dead three months in the bottom of a well out there west of Lakemore. But it's probably nothing, right?"

"Why, you miserable, rotten son of a bitch. You knew that and you let me keep talking! Goodbye, Marty baby."

She slammed the phone down and ran out of the room toward the stairs.

Fourteen

As soon as the bottom of the well had been so brightly floodlighted the long ladder could be placed without touching the body or the luggage, two men from the State Bureau of Investigation went down to the bottom, wearing masks, and cut away the brush from the sides of the shaft as they went down. Once at the bottom, they took pictures of the body from every possible angle before slipping it carefully into a rubberized zippered body bag. The body bag was placed at an angle into a large mesh bag shaped somewhat like a hammock, and men up at ground level hoisted it slowly up the shaft, with one of the technicians following it up the ladder, keeping it from bumping the sides or the ladder. Once the body was up at ground level, it was placed in a hinged metal box with a rubber gasket which made it airtight.

When the body box had been eased into the ambulance, the mesh bag was lowered again and brought up with the luggage which had been found resting on and against the body. There was an aluminum train case, two small suitcases and a portable typewriter. These items were placed in the ambulance as well, with every care taken to avoid smudging any fingerprints which might be on them, especially on the train case and the typewriter case.

The ambulance then proceeded to the city, sixty miles southeast of Lakemore, and drove to the basement entrance to the Southern Memorial Hospital, where they put the sealed container on a cart and rolled it to that section of the City Morgue equipped for the performance of autopsies.

The autopsy was begun at eight o'clock on the evening of the day the body was discovered, and was performed by Dr. George Ludeker, the Medical Examiner, assisted by Dr. Everett Johnson. Dr. Ludeker dictated each step of the procedure as it progressed. Dr. Johnson, from time to time, took pictures of the body for possible use in the investigation into the death.

The body was removed from both containers and placed face up on the dissection table. The clothing was soaked, soiled and rotting. There was a thin yellow blouse, a white brassiere, a dark blue cotton skirt, one white sandal with a medium heel. There was a gold chain around the neck, a Timex digital watch on the left wrist, a wedding band and a ring with a small diamond on the third finger, left hand, and a white metal ring containing a red stone on the index finger of the right hand.

When all items had been removed from the body it was subjected to close examination for distinguishing marks and characteristics. It was a female, one hundred and fifty-five centimeters in height, small-boned, fair complexion, pale blonde hair, impossible to determine what color the eyes had been. Approximately forty percent of the little finger on the right hand missing, with scar tissue indicating it had happened a long time ago. Decedent's age estimated to be between twenty and forty years.

Left side of face badly damaged, but impossible to tell if it was an injury prior to death or the result of the fall into the well. The body, in general, was in an advanced stage of decomposition, and so there was difficulty in determining what trauma had caused the death if, indeed, death had come as the result of an injury. Dr. Ludeker noted for the record that the body was not as badly decomposed as one might anticipate for a body which had been out of doors in the summer months at this latitude. Dr. Johnson said that the temperature at the bottom of a deep well might stay at about fifty-four degrees Fahrenheit, and apparently the well had been covered until the recent storm blew some of the boards off the top of it. That kept the body from the flies and the consequent destruction by maggots.

They were on close examination able to detect the existence of an appendix scar, and what had been a ridge of scar tissue across the top of the left foot. As was the practice, Dr. Ludeker examined the arms and legs carefully to determine whether he thought he might through tissue examination find any trace of needle tracks indicating some possibility of addiction or diabetes. But the condition of the tissues made any such search useless.

The body was then opened and the organs of the abdomen and chest examined in methodical fashion. They proved to be in normal condition, allowing for the state of decomposition and the resultant postmortem changes. There had been such degeneration of the soft tissues of the body it was impossible to determine whether the woman had been the victim of a sexual assault prior to death. The heart and the brain showed on close examination no indications of trauma. Small tissue samples from the reasonably stabilized areas of various organs were labeled and set aside for laboratory analysis.

It was not until they dissected the neck that they began to suspect a possible cause of death. They discovered that the cricoid cartilage, which is the ringlike structure of cartilage below the thyroid, was broken in two places. Neither doctor had ever observed this injury in a person as young as the decedent appeared to be. In the young the cricoid has enough elasticity to be able to withstand a considerable pressure. Once the cricoid has been broken, has been dented inward like a dent in a Ping-Pong ball, the victim will die of strangulation in a very few minutes. In a body recently smothered or strangled it is possible to find pinpoint hemorrhages in the whites of the eyes, far back under the lids. But she had been too long dead to provide this confirmation. Closeup color photographs were taken by Dr. Johnson of the broken cricoid and the tissues of the throat. In re-examining the tissues of the throat they could not find any evidence of the way the force had been used to break the cricoid. They reassembled the body, using large curved needles and a coarse thread rather than the customary staples to hold the edges of the incisions together, placed it in the metal case and rolled it on a stretcher into the cold room where the attendant would place it in storage and label the locker door.

After they had gone into the annex and showered and changed, they were surprised to find Lieutenant Coombs and Sergeant Slovik of the State Bureau of Investigation in the waiting room. It was quarter to midnight.

"What have we got, George?" Coombs asked Ludeker.

"So far it looks like death by strangulation. Busted cricoid. No other physical indications of strangulation."

"Manual strangulation?"

"We talked about that. When the stuff got thrown in the well, the edge of, say, the typewriter case catching her just right. No chance. That would have given us tissue damage massive enough so that we could see it. But if somebody wrapped their hands around the throat, we'd probably be unable to see any evidence of that. Our guess, and it's just a guess, is that somebody rested a big beefy forearm across the little lady's throat, probably to shut her up while raping her."

"Evidence of rape?"

"Not after three months."

"Doctors, I want to spare her husband the chore of a physical identification, and the State's Attorney's office says we can do it this way. Mike here was with me when we questioned Owen about distinguishing marks. I've got the list. What did you come up with?"

"Nearly half the little finger right hand missing. Scar on her left instep looks like she dropped a cleaver on it. Appendix scar."

"Perfect! Any jewelry he can look at?"

"Three rings, a necklace and a digital watch. I locked them up in there. They're soaking in alcohol."

"The watch too?"

"Yep. Fabric strap. Damned thing was running. Two minutes fast."

"Not anymore, it isn't," Coombs said. "I'll look forward to getting the written report and the pictures. And send the jewelry over in a plastic sack. He can look at it when we run it up there tomorrow."

"And the body is that of a woman in her early thirties?"

"That fits closely enough. You won't get the report until Monday late," Ludeker said.

"I know. Right now it just turned Friday. That's okay. We're going to have to move fast and good on this thing. When she was missing, it wasn't much of a story. But this is going to bring the media into Lakemore like an army. And the cause of death . . ."

"Is not news until the State's Attorney says it is," Johnson said, smiling. "See, Lieutenant? I'm learning." He stopped smiling, shook his head. "I don't want to talk about this one anyway. Ever. Once upon a time that was a fine-looking little woman. Bums that get knifed in an alley, I can handle. All the time, working on this one, I keep thinking —what a hell of a waste. Hope you guys catch him."

When the first red edge of the sun rim showed between two gentle hills in the east, Roy Owen and Peggy Moon had turned around and they were heading back toward the motel, walking briskly along the edge of the paved surface. She was glad he had talked so much to her about Lindy and Janie and his relationship to both of them and their relationship to each other. It made her feel as if they were moving more irreversibly into a relationship of their own. At times he had stopped, frowning, groping for the right way to say something. All he had wanted from her was the occasional murmur of understanding.

Finally they were so close to the motel he could look across the fields and see, above the trees that concealed the distant dirt road, the portion of barn roof.

"I've walked along that road half a dozen times," he said. He stopped, hands on his hips. "Right by her. I can see that barn roof from my window. She probably looked out that window and noticed it. Damn him! Whoever it was, damn him to hell. Thrown away like trash. Like a run-over animal. Chunked her in there and threw her stuff down. Three summer months down a deep well. Thank God I didn't have to identify her. What I told them about her matched up. That's what they came here at two this morning to tell me."

He started walking again suddenly, and she had to take several running steps to catch up and walk beside him. Though she was a few inches taller than he, it pleased her that in their walks their stride seemed to match perfectly.

"When are you going to call her mother?"

"Soon as we get back. I don't want her to hear it on the news. And I want her to keep Janie home and keep the news turned off. Then I'll have to call the office. And then find some way to make the arrangements that have to be made. We agreed a couple of years ago that we'd both like to be cremated. So I don't have to wonder about that. I guess the thing to do would be to get it done here, when they release the body, and then take the ashes up there and have a memorial service. There's no point in her mother and Janie coming down here."

"No point at all."

"They wanted to know what kind of a purse she carried. I said I didn't have any idea. They couldn't find it."

"Kind of a white canvas shoulder bag with brown leather trim and a brass latch."

"I'll tell Lieutenant Coombs. Thanks."

"They know that already. It's in their file. I described all her stuff, back when she had been reported missing."

"They're going to bring me an inventory of everything that was . . . with her. And her jewelry to identify."

"She always wore that heavy gold chain every time I saw her."

"I gave it to her on our fifth anniversary. I was afraid somebody might snatch it off her in New York, but she said it was too big to look real. They're bringing it and her rings and watch to me to identify."

"Today?"

"Sometime today."

At that moment they were both startled by a small woman in sweaty brown clothing and a yardbird hat stepping out from behind a highway sign and motioning to them to stop.

"Hey!" he said. "Carrie. Meet Peggy Moon. She and her brother own the motel."

"I know. Fred told me this might be a good place to catch you. Peggy, I'm Carolyn Pennymark. I worked at the same magazine as Lindy. Look, I have to make this fast, guys. There is really a mob scene right back there at the motel. Two television trucks, wire service people, syndication people."

"What the hell do they want?" Roy asked.

"What they . . . we . . . always want. News is the process of making not very much out of practically nothing. How does it feel to find out they found your wife's body at the bottom of a well? Why did you stay down here? Did you have some kind of a hunch?"

Peggy said fiercely, "That's the *last* thing he needs right now!"

"I know that, sugar. Why do you think I'm here? There's not much time. Look, what I do mostly in life, I make deals. Okay. Give me the exclusive rights, and I'll keep those clowns off you. I can't offer money because that would be in terrible taste. But we can put a thousand-dollar bond in your kid's education fund."

"That's tacky!" Peggy said loudly.

"Hush, dear. Life is tacky. Okay? I'll get you through the picket line, Roy. We had a nice talk. I think we understand each other. Don't get downwind of me. I have been on a dead run for quite a while, and I smell like a horse barn. Okay? Peggy, sweetie, the best place would be whatever you've got behind that office of yours. Less ground to cover. Okay?"

"It's where we live, my brother and I. There's a kitchen and then—"

"I've got Fred all set to lock it after we come galloping through. Peggy, have you got a typewriter I can use?"

"A Corona old as the hills."

"Good. I learned on one of those. Okay, you guys. What we do, we walk absolutely straight and steady. No glances to left or right. Ignore the mikes they'll stick in your face. Walk right through them. They'll pull them back. Ignore bad language and, Roy, you ignore any rotten thing they'll say about you or Lindy to get you going. Just pretend it's all in a language you can't understand. They'll have some choice things to call me too. Okay, troops? Off we go. Blind and deaf and steadfast."

Once they were in the office and Fred had slammed the door and bolted it, Roy knew that without her coaching it wouldn't have worked. He would have felt compelled to turn to them and tell them what he thought of their sick questions. Which, of course, was what they wanted. They circled the office and rapped on the windows, banged on the door. Peggy pulled the draperies and they turned on the lights. Fred was delighted by the whole thing. He had told their three customers that they wouldn't be answering the switchboard, and so when it shrilled at them, Peggy ignored it. In about fifteen minutes they heard car doors chunking and the engines starting up and the cars leaving, squealing their tires when they turned angrily onto the state road.

Carolyn looked at Peggy. "Didn't I hear you say something when we pushed our way through out there?"

Peggy shrugged and twisted from side to side. "Just two words. That's all. I figured they couldn't use words like that on the air."

"Have you ever thought of trying my line of work?"

Peggy smiled sweetly at her. "Not seriously."

Carolyn turned to Roy. "Okay. Here's our interview." She handed him the sheet she had typed.

"But we didn't do the interview yet!"

"This is what I would have asked and this is what I think you would have answered. If you don't like any part of it, make your mark and we'll go over it."

He sat and read it, with Peggy leaning over to read it with him, standing beside the chair, her hand on his shoulder.

"I think it's pretty good," he said. "No changes."

"It even sounds like him," Peggy said.

"Sweetie, I am a pro. And thank you. Now initial on the bottom there indicating your approval, Roy. Thanks. Peggy, can you put me through to New York? Here's my phone card."

A few minutes later they heard her say, "Marty? Marty, love? Is it really you? In spite of the way you tried to delay me and frustrate me, I have an exclusive with the bereaved spouse. Of course it's approved and signed. Put this onto the machinery and I'll dictate. And when you vend it to our sister daily, I want my piece of the action. Oh, and you approve a thousand-dollar bond for the little girl who lost her mother. Okay? Okay. Am I on? Right. At the sound of the beep, I shall proceed."

As Carolyn began dictating, Peggy took Roy's arm and led him back into a small room with a big television set and piles of books and magazines. "What I wanted to say, Roy. When she's through and you can get on the phone, don't try to tell Janie."

He stared at her. "She has to know, doesn't she?"

"Of course she has to know. But do it the best way for her. Tell her grandma how to do it. Let her grandma hold her on her lap and hug her and tell her, okay?"

"Yes. That's better. You're right. I couldn't have done it."

"You could have done it," Peggy said. "You could have done it as well as anybody could. Over the phone. But holding is better. Arms around you are better. And I'm kind of an expert."

And a little later, after Carrie Pennymark had left, he heard the phone ringing, up in Hartford.

Bruce's mother woke him early on Friday morning and told him she had something to show him in the kitchen. He followed her out. Baron lay on the cool tiles in front of the kitchen sink. When Bruce spoke his name and knelt beside him, the dog lifted his head and yawned, tongue lolling, then lowered his head and closed his eyes and his tail thumped a couple of times against the floor. He was very thin and filthy, his red hair matted with burrs and twigs.

"I saw a dog pack trotting by," she said, "and one of them looked something like Baron, so I opened the door and called him, and he peeled off and came trotting in. He's been out with the boys, Brucie. He's a rascal."

He stood up and turned toward her, smiling, and then the tears came. He stood in the circle of her arms and cried like a little kid. It made him ashamed to be so weak, to cry like that, sobbing and snuffling. She held him and stroked the back of his head. He tried to make himself stop. He could hear his father in the bathroom. He didn't want his father to hear him crying. When he had walked away from the well where they had looked down and seen the dead face of the woman, in that moment he had given up any last hope of ever finding Baron alive anywhere in the world. And now, here he was. Bruce wondered if maybe he was crying because he could never again miss the dog so badly, no matter what happened. Some connection he could not understand had been severed.

At breakfast in the smaller dining room on the ground floor of the Manse, John Tinker Meadows listened to Finn Efflander and Jenny Albritton and Mary Margaret and finally said, "Why are we required to make some kind of jackass statement about this? Is there some rule that says we have to? When they investigated the disappearance, we stated officially that we knew nothing about the damned woman. And we still know nothing about her. When she was here, she stayed a long way from the Center, and she died a long way from the Center. We've extended every courtesy to that pair the magazine sent down here. We didn't have to do that. I sometimes think we're too sensitive about the media and what they might say or write."

"I think we should say *something*," Mary Margaret said. "Even if to say we're sorry this happened to any woman in this county whether we know her or not. We extend our sympathy to her loved ones and her co-workers, and so on and so on."

"Maybe," Finn said, "we could work in a little comment on how the permissive filth in our society inflames rapists and murderers."

John Tinker sighed and said, "All right, then. I'm outnumbered and outvoted. Finn, get Spencer McKay to work something up. Tell him to keep it short. Jenny, you bird-dog it, and get it to me ten minutes before they tape it."

"Where would you like them to do it?" Jenny asked.

"Any suggestions?"

"Well . . . I think if you were sitting behind the desk in your father's old office . . ."

"Agreed. Tell them I will give the statement and then take a few questions. Will it be network?"

"There'll be the area affiliates of CBS and ABC and I think maybe somebody from CNN, but they have no idea whether anything they do will be picked up."

"It probably will be," Finn said bleakly. "Anything that could possibly bring any kind of discredit on the Church gets a big play."

"How can we be discredited?" Mary Margaret asked. "For what?"

Finn shrugged and looked at Jenny Albritton. She moistened her lips and said, "The brutalized body of Linda Rooney has been found in the bottom of a dry well on an abandoned farm nine miles from the Tabernacle of the Eternal Church of the Believer. Police are investigating what connection there might be between the murder and the fact that Ms. Rooney was conducting an undercover investigation of the Meadows family and the Eternal Church of the Believer."

John Tinker looked startled. He whistled softly and then said, "Okay, I was definitely wrong. We have to make a statement and it better be a strong statement. Tell McKay to underline how open we are with all members of the media. Thank you, Jenny. We sometimes forget how vulnerable we are."

"And we better pray that no one at the Center was involved in this in any way," Mary Margaret said. "If they can make it sound so terrible when we never knew anything about her, think of how they could make it sound if one of our employees—like one of the maintenance men— did it to her."

John Tinker finished his coffee and the informal meeting adjourned. Mary Margaret left with him, and stopped him in the lounge area, saying, "I have to talk to you about Poppa."

"What now?"

"Willa Minter says that if she has to handle him alone, she's going to quit."

"What happened?"

"Apparently what happened, he was in the tub and she told him he'd been there long enough. She was almost hysterical, so I'm not certain how accurate this is. She took hold of his arm to try to get him to his feet and help him out of the tub. He reached up and grabbed her by the back of the neck and pulled her off balance and plunged her head under the water and apparently grabbed her around the neck with his legs, like a scissors hold, I think they call it, and held her there with her head underwater. She was terribly frightened and she wrenched herself free. She was on the floor beside the tub, coughing up water, when he got out of the tub and stepped over her and went into the bedroom and put on his terry robe."

"Dear Lord God," he said wearily.

"Don't blaspheme."

"You should have recognized that as a prayer, sis."

"There's more."

"Spare me."

"I can't. I went back there with her immediately. He couldn't understand what we were talking about. He had absolutely no memory of it at all. And what is worse, after a few minutes, he couldn't remember what I'd been asking him. And he wanted the 'sanseer.' "

"The what?"

"That's as close as I can come to the word he was saying. The sanseer. Whatever it is, he wanted it right then. And in a few minutes he couldn't remember wanting it. Willa Minter says it's getting more difficult to understand what he's saying. The rate of change is accelerating, Johnny."

"Can you get someone?"

"More than one. Even with increased sedation, she thinks it will take three shifts, two RPN on each shift. She says he seems to have gotten a lot stronger physically lately. And he's getting more incontinent. I can find them, and we can house them in the dormitory, and we can pay them a very good wage, but I can't guarantee they won't talk about his condition. It could get to be common knowledge. I know you don't want that to happen."

"Five more! I'll have Finn help you find them and interview them. He's good at that kind of thing."

"What are we going to do, Johnny? Whatever are we going to do?"

"Get hold of yourself, Mag. We do the best we can."

"When is Tom Daniel Birdy coming?"

"He's invited for the weekend of the twenty-sixth. He won't say yes or no. If he plays cute right to the last moment, when we send a plane for him why don't you fly down?"

"Why?"

"I have a feeling he'd find it easier to say no to me."

"If he says yes, we're going to have problems with Walter."

"You butter up old Walter. By the time he finds out how things are going, it will be too late to raise a fuss."

"He's been very loyal."

"Walter is loyal to Walter first. Then to Alberta, maybe."

"I always thought he'd go along with anything we thought best. But the other day he got so upset when I mentioned the Reverend Birdy."

"On the way back in the airplane with Birdy, explain about Poppa. Level with him. Otherwise he's going to wonder about not meeting him. From what you say, Poppa is through meeting anybody. Wait a minute. I don't think you should go down. We'll send the plane for him. If you go down we'll look too eager. Tell him about the old man when he gets to the Manse, or when you're showing him the area."

"Johnny. Are you all right?"

"Me? I am totally fantastic. What else?"

"Please," she said, but he walked away from her and did not look back.

Joe Deets finally devised an access code which pleased him. It fitted into the protocols of the cryptography which he had set up to protect the master data base from any outside invasion through the phone lines. He tested it by copying a small portion of the data base onto a hard disk on one of his personal computers, along with the program which not only protected the information but allowed for the orderly additions to the data base, and periodic file maintenance.

When the hard disk was ready, he added the trigger name and address he had devised, sending it to file just as if he were one of Jenny MacBeth's girls running her terminal, adding the new donors. And then he began printing out portions of the information from the disk. On the first run it was slightly faulty. By the seventh retrieval, the list was garbage:

Mfs Clnstkoyn Niudg.oh
8gw3 Eoimm Sxo
Pubrczz, YU 8in5x

He tried to work backward through the changes to reconstruct the original data, but he had made the changes progressive, based on a random-number generation, and found the task impossible.

He erased the disk and shredded the lists. The poison was hidden inside the data base itself, unresponsive to any command to reveal itself. It was an elegant little program. Too bad there would never be anyone else to admire it. It would hide in there until the trigger came in, and then it would activate itself and begin the random substitutions, a machine-language corruption of the codes.

He switched a personal computer to Dow Jones Retrieval, and as he stared at the incoming data on the screen, once again his attention wandered and he found himself thinking about Annalee Purves. The daydream had a consistent pattern. He wondered what his life would have been like had they met and married in their early twenties. She had touched something within him he thought long dead. Though she was faded now, she was still a strong and vital woman, strong-bodied, intense, loyal, with a native shrewdness about life and relationships. He knew he had given her a problem that might be beyond her capacity to handle. Or Patsy Knox had given her the problem.

When his thoughts drifted from Annalee back to her daughter, Doreen, he tasted a faint sour edge of self-loathing, an unfamiliar flavor, quickly suppressed, overwhelmed by his sensual images of her body and her soft cries, deliberately recalled as an antidote to the unfamiliar discomfort of an awareness of evil.

Is this the way it begins? he wondered. As she knelt and prayed, that startling image as of a curtain being opened to give a glimpse of wonders beyond, then quickly closed again, leaving me with the impression I am in darkness. Lost in a darkness. Is this the way the sinner comes upon a state of grace? To fall half in love with a woman who is not only a farm-woman, but is one of Brother Meadows' ignorant tithing multitudes, compartmented away from life and reality, charged with thinking only those thoughts which reinforce her state of captivity. But she sees something out there, and for a moment I almost saw it. It comforts her. And she was once a sinner. In an indirect way she made that clear.

What if perhaps I stopped intellectualizing all this faith, and, like they say, took it on faith? Relaxed and believed. Prayed without the self-conscious feeling of being a superstitious damned fool. If it worked, what would I have left? The intricate pleasures of practicing my specialty. The constant itch and ache for the forbidden flesh of young women. And, maybe, a slim little promise of eternal life. Annalee, Annalee, I think I need you to come back here to me and help me pray. If we pray, maybe I can release your daughter and beg your forgiveness, and the Lord's.

The law offices of Winchester and Winchester occupied an entire floor of the Central Citizens Bank Building in Lakemore. Charley had the largest office, a corner room paneled in fruitwood, with four windows, a hidden refrigerator and bar, a desk big enough to serve as a conference table, a worn leather couch, two matching chairs and the customary shelves of law books.

Charley had been dictating to Mrs. Miller for over an hour, scores of short cheery personal letters to dear close friends. Mrs. Miller, who had always looked close to death and who was as healthy as the Cowboy backfield, was so familiar with his style he had only to give the meat of the letter and then say, "Yattata yattata and so on," and it would all sound like him when the letter came in for signature.

At a couple of minutes before noon his brother Clyde came in and nodded and turned on the bookshelf television. The hilltop tower and the new cable brought in all three network stations in the city clear as any picture anywhere. It reminded Charley of John Tinker's phone call and so he dismissed Mrs. Miller, and on second thought told her she could stay and watch the young Reverend Meadows if she wished.

He was the third story on the noon news, right after the new after-shocks in California and some unusual and destructive tornadoes up in Pennsylvania. John Tinker looked very good on the tube. It had been cut to about three minutes, and it ended with him looking directly into the audience eye and spreading his hands and saying, "We of the Eternal Church of the Believer deplore all cruel and violent acts, physical, mental or spiritual. And we deplore the climate of indifference in our country that makes such acts not only possible but, to some warped minds, necessary."

When they began talking about a warehouse fire, Clyde turned it off and said, "The same mixture as before, hey, Charley?"

Mrs. Miller said, "He's wearing a little thin."

"Who asked you, Marian?"

"You'd be better off if you asked me about a lot more things, Clyde." She went out, setting her heels down hard, closing the door with an ounce more pressure than usual.

"She's right, Clyde," Charley said. "I can see it. You can see it. He's going through the motions. He told me the old man is worse. Walter Macy is all ruffled up about this Birdy that Finn and John Tinker think will be so good for the Church. The old man has taken a sudden turn for the worse. Tried to drown his nurse."

"Jesus!" exclaimed Clyde.

"One of the Angels, great big old girl named Lilly Louise, boobs out to here, has got herself pregnant and won't say by who. Nice nervous little woman named Glinda Lopez came sneaking to my house last night to see me by appointment and told me that some Jap has rigged up some kind of computer voice system where she can talk on the phone to people way behind in their donations, pretending she's old Matthew. She wanted to know if soliciting money using somebody else's voice was illegal."

"Good Lord, is it?"

"It never came up before. I told her I'd study on it. But it seems to me you get a personal letter supposed to be signed by Reagan asking you for funds for the Republican Party, that's kind of the same thing. But in another way, it isn't. She doesn't like doing it. She says it's very hard work, and she's not sleeping well because she dreams about it all the time."

"Wouldn't you think John Tinker would have checked it out with you before going ahead? Or Finn? Or somebody? There could be a big stink about something like that."

"Not as big as finding a missing lady down a well. Clyde, when things go bad, they go bad in bunches. Few years back all these things bunching up could have hurt the Church a lot. Not anymore. Too big. Too much momentum. Too much cash in the drawer. When you're big enough you can blame your troubles on your enemies and get believed. When you're little, all your troubles come from bad management. Where are you having lunch?"

"Murph's. With that zoning board consultant with the beard. I can't ever remember his name."

"Yates. Don't order the corned beef. It's been fat and stringy lately."

Lieutenant Coombs and Sergeant Slovik talked to Roy Owen in his motel room. He and Coombs sat in the chairs and Slovik sat on the bed. They waited while he read over the inventory list of her belongings.

"Look about right?" Coombs asked.

"I guess so. I mean, it would be the sort of things she'd have with her. What's this about a notebook, illegible?"

"Bad luck there, I guess. The suitcase popped open when it hit bottom, and the notebook slid out into the water and crud. Or it lay there until the rainwater came in enough to wet it. The lab might be able to raise something off the pages, but it looked to me as if a lot of them had been torn out. Another thing. Some of her stuff was neat, but a lot of it had just been crammed into the suitcases and train case as if she was in one hell of a hurry, or somebody did her packing for her."

"Then somebody packed for her. Even in a great hurry, she was always a very neat and orderly person."

"Okay. Here's the jewelry. All we want you to do is identify it right now."

"The chain is hers. And the rings. I don't remember that watch."

"Okay, and here's the clothes she was wearing."

Roy looked at the list. "One shoe?"

"We've got people searching the area looking for her shoe and her purse."

Roy started to hand the short list back and then said, "Wait a minute. You've got a bra on the list, but no underwear panties."

"She wasn't wearing any."

"I know . . . knew Lindy well. Really well. I knew more about her habits than I did about her attitudes. She would never, never, never put on a skirt without anything under it. Believe me. Never!"

Coombs glanced over at Slovik and said, "That backs up our suspicion of sexual assault. And makes one more item to look for."

"Why didn't he throw everything down the well?"

The lieutenant said, "I reconstruct it this way. It was night. It took everything he had to carry her, find the well, drop her down it and toss her stuff down. Then he pulled those boards off the side of the barn and put them across the top of the well. Then he went back and checked the scene of the crime and he came across the extra shoe and her purse and the pants he'd ripped off. He just couldn't handle going back there and dropping them in. He never wanted to go back there again. So he hid them someplace else. He stuffed the shoe and the pants into the purse and maybe he buried it. Maybe he just heaved it out into the woods when he was on his way down to the airport in her rental car. We'll keep looking. For the purse and for him. If I don't find him before I get to retirement age, I'll still keep looking. Believe it."

Roy looked down at his fists. "I believe it."

"I'll let you know when you can have her stuff. The luggage and the clothes are pretty well mildewed and ruined. But there's the pictures of you and your kid in the silver frames. Things like that."

"When will they release . . ." He couldn't say it.

"Soon, I think. After they finish the chemistry."

"She'll be cremated here and we'll have a memorial service up in Hartford. Can you recommend . . ."

"Sure. Stith and Sons. They're reliable. And about a half mile from the hospital. You talk to them and they'll arrange about getting the body when it's released."

He watched at the window as they backed the unmarked car out and turned around and headed for the highway. He saw Peggy Moon come trotting out and flag them down. She leaned in the car window and talked with them for a time, then backed away and they drove out. She turned and looked toward the unit and he wished she would come in and talk. Or listen. She had certainly been doing a lot of listening.

He called the office. "You busy?" he asked.

"Holding the fort. But Fred'll be back soon. Then I'll come over. People are still phoning you, trying to get to talk to you."

"But nobody on that list I gave you?"

"Not yet."

"Well . . . see you."

"Sure thing."

Fifteen

At half past ten on Saturday morning, Moses stopped cutting and stacking brush for a Mrs. Bennett, left the tools on the ground and drove away in his shabby red pickup truck. Mrs. Bennett was looking out the side window as he drove by. She trotted out onto the porch and shaded her eyes against the glare to see which way he was going. He stopped at the intersection a block away and turned left toward Lakemore.

That very morning she'd had a long phone conversation with a woman who often stopped by for morning coffee, but who said she was not going to go to any house where Moses was working. Mrs. Bennett's friend said that the old fool of a sheriff should have locked Crazy Moses up long ago, before he had a chance to kill that magazine woman. Mrs. Bennett told her friend that she did not think Moses had the gift of invisibility. If he had driven that woman's car down to the city and left it at the airport, somebody would have remembered seeing him there, or seeing him on the way back. Moses would attract some attention anywhere.

The woman said he was a lot more clever than people gave him credit for, and all that preaching on the street he was doing lately was to divert attention from the bad things he was doing. Even though she was an old friend, Mrs. Bennett had hung up on her, and now, watching Moses drive away without a word, she began to wonder if she had been too abrupt.

One of the inner voices had told Moses to drive to the Meadows Mall and walk into the Mall to the big fountain at the intersection of the wide corridors. The Mall was very busy. The rains and floods had kept people from their necessary shopping. But there were many there, young families and teenagers, to whom a hot Saturday in August meant a carnival flavor at the Mall. They came from the four-county shopping area. The young designed their own T-shirt inscriptions, had their ears pierced, bought giant cones, and, in the deafening blare of country and Western inside the MusicBox, they flipped through the bins of records, read the spines of the stacked boxes of tapes, spent too many quarters in the arcade games, met old friends, made new ones and set up dates and arrangements.

Moses had to cruise the parking areas for a time until he found someone leaving. Once inside the cool corridors of the Mall he was aware of how sweaty he was. His soiled tank top, his ripped and faded jeans, even his hair and beard were as soaked as if he had just walked out of the sea. He was aware of people glancing at him and moving quickly out of his path.

Ever since the heavy rains came, he had been aware of strange phenomena in his brain. It was as if some compartment sealed shut for a long time had begun to leak. Bits and pieces seeped into his mind and were gone immediately. The fragments had the quality of the fleeting memories of long bad dreams. There was a sound of lots of voices talking at once inside his head. Excited voices, with now and then a word or two words distinguishable. "Billy . . . other gun . . . operation . . . Ethel, Ethel! . . ." When he had stopped cutting brush and had stood out there in the bug-humming heat of the overgrown feed lot with his eyes shut, straining to hear more of what the voices were saying, they faded out entirely. And as he worked, another voice came into his head and told him where to go, and to go at once.

He walked through the people, staring straight ahead over the heads of all of them. When he reached the fountain there was a short time of hesitation, and then he knew what he had to do.

He climbed up onto the wide concrete shelf that encircled the water jets and the green pool. It was only two and a half feet high, a comfortable height for sitting when tired from shopping.

A lot of them looked at him curiously as they walked by. A few stopped and stared at him, alert for the slightest deviation from normal behavior on the part of anyone.

He spread his big arms wide. "Hear me!" he brayed in his great voice. "Hear me! Hear this, all nations! Pay attention, all who live on earth, important people, ordinary people, rich and poor alike! My lips have wisdom to utter, my heart whispers sound sense; I turn my attention to a proverb, and set my solution to the harp. Why should I be afraid in evil times, when malice dogs my step and hems me in, of men who trust in their wealth and boast of the profusion of their riches? But man could never redeem himself or pay his ransom to God: it costs so much to redeem his life, it is beyond him; how then could he live on forever and never see the Pit—when all the time he sees that wise men die; that foolish and stupid ones perish alike, and leave their fortunes to others?"

His huge voice overpowered the pervasive Mall music. More and more people gathered around. A security guard came pushing through the people and yelled up at Moses, "Get down from there! You get down from there!"

"You get down on your knees, brother, and pray for the dead souls of the Meadows family." The man grabbed at Moses, and Moses leaned over and clubbed him on the side of the head with a thick fist. The man was caught by the crowd before he could fall. He recovered his balance, shook his head and went unsteadily away to find reinforcements.

"Their tombs are their eternal home, their lasting residence, though they owned estates that bore their names. Man, when he prospers, forfeits intelligence; he is one with the cattle doomed to slaughter. So on they go with their self-assurance, with men to run after them when they raise their voice. Like sheep to be laid in the grave, death will herd them to pasture and the upright will have the better of them. Dawn will come and then the show they made will disappear. The grave is the home for them! But God will redeem my life from the grasp of the grave, and will receive me. Do not be awed when a man grows rich, when the glory of his House increases; when he dies he can take nothing with him, his glory cannot follow him down. The soul he made so happy while he lived, thinking all the time, look after yourself and men will praise you —he will join the company of his ancestors who will never see the light of day again. Man in his prosperity forfeits intelligence; he is one with the cattle doomed to slaughter, to a darkness everlasting, forgotten by man and God alike. And so this House, these Meadows, they have raised up an edifice they call a Church; it is but a possession, an earthly glory for them and their progeny, and it has nothing to do with worship, nothing to do with eternal life. I proclaim the everlasting life of the one who once lived who was named Paul Meadows. A holy man who died young and now has life everlasting in the kingdom of heaven—"

"You are under arrest," the tall young deputy said.

"What for?"

"Creating a disturbance. Disturbing the peace. Assault on a civilian security officer. Come on along."

The audience backed away from the officer. He took two steps back and unsnapped the flap on his holster. Moses jumped down lightly and said, "All right, all right. If that's what you want, all right."

When Eliot Erskine arrived at Rick Liddy's small office, Liddy was just finishing his sandwich and coffee.

He nodded, chewed, drank the last of the coffee and said, "Siddown, Elly. How'd it go?"

"All right. Dockerty had Moses in a little holding cell. He seemed calm enough. Lieutenant Coombs got there a few minutes before I did. Like you guessed, they're going to try to make him for the Linda Owen murder, but their hearts aren't in it. He'd been read his rights. He said he was willing to talk without a lawyer present. He told about driving the woman from the motel to the Center when she couldn't start her rental car. He said he hadn't known her name at that time, and didn't find out until much later when he heard she was reported missing, and Peggy Moon at the motel told him that was the same woman he had transported to the Center and back.

"Dockerty asked him why he had started preaching at the Mall, and Moses said that some voice had told him to. Dockerty wanted him to promise he wouldn't do it again, and Moses said he would be glad to promise, but if the voice told him to do it again, he would. Coombs asked him if the voice had ever told him to do other things, bad things, and Moses said that the voice, and other voices he couldn't understand, had started about when the big rains started. And he said that he did not believe the voice would ever tell him to do anything bad. He said he had been thinking about that voice, and he thought it was the voice of Paul Meadows."

Liddy nodded. "The kid brother."

"Moses was in the funny farm with the brother years ago. That's why he came here. He got religion from the brother."

"I heard about that from somebody. Maybe the Sheriff."

"Witnesses say Petersen grabbed Moses by the leg and tried to yank him off the side of that fountain, which is a damn fool thing for a spindly little guy almost seventy to try. Moses leaned over and kind of casually belted him alongside the head, which seems like an okay response to me. Woman told me it was more of a push than a blow. He went right along with the deputy, meek as a lamb. Petersen won't press charges. I ordered him not to, like you suggested."

"What's your guess about what will happen?"

Erskine shrugged. "There'll be a lot of pressure. I don't think the political pressure means much to Dockerty. He's too close to retirement. He's easygoing, but he's smart. He could have rousted Moses out of the area a couple of years ago. He decided he was harmless. If it turns out he isn't, it isn't going to hurt Dockerty. There was a television van there when I left, and some people with cameras. Moses was worried about his truck, so the Sheriff told a deputy to arrange to pick it up and take it out to where Moses lives, and explain to the woman there, Mrs. Holroyd, about Moses being detained."

Rick Liddy pried between his back molars with a toothpick and inspected the end of it, and dropped it into his wastebasket. "But you know and I know that holding Moses is a crock. We've got a pretty good idea, haven't we?"

Eliot Erskine tipped his chair onto its back legs and studied Rick Liddy. The man's expression was unreadable. He had a ruddy, rough-skinned complexion, big hands with the dimpled knuckles of the ex-brawler, a thick short neck as broad as his jaws, glossy black hair parted in the middle with such precision it looked like a wig, lots of meat on the shoulders and chest, pale eyes that looked out of the skull holes like creatures safe in caves. Liddy was one very hard person, one very good cop—with that law degree the FBI likes their people to have. Erskine was trying to determine whether or not Liddy was leading him into some kind of a trap, and so he decided that it was best to say nothing at all. He had learned that difficult feat in Atlanta during interrogations. It is awkward in one-on-one situations to say nothing at all. The silence finally becomes intense and electric, like a scream unheard.

Finally Liddy stirred and said, "When we talked last Tuesday, you were going to come back to me and tell me how Walter Macy reacted to your telling him you were stopping the surveillance."

"I didn't get to tell him yet. It wasn't anything I wanted to say over the phone to him."

Liddy closed his eyes, sighed, massaged his brow. "We were walking around it before the body was found. How does finding the body change what we had been guessing? It means she didn't pick up any hitchhiker, and she probably didn't have any car trouble."

"Coombs told Dockerty that all indications were that somebody had done some of her packing for her, jamming things in the suitcase any which way. Coombs said Owen said his wife was neat and tidy about packing and about everything else, apparently. Do we get any kind of a scenario from that, Rick?"

"I won't make any guesses until I know everything you know."

"I think you do."

"So why do I get the impression you're just a little bit edgier than you should be?"

Erskine sighed. "Okay, we've both been in the business too long. And I did more than I should have. Anyway, I found out that Alberta Macy has a sister with cancer down in Jacksonville. She had a bad setback last May and Mrs. Macy went down there on Friday the sixth of May, back on Monday the ninth."

"I kind of wish you hadn't done that, Elly."

"I know. I wish I hadn't. Sure, I've thought it through. You know the type. They go along for years and years, keeping all the dirt locked up in their heads. We nailed one of them one time in Atlanta, he had a secret hidey-hole in his house, a baseboard with a concealed hinge, full of some of the dirtiest books I ever saw. His wife died when he was sixty, and he took to bringing women home, killing them, arranging them this way and that, taking Polaroid pictures of them and then burying them in the side wall of his cellar. He nailed three of them before his luck ran out and the fourth intended victim knocked him down and called the cops. He confessed the whole thing before we could hardly get his name and address on the records. We push Macy just a little and he will fold, Rick. That's my hunch."

After a thoughtful pause, Liddy said, "Okay. So the scenario shapes up that he had about a minute and a half or two minutes alone with her before you came in, Elly. And she did some clumsy faking and got out. But he had set up a meet with her for Saturday night. Wife away. He had the pictures and the tapes and he had the innocence to think that any magazine or newspaper—not just the cheapest scandal sheets—would use garbage like that. So they were parked in a private place, maybe one of the old logging roads. It's dark. Maybe parking lights and dash lights. She's a city woman from the North, sweet-smelling, a work-ing woman. And so she surprised him by being offended by that junk you collected for Walter Macy. So he started to preach to her about how in the name of decency she has to help pry John Tinker out of the top slot in the great Church. Maybe the garbage turned him on while it was turning her off. So she tried to get away from him and didn't make it. When he realized she was dead, he had to stifle the impulse to drive away and leave her right there. So he left his car there and put her in the rental car and drove back to the motel. He had her keys. There's no restaurant there, hardly any traffic. He'd wait until he was sure the office was closed and the Moons asleep." Liddy hesitated, then continued. "He packed up her clothes and toilet articles and snuck out to the car with them. Left the key on the bureau. Drove out and probably didn't turn on his lights until he was on the highway. No traffic to speak of out there beyond Lakemore late at night. He would turn away from Lakemore, turn west. Two miles west you have a crossroads sign and a gravel road that leads over to the dirt road that parallels the main road. Weather records say it was a clear night. Would he have known about the abandoned farm and about the well? Maybe part of his job is looking at property in the area. Okay, so he'd gather her up out of the car and tote her to the old well, probably moaning out loud in the night, loaded with fright and remorse and guilt. He'd hear her go crashing down and thud against the bottom. Then he would drop her stuff, go find those boards and put them across the top of the well. And ever since then he's been trying not to think and trying not to remember. He drove down to the city and put the car in airport parking, and left the keys and the papers on the car in the glove compartment. Let's say he got there and walked away from the car about three-thirty or four in the morning. There's a Trailways bus that stops at the airport terminal at five in the morning, and comes down off the Interstate to let passengers off at Lakemore at ten of six. So he walked from there to his car, where he had left it in a place well off the road. Five miles? Six? Four?

"Put him at his car at dawn, looking around to find what he had not seen in the dark. One of her shoes, her purse, the torn panties. Nothing else. He puts the shoe and the panties in the purse. He wants to get rid of those things as quickly as he can. I would think he would probably open his trunk, take out a tire iron, walk thirty steps into the pine woods, pry out a hole big enough, force the purse into it, cover it, stomp the dirt down, brush the needles back over the disturbed place. He drives home, cleans himself up, changes, and he's at the Tabernacle an hour before the service. Did I miss anything?"

Erskine shrugged. "It covers everything, but a lot of it is what the lawyers call pure conjecture."

Liddy stood up. "Lately I can't seem to think straight inside the office. Come on."

They took a security car and drove out past the informal salutes of the guards at the gate, Liddy at the wheel. It wasn't until they were in the middle of Lakemore, headed west, that Erskine said, "I can't buy him being familiar with that farm and finding it at night. So I'd revise your scenario this way. On Saturday afternoon he drove around scouting the area, looking for a private place where they could talk. He checked out that little unpaved country road and when he came to the farm, he drove around in back of the barn. It seemed private enough. Maybe he walked around a little and noticed the well. He wouldn't have had any idea in God's world how he was going to use it, but later, when he needed to, he remembered it, and that roof over it would make it easy to find in the starlight. And that's where he left his car when he drove hers to the airport."

"So why wouldn't he chuck the shoe and purse down the well?"

"Maybe by daylight he felt too exposed. Maybe he heard a farm truck on that road. Maybe he could see somebody over on the next hill. He'd drive somewhere else and bury the purse."

"I wonder where she met him?"

"Maybe the Mall, early in the evening, after dark, and he asked her to follow him in her car."

When they reached the burned-out farm, there were three young boys throwing rocks at the barn. After Liddy had stood and glowered at them for a few minutes, they drifted away, looking back, then yelled something when they were a safe distance away.

Erskine looked at the tire tracks in the rain-soft earth and said, "Been lots of traffic in here."

"Gawpers and goopers, official and unofficial. Two cars could park here with no chance of being seen from that road." Liddy walked over to where the house had stood and sat on the fieldstone foundation, his legs in the tall grass.

Erskine said, "I think he's destroyed all the stuff I turned over to him. That would be a link. And he'll pretend to be annoyed when I tell him I've quit. But he'll be pleased."

"Where are we?" Liddy asked.

"Up some kind of creek. Especially me. It would take a very small push to open him up. And with or without the push, he is going to crack open, I think. Soon, maybe. A full and complete statement in which I am going to figure, along with John Tinker and Molly Wintergarten and Linda Owen. My services to Macy were illegal."

"But you came to me and told me what he wanted and you said you were reluctant to do it, and I ordered you to do it, telling you it could affect security, and that is our job."

"Thanks, Rick. That's a nice thing for you to do."

"Forget nice. Just hope it doesn't come up. Because we can guess what will happen if it does. The old man is permanently out of business. The number two preacher is on trial. John Tinker Meadows is in the papers as having an affair with the wife of one of the business executives who run the Meadows Center commercial interests. That bunch of affiliate ministers will run John Tinker out of the Church. And Finn Efflander didn't get where he is by having a poor sense of timing. He'll be off and gone the minute he's convinced what happened really happened. Elly, this whole thing is going to come tumbling down. When the elephant falls dead, all the hyenas come trotting out of the woods, licking their chops. Politicians, lawyers, commentators . . . "

"But we should give him that little push, Rick."

"These are nice jobs, yours and mine. This place does a lot for a lot of people. A very nice cash flow for a lot of good works."

"And a lot of perks too."

"Which wouldn't add up to much of a big percentage of overhead, Elly. How many weeks does it take to bring in enough to buy those two Gulfstreams? You worked the mail and money room. Take a guess."

"Eight to ten weeks."

"John Tinker has built up a lot of friendship in Congress, with Charley Winchester's help. It's like having a nice tent to keep out the rain. Something like this would blow the tent down. There would be a lot of things they'd start paying attention to. Like how many blacks they've got in the University. One on the faculty. Three students. Discrimination. Student loans go out the window. Like with Bob Jones University."

"You're trying to tell me something, Rick."

"Jobs are still tight. This thing develops a lot of employment. ECB Enterprises, the Mall, Lakemore Construction, Meadows Settlements, Meadows Development. With more big things coming, they say. Geriatric medical center and hospital."

"What good is it?" Erskine asked loudly. "Even without any push from anybody, he's going to come apart. He can't handle it. Where are you trying to go with this?"

"You're a member of the Church too."

"I know. I tithe, you tithe. All God's chillen gotta tithe."

"I wouldn't want you should get smartass, Erskine. The Church has come to mean a lot to me. I told you that before. And it means even more to Martha than it does to me. It is not going to come tumbling all the way down. Nothing with eighty something affiliate preachers and their little churches involved is going to lie down and die. But it would really cripple it for a long time, I think. I didn't know God was offering me eternal life until I found it here. Maybe I owe the Church some kind of sacrifice."

"Sacrifice?"

"The sudden death of Walter Macy."

"I didn't hear you say that."

"The sudden *natural* death of Walter Macy."

Erskine turned quickly and walked away, past the well house, out to where an old woodpile rotted away in the weeds. He kicked one of the rotten logs, and then he walked slowly back.

"I don't know how to say this. Yes, that would be neat. That would quiet the whole thing. And not hard to do. Lots of easy ways. Sap him with a sock full of dry sand, and run a sharpened piano wire between his ribs into the heart, poke it around a few times. But what I am is a cop. An officer of the law. Maybe that's *my* religion. I can't take life. I don't even hunt."

"We're employees of an enterprise more private than public, agreed?"

"Of course."

"We took our oaths a long time ago to different entities. Official oaths about official duties."

"Right."

"As paid security officers, we are, on the average, civilians, Elly. We can think as civilians, and we have the right to take any risks we think should be taken. As civilians."

"In spite of all that, I can't have any part of it, no matter how it neatens things up, and no matter what kind of monster Macy is. Maybe he's dumped dozens of women down wells. It's against what I am, or maybe what I think I am. It is so impossible for me I can't even let you do it."

Liddy stood up and brushed the seat of his pants. He smiled and shook his head. "I knew that's how you'd jump. I had to try. Maybe, if I guessed wrong about you, I would have tried to go through with it. I don't know. I don't think I want to know. So there's only one thing I am going to ask you. Let's you and me not be the ones to give him the little push, okay?"

"Concealing the knowledge of a crime?"

"Tell me this, Mr. Clean. Are you absolutely positively certain that he killed that woman?"

"I guess not. Pretty sure, but not certain."

"Then you can go along with my suggestion that you leave it the hell alone?"

"On one condition, Rick. If they start to manufacture any evidence to tie Moses into it, I'm going to steer Coombs toward Macy."

"If that happens, we'll both do the steering."

"I appreciate that. I really do."

"Be my guest."

As they strolled back toward the car, Erskine said, almost laughing, "I can't believe we've been talking about what we've been talking about.

I come off as some kind of priss cop, obeying every rule. I used to hate working with one of those as a partner. Everything by the book. I always took shortcuts here and there."

"You come off as a man, Elly."

For a very brief time after the rains the humidity had been low but now it was back up again, very high, in the usual August range of ninety-five to a hundred, in a heat that silenced the birds and brought out ten thousand cicadas and tree toads, sounding like faraway picnics and road races.

Molly Wintergarten left the club at three o'clock on Saturday afternoon and did not make as good time as usual driving south to the next exit, due to the places where shallow water still flowed onto the Interstate to be whacked into fine spray by the speeding sixteen-wheelers. So she fully expected John Tinker Meadows to be there waiting for her at the double-wide trailer. After she had relatched the big cattle gate behind her, she drove down the winding muddy trace toward the trailer and the pond, looking ahead for the sheen of his blue Ford van in the shade of the trees. She was uncomfortably sweaty because something had gone wrong with the air-conditioning unit in the little convertible Rabbit. She had the top closed and the windows closed, but the huff of air from the vents seemed but faintly chilled, certainly not enough for a day like this.

She was so busy looking for his car she did not notice the trailer until she was fifty feet away from it, and then wondered why she hadn't seen it sooner. Burden Pond extended all the way to the steps and underneath, and she could see, by the mud line along the length of the trailer, the water had come much higher and had, in fact, floated or pushed it off the foundation blocks. The back right corner was canted down, the front left corner lifted high. She undid the padlock and climbed up into it. It was a sodden ruin inside, stinking of mud and mildew. She backed out and shut the door and hurried back to her car. The bugs had begun to find her. She ran the motor for the sake of the faint chill from the vents until the warning light went on, indicating it was overheating. She turned the motor off and rolled the windows down a few inches and sat fanning herself with an old *Time* magazine she found under the front seat. But the bugs were coming in, whining in her ears, and the sweat was running down her face and down between her breasts and down from her armpits, soaking her pink top and the waistband of her white tennis skirt.

Slowly she began to realize that John Tinker had really meant it this time. She had used their phone signal three times during the morning, and he hadn't called back from a pay phone until after eleven.

"How about like three o'clock, lover?" she asked him.

"Sorry."

"Sewed up with something again?"

"Didn't you hear me last time, Molly? This has been loads of fun and thank you very much, and I'll never forget you, and so forth, but this little game is over. I told you that."

"Bull! You don't get to say when it's finished."

"I'm saying it."

"You listen to me, Tink. Listen very carefully. I am going down there and you are going down there. Today. And you are going to be affectionate and loving, and you are not going to talk crap to me about this being over. It isn't over. You are going to be there because if you are not, I am going to make you the sorriest preacher in the state and the nation. I'll geld you at the entrance to your stupid Tabernacle, pet. Or I'll hand Rolf the knife. Let me see. How does that work? I cry and cry and cry and finally tell him that you've been making me sleep with you because if I didn't he was going to be fired. Rolf will believe everything I tell him. I am yanking on your leash, Tink. So heel, goddamn you! See you at three-thirty." She had hung up as he had started to say something, and when the phone rang again moments later, she did not answer it.

And now she was totally miserable in the heat, itching and angry. She looked at her watch and said she would give him until quarter after four and then that was it. And he was going to pay a very heavy price for every single minute of her discomfort. Worst of all, she had awakened this morning wanting him, awakened from a dream about him. There'd been, by her own careful count in erotic reverie, sixteen men, beginning when she was fifteen, but never one who'd been able to satisfy her as completely as Tink.

She started the car and went fishtailing up the muddy track. When she got to the crest she put the top down so as to cool herself in the rush of air, and blow the bugs out at the same time. She started to slow down as she reached the gate, then clamped her jaw tightly and stepped on the gas. Big splinters of board flew up in the air and fell behind her, and she heard in the impact the thin tinkle of the glass from her broken headlights, and thought for a moment of the various ways it could have happened, and selected the most plausible one to tell Rolf.

A few miles later an air horn blared at her as she moved from the access strip to the traffic lanes on the Interstate and a tanker went by her at a speed that twitched the steering wheel in her hands. She put the pedal to the floor and within a few miles she went by him at better than eighty-five. The wind snapped her hair against her forehead and ears. The speed climbed slowly.

She saw a sheen of water across the two lanes a hundred yards ahead and held the wheel more firmly. She was in the passing lane. Just as she reached the water, the great air horn roared again, and in the rearview mirror she saw that same tanker tailgating her, the cab with two figures in it high above her. So you win, she thought, and twisted the wheel to move over to the right lane. But the water was causing the front wheels, at that speed, to hydroplane, and when there was no effect, she turned the wheel further clockwise. Beyond the water was dry pavement. When the cramped tires snubbed sidelong against the dry concrete, the little car tripped over, throwing her out high and to the left toward the median strip, breaking her legs against the steering wheel as she was catapulted out.

There was the great shock, the jar, and a slow wonderment in her mind. The sky and the road and the green fields were circling around her, and in one glimpse she saw her beloved little yellow car bounding and whirling itself to death, bits flying off it. The grass swarmed close then, and she went down into a green thud, a great flash of white light and nothingness. The cars began to slow and stop, and the trucks began to call in on Channel 9.

At four o'clock on Sunday afternoon, Carolyn Pennymark waited for her flight in the Pan Am Clipper Club at the city airport an hour from Lakemore. Her flight was delayed in Tampa. Her giant purse which served as carry-on, suitcase, toilet case and camera bag was on the seat beside her. She had changed to a wrinkled white blouse and a sharply creased pair of pale blue polyester trousers too big for her, with the cuffs turned up. The blue denim work hat was squashed down on her springy hair, and her lavender lenses sat slightly askew. From time to time, as she talked, she dipped quickly to take a salted peanut from the bowl on the low coffee table in front of her, or take a quick sip from her bourbon on the rocks.

While she talked one part of her mind was busy trying to remember the last name of the man she was sitting next to and talking to. The first name was Sam. He was with one of the networks, but not in front of the camera. She hadn't seen him in perhaps three years and there he was, smiling at her and beckoning to her when she turned away from the desk after clearing her business-class ticket and her membership card with the Clipper Club woman.

"Anyway," she said, "where I am now, doing what I do, what chance do I get to have to look at dead bodies? I mean, you take something like *Out Front*, you don't go yelling for anybody to stop the presses, not that anybody ever did except in old movies. The thing I feel ashamed of is where I put the knock on Lindy Rooney talking to that PR bitch with all the teeth because I guess there was something about her that bent me the wrong way. In all honesty maybe every big lively beautiful blonde bends dark dim ladies like me the wrong way and we resent hell out of it. But who do you blame for genetics? Like I always say, we're lucky to be here at all, right? But it wasn't fair painting that picture of Lindy, because she wasn't all that bad. I mean, she had the makings of a pretty good tiger, but she'd never had the newsroom background to teach her the moves. When we worked together, it was okay, really. And I told that cute little husband of hers with the big mustache that Lindy was okay loyal when she was out of town. What did that cost me? Because she was, but I knew something about her I didn't want to tell him. One night in a motel God knows where Lindy and I got sloshed pretty good on the grape, a bottle apiece and a third one to split, and it got to be confession time and she said, not right out, but sort of crosswise, that she and the little guy with the mustache didn't make it too good except once in a while because he was, she called it, unresponsive. He didn't ever seem to pick up on the clues she'd give him when she was really ready and willing, and always seemed to want to make it at the wrong time. I tell you, Sam, he was just cute enough I was tempted to hang around and give it my best shot, which isn't a whole hell of a lot, but the best I got, but the way it looked to me, the lady owns half the motel with her brother was already pounding in the stakes and stringing the bob wire. Kind of cute in a monkey-face kind of way, she is. You know the type, and I would say maybe getting a little bit long in the tooth if it wasn't I've got the same problem myself. She moves young, though, you know what I mean? Like quick-slim. Anyway just about the worst move I made in this whole thing, I went through all my little routines until

I finally got a look at a little stack of eight-by-ten glossy black and whites of during the autopsy, and believe me, Sam, you never want to see anybody you have ever known looking like that. It is worse than any kind of picture you can get in your head from reading Steve King. It shook me, pal. That experience was a bitch. You know what I mean. We've seen bodies in worse shape, like when they pull them out of the Potomac after a long winter, but always nobody you knew, you've laughed with, walked with, worked with. I told Marty on the phone that it was my feeling they weren't ever going to make anybody for killing her, and the place was so crawling with media it wasn't worth me hanging around for the magazine. I should have stayed, I guess. I know I could have dug up some stuff, some of it pretty raunchy to be going on in the middle of the Bible lessons, but to tell the truth I was beginning to feel pretty strange about that whole operation. It made me begin to feel like a little kid again, and it made me feel as if doing my digging and prying was kind of like when you were little and they shushed you for making too much noise in church. I got the feeling that if I unmasked some of the kinky ones and we did a big story on sin and corruption in paradise, what I would be doing is hurting the Eternal Church of the Believer, and somehow I didn't want to do that. I'm not hooked on it, but a lot of people are. You see what I mean, Sam? It's the whole world to them, and heaven too, and it keeps them going in hard times, making them feel like this world is just a passing phase and sooner or later, off you go, with golden trumpets and all that. Funny, I've got no scruples about knocking institutions every chance I get. Conglomerates, banks, movie studios, government bureaus, political committees. I know they've got rotten spots and I can dig until I come to one and then open it up to daylight and let the people take a look. You probably read how those right-wing bastards tried to car-bomb me out of Guatemala City, but all they got was the chauffeur and the guard assigned to me. It went off when I was coming down the steps from seeing the minister of something or other, and it knocked me back up the steps on my ass, but I got some shots they used of the car burning and the guard there face down beside it with his uniform burning in back. Maybe what it is about that place, Sam, there has to be things people believe in, good or bad, and Sister Mary Margaret Meadows, she really does believe and she's doing her best while everything seems to be kind of falling down around her lately. That's what we do with what they give us, right? We take our best shot. Sam, how about you go over and get more peanuts in the bowl, and while you're at it, a real weak little bourbon on the rocks, about this high? Thanks, love."

The Southern Memorial Hospital occupied four blocks on the west side of downtown, twelve miles from the airport. At the time Carrie Pennymark's flight was loading, Rolf Wintergarten waited in a small room down the corridor from Intensive Care for them to give him his once-an-hour installment of five minutes with Molly. Down in the basement, behind a labeled drawer front with a stainless-steel handle, reposed the refrigerated remains of Linda Rooney Owen, awaiting final reports on the laboratory tests of the tissue samples taken by Drs. Ludeker and Johnson. If no further tests and samples were recommended, then the body could be released to the immediate family for disposition.

Wintergarten flipped through tattered travel magazines with color photographs of canals in France, villages in Crete, beaches on Pacific islands. He wondered vaguely who had decided that the waiting rooms for Intensive Care should be stocked with travel magazines. Get away from it all. Stop thinking about it all. Sure.

He wondered when his sister would arrive, if she would look for him at the airport, if she could find him on her own. A little old man shared the small waiting room with him. He was bald and cadaverous, in a suit too big for him. He had a thick book on his lap and he was bending over it to read, moving his lips, taking a long time between pages. Wintergarten wondered if the book would last the man the rest of his life.

The nurse beckoned to him from the doorway, filling his mind with panic. The hour would not be up for another fifteen minutes. She said Dr. Menirez wanted to speak to him. Menirez waited in the alcove outside the Intensive Care double doors, looking out the window at the glaze of heat over the Sunday city. He was too young, Wintergarten thought. Entirely too young.

"What's wrong? Is something wrong?"

"Let's sit down. I told you this morning that she's got some big problems, but I didn't know how big. We've been keeping a close watch on her, evaluating the damage. When she was brought in, Dr. Hendrin in Emergency diagnosed primary brain stem injury, and I confirmed his diagnosis. We had coma, stertorous breathing, pinpoint pupils quadrispasticity, all of which could have come from intercranial bleeding, but there was no raised intercranial pressure, so no point in going in to find or stop any bleeding. Okay? Are you following me?"

"I think so."

"We know now that she suffered some thoracic damage, damage to the chest, and we've been getting edema, hypoxia, unstable circulation and a fluttery heartbeat. We took a brain wave pattern a few minutes ago. It isn't entirely flat, but it's getting there. I'm sorry, but we have a really lousy prognosis here. She was just too badly damaged. I'm really sorry. I don't think there's anything we could have done or could do to save her."

"She's dying!"

"That's right. She's going whether we keep her hooked up to the equipment or not."

"Oh Jesus. Oh God. Oh Molly honey."

He leaned over and put his forehead against the cold metal of the right-hand arm of the chair. The young doctor put his hand on his shoulder. "You could come in and hold her hand. It won't be long."

They had drawn the curtains around the bed. Her hand was slack. Half her face was a swollen purple bruise. A tube was fastened to her throat somehow, and it pumped air into and out of her. The eye that wasn't swollen shut was half open and all he could see was the white. There was no particular moment when it happened. He suddenly realized her hand was cooling off. He called the nurse and she came and listened for a heartbeat and told him he should go. He walked out through a blear of tears and when he was halfway down the long corridor toward the elevators, he remembered to keep his head up and square his shoulders and walk briskly. And then he remembered he did not have to do that anymore.

He saw his sister come out of the elevator. He had not seen her since the wedding. It startled him to see how old she looked. He hurried to her and put his arms around her and sobbed once and said, "She's gone, Allie. She's gone."

The sister held him and patted him. "There there," she said. "There there. Rolf? The taxi charged me eighteen dollars to come in from the airport! Can you imagine?"

•

Sixteen

Finn Efflander was mildly surprised when John Tinker Meadows delayed their usual Sunday discussion until Monday, and then suggested they meet in the old man's office on the fourth floor of the Manse. It was as if he had anticipated the bad news Efflander was bearing, and thought to armor himself with the old man's aura.

When Finn knocked and went in, John Tinker was sitting in the big black leather armchair behind the big slate-top desk, surrounded by all the talismans of the old man's past victories. He was wearing a pale blue terry bathrobe and old sandals. It was ten in the morning. His hair was uncombed and there was a visible shadow of beard on his cheeks and jaw.

"Sit down, old friend," John Tinker said. "I have been sitting here for four hours. Not all the time. I've roamed around, but mostly I've been sitting and thinking. Where are we going? What have we been doing right? And wrong? Making lists, I guess."

"The long view?"

"Right. Anything I should know in the routine reports?"

Finn opened his folder on the desk. "No report from Rolf, of course, but his assistant, Jorgland, reports progress. Occupancy up, rentals up, traffic up. He says Wintergarten wants to discuss additional motel space with Harold Sherman. Ben Harvey reported on Lakemore Construction. The thirty houses in Section F of the Settlements are nearly done and all spoken for, and he has begun foundation work on G and H. Then he reports, wearing his other hat, Chairman of the Board at the bank, that the maintenance people did not keep the big pipes clear that lead through the wall around the flat roof of the bank. So they were blocked and a big tonnage of water accumulated, which broke down one corner of the roof and flooded through all the way down to ground level. He's getting the damage looked at and an estimate of what it will cost to repair structural damage. Charley is researching the insurance coverage.

"Because of our housing shortage here, I asked Walker McGaw to ease up on the radio promotion of the Settlements for a while. The radio coverage is on a twenty-four-hour basis and they have added two more languages to cassette distribution. The television transmissions are seen now in two hundred and thirty-one national markets. Spencer McKay on television production and McGaw on radio are both enthusiastic about the market survey technique Joe Deets worked out, relating specific test programs to response in selected areas. McKay calls it a wonderful device for fine-tuning the program content.

"Security had nothing to report, and neither did Maintenance and Grounds. Our University president, Dr. Hallowell, says that they have accepted a hundred and forty applications for the freshman class. It will include three Vietnamese and two blacks.

"Jenny Albritton did a good job with the editing of the interview you gave regarding the Owen murder, and it has been played at least three times over every television outlet. She appreciates the way McGaw and McKay worked with her on it. She also reported that she has all her ducks in a row for the arrival of Mr. Williamson, one of the new Founders of the Society of Merit. He and his family will get very special attention.

"Joe Deets reports receipts up five-point-two percent for the year ending August fifteenth, compared to the previous year. And the ratio of all expenses to all income from all sources is down by eight tenths of a percent. I have no report from Walter Macy."

"None at all?"

"He promised it and then he said he had been too busy. Too many things had piled up. He said he would get around to it."

"Did he know you wanted it for our weekly meeting?"

"Yes, he did. He seemed very upset about Molly Wintergarten."

"Everyone is upset, of course. Would he have had anything special to report, as far as you know?"

"I don't think so. He just seemed nervous and irritable and confused."

"Go ahead, then. Anything from my sister?"

"She wants to set up a music scholarship so she can attract some better voices for the choir. She's very anxious that everyone try very hard to show the Reverend Tom Daniel Birdy how happy we'd all be to have him here. And she suggests heavier concentration on our mission effort in Guatemala and Peru. That's about it."

"Which brings us down to your special little chores, Finn," John Tinker said.

"Which one first?"

"The media coverage of the Owen murder."

"That's softening up fast. They're leaving. I've talked to Coombs and Dockerty, and I've checked it out with Rick Liddy—checked what the officials told me—and the general feeling is that nobody is ever going to find out who killed her. Too much time has passed. To keep a story going you need little additives. Even that magazine, *Out Front*, called their girl back to New York. The husband is waiting for them to release the body for cremation, and then he'll leave."

"Why are they keeping it?"

"Chemical analysis. They might want to do more."

"How about accreditation?"

"All the colleges with a religious orientation have come in except two, and I have promises from them. So we're looking for the right names with lots of degrees. I've suggested we set up the office in Cambridge. Borrow some respectability from proximity."

"How about the medical complex?"

"We have some problems there."

"Like what?"

"It's difficult for me to explain."

"You better give it your best shot, Efflander."

Finn sighed. "I guess we got off on the wrong foot in the beginning, John. Somehow I've given you the feeling that you can alarm me, personally. Okay, you've detected alarm, but it is just alarm about what might happen to the things I've built around here, the administrative structures, the personnel structures. So when you threaten me and say, 'You better give it your best shot, Efflander,' in that harsh tone of voice, all I want to do is try to keep you from meddling in the structure, in the lines of authority and responsibility."

"Why should my meddling, as you call it, alarm you?"

"I've spent six years creating something that works. It works in spite of all the reasons it shouldn't work. I don't expect you to be able to understand how delicate that structure can be if you push it in the wrong direction. I've seen a new CEO come into a fairly healthy company and drive it into the ground in eighteen months. I have a lot of loyalty to what I've built."

"And no loyalty to me?"

Finn smiled. "I do what you tell me to do as best I can."

"And it ends up being done your way."

"Sometimes, John."

John Tinker Meadows sat silently for thirty seconds. Finn could hear the huff of the air vent, a subsonic rumble of compressors, the clatter of elevator doors.

Finally John Tinker said, "So I am not as subtle and wise and all-perceiving as you are when it comes to managing all the little departments and compartments of this place. But I have one damn good idea of direction. I set policy."

"That is quite correct. I carry out the policy you set. And now I have some problems carrying out the policy you decided on for this medical complex. The problem is personnel."

"Why should it be a problem when we have the money to hire the very best? And what a temptation it could be for a good man to be in on it from the beginning."

"In a sense," Finn said, "I anticipated what the problem would be. The land is no problem. We can pick up three thousand acres northwest of here, between our rear line and the Interstate cloverleaf, for two million two. Or the same acreage ten miles south of here for one million seven. Money isn't a problem, according to Joe. He can earmark two hundred million and keep it in securities we can get out of very readily. Both of these would be clean deals. No kickback charitable donations. No overpricing. No planning and zoning problems at all."

"I can't see the point in setting up ten miles from here."

"Let me work around to that," Finn said. "The whole thing is one hell of an idea. A teaching hospital, medical school, hotel for outpatients, nursing school, campus, dormitories, nursing homes, therapy center, all focusing on the problems of aging. It is a fantastic fit with what you have here. It makes good sense. However."

"However what?"

Finn took a typed letter from the folder on the desk. "I want to read this to you. You remember I told you that in searching for staff I wanted to use an old friend with an executive search group in New York. He's been working on this for six, nearly seven months. Here's what he has to say:

" 'Dear Finn, It seems to be time to play a little showdown and time for me to stop kidding you. As you outlined it, it is a dream project. And, as you told me, Doctor Meadows charged you with bringing in absolutely top people for interviews down there.

" 'So we have been going after the best. Nose to nose, because phones and letters are no good for this kind of project. The key man, of course, is the medic who would head up the medical school, research wing, teaching aspects of the hospital, etc. Ideally, because this is long-range, we'd hope to find a man in his forties or very early fifties, with good tickets, good track record, well known, an administrator and a persuader as well as a top scientist, the kind of man whose name connected with anything has given it a cachet of both dignity and success in the past and will continue so to do.

" 'Here is what has happened. Without naming names, we identified and isolated six men who have the characteristics you people seek. I can tell you that on the basis of the bare outline—to be in charge of a huge geriatric medical center and be in on it from the ground-breaking ceremonies, and not have to get involved in fund raising, at least for many years to come—these dudes really salivated, Finn. I saw each one of them personally.

" 'They kept on salivating right up to the point where I told them that this was being promoted and financed by the Eternal Church of the Believer. That's when things got frosty. When they said they would consider it, I knew they meant no way.

" 'Old buddy, you are not going to attract top talent for that project. I'm sorry. You are dealing here with dedicated and intellectual people. These sects, these electronic ministries, give far too strong a suggestion of trading on ignorance, fear, bigotry . . . you name it. If it isn't in the Book, it ain't so. Believe, or you'll plain go to hell. Evolution is only a theory, they say. The six men I dealt with know that evolution is a fact. They know about the fossil sea creatures atop Everest, about ferns captured in stone two billion years ago. Every surgeon who has dissected the body of a human being has seen the faint traces in the throat structure of what were once gills a few million years ago, before we came up out of the sea. These men know that the Holy Bible is a great document, that the teachings of Christ are eternal, as are the teachings of Buddha and Mohammed. But they also know that it has been translated and retranslated so many times, many portions of it are so vague and muddy that unscrupulous men can interpret it in any way that suits their ambitions of the moment.

" 'These are the top people, Finn, and they cannot afford to compromise their reputations and their futures by becoming entangled with those Meadows people and their anti-intellectual message. They are too wary of some of the precepts of that particular sect coming in conflict with sound medical practice. They do not wish to endanger the peer respect and confidence they now have. You and I know that almost a quarter of the people in this great nation can't read or write. That gives men like the Meadows great scope to use fear, superstition and false hope as their leverage. If you can lower your sights and go second class, I can find you some imposing hacks who will jump at the chance. But your geriatric medical complex will never be first class under their guidance.

" 'I followed through on your suggestion of recontacting them on the basis that the complex would be located at least ten miles from Meadows Center, and would not have Eternal or Believer or Meadows in the name. But they said that made no difference in their decision. They wanted no part of it. Sorry, fella. Let me know what you want me to try next. ' "

John Tinker held his hand out. "Let me see that!"

Finn handed it to him. He read it, frowning, handed it back and said, "This Jew Commie bastard heretic is a close friend of yours?"

"Willis has been a good friend for a long time. I've never had any occasion to wonder about his politics or his religion."

"They're cute, you know. They develop wonderful cover stories."

"Cover story or not, you can depend on him to tell the truth, to give you the facts, regardless of how they might hurt. You realize that he could have tried to ring in a hack by puffing up his reputation. When I was thinking of taking the offer here, Willis advised against it."

"Did he, now?"

"I came here because it was a challenge. And I have no standing in the scientific community to protect. I had never seen or heard of any organization in such a dynamic state of growth that was so totally devoid of controls, of any administrative know-how."

"And because the money was very good. Don't forget the money, Finn."

"You never believe me when I say it just isn't all that important to me. I like being paid what I am worth, and I enjoy living well, but I came with you people because I'm neat. I hate all unnecessary confusion. And I wondered if it was possible to create order out of total chaos merely by managing the people properly."

"Not exactly chaos."

"John, take my word for it. You do not have the background to be able to see just how bad it was, just how many simultaneous disasters this operation was heading for."

"Funny what a different impression I have, Finn. We were getting along. We had loyal and devoted people working for us. The contributions were flowing in. My father was building the Church tall and strong. Neither of us had time for all the little details, so we went out and bought us a man who could take that burden off our shoulders. I can't recall any threats of chaos."

Finn leaned back and gave him a lazy smile. "You know, John, you may just be right after all. A man can get so stale in a job he loses his perspective. Maybe I have an exaggerated opinion of my own importance. I think I'd like to take a leave of absence. Say a year."

"You could make it permanent if that's what you want."

"We'll know better what each of us wants after the year is up."

"By the time the year is up we will have a man of the first quality here directing the building of the medical complex."

"I hope so. I think I can get away in thirty days. I'll find a good man to run the store for you."

"Finn, old friend, I don't want to put you out like that. I want you to start enjoying your long vacation as soon as possible. And living well on that money you've saved. I'm sure Harold Sherman can handle the odds and ends."

Finn Efflander hesitated, torn between loyalty to his organization and his people, and a dirty glee at what he thought might happen at Meadows Center under Harold Sherman. Character won, and he said, "I don't think Sherman is right for the job."

John Tinker Meadows got up from behind the great desk. "We had the judgment to pick you, Finn. I think we have the judgment to pick the man who'll fill in for you or replace you, whatever the fates decide. Drop us a card from some island resort, please. We all want to stay in touch with you, of course."

After Finn left, John Tinker Meadows looked over at the wall at the familiar photograph of Matthew Meadows standing beside General Dwight D. Eisenhower at some ceremonial occasion. The General was holding a salute and the preacher had his hat in his left hand and his right hand over his heart.

He remembered his father telling him what he did in moments of stress and confusion. He started to flip the Book open at random. It was the Oxford Bible, handsomely bound in heavy leather, one of the many gifts his father had received. But instead he turned to a familiar passage. His finger came to rest on the fifth chapter, seventeenth verse of Galatians. "For the flesh lusteth against the Spirit, and the Spirit against the flesh: and these are contrary the one to the other; so that ye cannot do the things that ye would."

He closed it and took the more familiar Jerusalem Bible and turned to the same verse. "Let me put it like this: if you are guided by the Spirit you will be in no danger of self-indulgence, since self-indulgence is the opposite of the Spirit, the Spirit is totally against such a thing, and it is precisely because the two are so opposed that you do not always carry out your good intentions." He read on. "If you are led by the Spirit, no law can touch you. When self-indulgence is at work the results are obvious: fornication, gross indecency and sexual irresponsibility; idolatry and sorcery; feuds and wrangling, jealousy, bad temper and quarrels; disagreements, factions, envy; drunkenness, orgies and similar things. I warn you now as I warned you before: those who behave like this will not inherit the kingdom of God."

He came out from behind the desk and walked slowly through the long conference room and into his suite. He walked into the bathroom and stared into the mirror and fingered his crust of beard, hearing the scratchy sound it made. He thought he should take a shower. His body felt stale.

By habit long ingrained, after he had stripped, he lowered himself to the cool tile floor for the series of push-ups. But after three he let himself settle naked against the tiles, cool against his chest, belly and groin. He thought about Molly. He thought about her being hurled up into the air when her car tripped over. He tried to feel pity, sorrow, loss. There was nothing. So he tried to feel relief, gladness, relaxation. Still nothing. He created the most vivid pictures of her in his mind, trying to create at the very least some faint visceral stir of longing. Nothing. Nothing at all.

He rolled up onto his knees, and with hands in front of his chest, palms pressed together, chin down, eyes closed, he said, "Father in heaven, please tell me what is wrong with me."

It was a long time since he had tried any kind of direct prayer. He had prayed, but it had been an easy, practiced thing, words without any anticipation of an answer. Always before when he had tried direct prayer, there had been a kind of an answer. There had been somewhere in his consciousness a resonance, as if his own words echoed in the back of his skull, and in their echoing they set up a sympathetic resonance with some part of his spirit, giving him comfort and the sense of having been heard.

This time his words were totally flat. They seemed to rise to a place not more than six inches above his head, and were there deadened and dispersed, as if absorbed by a slab of cork. He looked up at the light fixture in the center of the ceiling and said loudly, "Father, please tell me what has gone wrong!"

But no one heard. No one was listening. The hoarse sounds died without echo or emphasis. All his life he had thought of himself as being alone. But not like this. Not so totally alone. Not so totally empty. Not this close to death.

"Paul!" he whispered. But Paul was gone too. Along with Poppa and all the rest of them. Paul had looked up to him. And this had made him a better person than he was.

Lieutenant Coombs and Sergeant Slovik of the SBI sat in Mrs. Holroyd's living room amid the overfurnished clutter of forty years of marriage and eight years of widowhood. The draperies were drawn to close out the heat and sunlight, and in the gloom a large ceiling fan turned slowly.

"I know what they're saying," she said, "but they don't say it in front of me more than one time. Moses is a gentle person."

"But you said he has seemed different lately."

"He's been doing more preaching, that's all. He has a really fantastic memory, Lieutenant. He preaches about God on street corners. Is that illegal these days?"

"Only when he does it on private property without permission."

"I told you. I am a light sleeper. That dreadful old red truck of his is very noisy. As you maybe noticed, my driveway out there is full of lumps and holes. When he drives in or out it sounds like somebody banging on garbage cans. And there is no way he could leave during the night and come back at night without my hearing him. It would make me very nervous to have him leave at night because it means I'm alone here. It makes me nervous to have him in jail. Do you think I'm lying to you? I'm old, but I have a fantastic memory. Moses would not do anything so sinful. He is a hard worker. He does not drink or smoke or use bad language. Sheriff Dockerty checked his record, you know. And he has never done anything bad in all his life. My doctor says he probably had schizophrenia, and some people do get over it and can live out in society. They are dumping them out of the sanitariums all the time lately. Saving money, they say. But they won't remember to take their medication, even if they are able to afford it. We should all be glad that Moses can support himself—provided, of course, you don't have to use him as a scapegoat for a murder you can't solve."

"Mrs. Holroyd please. We do honestly want to find out who murdered Mrs. Owen."

"Then you should get right to it, and let Moses come home. Some wretched children have vandalized his old school bus since the rain, and he should come back and fix it before more rain comes."

"May we look at it?"

"If you have Moses' permission."

"We do."

"Then go right ahead."

They found six smashed windows, and a sour pile of clothes and books on which had been dumped the contents of opened cans of peaches, beef stew, evaporated milk and a variety of canned soups. With gingerly care, Slovik extracted the books, wiped them just enough to find out what they were about. "No porn, Jerry," he said at last. "Travels in the Holy Land. History of the Crusades. Living in Christ's Name. Stuff like that."

"They look old."

"They're like, you know, from garage sales."

They searched with care but found no letters, no photographs, no medicines, no magazines or newspapers.

"The kids could have taken stuff," Slovik said.

"Somehow, I doubt it," Jerry Coombs said. "I was thinking maybe we could hang on to him so if whoever did it is still in the area, they'd feel safe and maybe do something stupid. But it isn't fair. Let's let the son of a bitch go. He's got a lot of work to do here. Look, those little bastards even let the air out of his tires."

When they got back to the County Courthouse, Coombs called the State Attorney General's office, explained his recommendation to release the suspect and got permission to so advise the Sheriff. There were no charges to be filed.

After Moses, back in his own clothes, was released and had left with a deputy who would drive him on out to Mrs. Holroyd's place, Sheriff Dockerty called Rick Liddy at the Security Office at Meadows Center and said, "You wanted to know about Moses. Coombs got permission to let him go. No way he was involved. But he sure was a popular suspect. People were right willing to believe he done it. Coombs says some kids trashed his school bus while he was my guest. Expressing the opinion of their folks, I'd guess. If we had somebody else nailed for the

Owen murder, I'd feel better about letting him go. People get that vigilante feeling about people who look and act different. And these days they think the law favors the criminals. Which is no news to any law person. I'm too short-handed to do much but I'm going to try to check on him now and then. It would be a real big help to me, and to Moses too, if you could hand me another suspect."

"I would if I could. You know that."

He beeped Eliot Erskine after the phone call and when he called back in, told him that they'd let Moses go. He could hear the relief in Erskine's voice.

In the late afternoon Finn Efflander met with Charley Winchester in the offices of the law firm in downtown Lakemore. When he heard the news, Charley stopped being the mild and jolly joker, and became agitated.

"I'll talk to John about this. It's just a little rift. It can be mended. We need you around here."

"It's not a rift. John and I understand each other. All I want to do is get away for a while. Haven't I earned that much?"

"But you're the one holds this thing together!"

"Nonsense. It was a mess when I got here, but I've had a few years to straighten it out, set up systems, work out the checks and balances. I've been kidding myself about how essential I am. I'm not, really. I've been going a little stale."

"How? What do you mean?"

"I'm a problem solver. Personnel relations was a big problem here. Equitable pay increments. Job descriptions. Reporting procedures. Security measures. Advance planning. Okay, so I've got good people now in all the key slots, and I've been letting Harold Sherman sit in on almost every meeting I set up. He's pretty humorless but he knows how everything works. And I haven't any choice, actually. John Tinker says Harold can fill the bill, and John Tinker is the head man. I've been creating problems so I can find the answers. Running in place. I've been butting into lower-level things where I don't belong, like McGaw's little production operation, and checking the maintenance schedules on the aircraft. When I finally told John I thought I needed a break, I felt a genuine sense of relief."

Charley got up quickly and went over to the windows to look down into the State Street traffic, his hands locked behind him. Finn realized that from that angle Charley looked a lot older than he did head on.

"Your man in New York couldn't find anyone, eh?"

"Anyone good."

"Same with the University. We couldn't find anyone good for that job. So we finally hired Hallowell."

"He was here when I came aboard."

"Due to family contacts he got all the right tickets. He's fairly bright. But his problem is narcolepsy."

"I knew there was a word for it. I think the second or third time I saw him, I was in his office and he was asking me a question and he paused and all of a sudden he was snoring. So I went out and asked his secretary if he was all right. She went in and came out and said everything was just fine."

Charley came back and perched a heavy haunch on the corner of his desk. "I just don't like the way things are going, Finn. I don't think Rolf is going to stay on here. He is completely broken. That young woman was much too important to him. Maybe she was his chance to stay young a little longer. Matthew is out of it now. For good. He had such a bad day Saturday Mary Margaret came to me to find out if there isn't some way we can get him institutionalized under some other name, in some good place."

"Can you do that?"

"I think so. Switzerland, maybe. But then her conscience is going to turn her sour. She's having trouble finding nurses. I told her to hang on for a while."

"Hang on until the big medical complex is next door," Finn said. "It ought to be able to provide nursing care."

"Oh, John Tinker will go ahead with it," Charley agreed. "The money is available. And he has a compulsion to buy all the respectability he can get. He knows that Matthew Meadows' orders to his flock to avoid doctors and hospitals made the whole ECB operation suspect to a lot of people. Now he can go the other way, and change public opinion a little bit. Finn, you're right. If it isn't first class it isn't going to kill the patients. John Tinker worries me lately. He seems to be withdrawing somehow. There's no lift. No sparkle. He's not enjoying life. The sermons are mechanically good, well rehearsed, full of camera cues. I think Mary Margaret is gaining a couple or three pounds a week ever since Matthew got so much worse. Who have we got left around here? Walter

Macy? He could do well running a little bit of a church in a rich parish, and play politics with the deacon list. He's not up to operating anything this big.

"Joe Deets can't keep his hands off the pretty little girls. So he's going to get into very big trouble. Finn, you can talk all you want to about taking some time off, having a nice rest, but you are leaving what begins to me to look more and more like a sinking ship. Ever since Matthew's trouble started, the long-term membership trend has been turning down. Very slowly, but definitely down. An institution like this needs constant attention from somebody who knows the whole picture and knows what he's doing."

After several moments of silence, Finn shook his head and said, "No. No, thanks. For several years now old friends all over the country have been saying, 'What in hell is Finn doing down there with that bunch of weirdos?' I haven't been paying conscious attention. I've told myself I don't care. But I guess I do. This may be a rude question, Charley, but how do you rationalize it?"

"I don't have to rationalize a thing, friend. To me and Clyde, the ECB is a nice piece of business. Without us it would have gotten into a lot more trouble than it has, and paid a lot more taxes. We're advocates. And everybody at one time or another needs one. For my own personal private opinion, I can tell you this much. I can't see a whole lot of harm in bringing folks into church to hear the old-time religion. Lifts the hearts. Refreshes the spirits. Makes them feel like they're part of something real special. This place is like a shrine now. They come from all over the country to listen to the biggest loudest electronic chimes in the known world."

"And if you weren't taking care of their legal problems, somebody else would be?"

"Let's not get philosophical-tricky, Finn boy. What's your departure schedule?"

"By tomorrow noon, I'll be long gone, provided you can disentangle me from some of the things I've had to sign. When I get an address, I'll let you know."

"Got any destination?"

"Vermont, I guess. Haven't seen it since I was a little kid in camp."

"Well, let's check the paperwork. And then we'll have a drink."

. . .

The Hemstead Brothers Funeral Home sent one of its hearses down to the city Sunday evening and brought Molly Wintergarten's body back to Lakemore for processing. The sister-in-law of the deceased brought in a dark blue Halston dress that same evening, and some of Molly's cosmetics from her dressing table.

The sister-in-law's name was Alice Berns, a tall, pale, gray-haired woman in octagonal eyeglasses without rims. She told Buddy Hemstead that she had the authority to select the casket, and she picked a steel box with a bronze metallic finish, white satin interior, and an outer container of waterproofed concrete. She said that Mrs. Wintergarten's mother and sister had been informed, and they would be coming down for the service, scheduled for noon on Wednesday in the small chapel on the grounds of the Meadows Cemetery. She said that the Meadows Center would be providing the music, the service and the actual work at the grave site. Buddy Hemstead said he was familiar with the system as he had taken care of other people from the Church who were buried there, including young Paul Meadows, who had died at an early age.

He took her into the office and explained that he and his best employee had inspected the body and it was their judgment that they would be able to make the side of the face presentable, so that there could be a viewing, if so desired. "Have to keep her head turned just a mite left," he said.

Mrs. Berns said she did not believe that her brother contemplated any sort of viewing, but to go ahead and make her look as good as possible in case he changed his mind. He worked out the bill, which included picking the body up at the city hospital and then taking it out to the chapel. He said his people would coordinate with the cemetery people and have the outer watertight box in place to receive the casket, and they would supply the lowering device. The bill came to thirty-eight hundred and seventy-five dollars, or four thousand and thirty with tax. She said she would make certain it was paid promptly. He said he appreciated the business, and please express his condolences to the bereaved. He asked if John Tinker Meadows himself would be officiating, and she said the family had decided that Mary Margaret Meadows would perform the service. He said she was a lovely woman, and Mrs. Berns said she was sure she was, but she had yet to meet her.

Roy Owen received word from Lieutenant Coombs late on Monday afternoon that Linda Owen's body could be released to any designated and licensed mortuary at any time. He had made arrangements with a firm down in the city named Stith and Sons. He phoned them from his room at the County Line Motel and they said they would pick the body up at nine in the morning and take it directly to their crematorium ten miles south of the city, on Route 887, a white building on the left, set back, just beyond the Pepsi Bottling Works, you can't miss it. And it would be performed at ten o'clock. He then phoned the hospital and told them who would be coming for the body. They told him there were some charges and they could not release the body until they were paid. Six hundred and eighty-one dollars and forty-one cents.

He located Lieutenant Coombs through the Sheriff's office and told him that he had no intention of being cheap, but he had not requested any hospital services, certainly not over six hundred dollars' worth. Coombs cursed the hospital, the state, the federal government and every paper shuffler in the known universe. He called Roy back twenty minutes later and said the matter had been settled and there were no charges to him, that the charges were an obligation of the state and the county, and the hospital was prepared to release the remains to Stith's people.

Peggy Moon tapped on his door, and when he opened it she came in barefoot, wearing cutoffs and an old yellow T-shirt with "Pac Man" printed on the front of it. She took hold of his wrists and looked directly at him, frowning with concern.

"I was listening," she said.

He tried to smile. "Isn't there some law?"

"I'll go down there with you, okay?"

"No. It's all right. I'll manage, Peg."

"You *can't* go alone! Really. You can't. I won't permit it."

"What did you say?"

She swallowed, flushed and said again, thrusting her chin upward, "I won't permit it."

He smiled at her. "In that case, what choice do I have?"

"Absolutely none. I'll expect you for breakfast at eight and we'll be out of here by eight-thirty, to be on the safe side. No, come at quarter to eight and we'll leave at eight-fifteen."

"Look, it means a lot," he said, and turned away from her as his eyes began to sting.

"Nobody should ever be alone. Not ever," she said.

Seventeen

When he came pedaling up the hill just at sunrise on Wednesday morning, Doreen was waiting for him under their tree, smiling at him, teeth so bright in the lovely tanned face, her right hand resting on the handlebar of the new bike he had bought her, silver and blue, ultra-lightweight, but with the broader cross-country tires and fifteen-speed dérailleur. She was glistening with sun oil and bug repellent, and she had their breakfast picnic strapped to the luggage carrier.

"Hey, Joe!" she called. "It's really great. It's really a wonderful machine. It must have cost an awful lot."

"You're not supposed to ask how much presents cost, Dorie."

She reached out and patted his cheek as he came close enough. "So you're going to teach me manners too? I've been like two miles up the road already and back, just trying it out. I thought at first maybe it was too big, but it's just the right size frame, really."

She swung aboard and as soon as she had a little bit of speed she bent over and pulled each toe strap tight. She grinned back at him and yelled, "Catch me if you can, dads!"

After a mile he nearly did catch her, but she looked back in surprise and increased the pace. He looked at those muscular and elegant little haunches ahead of him, working away under the tight fit of her white short shorts. There was bare brown skin between the shorts and the yellow halter. Wind whipped at her hair. It was pale spun gold in the sunlight, touched faintly with the red overtones of the rising sun.

He began to be increasingly uncomfortable, sweating too heavily and enduring the pain in his side. He was panting for air, and he could feel the beginning of a cramp in his left calf. Damn the girl, he thought. Damn her. Fifteen speeds forward gave her too much of an edge. He wished he'd bought her one with no gears at all.

Sweat was running into his eyes as they passed the old Addy place that had been deeded to the Church when the Addys moved into the Settlements and sold off their pigs and chickens. He had hoped she had decided to turn in there where they had picnicked on other mornings. But she went sailing by, and she was singing something. Fragments of the song came back to him on the morning air. It didn't seem to have any words—at least not any he could understand. She turned off on the path which followed the fence line a mile beyond the Addy place, and then left the fence line and curved downhill to the shore of the creek.

She stayed aboard, but he could not risk his thin tires on all the roots and stones of the path, and so he swung down and walked the bike down. She was long out of sight. He stopped for a couple of minutes to catch his breath and massage the cramp in his calf. His blue cotton shirt was sweat-pasted to his chest in spite of the transient and deceptive coolness of early morning.

When he arrived at the bank of the stream he found she had spread the light blanket in a different place than before. He soon saw why. The creek, when it flooded, had spread a layer of mud and debris up over the bank and the slope of tufted grass where they had lain before. It was drying and cracking, and smelled faintly of vegetable decay. So she had settled them further up, under a stand of longleaf pines, on the carpet of brown needles between two long roots that stretched down toward the creek.

"Okay here?" she asked.

"Sure."

"What took you so long?"

"I had to walk my bike down from the road."

"You should get one like mine, sweetie."

"Maybe I will. Maybe I will."

She had bought the breakfast at a fast-food place beyond the motels. Two quart cardboard containers of some kind of reconstituted orange drink. There were eight honey buns, which seemed to be some dark sweet stickiness speckled with pecan parts, spread on bread dough containing the occasional raisin, and a stubby thermos filled with acid coffee laced with artificial cream and too much sugar. She laid the breakfast out on the blanket and, with a certain ceremony, handed him his paper napkin and empty foam coffee cup with plastic spoon.

Doreen sat cross-legged, beamed at him, ate hungrily and said, "Eerie ice ear."

"What's that?"

She swallowed. "It's really nice here. With the sun slanting in like now."

"Really nice," he agreed. His honey bun had turned into a glutinous paste and he could not swallow it down without the help of some of the simulated orange-type drink. As soon as it was down, he realized a sharp crumb of pecan had worked its way under the partial bridge on the right upper side of his mouth. He managed to sluice it out with some of the sugary coffee. He refused a third sticky bun. She ate it and the rest of them and finished off his orange drink and what was left of the coffee.

With speed and efficiency of movement she bundled the trash into the paper bag the juice had been in, and strapped it and the coffee thermos to the carrier on her new bike. She came back and, grinning down at him sitting there on the blanket, she quickly slipped the white shorts down and off, pulled her halter off and fell upon him, working at the buttons of his damp shirt, wearing a pretty frown of concentration, breathing through her open mouth.

When the morning sun was an hour higher, she lay beside him, her breathing slow and deep. Her left leg lay slack across his naked waist, and it felt uncommonly heavy. Her eyes were closed, the white curling lashes so close to him that he could not focus on them. They were a pale blur. Her mouth lay half open, the lips puffed. He could see the amber speckling of faint freckles against the golden tan of her left shoulder. Her head lay heavy on his left arm, numbing his fingers. Her face was the face of a child in sleep. The honey buns and orange drink were a leaden mass in his belly. He had not removed all of the pecan from under the partial bridge. The pain that had alarmed him when he was cycling hard to catch her had come back again fleetingly in the midst of lovemaking, giving him a momentary feeling of impending doom, quickly lost amid her dauntless energies.

He turned his head slightly and looked up through the pine boughs at patches of pale blue morning sky. A scouting patrol of crows came wheeling through the pines, cawing about successful raids. A blue jay stood on a low branch, tilting its head from side to side. He could hear the murmurous sound of the creek, and the cawing in the far distance, and the sound of a jet somewhere. The morning seemed uncommonly drab to him, as if all his senses had become dulled, faded by overuse, a morning of postcard scenes thumbed through too often.

The left calf was beginning to cramp again. She made a small buzzing snoring sound and he felt her breath against his chin and throat. With his passions spent he could look upon her asleep and see her as a vital, healthy, boring child. There was a certain grossness to the appetites he had helped her develop. Six months from now she would be recovering nicely from the physical infatuation she had thought deathless love. And six years from now she would have to stop and think to remember very much about him or their affair.

God help me! The three words appeared in his mind so suddenly and unexpectedly he thought for a moment he had heard someone else speak them. But with his voice.

Forgive me, Father, for I have sinned. I want to stop this. It demeans me. It makes me feel small and dirty and wicked and cruel. Or perhaps, pointless. Maybe that is the worst of it. To feel that one's life has no meaning other than pleasurable sensation. A manipulation of nerve ends, achieved through lies and deceit. A strange thing happened to me when this girl's mother prayed . . .

And it happened again, just as quickly. As if a curtain had been pulled aside and then closed, giving him a glimpse of some wonder beyond his ability to comprehend. It made his eyes fill again. Vision. Revelation. But without body or substance.

She woke with a start, sat up quickly and slapped her thigh. "Darn fire ant," she said. "And here's another. And there's one on your ankle, Joe."

They killed the ants and got dressed. She put on the other clothing she had brought, clothing suitable for going back through the campus gate—a gray skirt and a short-sleeved white blouse. She shook the blanket out and folded her shorts and halter into it and placed the bundle under the rubber straps on her carrier.

They both wheeled their bicycles up the curving narrow path toward the road. She was in the lead.

Turning her head halfway around to speak back to him behind her, she said, "This guy named Roger something smuggled a recording of the sound track of *Flashdance* into the dorm. We're not supposed to have music from any movie that isn't on the list, you know?"

"No, I didn't know."

"So Bobby made cassettes from the record, and he gave one to Lolly. She came sneaking into my room last night with that Walkman she has with the two sets of ear things, and we listened with the volume turned high until we like to freaked out, you know?"

"You can injure your hearing doing that, Dorie."

"So back there when we were doing it, that music was jumping around in my head, right to the same beat and everything. Joe, honey, could you get me a Walkman like Lolly has? I mean, get one for us, because if we were both hearing that same music at the same time, it would be fantastic, I think. I mean, it would be so much better and louder than those funny old records you play. That music from last night is still going on in my head."

" 'Funny old records'?"

"You know. Like classical. Like in church almost."

He shut his jaw hard and winced with the pain under his partial bridge. His left calf was so knotted he limped badly. He felt as if he might throw up his orange drink and sticky buns. His body was wet with a cold and oily perspiration.

They had reached the road. She turned to him and said, "You sure don't have very much to say this morning, Joe honey. You know, you look a little weird. You're kind of a funny color."

"I'm fine, really."

"Look, what about the Walkman? Will you get us a Walkman with two ear things? There's two holes on the top you plug into, so we both will be hearing the same music."

"I'll think about it."

"I can tell you don't like the idea. You've got that look. How do you know you won't like it unless we get one and try?"

He sighed audibly. "Where do you get them?"

She grinned at him. "Hey, that's wonderful. They got them at the MusicBox in the Mall, like for ninety-nine fifty for the best one." She frowned at him. "You act real down. Is anything wrong?"

"I guess I'm thinking about how much work I have to do. I've gotten a little behind."

"Would that be my little behind?"

"For God's sake! Don't be so goddamn coarse!"

"So pardon me for living! You've got no sense of humor today, Joe. You're kind of boring."

"That feeling could be mutual."

She stared at him, her face immobilized by shock and hurt. Her eyes filled, and she mounted the bike and pedaled away, hard and fast, bending low over the handlebars.

As he had expected, she was waiting for him at their big tree. As he dismounted and balanced his bicycle against the tree, she said, "You better say you're sorry."

"You just didn't understand what I meant."

"I know what you said."

"I meant that my general disposition this morning is boring both of us."

"Wasn't it any good for you back there?"

"It was beautiful, dear. But we're going to have to ease up a bit. I'm in the middle of a big computer project and working very long hours, and it's sapping my energies."

She was immediately concerned. She laid her hand on his arm. "Poor honey! I guess at your age it could be—"

"I wish you wouldn't get onto age so often!"

"Don't be cross. Listen, I don't think of you as an old person. I really don't. My dad is not even as old as you are, but he seems really old to me. He is all grown up, and you aren't really. I don't know how to say it."

"I think there's another thing wrong with me, Dorie. I'm beginning to feel . . . reluctant about what we're doing. It's beginning to make me feel guilty."

"But, honey! Right from the very first time, we both said we both know it is a terrible sin. We couldn't help ourselves. It was the weakness of the flesh. And besides, without me, you said all your job responsibility and so on would be too much for you. Gee, I feel guilty too, lots of times. But not much lately."

He put his hands on her shoulders and kissed her quickly and gently on the lips. "I know we love each other very much, but maybe we ought to try to be stronger."

"I . . . I don't think I can."

"We can at least try, can't we?"

"Well, I guess so. If you want. But I don't see the point."

"It will be good for us. A test of strength."

"When will I see you again, Joe?"

"I've got conferences the rest of this week. Because of Efflander leaving and Harold Sherman taking over."

"How about early next Sunday?"

"I may have to go to Atlanta to a weekend meeting. I'll let you know, okay?"

"I don't like all this. It makes me feel funny."

He kissed her again, and smiled at her. "Trust me. If we can show a little character, our relationship will be that much stronger. Believe me."

"Well, okay. But it just—"

"Run along, Dorie. Have a good day."

And then she was gone, down the graded road and out of sight around a curve beyond the trees. He leaned against the tree and looked down toward where he could see, through a gap in a tall hedgerow, a small segment of the paved asphalt road that led down to the Settlements and the rest of the complex beyond. He could see the white roofs of a few of the Settlement houses, and a cemetery slope off to the left of them where, at noon, he would have to attend the funeral of Molly Wintergarten.

He estimated that it was time for Doreen to appear, and a moment later, there she was, moving very swiftly, pedaling on the downslope. He imagined that the hot morning wind was drying her tears. He belched orange-flavored gas and had a moment of nausea which passed quickly.

He felt obscurely pleased with himself for having begun the process of giving her up. When he thought of praying for the strength to end the affair, he was sadly amused at himself. It is ever thus. When each of them begins to seem increasingly fleshy, brimful of her hot juices, huffing and grinding and moaning, then I begin to be offended by her, and to ease whatever conscience I have left, I pretend to find strength in prayer, strength to relinquish her. And when I have cut her free, with as little pain to her as I can manage, then I must rest for a time and go a-hunting again—hunting for shyness, fright, reserve, reluctance, timidity, and the long delicious process of turning all that into the avidity which in time must turn me off.

But now there have been these two odd episodes, once with Annalee Purves, once back by the creek when I was thinking of Annalee, that image of a curtain opening quickly and closing again, giving me a glimpse of something I cannot describe—a holy light, a revelation that would make me into the person I thought I once could become—a promise of childhood coming true. I need instruction in this. I need to talk to some man of God who can tell me what it could mean, and how I might be able to open the curtain wide enough to see what is beyond. Who is there to go to? Not one of the instant pastors created in the same way I was. Certainly not John Tinker Meadows, who exists only in some technical audiovisual sense. Not Mary Margaret, who despises me because I represent what she fears the most. And not Walter Macy, who would not be able to understand any part of what I say.

And suddenly he thought of Annalee Purves. What if they prayed together for the soul of Joseph Deets? What if, with her, he could pray with that same simple and honest heart she had displayed in the motel.

Perhaps if she could visit her daughter again, and he could talk to her, and this time tell her the complete, dreary, self-serving life of Joe Deets. Beg her forgiveness. And the Lord's.

Because he had no morning classes on Wednesdays during the short summer session, Professor F. Vernon Laird was on his hands and knees in his small front yard in the Settlements, digging out clumps of crab-grass with a small red trowel in the relative cool of early morning, when Joe Deets came coasting slowly down the hill on his bicycle. Laird returned his half wave, and looked at his watch. This time there was a seventeen-minute hiatus between the high-speed passage of the pretty little Purves girl and the slow descent of Deets. Usually it was a shorter interval. He told himself it would be wise to put all such thoughts out of his mind. He had lost his tenure at a famed university over a very ugly scandal involving a freshman girl, and he considered himself fortunate to have found this post, even though he served in a department staffed with misfits and incompetents, and was forced to use course materials that had been out of date in 1923.

He stabbed at the next clump with such force that he hurt his wrist. His wife came around the side of the house and said, "Vern? Don't you think it's getting a little too hot for that kind of work?"

He put one palm on his knee and levered himself up to his feet. He turned and as he smiled at her, he thought briefly of sticking the red trowel into her wide white throat. "I guess it is, my dear."

"There's iced tea in the fridge."

"Thank you, my dear."

By decree issued by John Tinker Meadows, a half day of mourning began at noon on Wednesday, August twenty-fourth, with all work suspended at Administration and Communications, with afternoon classes at the summer session canceled. The funeral services were at noon at the small cemetery chapel, and the memorial service was scheduled for seven in the evening at the Tabernacle.

The maximum capacity of the chapel was forty persons, five rows with four persons on either side of the center aisle. Behind the altar was a glass wall which looked into the cemetery greenhouse, but in the hot months the effect was spoiled by the condensation caused by the chapel air conditioning. The first two rows on the right-hand side as one faced the altar were reserved for the immediate family, Rolf and his sister, Molly's elder brother and his wife, down from Boston, with Molly's father and her uncle. In the other two rows on the right were some friends of the Wintergartens from the Lakemore Tennis Club.

The left side of the chapel was occupied by key personnel of the Meadows Center: the Reverend Sister Mary Margaret Meadows, the Reverend Doctor John Tinker Meadows, the Reverend and Mrs. Walter Macy, the Winchester brothers, Joseph Deets, Walker McGaw, Spencer McKay, Dennis Jorgland, Ben Harvey, Dr. Hallowell, Jenny Albritton, Harold Sherman—Efflander's replacement—and Jenny MacBeth, along with two motel managers and a couple of people from Planning and Development.

A woman from the music department at the University noodled along at a small organ off to the right of the altar. The metallic casket gleamed in front of the altar, standing there on a wheeled cart with a spray of long-stemmed roses atop it.

As the Tabernacle chimes struck the hour, Mary Margaret arose from her seat in the first pew on the left and walked up the steps and took her position behind the rostrum. She was clad all in white, the rope of braided hair fashioned into a gleaming tiara. She looked half again life-size. She waited until the last echoes of the chimes died, and said, "I take the text from the Book of Wisdom, beginning with the twenty-third verse.

"Yet God did make man imperishable,
He made him in the image of His own nature;
it was the devil's envy that brought death into the world,
as those who are his partners will discover."

Before she could continue, Walter Macy emitted a loud, coughing sob, and buried his face in his hands. Alberta Macy turned her head sharply and stared at him in astonishment with a feeling of nervous apprehension. Walter was a known quantity, not very emotional at any time. This was a reaction so untypical it made her feel insecure. When the faint muttering and stirring ceased, Mary Margaret continued.

"But the souls of the virtuous are in the hands of God,
no torment shall ever touch them.

In the eyes of the unwise they did appear to die,
their going looked like a disaster,
their leaving us, like annihilation;
but they are in peace.
If they experienced punishment as men see it,
their hope was rich with immortality;
slight was their affliction, great will their blessing be.
God has put them to the test
and proved them worthy to be with Him;
He has tested them like gold in a furnace,
and accepted them as a holocaust.
When the time comes for His visitation they will shine out;
as sparks run through the stubble so will they.
They who trust in Him will understand the truth,
those who are faithful will live with Him in love;
for grace and mercy await those He has chosen."

She looked at the small audience, and she gave the impression of strength and calmness. "It is not our custom to give a eulogy for our departed sister. It is a dreadful shock to our small community whenever we lose one of those we have seen, day by day, among us as we go about our holy work. It is a greater shock to lose one so young, so vital, so full of life. It is a pity that she has been lost to us before we learned to know her as much as we wished to. But though her leaving looked like disaster, she is in peace, rich with immortality. Let us pray."

Walter Macy squeezed his eyes so tightly shut that starry skies blinked and stuttered in the blackness of his vision. The sob had so torn his throat that when he swallowed there was pain.

The same dream had come back last night, changed this time in only one particular from the memory that would never die. She was beside him again, so fragrant, so remote, so skeptical—her eyes like wet gems in the glow of the dash lights turned high, and she had told him to stop the tape, but he had wanted her to hear that part that would make her want to have the magazine destroy John and Molly forever. He had turned on the dome light to show her the photographs and she had asked him what made him think *Out Front* used filth like that. Hadn't he ever read it? Who did he think she was? What did he think she was down here to research? She reached to turn the tape off when he wouldn't, and he stayed her hand, and then the tape got to that terrible part, that clattery, rumpety, thudding, banging, with her yelling those words that had never passed his lips and never would.

But in the dream as in memory, she wrenched away from him and opened his car door on her side and scrambled out. He got out on the driver's side and ran back. She was parked behind him. She tried to come between the cars to get to the driver's door on her rented car, but he was there in time to block her. She turned and ran away from him. He was enraged. What made that city slut think she was so high and mighty in her silken clothing and her gold chains? Why was she pretending to be offended? Her life, not his, was just like that tape. She was here as the Antichrist, to destroy the faith of the humble and hardworking. When she turned to dart back, to elude his chase, he stumbled and fell, but as he did so, he reached out and caught one slender ankle and brought her sprawling down.

From then on there was no clear memory at all, just the writhing, struggling strength of her, her yelpings, pinning the narrow wrists, and the kneeing, tearing, and the deep quiverous heats of her invaded depths, then explosions, silence, heaviness, the whistle of his breathing, a nearby sound of crickets as well, the slow awareness of the slackness of the wrists he held in his right hand, of the utter stillness under the weight of him. He had scrambled up, knowing that the whole weight of his upper body had been on his right forearm and that the screaming had stopped under that weight across her throat.

No entreaties, no shaking, no breathing into her lungs, compressing her chest, could bring her back to motion and life. He wept over her and talked to her and told her he didn't mean it. He told her it was her fault. Then he wondered if anyone could hear his sobbing voice in the night, and he became as ice with sudden fear. He got up again and trotted to his car and turned off the dash lights and the dome lights, and sat there in darkness, sweating despite the coolness of the night, wondering what he should do. He planned it step by step before he took the first step, because he knew that after that first step, he would have to go through with all the others, as quickly as possible.

In the dream as in the prior reality, she seemed so dreadfully loose. He stood her up and got his shoulder into her belly and let her fall across his back. In the dream as in the reality, when he stood up with her there was that dreadful squawk of gases being expelled from the dead body by the weight of her against his shoulder, a sound so startling he nearly flung her away from him. He walked her to the well and dropped her in. In the reality he heard a crashing of brush and then a sickening thump. In the dream last night he heard nothing. He was trying to look down the well and he saw something coming up, a paleness floating up toward him, and he fell back. In the dream there was no roof over the well, and she floated up into starlight, wearing the familiar naked body of Molly in the photographs he had stared at so many, many times, and she was wearing as well Molly's wide and lascivious grin, her tongue licking her underlip. But she still wore the gold chain, and she floated above him and toward him, and he spun in terror and ran off the edge of the earth and awakened an instant before he landed on the red-hot stones of hell.

The prayer was over. Alberta nudged him and he straightened up to see that the prayer had ended, and the organ was playing a different sort of melody, and the pallbearers were wheeling the casket out the side door onto the concrete path that wound between the grave sites. They all followed along, with Mary Margaret in the rear. When Walter saw them place the casket on the contraption which would lower it into the grave, his legs weakened and he staggered against Alberta. She gave him a strong, angry push away from her and whispered, "What on earth is wrong with you? What's the matter with you?"

He did not answer. Nothing at all is wrong, he thought. Except that this is it all over again. The hole in the ground. And it is the Owen slut in the box, not Molly Wintergarten. They're all mixed up in my head, ever since Molly was killed. Nothing is wrong except that I have seen with my own eyes the red-hot stones of hell down there waiting for me. There is no escape. There is no possible act of contrition enormous enough to wipe it out. I have destroyed every picture of them, but I can see each picture clearly and in color as though printed on the inside of my eyelids. I crushed and burned the tapes along with the pictures, but in any random sound, as in running water or people talking, or traffic noises, I can hear as well the sounds of the tapes, of their obscenities and their shouts of fulfillment. I do not even dare pray anymore for fear God will notice me.

Roy Owen and Peggy Moon took their last long morning walk on Thursday. He had delayed his departure, and had lied to her about a flight being canceled. They walked south on a road where they had walked before, but this time took the right fork instead of the left. A mile further they came up on a small grove of peach trees so old that they could bear nothing but bitter fruit. Beyond the wild orchard were some live oak trees shading a small cemetery. The stones were crooked and some were toppled. They could see a deserted farmhouse a hundred yards away, windows broken, roof sagging almost to the ground on one side.

The largest monument was in the center of the small cemetery, and the name on it was Berrencourt. He noticed that most of the stones had that same name, or the name Hotchkiss.

"Those were big names around here long ago," Peggy said. "Some died and some moved away. I never knew this was where any of them lived."

They stepped over the place where the iron fence around the cemetery had rusted away and read the names and dates. The old marble was so weathered the inscriptions were difficult to make out.

He read one to her, slowly. "Edith Anna Berrencourt   January 10, 1821   July 30, 1837   Died of Fevers   God rest her gentle loving heart."

His voice had started to break on the last two words. He went over and sat on the raised base of the central family monument. She sat at his right, so close their shoulders touched. "Just sixteen," she said. "Poor Edith Anna. Don't you wonder sometimes if anything at all makes any sense?"

"I wonder a lot lately."

"Of course. That was a fool question."

"Look, the question was okay. I just gave a kind of dumb flip answer. Nobody could have been better company in . . . in this whole mess, Peg. I'm very grateful."

"All I've done is hang around."

"For which I am grateful. So there she is, back in your unit number sixteen, in a chubby little bronze pot with a screw top, fastened on with wire and red wax, and around the belly of the fat pot is a whole parade of elephants, little elephants each holding the one in front of him by the tail. I ask you, what the hell have elephants got to do with anything?"

"Maybe they buy the urns in India or someplace like that."

"Sensible guess. She was scared of elephants. She was scared of a lot of things. She was scared of growing old and scared of dying, and scared of not doing her job better than anybody else in the world could do it. So coming down here to die makes as much sense as having elephants on the urn. But the standard response, of course, is to say that she died as a tiny part of some vast plan so complex that our little earthbound souls can never understand any part of it. Which is cop-out or comfort, I don't know which."

"I guess she was some kind of perfectionist."

"About a lot of things." He looked at her and at her rueful smile. That smile and that mildly weathered face, and that obscurely simian look of her had become more dear to him than he had dared tell her. She had made no demands at all. She had been the handy wailing wall. And he had said things to her about his life and his thoughts he had never expressed to anyone before, and did not even know in their full dimension until he said them aloud to her. She had the knack of teaching him who he was without ever saying a word.

"Got to tell you something," he said. "Don't be mad."

"Mad?"

"There was a very shrewd writer a time ago named Saki who said a few very sensible things. For instance, a small inaccuracy can save hours of explanation."

"I like that! What's to get mad about?"

"The small inaccuracy was that the airline didn't cancel. I did."

She looked at him, frowning and puzzled. "But why?"

"It was an impulse. I didn't want to leave you yet. I can't explain it. I just wasn't ready to leave here yet. Nothing about the place to keep me here, God knows. But it was leaving you."

She looked at him wonderingly. "That is supposed to make me mad?"

"I lied to you."

"Roy, it was a small inaccuracy that saved hours of explanation. Now I'm ready for those hours of explanation, fella. Take a couple of them and tell me why you couldn't leave me."

"Well . . ."

"Or this way," she said, and put her arm around him and pulled him close. They kissed awkwardly, and then stood up and kissed again. It was the first time he had held her close. There was a feminine softness, a yielding, that he had not anticipated. Her mouth was sweet. She was the taller, but they seemed to fit as though designed that way. They were both breathing audibly when they stopped.

He looked at her with delight, seeing for the first time how lovely her eyes were, how crisp and handsome the line of her jaw, saw the delicate miracle of the dark hair springing so alive from the tanned brow.

"Well, I don't want to lie either," she said, "so I have to tell you I've been wanting that to happen for a very long time, not from the day you registered, but it started to happen pretty soon after that, Roy. It really did. That marriage was so rotten, I didn't think anything like this would ever happen again, that I'd ever feel this way again. For the love of God, make me stop talking. Hold your hand over my mouth or something. I can't stop."

So he kissed her again, and they talked some more, and they walked slowly back the way they had come, holding hands.

At the door to the office he said, "The flight leaves at three thirty-five. I hate to face the whole situation up there. Could you come with me?"

She cocked her head and then shook it slowly and sadly. "No way, my friend. Your mother-in-law and your kid have got enough trauma going on without your showing up with another lady. It would be vulgar in a way neither of us want or would intend. Okay? You go up and do the memorial service thing and get back on top of your job and spend just as much time as you can with your daughter, and hug her a lot and hold her a lot, and read to her and walk with her and all that. I had that same kind of bad time a thousand years ago and it takes a lot of hugging. Then, dear friend, next spring you bring her down here on a vacation. I'll be here. And I will take her to all the places where I did my growing up around here. And with any luck, she and I will become friends. After we do, then you and I will see how well whatever we found today is lasting. If it is, I'll be open to any suggestion at all, at all."

She went inside and watched him walk back toward sixteen, thinking how much she loved him, and how much temptation it had been to agree to fly North with him.

Brother Fred came in from the living area, eating a jelly sandwich. "We got us a couple raggedy pilgrims in twenty-one. Couldn't afford the rates the other side of the Interstate. You nail him?"

"Nail what? Who?"

"You pin the little guy with the mustache to your trophy-room wall, Sis?"

"What gives you a dumb idea like that?"

"Look, I have been living here. I have been watching you and the little guy. Don't try to kid me or yourself."

So without warning she was crying and he put his arm around her and gave her a jelly kiss on the forehead and told her that he thought she had roped herself a real nice little guy, all man in spite of the size of him, and apparently doing okay in the world, and if she ever wanted to take off, don't worry about leaving him stuck with the motel. No problem at all. No problem at all, Sis.

Eighteen

On Thursday, Jenny MacBeth supervised the mail and money flow under the watchful eye of Finn's replacement. He seemed always to be about three steps behind her, never directly behind, but either off to the left or to the right. She kept darting a glance back to see where he was, and she had the feeling this amused him in an obscure way. He was a stringy, swarthy, hollow-chested man in his fifties. He combed his graying hair straight forward, covering the bald front half of his skull, and it was cropped in a straight line an inch above his heavy black eyebrows. With his posture, glasses with the top halves tinted, and his curiously wide jaw with bulges of muscle at the hinges, he made Jenny MacBeth think of some sort of oversized insect.

All she knew about him was that Finn had told her Harold Sherman had worked for a now defunct airline in accounting and control and had infinite patience and a talent for streamlining detail work, using time and motion study analysis. He had been around for over a year but she'd had very little contact with him.

It bothered her that he was observing her operation when, due to the unexpected quantity of incoming mail, it was not functioning smoothly. Yesterday they'd had to cease operations at quarter to noon and lock all the unprocessed materials in the big vault. Today these had been added to the incoming mail, and her people were flustered not only by the quantity but by the observer. They tried to go too fast and they made more mistakes than usual. Whenever a mistake was made, Harold Sherman was right there, expressionless, a step behind her, watching her correct matters and get the smooth flow started again.

It wasn't until three in the afternoon that she was able to let the last of her people go. She followed Sherman through the Outgoing Mail room, through the continuing roar of the Xerox Diablos to that small office which had been Finn Efflander's.

The room was bare. All personal items, all decorations had been removed. There was a desk, a table, two chairs, two tall file cabinets and a computer terminal.

He asked her to sit across the desk from him. He looked at her with his head lowered, so that she could not read his eyes through the shaded top halves of his lenses. He did not speak. Though she was becoming increasingly uncomfortable in the silence, she vowed not to speak and then heard herself saying, "When the deposit has gone, that's when I usually have lunch."

"Of course."

"You haven't had any lunch either."

"I am quite aware of that, Miss MacBeth."

"What do you think of the operation?"

"Those shoes you wear are very strange."

"These? Yes. The floors are hard. I spend seven or eight hours at a time on my feet. I have foot trouble. Mr. Efflander gave permission."

"Everything Mr. Efflander left behind is subject to review."

"I'm aware of that, Mr. Sherman."

"There are more advanced and faster letter-opening devices than those three you are using."

"I'm aware of that. We've tested some of them. The mail is so varied in size and thickness, they don't work properly for us."

"Maybe with some experimentation they can be made to work. And then you would need only one operator instead of three. Your operation is very labor-intensive."

"That would be a primary consideration if we were ... out in the real world where we had to pay going wages, union wages. But here, it really doesn't—"

"Good policy works anywhere. And I was not told that you are in a policy-making position."

"But I set up this whole system when we were handling thirty percent of what we handle now!"

"I'm aware of that. It's all in the records. I will set policy. You will do your job."

She selected her words with care. "The distinction eludes me."

"It will become clear to you in time, Miss MacBeth. My first policy statement to you is to continually examine the number of people you are using out there, and see where and how the number can be cut."

"It could be cut tomorrow. Fewer work stations. And then we would finish too late for deposit and we would lose a full day of interest on the money we turn in. I have been operating with the minimum number of people to get everything processed on time."

"It was not finished on time today."

"Because we had only a half day to work yesterday."

"I know that. I was merely commenting that you did not finish on time today. What do you think that cost in interest?"

"I have no idea."

"Assuming eight percent, Miss MacBeth, it should be about a hundred and thirty-one dollars and fifty cents."

"That little!"

"That is why I would rather you did not involve yourself in policy. Is the distinction a little clearer?"

"Not very."

"Those women seem very wary of you. You seem to me to be quite harsh with them."

"When they make stupid mistakes, yes."

"You were equally harsh with the operator the time the terminal broke down."

"Was I? I guess it was because I am not used to being followed and watched all day long."

"If I did not follow you and observe you, I would never learn the functions of your department, would I?"

"I could tell you how it works."

"Personal observation is better than something filtered through the mind of an untrained person."

" 'Untrained'!"

"In matters of policy. And I might say that you could use some help in actual procedure."

"I beg your pardon?"

"Your work stations are laid out inefficiently, causing wasted time and a certain amount of confusion in distributing and collecting materials."

"I *know* that! If you will kindly turn off the U.S. mail for a week, I will have that room reorganized. There is a lot of wiring to be rerouted."

"I don't believe impertinence is going to help either of us."

" 'Impertinence'?"

"Sarcasm is a form of impertinence, Miss MacBeth. We both know I have nothing to do with the mail service. I am delighted that you are aware of the inefficiency of the layout. I want from you a detailed plan showing how the needed changes can be phased in without interrupting your basic service. We need have no further contact until that phased plan is ready for discussion. And at that time I will want to hear your report on the feasibility of a more advanced letter-opening device than those now in use. Thank you for your time."

She stared at him, her mind quite blank, stood up and nodded at him and left the office. She went into her department and looked at the empty tables and desks, the empty computer terminal stations. The pride had been snatched away. A certain tough-minded joy was gone for good. She missed Finn at that moment as desperately as she sometimes missed her dead parents.

Finn had told her to always keep trying to figure out ways to beat the system, and to block them before anyone else moved in. The money of the faithful came through the room like a green river flowing. Joe Deets's microchips provided almost too many checks and balances. Almost. Nibbling here and there was no good. It would be caught. Complaints would come in from donors, about incorrect receipts. The place to intercept would be after the cash was all bound, tagged and bagged for deposit. Two people watched the cash bags at all times. Each day, for a short time, toward the end of the day, she was one of the two.

She slowly traced the route of the deposit bags, out to where they were guarded while awaiting pickup, in an anteroom behind a waist-high counter near the door to the vault. She lifted the gate and went behind the counter and walked over to one of the storage cabinets and opened the door. There were three spare money sacks, folded, placed neatly on a shelf. She closed the door and went to the counter and leaned upon it, arms folded, head bowed, devising and discarding scenarios, measuring risks.

Late on Thursday afternoon Sheriff Dockerty phoned Rick Liddy at the Center. "Got a little bit of news on the Owen thing," he said.

"Sheriff, okay if I put you on the office speaker here? On account of I happen to have Elly Erskine here with me."

"Doesn't matter to me. Both you boys have taken a pretty keen interest in this, and there's nothing to keep me from telling you what is going on. I mean, it isn't going to screw up any trial testimony because we haven't got any suspect yet. You know my people have been helping the state people looking for the purse.

"Anyway, they found it about noon today down at the bottom of a place where there's a deep cut where the Interstate crosses about fifteen miles south of here. You know the place? It's where the median is more like a ravine, and they put in the concrete culverts under the two sides of the Interstate."

"I know where you mean."

"To reconstruct it, what the driver of her car would have done was go over into the left lane and fling it out the driver's side window down into that artificial ravine, all brushy at the bottom. It was a good shot and he hit it in the middle, but the bag had a big shoulder strap and what that did was loop right over the top of the stump of a dead tree. That way, in the rains, when the water came up so high there, the shoulder bag didn't get washed away. But you can understand it was a real mess. The shoe was in there and the torn pants, and her personal stuff. Any papers or paper money got turned to mush and washed out of there, but the credit cards were pretty much undamaged. Coombs's people took it to their lab to see if they can learn anything from it. If it hadn't hooked on to the tree, it would have been washed down to God only knows where. Good aim, good idea and bad luck."

"It happens that way."

"But I saved the most interesting part till last, boys."

" 'Interesting'?"

"I've gotten the idea, I don't know where or how, that you two might know a little bit more about the Owen thing than you've told me. Maybe it is just a hunch or a suspicion on your part, and you don't think it's enough. But here's what happened. This morning Moses went back to where he'd been working when he got the notion to go to the Mall and preach. Mrs. Bennett's little place. He finished the work and gathered up his tools and got paid and drove on back to Mrs. Holroyd's place and parked out back behind the barn where she likes for him to park that old wreck. When he was walking from his truck to the school bus, shots were fired. She called me, all shook up, and I went out there. All three missed him, and it isn't hard to see why. I was able to get a good line on the direction because one of them came through the windshield of the bus and went all the way through and out the screening at the back, about two feet lower than where it came in. One smashed the handle of his hoe and stuck some slivers from the handle into his thigh. No telling about where the third went, but he says he heard it make a kind of *thup* noise as it went by, so it was pretty good velocity, and close.

"I paced it back and got myself pretty winded before I found where it had to come from. The ridge back of her place is a good seven hundred yards, and when I moved to the right spot and looked around I found where the grass was flattened down and somebody had mashed four cigarette butts into the dirt while they waited. Now what I want to tell you boys is that here we've got somebody as unglued as Moses himself, and he thinks that we're a bunch of Supreme Court liberals here who had to let Moses, the killer, go free on account of the rules of evidence or some damn thing. So this tower of moral judgment is going to blow Moses away mostly because he's different, not that he's done anything.

"But he tried from too far off, and I guess he'll think it over and try from closer. You boys got anything to say to me?"

Liddy knew the silence was lasting too long, but he couldn't find the right words. "I guess I just don't know what you mean."

"I think you boys know what I mean all right. You are, or were, good cops, both of you. That outfit you're with seems to want to go down its own road, wash its own underwear, sing its own songs. But there has to be a structure, a network of law and law enforcement. I'm not telling you anything you don't know. Taking in two or three hundred million a year doesn't make you people immune any more than it makes the telephone company immune. I'm not going to push on you, hear? But I kind of like that Moses. I wouldn't want anything to happen to him that could have been prevented by you boys. Okay?"

"Okay, Sheriff. Thanks for calling."

Liddy hung up, leaned back, knuckled his eyes, faked a yawn and ended it with an expiring sigh. "How do you want to do it?"

"How *we* want to do it?"

"You see him come out of the chapel yesterday? No, you weren't there. You heard about death warmed over. There it was with that little old wife of his sort of holding him up, and snarling at him every two steps."

"Rick, you're not going to get a confession."

"I know that! I'm not foolish. If we get one, it'll be in a note found near the body. And the odds are against it. We'll start nudging him. You're in the best position to give him the first little push. Let's figure out what you should say to him. What are you after? What do you want?"

"We'll have to write some kind of a script that will play."

When one of the new nurses leaned over his chair to adjust the volume on the television set, old Matthew Meadows reached up and squeezed her left breast like an old-time motorist honking the bulb of the horn on his vehicle.

She yanked herself away, glowered down at him and gave him a ringing slap across the face. His look of mischief faded slowly into hurt and shock, and he began to sob into his hands. "Maamaa," he cried brokenly through his sobs. "Maamaa, oh maamaaa."

Mickey Oshiro and Glinda Lopez were ordered to meet with Harold Sherman in the small lounge on the second floor of Communications at 5:00 P.M. on Thursday. Oshiro arrived five minutes early and found Harold Sherman already there, sitting on the big blue Naugahyde couch, leafing through the papers on a composition clipboard. They said hello and Oshiro went over to the coffee machine and got the steaming cup of black, too hot to drink, as usual.

"I never drink coffee," Sherman said.

"I beg your pardon?"

"I said I never drink coffee."

"Well . . . some do, some don't." He sat in a straight chair against the wall. It had one wide arm like a lecture-room desk in a school.

"Coffee has as yet unknown effects on body chemistry," Sherman said.

Oshiro frowned at him. "Are you trying to make me give it up or something?"

Sherman looked mildly surprised. "I was making conversation. I was making general comment. Would you prefer to talk about the weather? It is very hot here this time of year."

"Which also has an unknown effect on body chemistry."

"Is that a joke?"

"Take it any way you want, Mr. Sherman."

"I was curious. I hadn't heard that you people had much sense of humor."

"Computer consultants?"

"You're Japanese, aren't you?"

"Racially, yes. But I was born here. I am an American computer consultant of Japanese heritage, and I sometimes make jokes."

"Are you trying to get our little meeting off on the wrong foot, Mr. Oshiro?"

"Heaven forbid!"

"Miss Lopez is late."

"Mrs. Lopez. And my watch says two minutes past the hour."

" 'Mrs.'? Excuse me. Ah yes. Here it is. It is indeed Mrs. Lopez. And, of course, late is late. How much late is a secondary consideration."

"Here she is," Mickey said. "Hi, Glinda."

"How you, Mick? Hello, Mr. Sherman."

"Please be seated, Mrs. Lopez. I have been reviewing your special project. I have listened to the tapes made at intervals over the period of this project, and I have noted the improvement as time passed. Mr. Efflander brought me up to date on the details of the inception of the plan, and so forth. And I have made my own study of the cost effectiveness of the experimental program as it is now constituted. I see no special reasons for any further tinkering with the program, which of course means that we can terminate Mr. Oshiro's consultant contract and save sixteen hundred dollars a week."

"Now wait just a minute!" Glinda said.

"Allow me to finish, Mrs. Lopez. From the telephone records I find that during this experimental phase you have been calling delinquents on a schedule of four hours each working day, and you have not been training more operators. You began and then stopped. Why?"

"They couldn't do it."

"I don't understand. If you can do it, they can do it."

Oshiro answered the implied question. "Mrs. Lopez has some very rare and special qualifications for this kind of procedure, Mr. Sherman. She is quick-witted, inventive, very fast and she has a useful grasp of what Doctor Matthews would have said under almost any sort of circumstance. She has to concentrate totally, so much so that I am surprised she can handle it properly for four hours. I don't think I could last two hours."

Sherman stared at him for a time without answering, and then said, "No one else has this earthshaking talent you attribute to Mrs. Lopez?"

"No one else working here," she said.

Sherman leaned back and put his clipboard aside. "Let me make an observation. Let us put everything in its proper perspective. In my years of varied experience I have learned that whenever people—from factory workers to executives—become involved in a new technique, they tend to think of it in terms of it being some sort of mystique. And that, of course, is nonsense. We have a tendency to humor ourselves, and while doing so, make routine tasks seem far more important and difficult than they are."

"I would like to see you try to—"

"Hush, please, Mrs. Lopez. Mr. Efflander ran a very loose operation here. That is becoming more evident everywhere I look. He was, as you know, a very relaxed and languid person. I have the hunch he was a person of limited energies. He let all of you go your own way. He allowed too much free rein. That is not my way of directing complex operations. I intend to keep on top of every detail, every bit of procedure and policy. In your case, Mr. Oshiro, and in yours, Mrs. Lopez, Efflander permitted a slackness I will not stand for. Your free ride is over, Mr. Oshiro, as of the end of the business day tomorrow. You have not made any changes in the last week in the basic synthesis program. And as for you, Mrs. Lopez, from now on you will operate the program as an ongoing and permanent aspect of our solicitations, getting your prospect list each day from Deets's people based on degree of delinquency. You will work the program for six hours each day, and during the remaining two hours you will train two more operators. I estimate that ten hours of training should suffice for each one. Deets's people will set up the new work stations when you get the other two women trained, and we will then have a man-hour total of twenty-four hours a day of solicitation using voice synthesis. I have thought this through very carefully, and I am willing to reward you, Mrs. Lopez, for special effort, say a ten percent pay raise. Please be on time the next time I want to meet with you."

As Sherman started to rise, clipboard in hand, Oshiro said, "Can you believe this clown, Glinda?"

She shook her head. "I can hear him and I can see him but I don't believe him. Where did they get him anyway?"

"Listen, Harold baby," Mickey said. "I've been assembling a work manual as we went along. It's all there, right beside the work station. I wouldn't want to take it away and give you a lot of excuses. So you go right ahead, bone up on it, break in some new people, have your fun. You'll really know how it works when you get through."

"Are you people trying to tell me you are irreplaceable?"

"I'm not trying to tell you anything," Glinda said. "The only reason I kept going was because I was trying to please Mickey here. I mean, he worked it all out and I guess I was trying to please him by making the darn program work. But every day I've been hating it a little bit more. I couldn't have kept going. Those poor people, losing their houses and their cars. Sick kids. Death in the family, hospitalizations. Car accidents. And there I am, sucking up to them in the old man's voice, wheedling, telling them that their tithe is their prayer to the Lord, and when they are having hard times, that is the worst possible time to stop giving, because if they keep giving to the Lord, He will help them out of their troubles. And, Mr. Sherman, that is a crock. A real crock. The worst of it is, they believe him. They promise they'll get the money somehow. And when I hear that I want to bust in with my own voice and say, Hey, don't listen to that shit! Get yourself out of the hole first. Pay your bills. Save your house. And then come back to the Church and make your tithe." She spun and looked at Mickey. "The old broad that needed the operation, you remember her, on Monday?"

"Yes. I remember her."

"It's wicked work I've been doing, Mr. Sherman, and I couldn't have kept on much longer with or without Mickey."

"I'm glad to hear that," Oshiro said quietly.

Harold Sherman said, "Those people who touch your bleeding heart pledged their support. They made an agreement. If they can't live up to it, they should resign from the Church. And I believe you owe the Church some consideration, Mrs. Lopez. From your personnel records I believe you came here to us because you were emotionally disturbed, and we found work for you."

"And I did more than enough to clean the slate."

"Mrs. Lopez, I find your attitudes distasteful and unpleasant, and not in keeping with the discipline I intend to establish in this organization. You are really not a person I would wish to have working on delicate and confidential matters. Two weeks' termination pay will be arranged. Do you have any personal things in this building you wish to retrieve? Either of you?"

They shook their heads.

"Then I will go with you to the gate, and leave orders you are not to be readmitted to this area."

"He didn't even realize I'd already quit!" Glinda said wonderingly.

"I told you he's a comic. He's got a great routine there."

"Wow, he's really going to keep this place on its toes, isn't he, Mick?"

"Right up there on tippy toe, saluting every minute."

As they got to the doorway, it was evident that Harold Sherman actually intended to accompany them to the gate.

Oshiro spun, went into a half crouch, hands all poised for the judo chop. "Try to follow me, round eyes," he said, "and you have a long painful recovery, if you recover."

"You are threatening me!" Sherman said in a thin small voice, backing away.

"Damn right."

When they got to the stairway they looked back. Sherman had not come out of the room. "Hey," Mickey said, "that stuff is pretty good. I keep seeing it in the movies but I never tried to use it before."

She giggled all the way past the security station and she finally had to stop, breathless, and lean against the concrete wall, hugging her stomach.

"Oh, I haven't laughed like this in so long, Mick. Oh boy. That was absolutely wonderful. 'Round eyes'! Did you see his face?"

"Hell yes. I wondered what I'd do if he knew judo. They say you're supposed to watch their eyes. But what do you watch for?"

As they strolled on, the laughter died away and she said, "Okay, so what am I laughing at? Unemployment insurance?"

"What do you plan to do anyway?" he asked.

"Find work, but not here, and not up home either. Bad memories up there, my friend."

"Tell you what. I'm willing to invest in a plane ride for you. Coach. I'm basically a cheap Jap."

"To where?"

"Out to this little company I told you about. MacroMix. I want you to meet my partners. I want to set up a rig like we had here and you give a demo."

"No solicitations!"

"Nothing like that. Well, maybe some kind of advertising. If we could line up the rights, suppose some lady answers the phone and it is Paul Newman inviting her to come down to her whatsis agency and drive one of the new models."

She looked sidelong at him. "What am I being so picky about? I'm unemployed, right? And I've never set foot in California, ever."

She put her hand out and once again they shook hands, grinning at each other.

At ten o'clock on Thursday night, Jenny Albritton sat Buddha fashion on her bed, wearing a brief yellow nightgown, facing Jenny MacBeth, who lay supine on her own bed, telling about Harold Sherman's conversation with her.

The single light was behind Jenny Albritton, leaving her lovely face in shadow. The coolness from the air-conditioning duct in the wall behind her stirred the strands of long blonde hair.

"He's such a self-satisfied little turd," Jenny MacBeth said. "I have tried to tell myself that management theories and practice differ from one manager to another. But I can't believe he is any good at all."

"It makes me furious to think anyone could be rude to you."

"Wait until he gets around to Public Relations. Then you'll find out what he's like. He just doesn't have the slightest idea how *good* Finn was, how he was subtle and tough and elegant all at once and how much fun it was working for him and pleasing him. I think it is going to be pretty terrible around here from now on. Old Matthew would never have hired a man like that, and certainly never have put him in charge. What is John Tinker thinking about?"

"I heard that Finn Efflander recommended Sherman."

"Not so. He wouldn't do that to us after how hard we've worked for him. I've got it right from the source. Finn wanted thirty days to bring in somebody and train them but John Tinker turned him down and appointed Sherman. And everything is going to go to hell, no pun intended, while the preachers learn their sermons."

"And that'll give Sherman time to really mess it up."

"Are you happy here?"

Jenny Albritton took her time thinking it over. She shook her hair back and sighed. "Well, on balance, yes. I guess I'd be pretty happy anywhere with you. But I guess there could be better places for us in the world."

"I'd like to leave. That damn man took all the fun out of it in five minutes by the clock. There are places where we'd be more accepted, hon. San Francisco, Dallas, Fort Lauderdale. Colonies where people would understand and be glad for us. But before we go, I would really like to clip that money room for a very large chunk."

"Hey now, Jenny Mack, anywhere doesn't include jail."

"Oh, I won't do it if there is the slightest chance of our getting caught. I say 'our' because I think I am going to need your help. I mean, a very vague plan is taking shape. It is going to take weeks and weeks to work out all the details. There will have to be a couple of dry runs. Both of us, you and I, will have to agree that it is going to be worth the chance. I'm going to depend on you to look at the plan like some kind of cop, and punch holes in it."

"How much are you going to try to take?"

"Three hundred thousand in fives, tens and twenties."

"This is probably a very dumb question, but won't they miss it?"

"You can bet your sweet whatever they'll miss it. It'll be like kicking over a beehive. What has to be worked out is the absolute and complete impossibility of my having taken it, or arranged for it to be taken."

"You can do that?"

"I don't *know* yet. I won't know for weeks and weeks. But until I either decide I can or decide it's too risky, I am going to keep my head down. I am going to be humble and cowed, and I am going to tell Harold Sherman what a great man he is, how bright, how intelligent, how shrewd. Over and over. That's what will work with him. I can tell. And you and I, we'll go over my plans. Over and over and over, as I refine them. You are very bright, hon. I need your advice. There may be things I can't see because I am too close to them."

"But what does it involve?"

"Substituting one money bag of newspapers for one money bag of money. And some indirection. And some way I can manage to be in two places at the same time. And some way of implicating one of the security men. I have a nasty one in mind. He leers and smirks and, on occasion, gives my roller-skating Angel a little pinch on the fanny."

"But if we leave right after that, won't they . . ."

"Leave? That would be dumb. We'll plan and plan and plan, and then we'll walk through it a few times until we know it's foolproof, and in the meanwhile we'll have worked out a good place to hide the bag of money, where nothing can harm it. And then, say six months later, while they are still sniffing around after the money, and they have interrogated me five hundred times, we might get just a little bit careless about our personal life. And they'll throw us out into the street, believe me, with Mrs. Macy calling the signals. And we go away without the money and maybe get jobs and work for six months or a year. And then we come back here, quietly and carefully. We make certain we're not followed, we go gather up all that money and repackage it somehow, maybe into cute stuffed animals, and off we go into the sunset. Palm trees, beaches and rum collinses, dear."

Jenny Albritton looked troubled. "But if it should go wrong, couldn't it turn out to be very, very ugly? Like jail?"

"But, my darling, I keep telling you. Unless we can come up with an absolutely perfect plan, we just won't do it at all."

"Don't be cross with me."

"I'm not cross, Jenny A."

"I guess you've been thinking about this for a long time."

Jenny MacBeth smiled across at her young lover and winked and said, "Practically all my life."

Nineteen

When the Reverend Walter Macy arrived at his office on the ground floor of Administration, Eliot Erskine was waiting for him, sitting on the couch across from the desk, under the photo mural of the Meadows Center, sitting so stolidly, impassively, Macy had the momentary impression the man had been there all night.

He did not arise or move or speak when Walter Macy came in, merely watched him with his small pale eyes, slack fists resting on the big thick thighs. There was a faint blush of sunburn on the fair skin of Erskine's forehead and cheeks.

Macy stared at him, then turned and closed the office door quickly and said, "What are you doing here? What do you want?"

Eliot Erskine gave himself a slow count of five before answering. It was a device he had used when he had been on the interrogation team in Atlanta. It had been easier there, because they could rotate—play good guy, bad guy, skeptic, old buddy, maniac barely under control—whatever the situation seemed to require. And when one approach began to work a little bit, they could use that to pry the suspect open. He had used the slow count in poker games, before betting or folding. It worked well there too.

"I just thought it was time we had a little talk."

"But I told you not to come here. Not ever. I mean, unless it is about something else."

Slow count. "This isn't about anything else." He thought Walter looked bad. His color was bad. His hand trembled as he went through a charade of sorting the opened mail on his desk. His cheeks sagged and there were dark blotches under his eyes. The skin of his forehead and cheeks looked mottled and scaly.

"Erskine, you said that you decided there was no point in continuing because it was all repetition. So it's over, isn't it?"

He gave him a longer count and then said, "Over?"

"Over! Finished! How else can I say it?"

Erskine stared at him with expressionless intensity, like a man looking into an aquarium. "Do you have the pictures and the tapes?"

"Of course not! I destroyed them."

"When?"

"Well . . . as soon as I heard about Molly's accident."

"You had me collect those materials because you wanted to use them to force John Meadows out so you could be top preacher."

"No, no, no. Nothing like that. That's your conclusion. I told you nothing like that. He doesn't like me. He's made that clear. I was afraid he would try to force me out sooner or later. So I wanted to have evidence I could show him. If he knew I could destroy his reputation, he wouldn't dare force me out."

This time Erskine gave it a very long count, and he allowed himself to look puzzled, troubled. Walter Macy said, "I really have a lot of work here."

"If that's why you wanted evidence, why did you destroy it? Wouldn't it work just as well whether the woman is dead or alive? Maybe her being dead would make the case stronger."

"I . . . I destroyed it on impulse. I was upset about her getting killed that way."

"And have you regretted destroying it?"

"Well . . . I guess so. A couple of times."

"Then you can relax. I've got duplicates, Wally."

Walter went pale, then red with anger. "I told you in the beginning there was supposed to be just the original, nothing else. You promised."

"What you had me do is illegal, Wally."

"Stop calling me Wally! It's . . . disrespectful."

"Okay, Reverend Wally. It was illegal and I did it. There is an old saying around every courthouse in the country, C.Y.O.A. It means Cover Your Own Ass. You wanted that stuff because it might be useful against somebody. I wanted copies because they might be useful against you if you got to be top man somehow and tried to boot me out because of what I know about your methods."

"I order you to destroy the copies!"

"The only person giving me orders is Rick Liddy, and what I would have to do is go to him and explain the whole thing, show him the stuff I've got and ask him if I should destroy them the way you have ordered me so to do."

"No, don't do that. Where are those copies?"

"In a safe place. Every set is in a different safe place."

"Every set?"

"Along with a little statement from me about how I came to take the pictures and bug the trailer, and who I gave the originals to. It's what's called a form of insurance."

"Oh my God!"

"Don't get so upset, Wally. I'm not going to peddle them. I had the whole operation figured wrong, I guess."

"What do you mean?"

"The way I had it worked out, once you had the evidence that would ruin John Tinker, you were going to try to slip it to somebody who'd give it a lot of exposure, like in newspapers and magazines. I thought you were going to get him dumped that way, and nobody would know you were the one behind it. Except me, of course."

"I just told you why I wanted the pictures and tapes!"

"When that little blonde woman got in to see you that day in May, she acted so weird and I followed her in, remember?"

"In May? I see so many people every day."

"It turned out she was the one from that New York magazine outfit, they found her body in the well the other day."

"I spoke to that person?"

"Right here in your office. She had some kind of dumb story that didn't hang together about icons. I guess it was my imagination, Wally, but when I came in I had the feeling the two of you had suddenly switched the conversation to something else."

"Ridiculous."

"I guess I had that feeling because it seemed to me that if you could meet her on the sly and give her the materials, maybe she could use some of the stuff in the story she was writing about the Center."

"Absurd, Erskine!"

"It would have been an okay weekend to meet her, your wife being out of town and all. But I guess I'm letting my imagination run away with me. Because after that woman turned up missing, you still had me on stakeout picking up more stuff on Johnny and Molly."

"Maybe you have been watching too much afternoon television."

Erskine stood up slowly and smiled at Macy. It was his first smile of the morning. "Pretty dumb of me, huh? Because if it did fit together it would mean that you, good old Reverend Wally, are the rapist-murderer, smart enough and clever enough to almost get away with it."

He had dropped the key word in there. *Almost.* He watched Macy intently and saw the impact of that word, saw Macy rolling it around in his mind while his eyes looked through Erskine and through the wall into the far distances of memory. Giving it too much time. Coming back with a start to here and now. Pulling himself together.

"Mr. Erskine, I would really consider it a very great personal favor if you would arrange to destroy those copies. I am not going to pose any threat to your employment here. I think we should both forget the entire incident. It was an unfortunate lapse of judgment on both our parts. And there is no need to ever discuss it again."

Erskine rocked slowly back and forth, heel to toe. He sorely missed the other members of the old team. Right now the one to send in would be Crazy Lew Yolen. He wondered if he could manage to be Crazy Lew for a couple of minutes. What the hell, it was worth a try. Crazy Lew would come in with the information about the shoulder bag. As he silently rehearsed, Walter Macy said, "Good day, Mr. Erskine," and picked up one of the papers from the pile on his desk.

Crazy Lew gave a sharp hard yell of laughter and jumped into the air and landed closer to Macy's desk. He slapped two hard palms on the desk and Walter nearly jumped out of his chair, mouth and eyes wide.

"They found her purse, you old freak! Hey! How about that! Right where you threw it off the left lane of the southbound Interstate fifteen miles south of here, right where the shoulder strap got hung up on a tree, so it didn't wash away. It's up in the lab now. Shut up! I'm talking to you! You sure that shoe of hers didn't take a fingerprint on the shiny leather? What if it didn't! You in the clear? Bullshit. I'm going to chase your flabby old ass up and down the woods and the fields until you fall on your sorry old knees with the tears running down your face and tell me just how you came onto her like an animal and crushed her throat to stop the screaming. Shut up, you old freak. I'm on to you now and from here on in, and I am going to see you in hell." He leaned across the desk and yelled into Macy's face, "IN HELL!"

He spun and took three long quick strides to the door and went out and slammed it behind him. That was part of Crazy Lew's technique.

Don't give them time to respond. Let them do the responding to somebody else. He didn't know if it had worked at all, but he knew that there had been pure terror on Macy's face as he tried to get further back from the loud yelling, as he tried to roll his desk chair back through the wall behind him.

One of the secretaries was standing beside her desk, looking at him with concern and astonishment.

"What was happening in there?" she asked in a small voice.

"We were rehearsing for the pageant," he said in a tired voice.

"Pageant? Pageant?"

He brushed by her and went out into a fading sunlight that was being extinguished as the big black cloud from the west swallowed the sun. Thunder boomed in the distance, rolling and re-echoing. His palms were wet. He had a faint dull headache. Old Wally had given all the wrong responses, confirming everything. Courts would not accept Erskine's intuitions, his professional perceptions. It was, he thought, much like buying a used car. You buy one every two years and you go in and expect to outwit the salesman on the lot and the sales manager in the little house. But they have been selling thirty a day ever since you bought the one you are driving now. Maybe eighteen thousand potential customers have come in with every intention of making a better deal than they deserve. Thus it is with the one-time or the sometime criminal confronted by an experienced officer. They might stand a chance in the courts, but no chance at all with the officer. No chance at all. But it wasn't a hunting license, he thought. Too bad. Our trouble is that too many times we all wish it was. Pow, pow, pow. End of case. Blow away the smoke and reholster. The next step was unpredictable. Old Wally could not try to regroup by demanding the firing of one crazy person named Erskine. He might try to feed Erskine an alternate theory on the death of the Owen woman. Very hard to say. The man was on the edge. He had been pushed, just a little, but he was still on the edge, waving his arms for balance, aware of the chasm in front of him and too scared to look down.

Joe Deets went down to the city Friday morning on the bus, and took a cab from the bus station to the airport. Her feeder flight was on time and soon she came walking out past the people waiting to go through the security check, looking from side to side until she saw him and came directly over to him. She wore a white cotton shirt-dress with short puffed sleeves, a black collar, black bands on the slash pockets and two black buttons on the double-breasted front. She wore black sandals with medium heels, and carried a large red shoulder bag. She wore big sunglasses with very dark lenses. He had the feeling she had selected what to wear with great care. She looked more slender than he remembered her. She did not smile at him.

"So glad you could make it, Annalee."

"You didn't give me much choice, Joe. I meet you here or you come down to my house."

"I had to see you."

"Sure."

"I got here early, so I found a place we can talk. There's a motel pretty close. Walking distance. With a coffee shop."

"We keep meeting in motels, people'll start wondering," she said.

He laughed. "I'm glad you can joke."

"Not too much choice there, either," she said.

It was a huge motel complex, and the coffee shop was off to the left of the lobby. He led her to a red plastic booth in a back corner. They could look out a gold-tinted window at traffic the color of old brown newspaper photographs. It was a booth for two, with a narrow table between them. The air was chilly. She rubbed her arms, then pulled a red sweater out of her shoulder bag and put it around her shoulders. He ordered a pot of coffee and some toast. She asked for tea and Danish. She looked at her watch and said, "I got to get back over there by quarter to noon to get my flight. It wasn't easy to arrange. I'm not a very good sneak. What's this all about anyway?"

"Coming down on the bus I had a pretty good idea of what to say and how to say it, but it's gone."

"I don't know what you mean?"

"It's gone because it was crap. Posturing. I'm trying to peel myself down like an artichoke, one dead leaf after another, to see if there is anything at all left in the middle."

"Is something wrong with Doreen?"

"She's fine. Splendid. Healthy, full of life. I bought her a new bike."

"How terribly wonderful of you."

"I know, I know. It was news, not a request for a gold star."

"You must want a gold star for something."

"You can see through me. All right. A gold star for cutting her loose. For trying to push her out of the relationship."

She leaned forward slightly and took the glasses off and clattered them down on the tabletop. "First you seduce my daughter and then you want a round of applause for leaving her alone? You are a weird man. Do you know how really weird you are?"

"I get a notion of it once in a while."

"Did you come down here to make me feel good so you could feel good?"

"That wasn't it."

"Then what was it?"

"When we talked that time . . . This is hard to say, Annalee."

"And hard to listen to."

"I know you couldn't care less. But something happened to me in that cut-rate motel room when you prayed. I'm sorry, but it never happened to me before. I know it bores you, but I came here to see you and tell you about it. It seemed to me as if something opened up inside my head or my heart. I don't know where. Like some strange flash of light. And it happened once again since then. It happened when I was thinking about you praying. Listen, ever since it happened I've had a kind of increasing contempt for myself. A contempt which comes, I think, from self-knowledge I didn't have before. I'm what they called in the olden times a libertine. I seduce women."

"And children."

"If you want to call her a child, all right. It's always been like a hunt. The right wind direction, camouflage, weaponry. All the right words. Walk lightly and move ever closer. Never be hasty. Never give up. It's been my avocation. And once they are caught, and when finally the novelty is gone, and the loving is getting too familiar, then I shuck them, as gently as possible, leaving as few scars as I can. And I've always been able to justify it by twisting the facts around. Doreen had been treated badly by her dead motorcycle friend. So-and-so's husband has been neglecting her shamefully. What's-her-name has never realized how attractive she is and it needs to be proven to her."

"What's that got to do with me? Just drop her as quickly as you can and try not to hurt her anymore. Don't bother either of us."

"I'm bothering you because you gave me the feeling that there is something in the world I didn't believe existed. Whatever it is, God or destiny or eternity, it's as if you're the only doorway I know about. Why are you laughing? Am I that ridiculous?"

"I'm laughing because you're just beginning to find out what the Lord is all about. And I've felt my faith slipping away from me ever since I first met you. Our place got flooded and most of the chickens got drowned, and the kitchen garden got washed away. That was part of my punishment for beginning to doubt. But I can't stop doubting. I went up there twice, you know. Everything is so rich and fine. All you people live so good. And right in the middle of all that religion, all those big chimes and singing and preaching, my little girl is being screwed by a preacher older than her daddy. I just can't keep my faith up in the front of my mind anymore. I pray and the words don't come right. I read the Book and parts don't make the same sense they used to. We send in money and I wonder for what. I keep wondering why God would want to reach His flock through a place like the Meadows Center. If He does, then He really doesn't care much about His people."

"Just tell me what it used to feel like to you, to have faith."

"I can't tell you exactly. It's a kind of *knowing*. It's such a great big *sureness* about things. You know the Lord is watching over you. You feel a kind of warmth and glow of His presence. Sometimes it's so wonderful you can't take a breath deep enough. It makes you want to live your life the best way you can and then you can be certain of your reward in heaven. But I've been losing it. It's been going away from me, Joe Deets. Like in a drifting boat, looking back up the river where you've been, where it was so nice."

"Maybe all I've got is some kind of brain tumor giving me flashes of light."

She reached quickly and touched the back of his hand. "I shouldn't hate you like I do. I'm sorry. I was a sinner too. I was a real mess. It was just luck I ever landed on my feet, and found God."

"Can you remember what it felt like? Was it some kind of sudden thing, Annalee?"

"I walked down the aisle to the preacher man feeling foolish every step. I went down to the altar rail because my friends were going down there. I thought I would go through the motions and I knew they didn't mean anything at all. The preacher man looked into my eyes and he was looking right on through them, right down into my black heart. He put his hand on my head and he told me my soul was in great pain because it felt lost forever. If I would give myself to God I would be healed forever. And I did and I was. I mean, I thought I was. I thought I was, right up until recent."

"Can you pray for me?"

"I'll try."

"I mean here and now."

"Now? I don't know. I don't know if I'm worthy to pray for anybody. Last Sunday she was close up on the screen again, singing, looking so beautiful it could have broke my heart. And I watched her, thinking about you and her, and about how I could feel everything slipping away from me. I don't think I can pray for your soul."

"There's nobody else who can, Annalee. Try. Please."

She seemed ready to decline. There were two deep frown lines between her brows. Her lips were compressed. And then her face changed. He could think of it only as a calmness, a look of peace and of rest. She nodded.

They bowed their heads. "Lord God, please forgive me for what has been happening to me lately. I've been trying to hold on, but it's been getting away from me. It's like a big door shutting, real slow. It's half closed now, and nothing I can do to stop it moving. I don't know if You can help me, and I would appreciate it if You would, but this man here, Joseph Deets, he has been leading a mean and sorry life and he has just now started to feel Your presence, and he is scared. He is scared sick all the way through and he needs to find his way to You somehow. He's probably more than halfway through his life and it has all turned to ashes for him, and he is beginning to learn he has been the pawn of Satan, and his soul will roast in the roaring fires of hell forevermore. He thinks he can find his way to You through me, but he should have found somebody who's in closer touch lately than I am. I need You, but he's more needy than me, and if You can show him the way, I would surely appreciate it. Amen."

When he lifted his head and opened his eyes, the tears ran down his face. "I . . . I just . . ."

"Hush now," Annalee said. "Hush up." She handed him a tissue from her purse. "Everything is okay."

"For you to do that means . . . so much."

"What did it cost me? Three minutes out of my life."

"Speaking of cost, I told you on the phone I'd pay the plane fare. Here."

"That's more than it was. Like twice more."

"Please take it. Buy something for Doreen. I promise on my word of honor that after we split up she'll be okay. I've got some other things to . . . to mend also. I don't know why the tears. It's not like me at all.

I've felt so strange lately. I thought I had the world figured out. But it isn't the way I thought it was."

She put the money away. "Thank you. If I helped, I'm glad. But it's hard to believe I did. Funny, you being right in the middle of things up there, and being ordained and all, and never realizing God was watching you every minute, waiting for you to come around."

"I'll walk you over there."

"If you don't mind, I'd just as soon you wouldn't. Lots of people from down our way come up here a lot. It would just make me more nervous than I am already." She slid out and stood up and looked down at him. "Good luck to you anyway. I'm going to try not to think about you with hate anymore. I think I'm more like ashamed for you."

"So we both are. Okay. And thanks."

He watched her leave and watched her come by the window on her way out to the sidewalk. She had a sturdy and determined walk, just like her daughter, chin high, head and shoulders back. He blew his nose. It had worked. He had been in the light for a little longer this time. And he was going to have to learn how to make it happen by himself. And then his life would begin to have some kind of meaning that he could not even guess at. And he could not imagine what kind of man he was going to become. All he was sure of was that he would be nothing like the man who sat here.

He studied the bus schedule and decided he had time to walk to the bus station. But he would have to walk slowly, because of the heat.

Roy Owen phoned Peggy Moon from Hartford in the early afternoon of Friday, August twenty-sixth. She took it at the little office switchboard, leaning back in the battered old oak swivel chair, smiling with pleasure.

"How's it going?" he asked.

"Let me see. Thunderstorms this morning but they didn't last long. Cooled the air and now it's back where it was, unbearable. What else, let me see. Three rooms rented already. Lots of people coming down here with their kids before school starts again. Fred is prowling around, spraying for roaches. I've been catching up on the books. And I've been missing you something terrible."

"And I miss you, and the heat and the bug sounds."

"I almost forgot. Somebody shot at Moses and missed. People think it was because somebody believes he was the one killed Lindy. The deputies are keeping an eye on him and on his place. What's with your kid?"

"Janie is okay. She's happy to have me back, I think. But it is a little hard to tell. She's playing the whole scene very mellow and laid back. I think she's being somebody on television, but I can't figure out who."

"Hug her a lot."

"I try, but she scuffles. Elbows and knees. She resists hugging like you wouldn't believe."

"Roy, you keep at it, hear? Hang on to her and one of these times the dams will bust and she'll cry her eyes out. The laid-back thing is a pose. I remember how it was with me. I didn't want anybody to know how torn up I was inside. It seems as if it happened to me a hundred years ago. But I'll never forget it. When her mother left her and went to New York—which to a kid can be the other side of the moon—she wondered if it was because there was something wrong with her and her mother didn't really love her. That it was all just pretend. But Mother came back with hugs and presents. Now she is gone for good and Janie is wondering again if she is unlovable. So she is keeping people at arm's length. Okay, so that's parlor psychology, but give it a try. Okay?"

"Okay. I'll try it. Lindy's mother is pretty down, of course, and so I've left Janie with her maybe more than I should have. But she has a married brother in Toronto and they are coming down for the memorial service and they've asked her to go back up there with them for a while before the cold weather starts. I'm going to encourage her. Then Janie and I will have a lot more time together."

"When's the service?"

"A week from tomorrow. A lot of the magazine people will be coming up for it. I really miss you, Peg. It doesn't seem to be letting up at all."

"I wouldn't want it to. If I go through it, I want you going through it too."

"When I promised Janie a trip down there for Easter vacation, she just raised one eyebrow and looked at her fingernails and said, 'How terribly nice!' Big reaction, huh? Easter seems too far away from where I sit."

"What we got to do is both hang in there."

"On the way back up here I decided you are right about holding off until the spring."

"How goes your work?"

"I kept in pretty close touch, you remember. A few loose ends. Not too many. We jumped a little too soon on some things, and a little too late on others. Name of the game. All three funds look very solid right now, and down at the shop they smile at me whenever they see me. Listen, would it bother you if I called you up quite a lot? Even when there isn't much to say?"

"I would like that quite a lot, Roy."

"Good. Got to go. Consider yourself kissed."

"Likewise. Bye."

In the middle of the afternoon, John Tinker Meadows ordered a car from the vehicle pool and drove down to where he had failed to keep that final date with Molly Wintergarten. The gate had been destroyed. It seemed to have exploded outward. He got out to examine the pieces and he found the small shards of headlight lens glass in the dirt and realized then how angry she had to be when she drove out. She had driven right through the gate. He had a mild sense of wonder.

The double-wide had been shoved off its foundations by the high water. It was unlocked, the door ajar. He climbed up to the door and looked into the shadowy interior. He smelled wet rot and mildew. He jumped down and dusted his hands and strolled about under the trees, picked up a few stones and tossed them out into Burden Pond. He had the habit of thinking in terms of symbols and how they could be worked into sermons. The house off its foundations. The shattered gate. The smell of decay. The ripples that spread from the small stones he threw.

He could interpret them as symbols, and figure out all the sad and touching ways they could be used, but they were without impact upon him, just as her funeral service and burial service had touched him no more than would a public television special about coming of age in Samoa. It seemed to him as if there was some sort of membrane stretched across his mind. It had a springiness about it. Everything dented the membrane imperceptibly and bounced away, leaving what was underneath quite untouched. He saw that the importance or unimportance of the event made no difference in the degree of penetration and the height of rebound. A bug song was as significant as thunder, a hangnail equivalent to death. Perhaps, he thought, the membrane is stretched across nothingness. Perhaps, without knowing I was doing it, I have used myself up. So now there is nothing left to feel any emotion with. Perhaps I have achieved true holiness in the Hindu sense—a person who is not affected by anything and who has no effect whatever on his environment, who lives in a holy condition of total indifference to time and space. And he remembered, without surprise, from his study of the history of religions, that the truly holy man in the Hindu religion used total sexual debauchery as one of the tools for attaining the ultimate holiness.

It is, he decided, a kind of warped freedom. I can stay or go, live or die, laugh or cry, and it will not mean anything of any importance to anybody, ever. I have used everything up.

He looked at the time. Mary Margaret wanted him to join her in more preliminary discussions with the Reverend Tom Daniel Birdy. The boys had taken a Gulfstream down and picked him up and brought him back this morning, and Mary Margaret had been guiding him all day, and no doubt answering a few thousand questions. He hoped the Reverend Birdy would jump right in, hopping and whirling with energy, ready to take a big preaching load as soon as the audiovisual people smoothed some of the rough edges.

He walked over to the car and it looked curiously unfamiliar to him. Had not the one he had driven down been a darker color, a deeper maroon? This two-door was red. The interior did not look the same. The dashboard array had that same unfamiliar look. Yet he knew he drove it down. It had been standing in the shade in the corner of his vision, and he was totally alone.

It gave him a feeling of apprehension which he quickly shook off. Little things had been happening for at least a year. Maybe longer. One of the office women would bring him a letter transcribed from a tape he had dictated, and he would not be able to remember saying any of those things he read in the letter. But it would be a letter so bland and unimportant it could not possibly be any part of some kind of conspiracy. He would find himself in front of a bookshelf with no idea of what book he was after, or why he was looking for it.

He got into the strange car, started the engine, turned up the air conditioning and slammed the door. He drove back to the gate and stopped and got out and stared blankly at where the gate had been, at the shards of wood spread about, and the glitter of glass, and suddenly remembered that Molly had driven right through it. She had been very angry. He decided to tell Finn Efflander to unload this piece of land for whatever they could get. It was too far from the Center to be of any possible future use to them.

He was back on the Interstate before he remembered that Finn was gone for good. So he would have to tell that Harold Sherman to sell the property which had been given to the Church in a codicil to a will. It depressed him to think of talking to Harold Sherman. The man seemed forever on the verge of bowing to him, or dropping to his knees. Please, sir. Yes, sir. No, sir. And he had an irritating habit of dry-washing his hands while talking. Though he seemed competent, he did not have Finn's knack of summarizing the operations in a brief verbal report. When asked about anything, Sherman brought in pounds of paper, ring binders, printouts. And Sherman kept telling him not to worry about anything, not to try to get into the trivia of operations, telling him he had far more important work as the spiritual leader of the worldwide flock. He kept saying everything was under control, that he was busy installing new controls and procedures which would make everything run more smoothly than ever before.

He slowed down at the place where Molly had been fatally injured, but he was not certain it was the right place. There was no remaining sign. He pulled off onto the wide shoulder and got out. Trucks slammed by, gusting hot air and diesel stink at him, an instant gale that rocked his car on its springs. He walked a hundred yards north, waited for a gap in traffic and then walked back on the grass of the median until he was opposite his car. The sun was a weight upon him. He walked the same approximate distance south and as he was waiting to cross back over to the side where he had parked, he saw a metallic glint in the grass another fifty feet further south. As he approached it he saw that it was a chrome door handle. He picked it up. There seemed to be a certain familiar contour to it, the way it fit his hand. He had opened the door of her little yellow car for her many times. It had been ripped off the door. He then noticed the ruts in the soft turf where probably the ambulance and the tow truck had driven onto the median. The door handle was sun hot, almost too hot to hold comfortably. He flipped it away. It was tangible, but not a bridge to memory of her. In eulogy, all he could think of was the trite and borrowed "Alas, poor Molly!" More tangible than the door handle was the memory of the sweat-tang scents of her body, fresh from the contrived misdirection of the tennis club.

He was almost across the highway when he heard the shocking blare of air horns, scream of tires, and he dived to safety as the lumber truck thundered by, a man up in the high cab shaking his fist. It upset John Tinker Meadows to realize he had crossed without even looking for northbound traffic. He could have died more quickly than she, and very near the same place. Everything today seemed to be turning into symbols and hidden messages. He remembered to look for a long gap in the traffic before he drove back into the right-hand lane.

Twenty

The Reverend Tom Daniel Birdy was nothing like what Mary Margaret Meadows had expected, and in fact was not like anyone she had ever met anywhere. He was much larger, for one thing. Six foot five, she guessed, and weighed at least two-fifty. When they walked together he made her feel dwindled. He wore a white suit so wrinkleproof it presented a smooth and dazzling expanse of back and chest. He wore a blue shirt with blue lace ruffles, and a starched ministerial collar. He wore a broad-brimmed planter hat with a blue bandanna band. The white cuffs of his trousers were tucked into dark blue boots of western style.

His head was huge, his face broad and brown, the features thickened by time and weather, from potato nose to scarred jutting brow. The wide lips lay firm and level, showing nothing, asking nothing. He moved slowly and with a ponderous courtliness, stepping way back with extravagant half bow to let her precede him. He made so little comment on what he was told she began to hear her own voice in her ears, prattling along, full of empty little nervous giggles. He was not content to ride past anything in the air-conditioned limousine. He asked politely each time if he could get out. "Of course!" she kept saying. But he kept asking. His black hair was coarse and touched with gray, his eyes a vivid and memorable blue.

There is not much you can say about an airstrip and a small control tower, five aircraft including the helicopter. "Those are all the airplanes, and those are the men who fly them and maintain them. The tower has reception from the weather satellite that covers this whole part of the East from Washington to Jacksonville."

He climbed up into the tower with the heavy agility of a big polar bear. He stayed up there talking to one of the employees for ten minutes while she waited in the shade of a hangar. After that he went into the larger hangar and talked to the boss mechanic. He did not volunteer any information as to what he had talked to them about, and she felt a reluctance to ask him.

He seemed fascinated by the Mall. He covered all of it, strolling slowly, stopping to look into every store and walking through the larger ones, up and down the aisles. He stood for a long time without comment, his back against a wall, watching the traffic flow of people. Many turned and stared at him, then asked each other low-voiced questions.

Rolf Wintergarten had come back to work that morning. She took Tom Daniel Birdy up and introduced him. For once he did not stay and talk, but went back out into the corridor and said, "What's wrong with that there man?"

"His wife died very recently. We buried her here Wednesday at midday. She was in an automobile accident and never regained consciousness. They hadn't been married very long. She was much younger than Rolf. She was his second wife."

"You wait right here," he told her, and he turned and went back in. Before the outer door closed she saw him taking big strides toward the door to the inner office and saw one of the women trotting after him saying, "Sir? Sir!"

It was twelve minutes by her watch before he came back out. He took out a big white handkerchief and dabbed at his eyes, then blew his nose. "Might be to he'p him a little maybe."

"I beg your pardon?"

"I made him up a para-bell."

She frowned at him, puzzled.

"Para-bell, para-bell," he said impatiently. "Jesus Christ went around telling them to folks."

"Oh yes, of course," she said, realizing he meant *parable*. "What kind of . . . what did you tell him?"

"That's between him and me. It's his now, like I give it to him to hold his life stitched together. He wants to tell anybody, he's free to do so. It don't belong to me no more."

"That's a very . . . unusual concept, Reverend Birdy."

"Not to me, it ain't. Of course, I've been doing it for years. And I maybe got one I can make up for you." As he spoke he turned to look directly at her, and she felt that he was seeing her for the first time. There was an extraordinary impact in that clear blue stare looking down at her.

"Well . . . that will be nice, I'm sure."

"Some are nice and some aren't nice. They has to fit the person. Fit them the way I see them, which sometimes it isn't the way they think on themselves. So it comes to them as a shock. But it is kind of the word of the Lord, filtered down through me. When He tells me what to say, I say it."

"I was very impressed by the way you conducted that revival that was taped. It was very stirring."

"The camera and the lights kept me from getting all the way up where I wanted to be. It was too much like acting. I'm not an actor. What do you show me next?"

"I don't imagine you want to look at the motels and the restaurants."

"Sister, like I said back there when I got off the airplane, I want to see the whole thing because maybe I won't be back."

"We hope you'll be back to stay."

"I know."

And so he made long and careful visits to the motels and the restaurants, and to the University—the classrooms and dormitories and gym and swimming pool. And the University theater. He accepted the fact he could not see Matthew Meadows, that he was too ill to see. He inspected two new houses in the Settlements that were not yet occupied, and he talked to some of the workmen putting up more. They went back to Communications and he listened to the taping of a radio talk show. He went up to the roof and looked at the big GTE dishes. He listened to Walker McGaw's set speech about the number of television stations they reached, and the number of hours they were on the air both in radio and television. He roamed through the noisy room where the women were composing the boilerplate letters on the word processors linked to the Diablos, and where the mechanical pens were making the facsimile signatures on those outgoing letters. He picked several up and read them carefully, his lips moving. It seemed to Mary Margaret he took a long time to read each letter.

They strolled the Garden of Mercy, and they went up and walked through the cemetery. Her tent dress was getting so damp with the perspiration of long effort in the sun, it was beginning to cling to her shoulders and flanks. When at last there was nothing more to see, he said, frowning at her, "Where's your brother? Wasn't he supposed to be here? Friday a busy day for him?"

"Something probably delayed him. He might be looking for us right now."

"Where can we talk, you and me? I'd like it if we'd talk in that place where you live. The Manse? In your place. I want you to be in a place where you feel most at home, and I'm the stranger."

She hesitated, wondering what he meant, then agreed. The limousine took them back to the Manse. They rode in silence in the automatic elevator to the third floor and walked diagonally across the wide foyer to her apartment. It was never locked. With the intense security at the Manse there was no need. She phoned Security and Reception and told them that when John Tinker arrived, she was in her suite having a discussion with the Reverend Birdy. While she phoned, he roamed around, looking at the spines of the books on the shelves, looking at her small collection of primitive Balinese and Haitian paintings, curious amalgams of innocence and sophistication.

"What's this here one about, Sister?"

"That's from Bali. Those are fruit bats."

"Ugly little devils, aren't they?"

"The way they arranged them is very pleasing, I think. It is a nice pattern, a nice composition."

"Buy it yourself?"

"Yes. I bought that one and those two over on that wall of the fish and the butterflies when I went with Poppa to Denpasar years and years ago to a Christian Action Conference about the missions."

He continued to look at the bats, rocking back and forth, heel to toe, his huge brown hands clutching the wide brim of the planter hat he held behind him. He said, almost to himself, "Lots of people, I guess they can take the ugly in their lives and they can make a nice design out of it. Put it just so, a little dab here, a little dab there, and then it is a design instead of evil and they can have folks in to admire it."

It annoyed her slightly and she raised her voice and said, "Won't you please sit down, Reverend? I'm sure you have a great many questions to ask about Meadows Center now that you've seen it all."

He looked around and selected the big leather armchair she had acquired to make Poppa more comfortable when he came in to see her for one of their long talks. She was on the small needlepoint settee nearby. He dropped his planter hat on the floor beside the chair.

"I got no questions."

"None at all? Oh, come now! You must have some. If you don't have any questions, do you have any comments?"

"Anything I want to say about it, I'll save until your brother gets here. I promised you a para-bell, didn't I?"

"I . . . I guess you did."

"The way it is coming to me, it might sting you some, but it might also he'p you some."

"Help me what?"

"He'p you live your life. It's the one thing all of us got in common. How to live the life."

"Well, go ahead then."

"In a minute," he said. "Got to arrange it into words." He closed his blue eyes for a long thirty seconds and then opened them and looked directly at her.

"A long time ago there was a little girl lived in a village by the sea." His voice was deeper and slower, and he was selecting his words with more care. "This little girl had an important father, a chief in the village. And she had two brothers, one older than her and one younger, and they were both handsome and brave and smart and everybody knew they would grow up to be chiefs.

"The little girl did not know what she would grow up to be but she believed it was her fate to become a wife and bear children. But she was the middle child and people did not pay attention to her very much. She worried about herself. She didn't know if she was pretty or if she was ugly. It was on her mind all the time. She was scared of the young men of the village, scared about what they would think about her, scared of walking on the beach with them in the evening. Her fears got worse and worse. She did not know what to do.

"So one day she was down on the beach alone and she saw an ugly kind of seaweed that always washed up there. It had fat pods and wrinkled leaves. She wound two strands of it around her waist. She wore the strands all day long. They made her feel better. She did not know why. Every day she added more weed. And she felt better toward herself. She became the seaweed girl, and no young man wanted her. It had solved her problem. She would never have to find out if, under all the weed, she was pretty or she was ugly. It would never have to come up. She could stop being afraid of the young men because no young man would ever ask her to walk down the beach in the evening, and she would not need to worry about what might happen."

He seemed to be through. She stared at him. "What happened? I don't know what you mean."

"Your seaweed is butter and cream and cheese and chocolate cake and ice cream and cookies."

"Now you listen to me!"

"You used a knife and fork to cover your own self up so you wouldn't have to worry about yourself—so nobody would come and try to take you away from Poppa."

"That is ridiculous!"

"Look at you! There was something you didn't realize. You are a creature of God, Mary Margaret. God has told us to be fruitful and multiply. You turned your back on your own God-given body so you wouldn't have all that responsibility. And by doing that you turned your back on God. You turned your back on your own life. Your way back to God would be to shed all that blubber. Shed one pound a week. That isn't hard to do. Fifty-two pounds in a year. My guess is there is maybe a handsome woman buried under all those chins and that big belly and those hips and thighs big as bushel baskets. You got all winded just walking around with me. That's pitiful. You're a young woman. Tell you what I'll do for you and the Lord. I'll come back by here a year from now and look at you. And I'll pray for you to have the strength to do it. And if I come back here and you haven't done it, then you and me are going to go around and around, hear?"

"I have never heard such total nonsense in my life!"

He smiled at her. "Never have, eh? Told you the para-bells tend to sting. That's because they get down to the roots."

Five minutes later when John Tinker Meadows tapped on the door and came in, the two large people were sitting side by side on the frail settee. She was bent over, sobbing like a child, and Tom Daniel Birdy was patting her on the back of her shoulder, making rumbling sounds of comfort.

"What happened? What's going on?"

The big man got up. John Tinker hadn't realized how big he was. He shrugged and said, "Your sister here, you could say I brought her a little personal message from the Lord."

"What happened, Mag?" John Tinker demanded.

She raised her stained and bloated face and glowered at him and said, "Oh, shut up, Johnny." She levered herself up onto her feet and plodded to her bathroom and banged the door.

John Tinker looked to the Reverend Birdy for an answer, and the man said, "Did her no harm. Maybe he'ped a little. It's her business and the Lord's, not yours, friend. Nice to meet you. Nice to shake your hand, Reverend Matthews. Met your daddy long ago."

"May I take it that we can welcome you to the Church on a permanent basis?"

"She showed me just about everything. I had a good long look at all of it. She told me about the medical center you're planning on and all that. She did her job. She put a good face on everything. Let's just wait until she comes on out. You two are the family. From what I gather, the old man's out of it for keeps."

"That's right. Did you meet Walter Macy?"

"No. He was under the weather, his wife said on the phone. But there was no real need to meet with him. I met a lot of the others in charge of different things."

"Few people realize what a large operation it is."

"It turns out bigger than I thought."

When she came back out she had changed her dress and fixed her hair. She gave Birdy a small shy smile, and went back to the settee. "You set there, friend," Birdy said, pointing to the leather chair, and John Tinker found himself obeying the voice of authority. It was the same knack the old man used to have, to give orders gently but with such confidence they would be obeyed, nobody questioned them.

Tom Daniel Birdy stood where he could face both of them. He smiled and said, "I've been making this speech up in my head all day long. I thought of so many different ways of saying things I got no idea how it'll come out.

"I'm pleased you thought of me and had the idea I could handle the number two or three preaching job here, or whatever it is. Any man should be flattered to be given a chance to reach all them people with the Word of God. Ride all over the world in those big pretty airplanes. Stay in the best places. Own fifty suits of clothes and twenty-five pair of shoes. Get onto first names with the heavy hitters. Senators and Ambassadors and all such. Buy land, build stuff. Wowee!"

He stepped closer to John Tinker and leveled a finger, aiming it at the middle of his face, a finger like a sausage. "But I got into this line of work to tote souls to Jesus! To tote them my own personal self without million-dollar satellites and million-dollar airplanes and five hundred pounds of computer forms. What this whole place does is separate you from your people, and that separates you from God and Jesus Christ."

John Tinker, keeping his voice level, asked, "Isn't that an inverted form of vanity? Isn't it the product of ego?"

"You are one smart man to ask that, because that's what I've been worrying on. It's the one weak place where my thinking isn't clear to me. I prayed to the Lord to make it come clear, but nothing has happened yet. I got my little church down there, and the people come from quite a ways around. No radio broadcasts, nothing like that. They come because somebody told them. If I grow too big for that little old church we'll build us a bigger one with our bare hands, me and my deacons. Working people. I baptize them, and I he'p them through sickness, and I comfort them in grief and I bury them, knowing they are safe with the Lord forever. Man, that's what this fool business is all about. It ain't quantity, Johnny. And it ain't money and power and airplanes and all. It is you beside a sickbed holding the hand of a dying boy and making sure he goes to heaven, and then it is you crying along with his folks when you comfort them. This whole place is too big. Way too big. All your members are little numbers somewhere down inside machines. Sure, you go into their living rooms and there you are on the screen, Johnny, your face big as the whole screen and you are looking at them and talking personal, and you want them to send in their money, and you ask them nice, and tell them their money is a prayer to God. Maybe it's a prayer to you and your father. I want my people to give what they can. And they do. You want them to give more than they can, and you never look them right in the face and see them. You don't know them. What good is that? How can you send a soul up to Jesus when you don't know the face it is hiding behind?"

"I don't think you understand," John Tinker said.

"Maybe neither of us understands the mystery of the Lord, my friend. Maybe it passeth all understanding, and what we got to have then is pure belief. And my way of living gives me more belief in one hour than you'll have in a whole year. I feel it in my gut that the way you people are doing it is *wrong!* You think you can haul in a great big pile of money and do a lot of good with it, along with doing yourself some good. I had a boy down there been dying of that AIDS thing. Picked it up, he thinks, living the low life in New Orleans, and he come on home with it. I'm not telling him it is the Lord God punishing him for doing abominations with other fellows. I'm not telling him he's wicked and dirty. What I'm doing, I'm setting there beside his bed at home—they got him home after the last pneumonia—and I'm holding his hand and kneeling beside the bed and praying for his immortal soul. And I am telling him there is room in heaven for anybody who goes out of this life sincere, repenting for any mean cruel things they done to anyone."

"Have you taken a vow of poverty?" John asked politely.

"It's pretty obvious we never have," Mary Margaret said.

"Shut up, Mag. I'm asking him."

"I live as well as I need to live, Johnny. We take up the collections and I take out living expenses, and what is left, half goes to the poor in the parish, the poor and the unemployed and the sick, and the rest goes into the bank waiting on the time we need to fix up the church or build something else. I couldn't have afforded to come here if you hadn't sent the airplane to fetch me. You know something?"

"Like what?"

"These days it's all like a big shooting gallery."

"I don't know what you mean, Tom."

The Reverend Birdy sat on a hassock with his big fists resting on his knees and looked across the room at them. "People are confused. Life has got all mixed up these days. Nuke-ular freezes that won't happen, and jobs scarce as buttons on a goose, Latins flooding in by the hundred thousand, drug busts, and politicians all the time raising their own pay, and them sheiks wanting to cut off the oil again, and Reagan saying one thing and doing something else, and the Supreme Court fogging everything up ever' chance it gets, with one law for the rich man and another for the poor. They got junk and garbage running out of their TVs and their cable onto the rug in the front room. They got a world around them being poisoned by companies so dang big they don't ever have to answer a letter unless it comes from a bunch of lawyers. People want to understand what their life is about and what is the meaning of it, and everything they see in the real world, why, it tells them that their life is no-account and meaningless. So they have this great need to turn to something that will give life meaning. That's why it is a big shooting gallery. It is shooting fish in a barrel. It is having so many rabbits in a field you can't walk without kicking them. It makes open season on hopeless folk for every freak religion and medication and diet that comes down the pike promising them everything. Used to be all the medicine men used to peddle their ointment out in California, but it has spread to the whole country. Your daddy worked in times when people were confident of their lives and the future, and it was a lot harder then to bring people to Jesus than it is now. You stand up there and promise them heaven, and they will send you money because they don't dare take the chance they might miss out by not sending it. You lock them into your big group of supporters and tell them they are better than any other group in the whole world. And that, forgive the expression, Sister Mary Margaret, is stable dressing."

"And what are you doing that's so great?" John Tinker asked.

"Whatever it is I do, I can't do it in the big store window on Main Street at high noon. I am a private person who belongs to the Lord God. I got my little flock of folks and I make certain they know what the Lord has promised them and what He hasn't. I take care of them, every one, the best way I can, and when I am gone I know where I am going. The only marks I leave behind will be on the souls I touched, the ones left behind when I went. And when all of them are gone from this earth too, there won't be left any sign or mark of me. No big buildings or trust funds or hospitals. I'm an evangelist, Johnny. That is my line of work, and I do it alone and do it the best I can. If it weren't for vanity I would never have let those people take that movie of me saving souls. I wanted to say no, but somehow I couldn't he'p myself. I don't have that trouble right now. I appreciate the offer, but I can say no with no trouble at all, and no regrets. If I find my way back to that little airport of yours, will they take me home?"

"They'll take you home," John Tinker said.

He bowed to Mary Margaret, adjusted the planter hat with care, said, "Thanks for your time," and left.

"Why were you crying like your heart was broken?" John Tinker asked his sister.

"Just go away. Okay? Right now. Please."

"We were wrong," he said. "Tom Daniel Birdy is a country clown. We don't need him. We wasted a lot of time on him."

"Please—just—go!"

He shrugged and walked out. She went in and opened the closet door that had the full-length mirror on the back. She stood there and looked at herself for a long time. She realized that on all the other times she had looked into it, she had looked at her face and her hem line. Nothing else. The rest of her had been invisible. It had been covered with seaweed.

Deputy Reeser brought the Lloyd boy in at three Friday afternoon. The boy was sullen and white-faced. He tried a tough swagger as he approached Sheriff Dockerty's desk, but didn't bring it off too well. "Just set there on the bench and shut up a minute."

The boy took his elaborate and mannered time in strolling to the bench against the wall opposite the Sheriff's desk and sitting down and crossing his blue-jean legs. "You got what I think you got?" Dockerty asked.

"This here is one of Dud Lloyd's middle boys. This here one is Parker. I waited like you said and he come along and settled down on the ridge there. This here is one of Dud's deer rifles. Six-power scope on it. It's empty now. No clip, nothing in the chamber."

Dockerty picked it off the front edge of his desk and sighted out the small window at the round Gulf sign on the station down the street. "Nice big field," he said. He looked over at the boy. "Shoot as good as it looks?"

"Throws just a hair high and . . . Screw it, I'm not saying nothing."

"Dud know you got this?"

"Ask him."

"Parker. You're the one works over at Burger King. Whyn't you working?"

"I go back on at . . ."

"You might as well talk to us, Parker. You cooperate and I think it might keep Dud from peeling all the skin off your ass, big as you are. What were you fixing to do?"

"Scare that freak so's he'd leave town."

"You weren't trying to hit him the first time?"

"Just scare him."

Dockerty shook his head. "Maybe you can handle a rifle, boy, but you can't handle one that good, so as to hit the handle on the hoe he's carrying, bust it to shit and stick splinters in his leg, not at no seven hundred yards."

"I guess that one came closer than I wanted."

"So if we give you the benefit of the doubt, what's it to you if he stays or leaves?"

"I got sisters and a girlfriend, and a de-gen-er-ate like him shouldn't be out of jail. He's a danger to every woman in the county."

"And Parker Lloyd is going to protect every woman in the county by shooting some poor weak-headed fella that never hurt anybody."

"That isn't what they say."

"That isn't what who says?"

"Everybody. They say you had to let him go because the only evidence on him was cir-cum-stan-tial."

"The evidence we got says he didn't do it, couldn't have done it and wouldn't have done it if he had a chance."

"You kidding me?"

Dockerty held up his hand. "God's truth, boy. I swear. I haven't lied in years. Out of practice."

"What . . . what's going to happen to me?"

"I don't want you to get off to a bad start, boy. I think we'll call this malicious mischief. You get yourself to the courthouse on Monday at ten in the morning, and I think Judge Muirhead will probably put you on probation and give you—oh, I'd guess a hundred hours of community service."

"But my old man is going to . . ."

"I'll have a talk with Dud. In return for that, Parker, I want you to turn into some kind of motor-mouth between now and when I say stop. I want you telling everybody the old Sheriff has proof Moses didn't do anything illegal except preach in the Mall without permission. You got that!"

"Yeah. I guess so."

" 'Yes, sir' sounds better, boy."

"Yes, sir!"

"Take him on home, Harry."

On Friday evening the early thunderstorm turned into a steady misty rain that lasted well into dark, making halos around the commercial lights of Meadows Center and around the home lights of the Settlements and the corner streetlights. Alberta Macy had broiled a nice piece of fish for them and baked two medium-sized potatoes. He pushed the food around on his plate. He said he couldn't eat. She asked him if he would call the doctor and tell him how he felt. Walter said he wasn't sick. She told him he acted sick. He said he couldn't help how he acted. He was not sick. He asked her to leave him alone.

After she cleaned up after the meal, she turned on the television set to the educational channel. Walter always liked *Washington Week in Review* and *Wall Street Week*. When she looked at him to see if he was enjoying *Wall Street Week*, he was looking off to the left of the screen, his expression blank, mouth ajar.

"Would you rather have something else on?" she asked.

"Would it be possible for you to leave me alone?"

"Pardon me for living."

She jumped up and turned the set off and went back to her mending. After about ten minutes he got up and went out into the kitchen. She did not know why he went out there until she heard the door to the carport shut. He raced the engine of the small dark blue Buick which the Church owned and which was permanently assigned to them. When he drove out she resisted the temptation to try to catch him in the driveway and ask him where he was going. She knew it was a very bad day for Walter Macy. He was heartsick. He had at last realized, as she had earlier, that they were bringing in this backwoods preacher, Tom Birdy, to take over a lot of the preaching chores in the Tabernacle, the work that Walter loved best of all. It was a terrible blow to him after all his faithful labor. In fact, a terrible blow to both of them. Probably that hick would be moving into the Manse. As soon as Walter regained some of his spirits, she decided she would ask him to rally the affiliated ministers to his side to reconfirm him as the first assistant to John Tinker. She was certain that between the two of them, they could get the affiliates to agree. That hick had no formal training at all as far as anyone could find out. Several times during the day she had tried to get Walter to talk about it, but he had looked at her as though she were some stranger butting into a private conversation he was having inside his head.

Walter drove the Buick down out of the Settlements in a slow and aimless fashion. He had to get out of the house, had to get away from her and her questions and her worry about him. He parked at the Motor House and went into the coffee shop. His stomach was empty and he felt hungry, but when he tried to eat a doughnut at the counter along with his cup of coffee, it turned into a kind of stale mush as he chewed it and he knew that if he swallowed it, he would be ill. He disposed of it in a couple of paper napkins and left them on his plate beside the rest of the doughnut.

One of the things that had bothered him most all day had been his inability to muffle the vividness of the memory of Erskine's eyes and his voice ". . . going to chase your flabby old ass up and down the woods and the fields until you fall on your sorry old knees with the tears running down your face and tell me just how you came onto her like an animal and crushed her throat to stop the screaming."

It kept coming back into his mind with such a force of prediction that he kept feeling himself being pulled in some strange way toward Erskine, toward confession. But that would be insane. There was no proof. There would never be any proof.

Two young Angels came in out of the rain, evidently with special permission to be in the commercial area this late. There was a rerun of one of the old De Mille biblical motion pictures at one of the Mall theaters. They had probably been to that. They sat at the counter. There were two empty stools between him and the nearest one. They whispered and giggled together. The nearest one wore beige shorts and a yellow blouse and carried a furled red umbrella. They both ordered chocolate sundaes. They were at his right. The long curve of the top of the girl's thigh was exquisite. He shaded his eyes to conceal the direction and intensity of his inspection of her. She hitched forward on the stool, her knees a foot apart, and he saw where the two lines of her thighs converged softly and gently to stop at a point just far enough apart to provide a sweet space, pouched in beige fabric, for the little curly chestnut thatch, moist pink lips, perky little clitoral button, her magic kingdom awaiting assault. And of course the cheap little teasing slut would know what she was doing by flaunting it around, and parading the rubbery cheeks of her taut little ass, and the swollen pink-brown of her nipples. She strutted about, defying God and man in her wickedness, challenging the thunderbolt, practically demanding that somebody take her up on her lascivious flaunting and teach her that the reward for evil was pain and fear and death.

He shuddered and realized that he must have made some odd sound, because they were all looking at him with a kind of bland and meaningless curiosity.

"Sorry," he said, "sorry." He left his coffee and went to the cashier and paid the tab and went out into the misted rain, wondering if he had really had those same thoughts back there during that night in May, or if he now merely imagined that he had thought things like that. Because if he had, then it was probably not an accident. But it had to be.

He drove west and took the on ramp and headed north on the Interstate. The phased windshield wipers swept and paused, swept and paused. There was little traffic. The tires made a hissing sound on the pavement. He noticed the speedometer and was shocked to see that it read in the low eighties. He slowed down at once and turned off at the next exit, forgetting that there was no southbound on ramp at that first exit north of Lakemore. When he realized his mistake, he pulled off the road and got a local road map out of the glove compartment. He saw that he could head east on a county road that would intersect a state road. He could go south on the state road and come out a few miles east of Meadows Center.

While he was studying the map he thought of the young girl's thighs again, and found that he was swollen large inside his trousers. There seemed to be an unwanted and unfocused sexual excitement in his body that made his face hot and his breath short and rapid. He willed it to go away but it remained. And he could not pry his thoughts away from the girl. The country road was narrow, but it had been recently resurfaced. He began to drive fast, thinking that if he could make himself nervous about the speed of the car, the erection would subside. But the sensation of speed and the vibration of the car, the sway of it as he rounded the gentle curves, seemed to enhance his tumid state.

He slowed down, and finally took his foot off the gas pedal entirely. The constriction of underwear and trousers was so uncomfortable as to be almost painful. He unzipped himself and prodded himself free. In the faint glow of the dash lights he saw that rigid pallid thing, under the bottom edge of the steering wheel. The car was almost at a stop. An old farm truck rattled by at high speed, startling him with the roar of engine, blare of horn.

Quite suddenly, and almost with a feeling of relief, he realized that the thing down there, that hard, yearning, gristled object, was the devil. It was Satan which had affixed himself to the body of the servant of the Lord, and thus held that servant in his power. Once long ago he had become drunk for the only time in his life. A fellow ecclesiast had sworn the tall refreshing drinks had little or no potency. And in his drunken state he had felt like this, he recalled. A kind of intense revelation, an awareness of great mysteries around him. A necessity for some kind of act, but he could not guess what it would be.

He moved the car slowly ahead, looking out through the sweep of the wipers, and he saw a small iron bridge. At first he thought he would pull off the road at the right, but it looked too overgrown to get completely off the pavement. He swung over to the left where there was a bare shoulder, pulled on to it, turned off the car lights and the engine. The wipers were stilled. The clear spaces became dotted with fine rain, visible against distant muted starlight.

The Reverend Doctor F. Walter Macy grasped himself with his right hand and opened the car door with his left. He stepped out into the night, feeling the prickle of mist on his face. He could hear a rushing and whispering of water. He thought he might best step into the thicker brush for what he was about to have to do.

When he took the second step, his heel slid on wet clay and he fell heavily onto his left shoulder and hip. He was on a forty-five-degree slope. He turned onto his hands and knees and pushed himself erect so he could walk up the slope. A wet branch slashed back across his throat and, in dodging it, he fell backward, realizing as he fell that it would have been preferable to have crawled up the slope on his hands and knees. He fell to the foot of the short slope and struck the back of his head on a shale ledge. It so stunned him that when he lurched to his feet, suddenly and desperately alarmed, he staggered to his right, put one foot deep into the rushing creek water and, with a cry of anger and despair, he fell into the creek, into floodwater boiling with energy and country topsoil. It rolled him over and over and he caught at an edge of the bridge support. He held on there for a time, and then the water yanked him free. He knew he would have to swim to shore, and shore could not be far away. He knew he would have to swim in the direction of the current. He swam into the smaller branches of a great tree which, undermined, had fallen halfway across the creek. He made swimming motions, ever more slowly until his lungs filled and he rested there, entrapped, deceased, his head and shoulders upstream, his legs swinging slowly back and forth in the changing pull of the muddy currents.

Ten minutes later a deputy sheriff, returning to the rural station in West Carrolton, came upon the car parked over on the shoulder on the wrong side of the road, just before the Knoll Creek bridge. As he pulled in to park nose to nose with it, he could see the driver's door was open, the dome light on. He got out with his big flashlight in his left hand, and unsnapped his holster before he moved toward the dark Buick. He walked slowly and cautiously all the way around it, shining his light in the windows. Keys in the ignition. Unfolded map in the seat beside the driver. Local tags. No luggage. A Meadows Center parking sticker on the rear bumper and another one on the front side of the rearview mirror.

If the car had run out of gas, it would have been on the proper side of the road, and locked. Same if some mechanical problem had occurred. The deputy's name was Walker Hendry and he had been six years in the department, long enough to feel uneasy when he came upon something in the night that did not make sense. The misty rain had stopped. He moved back around to the open door and shone his bright beam down the abrupt brushy slope, and saw a fresh scar in the clay, as might be made by the heel of a leather shoe. He saw two branches freshly broken. With care, he eased his way down the slick incline and, at the bottom, on the bank of the creek, he came upon a pair of eyeglasses with heavy black frames. The frames were twisted and the left lens was cracked. Had they been in that exact spot during the time of the heavier rains earlier in the evening, they would have been spattered with mud.

It was beginning to take shape in his mind, a process of cause and effect. Somebody, alone, in a big hurry to stop and get out, and that was why the car was on the wrong side. Too much growth too close to the hardpan on the other side. A drunk sick to his stomach, or a case of diarrhea, or an emergency bladder problem. So he slipped and pitched down the slope, landed hard and rolled into the creek. In the focused light the creek looked like sudsy chocolate milk.

He climbed back up to the car and walked out onto the bridge, thinking that the poor son of a bitch would be a couple of miles downstream by now. The rains had turned every trickle into some kind of Niagara. He stood at the iron railing and shone his light downstream. There was a big tree that had fallen at an angle, blocking half the creek. The body was in dark clothing and he could not determine its position until the light picked up half an ear out of water and the white temple.

Walker Hendry sighed and spat, and wished he had taken the other road in. This was going to hold him up for an hour anyway, to say nothing of the damn forms and reports. It would be nice, he thought, if it turned out to be somebody unimportant. It would take less time. As he reached to try the key to see if the Buick would start, he hesitated and pulled back. There was always the chance the whole thing had been staged, and the man caught in all those little twigs and branches of the great tree had been thumped on the head and dumped in. He went back to the county vehicle and his radio and called in, saying to the dispatcher, "Guess what I got, doll."

Twenty-One

On Saturday morning at eleven o'clock the Reverend Doctor John Tinker Meadows met with the press and the television and radio people in the fourth-floor conference room at the Manse and read the statement prepared for him by Jenny Albritton, Spencer McKay and Walker McGaw, assisted by Alberta Macy. They had begun work at midnight on Friday, and at six on Saturday morning, after Alberta had gone home, they rehearsed John Tinker, correcting the script wherever the lines did not sound quite right.

"Ladies and gentlemen of the media, I want to thank you personally for appearing here on such short notice. There will be no need for any of you to take notes. Mrs. Albritton has seen to it that enough extra copies of this statement have been prepared to give one to each of you.

"As all of you doubtless know by now, my trusted and valued First Assistant Pastor of the Eternal Church of the Believer, the Reverend Doctor Walter Macy, drowned in an unfortunate and terrible mishap last night while on an errand of mercy. His grieving wife, Alberta Macy, has told us that Walter was quite distressed all day yesterday, worrying about a family of members of the Church who live in West Carrolton. They have had bad fortune recently, and they have written me several times, asking if the Church might be able to help them. I had asked Walter to look into it when he had a chance.

"Those of you well acquainted with the area know that West Carrolton is on County Road 88-Z, a dozen miles west of the next exit north on the Interstate. Mrs. Macy has told us that Walter said to her that he was going to go visit with that family and find out how the Church might help. It was quite dark last night, with a persistent drizzle and ground mist. What we are assuming is that Walter got his direction confused when he came down off the Interstate and headed east rather than west, as was his intention. After ten miles or so, he apparently began to realize that he was not passing any familiar landmarks, and so he pulled well off the narrow road—it was County Road 88-Z—by a small bridge that crosses Knoll Creek and one must assume that he studied his road map. It was open on the seat beside the driver's seat when the alert deputy came upon the empty vehicle with its lights out, engine off, and the driver's door open.

"There is little point in speculating on why Doctor Macy got out of the car. It is sufficient to say that careful expert examination of the scene shows that he slipped on the clay bank, fell to the bottom, struck his head on a shelf of shale rock and rolled into Knoll Creek, where the water has been high and fast for many days. The cause of death has been established as accidental drowning.

"This is another sad blow to all of us. Last week we lost Molly, the wife of one of our valued executives, Mr. Rolf Wintergarten, in an automobile accident. And just recently, though there was no connection to Meadows Center and our work here, the body of one of the members of the press was discovered, long dead, in the bottom of a well within twelve miles of here. It has indeed been a tragic summer thus far in the annals of the Eternal Church of the Believer.

"The Reverend Doctor Walter Macy will be buried up on the hillside behind the Manse next Wednesday at high noon. There will be a small service at the chapel on the hill and at the grave site, and the whole community will be present at the candlelight memorial service at dusk that same day.

"We are sorry to lose these people out of a life of piety and service and self-sacrifice. But we know they have, in the midst of life, been harvested by the Lord and taken to His kingdom for life everlasting.

"I am prepared to answer any questions."

"What's the name of the family he was going to see?"

"I'm sure you all understand why I must keep that information confidential."

"Don't you think that sounds as if you're covering up something?"

"I am. I am covering up their identity to save them from harassment and embarrassment."

"Do you know if there are any clues in the case of Linda Owen?"

"I haven't heard of any new developments. My personal guess is that it will never be solved. The trail was, as they say, too cold."

"How much money will the Eternal Church take in this year?"

"Next question?"

"Do you have a replacement for Reverend Macy?"

"I am appointing a search committee from among the pastors who head the affiliated churches. Perhaps one of the men on the committee itself will be found suitable. In the meantime my sister and I will shoulder the entire burden."

"Can your father take over any part of it?"

"Regrettably, no. He is not up to it. He is willing, of course, but his voice is too far gone for that kind of strain."

"Is it true that you fired your administrative officer?"

"Mr. Efflander? Not at all. He was told by his doctors that he had been under too much strain for too long. So we agreed to his taking a leave of absence. We all hope he will decide to return when he is feeling better. He developed a strong staff during the time he was here and so things are running smoothly."

"There is a rumor about a hospital here and a medical school and school of nursing. Is that in your plans?"

"All I will say is that if it is indeed in our plans, it is too far in the future to be discussed at this time. I believe that we do not have time for any more questions. I would like to close by telling you that I have been in consultation with Alberta Macy and it is her desire and mine that the Church, in conjunction with the University, set up a special faculty chair in Biblical History. Mrs. Macy will take an active role in helping establish this memorial fund and I need not add that she will remain on as a valued member of the Meadows Center family. Thank you all."

The bright lights were turned off and John Tinker slipped through the door that led to his own suite. He closed it and locked it and leaned against it for a moment with his eyes closed. It seemed to him that it had gone well. Better than he had any right to hope, the way Alberta Macy had reacted at first. It had taken a long time to convince her that it was beneficial to the Church to have a story everyone would accept. And as Tom Daniel Birdy had refused to come aboard, the scenario of Walter Macy storming out of the house, enraged and sick at heart at being displaced, would just not play. Every effort would be made to make life pleasant for the bereaved.

And Spencer McKay, with the backing of Jenny Albritton, had been right in saying that there was no point in stating, as had the accident report, that the condition of Macy's clothing indicated that he had gotten out of the car to relieve himself. Spencer had composed the sentence that said there was no point in speculation. It made the whole thing more dignified.

In the heavy heat and silence of Saturday afternoon, Eliot Erskine and Rick Liddy parked where the abandoned Buick had been found, and got out of the cool security car and walked out onto the bridge. Three little kids, scrawny and sun-browned, were standing by the rail looking down toward the tree where the body had been.

The tallest one looked at them and said, "They pulled a drownded man out of there, stuck in that tree. He was pissing in the river and fell in."

"You got it about right, kid," Rick said, "but you should learn better language."

The smallest one said, "There was a horse drownded in there a long long time ago. A big horse."

"You kids stay out of fast water," Erskine said. "It's tricky. It'll get you."

They walked back and got into the car and turned the air on high and drove slowly away, Liddy at the wheel.

"Cold beer?" Liddy asked.

"Fine by me. Now what?"

"What do you mean by this 'now what'?"

"Isn't there still a chance they'll try to make Moses for the Owen thing? What's to keep the new guy from moving on him when Dockerty takes off the end of the month?"

"I think it's all over."

"It isn't over until it's over. Yogi Bear."

"We're going to be around, aren't we?"

"Far as I know, Rick."

"The best chance is the new sheriff will clean up his area to save future trouble, and Moses will get the usual roust and become somebody else's problem five hundred miles from here. But if it doesn't happen that way, we keep an eye on it. And if they ever try anything that dumb, we can tilt the machinery a little."

"Mind telling me how?"

"What are you? Some kind of total straight-arrow warrior? It would take one of those notes made with letters cut out of the newspaper. 'Oh, sir, it has been on my conscience so bad, waking up in that busted-down barn and seeing that big preacher that drowned carrying a body to that well and dumping it in and covering it over with boards from the barn.'"

"Won't that open up the whole mess?"

"Doubt it. Charley Winchester would be in on it, and that note would go into the back of a safe in his office. Nice and quiet. And you can't try a dead man. And if Walter Macy and the rest of the preachers are right about what's waiting in the next world, old Walter is up to his glottis in boiling lava, bellowing his lungs out. That place ahead look okay for a quick beer?"

"I did it to him, Rick. I shook him loose from his life. I turned myself into Crazy Lew Yolen and pushed him into the creek and out of this world into the next one. Makes me feel weird."

"I asked you if the place ahead looks okay for a cold one."

"Okay, okay. All right already!"

"What's to yell at me about, Elly? The hotter it gets, the better cold beer tastes."

The Reverend Doctor John Tinker Meadows stood silent and motionless at the pulpit of the great Tabernacle of the Eternal Church of the Believer, staring at the stained-glass window at the far end of the building, and listening to the murmur and rustle of the enormous congregation as the sounds slowly diminished.

Once again the vast space was filled for an early-morning service, even in the heat of the sun belt in August. The three broad aisles which sloped down toward the altar rail at a slight angle cut the congregation into four equal portions, fifteen worshippers wide, sixty rows deep. Another thousand were over in the University theater, watching him on the big screen in closed-circuit color, and he knew that up in the control booth to the left of the stained glass, high above the entrance doors, the production manager and the director were watching the monitor sets, cueing the camera stations. The sound was being mixed with due regard for whichever camera was being used.

He felt a trickle of sweat on his ribs, under the cassock and surplice, and reacted with familiar exasperation toward the so-called experts who had designed the subterranean air conditioning. It had proven ample for the giant space even in midsummer, but had a built-in low-frequency rumble which made it impossible to use it at full throttle when taping. Finn Efflander had put someone to work on a filter that might keep the rumble off the recording. But even were it working properly, he knew that by the end of the sermon his clothing would be sodden. He perspired heavily whenever and wherever he preached. His face would be wet and shiny in the closeups, partially defeating the efforts of makeup to give him the look of a younger Charlton Heston.

He was aware of a slight change of the light off to his left and realized that someone in the control booth had pressed one of the buttons which controlled the movement of the huge translucent, fire-resistant draperies, to move one of them slightly to cut off an edge of morning sun, making the interior light whiter and more luminous.

He heard some whispering from forty feet behind him and a dozen feet above him, and he well knew the stare his sister would direct at the offenders. The choir of fifty young women, the Meadows Angels, was a chronic disciplinary problem. Had they been selected more for voice quality and less for beauty, he guessed the problem would be lessened a bit. When he thought of beauty he remembered his sister's recommendation regarding her oldest Angel, Tracy Bellwright.

John Tinker Meadows turned just enough to see the far right end of the loft, where he knew she would be. He looked directly at her and she saw him and began to smile and changed her mind, and then blushed bright pink. A lovely young woman indeed.

But he knew it was impossible, and did not know why. He saw her as though through glass, as though she lived in another world, or another time and place. It was like seeing in the oncoming traffic, stopped for a red light, an attractive woman driving a car. You saw her through the windshield. There was a mild pleasure in looking at her and a mild curiosity about her life, her problems, her joys. And then the light changed and you never saw her again anywhere, ever.

John Tinker Meadows knew that many in the congregation each Sunday were seeing the service in person for the first time, after years of faithful membership, generous tithing, much television viewing. To them the thrill of being in the same space, breathing the same air, as the famous John Tinker Meadows and his sister, Mary Margaret Meadows, was only slightly dimmed by their being such tiny figures so far away, unlike the living-room screen at home. And as the service proceeded, they would begin to realize that it ran longer than the fifty-minute version edited for cable.

It was time. When a child coughed, the cumulative silence made the small sound carry. He looked at them, feeling their tension and their excitement. He was a tall slender man with gray-blonde hair worn long at the sides, brushed back. He tried to fuel his own energies from their expectancy, from their belief.

It was time. He looked down at his opening lines, and at the marginal messages which would coordinate his talk with the marked scripts in the control booth. One more Sunday, he thought. I will get through this one somehow, and there will be another. And another and another. Somebody accepted an award once and spoke of prevailing rather than merely enduring. God, if You are there and if You will ever listen to me again, I no longer want to prevail. It will be enough merely to endure.